# Senate Cloakroom Cabal

Book 2 of the Laura Wolfe Thriller Series

by Keith M. Donaldson

Published in the United States by BQB Publishing
(Boutique of Quality Books Publishing)
www.bqbpublishing.com

Printed in the United States of America

ISBN 978-1-937084-22-6 (p)
ISBN 978-1-937084-24-0 (e)

Library of Congress Control Number: 2012944843

Book cover and interior by Robin Krauss, Linden Design, www.lindendesign.biz

# Other Books by Keith M. Donaldson

*Death of an Intern*
Book 1 of the Laura Wolfe Thriller Series

*Rude Awakenings*

# Dedication

*I dedicate this book to my wife, Barb, for her love and undying support.*

# Washington T

## Editorial

*The Washington Daily Star*

Usually a drug does not miraculously reverse a fatal illness. More, it reduces the risk of death by relieving symptoms. There are many variables, because diseases don't follow a predictable path.

The way to determine if an investigational drug's overall effects are favorable or adverse is in controlled clinical trials.

One of medicine's most celebrated clinical trials was Louis Pasteur's treatment of patients exposed to rabies. Everyone survived. Because untreated rabies was 100% fatal, it wasn't difficult to conclude that Pasteur's treatment was effective.

Today, one of life's most devastating diseases is cancer. There are numerous medicines providing a variety of treatments for the many forms of the disease.

Early studies of a new cancer drug coming out of Rogers Pharmaceuticals in New Jersey reports their clinical trials of a single drug revealed it to have a 90% cure rate in all forms of cancer. However, it is rumored that unspecified side effects may derail this purported miracle drug, a position that some powerful people are advocating.

What if . . . ?

T he Goose, a small restaurant bar on Capitol Hill, was bursting with lusty, charismatic twenty- and thirty-somethings. It was happy hour, and the crowd was buzzing. Barstools sat askew, each surrounded by a gaggle of drinkers. The wooden tables and chairs, jammed into the small dining area past the end of the bar, were fully occupied with standees squeezed in around them.

Congress was in session.

The crowd was as diverse as were the people on the Hill. Gays and straights, males and females, color—it made no difference here. Happy hour at this popular watering hole belonged to the aides and staff who worked on Capitol Hill.

They played like they worked—at a blistering pace. They gossiped with great glee over what a senator or congressperson did on the floor or in committee. Their faces were bright with the eagerness of youth as they shared tidbits of congressional gossip, always on the alert for a new spin.

Unlike modern glass-and-brass eateries with TV sets or jukeboxes, the entertainment here came from the patrons themselves. They wanted it that way—no competition. Their burning desire was to share some ripe new morsel of inside information. Between their rush of words, they gulped in air or took a swallow of their favorite libation.

Two men and a woman sat at the end of the bar with their heads practically touching. The sandy-haired man with a rumpled and haggard look was Michael Horne, administrative assistant to Senator Roanne Dalton. He spoke in a forced hush tone to fellow Hill staffers Nancy Morris and Tyrell Ward.

"I'm telling you, Senator Dalton's not going to cave in."

"She could lose her seat on the committee, Michael," Nancy said, as she tucked some of her long, light-brown hair behind an ear. "Tom Kelly is not someone a junior senator—"

"Or any senator," warned Tyrell, a trim African-American male. "You remember what happened to Wolford. Kelly demoted him to an afterthought."

"The Majority Leader's not putting my senator on a scrap heap."

"Such loyalty," Nancy parried, flipping her hair for the umpteenth time.

"Yeah well, we're working on some stuff that should make Kelly sit up and listen," Michael replied.

"He's a fourth-term senator and fifth-year Majority Leader whose sights are set on higher things. I doubt there is anything—"

"He would do well to curry favor with Senator Dalton, Nan. He does *not* want to take her on in open session. He's ornery, I'll give you that, but not stupid. We've attempted to sit down with him, but he keeps giving us the cold shoulder."

"Why do you care, Michael?" Tyrell pressed. "Aren't you the guy who was moving on once Senator Dalton got her feet wet? I mean, she's duly elected to a full term now. You said—"

"And I may. I'm just not in any hurry. Besides, she's savvier—"

"Yeah, yeah, we know how political those beauty pageants can be. Didn't you also say you weren't interested in working for a beauty queen living on her late husband's reputation?"

"Don't be too harsh on our confused friend, Tyrell. He may like his female senator more than we think." Nancy winked at Michael.

"Oh please, give me a break, Nan. The only switching I'll be doing is in the job market."

His companions laughed. Actually, Michael did like his boss. His being gay may be to his advantage; he wasn't sexually attracted to her. He had never expected her to run for the Senate office she had been appointed to after her senator husband was killed in a plane crash that also took the life of his AA.

"Go on and laugh, but the current Senator Dalton is not riding on her late husband's coattails. She has a PhD in history and has been, as you so deftly pointed out, through the beauty pageant wars." Michael downed his drink. "I need to get going."

"Why?" Tyrell asked. "I thought we were going . . ."

"Standing us up?" Nancy pouted.

Michael caught the bartender's eye. "My bill, Sal."

"Gotcha," the bartender replied from down the bar.

"Help me out here," Michael asked. "What can Kelly and others gain from a cancer drug being turned down?" He didn't add Senator Pembroke's name because he chaired the Health, Education, Labor, and Pensions (HELP) Committee, where Nancy worked. Her committee had oversight on the FDA.

"Oh, come on," Nancy protested.

"You're not saying a United States senator—?"

"Put it any way you want, Ty," Michael shot back. "The drug lobby is second only to terrorism and the NRA when it comes to putting on the pressure."

Nancy became concerned. "Maybe I shouldn't be hearing all this."

Michael knew she was right. What kept the three such good friends was never getting into serious stuff. Besides, gossiping and rumor-mongering was more fun and less dangerous.

"We're not talking policy." Tyrell grinned. "Besides, what do we know anyway?"

"True," she said weakly. "I just don't like to hear things like that."

"How do the spy boys say it? *We never had this conversation*," Tyrell smirked, eliciting grins from both. "That's better. This is a place for gossip and conspiracies, nothing real or serious."

Bartender Sal slapped a bill down in front of Michael. "How about you two?" he asked, as he backed toward a beckoning voice.

Tyrell looked at Nancy. "You good for another?"

"Sure, I don't have anything except a pile of laundry to go home to."

"Another round, Sal," Tyrell called out.

Michael put some money on the bar and picked up his briefcase. "I've got new stuff to read before I meet with the senator first thing in the morning. One envelope was dropped off as I was leaving the office with just my name on it. I opened it only to find a sealed letter with a note taped to it that read: *Do not open this where anyone can put their eyes on it*. There was no author."

"Sounds mysterious. Maybe a new admirer?" Nan quipped.

"Who knows. I'll find out after I get home."

Tyrell grinned. "Ah, no rest for an AA."

Michael smiled. "I'm taking the train up to Baltimore tomorrow evening, so I won't . . ."

Sal arrived with two drinks and cleared Michael's bill.

Tyrell frowned. "I thought you weren't seeing him anymore."

"I'm not. Just tying up some loose ends. Maybe we three can catch something in Georgetown over the weekend."

"We'll talk," Nancy said.

"Take care, bro," Tyrell added affectedly.

"Always do." Michael gave them a half wave and squeezed his way through the standees and onto Pennsylvania Avenue. He was dressed for winter, but a warm front had come through during the day, turning the evening into a balmy one.

He liked living on Capitol Hill and being close to work. He also liked the village atmosphere. The Seventh Street Market gave him convenient shopping. Although Michael had the look of an overworked, out-of-shape, young college professor, he was an avid biker, spending many weekends on the paths along the National Mall and Potomac River.

He enjoyed working for his female senator. Barely six years his senior, she had promoted him to AA when she decided to run for the seat to which she had been appointed. Roanne Elizabeth McAllister Dalton was a beautiful woman, was very intelligent, and knew how to win.

He crossed Pennsylvania Avenue at 2nd Street SE and walked east on Independence Avenue. Senator Dalton had surprised him with her panache. They had met during the five years he had worked as staff for her husband, but they'd never talked beyond pleasantries.

He turned left on Fifth Street, walked a couple of blocks, and then turned onto his street. His apartment had a large bedroom, a private bath, and a closet kitchen on the third floor of a converted house. Maybe someday he'd be able to buy one of the smaller townhouses. That was too far off to think about now.

He neared his building and reached for his house key. Hearing a rustling sound, he started to turn around, but never finished his move. He felt a sharp pain on his head and sensed he was falling. Then everything went black.

Across the street, a woman looking from a second-floor window witnessed the mugging and immediately called 911. She watched as the assaulter hurriedly rifled the victim's pockets and then dragged the lifeless body off the sidewalk, rolling it down the short flight of stairs that led to an English basement apartment. The mugger picked up a briefcase and ran off, just as the witness's emergency call was answered.

# 2

Tom Kelly sat patiently in his black leather chair behind an immense, mahogany desk. He stared at the back of a wiry man of medium height dressed in a hand-tailored, silk suit, the cost of which could feed a family of six for three months. The lobbyist was looking out the window that faced the US Capitol.

"I've always admired this view of the Capitol Dome from your vantage point, Tom," Stanley Horowitz, the top pharmaceutical lobbyist in Washington, said, turning to look at the Senate majority leader. "It's awesomely patriotic and inspiring, especially at night with the lights shining on it."

Kelly smiled. He always preferred to meet the feisty lobbyist here, in his private senate office, instead of his more public office as majority leader. Kelly had occupied this space for the last twelve of his twenty-two years in the Senate. Black-and-white photos of smiling faces adorned his walls . . . trophies of a gilded past.

He said, "That it is, Stanley. However, I'd trade this view in a heartbeat for the one looking south at the Washington Monument."

Horowitz smirked. "Can you actually see the Washington Monument from the Oval Office? I can't remember."

"You can see it clearly from the president's bedroom."

"Ah, to wake up and see the rising sun reflecting off that white obelisk."

Kelly laughed. "Don't go poetic on me, Stanley. I can't stomach it."

"Poetic I'm not, Tom, but a realist I am."

*And so much more,* Kelly thought. The pharmaceutical lobbyist was a hard-nosed bastard. He had no soft edges. Even his smile had down-turned lines.

"And for you to realize your fondest dreams of waking up and catching that view," Kelly said, sweeping his hand toward the window, "we need to tend to business."

"Senator Dalton is a member of *your* caucus *not* on board, and for that I blame her overly eager administrative assistant, Michael Horne. He's the one doing the digging."

"She'll come around," Kelly half mumbled.

"Aren't there a couple of other wafflers?" Horowitz snapped.

"Gavin Crawford and Jean Witherspoon are cautious senators. Nevertheless, they always follow the caucus when unanimity is required. They were never not on board, Stanley."

Horowitz moved to the front of Kelly's desk. Leaning in against it, he said emphatically, "It wouldn't look good for a potential presidential nominee to be incapable of roping in his own senators on something so simple."

"It's a done deal," Kelly said indifferently, meeting the pharma's gaze. Horowitz thrived on intimidation. Kelly often wondered what the man's life had been like before he had built his high-priced law firm and taken over the pharmaceutical lobby. He was considered to have more power than any non-legislator on the Hill.

Horowitz's eyes were like slits. "Rogers's cancer drug *cannot* be approved. We've done our job on the FDA's administrative committee. They like the tens of thousands of reasons we've given them to see it *our* way, and I don't want—"

"Harley Rogers is a tough old egg, admired."

"He doesn't have the clout of a two-year-old. His crumbling company proves that," Horowitz said intensely, some of his spittle landing on Kelly's desk.

"He's a decent, well-respected guy, Stanley."

"Don't get all wishy-washy on me, Tom," Horowitz warned. "It doesn't become you. Harley Rogers went back on his promise to reduce the scope of Tutoxtamen to curing only one of the cancers. He tricked us into thinking he was going along. Well, now he'll suffer the consequences. Do you understand what a ninety percent cure rate would do to the economy?" he asked, as he slapped the desk for emphasis.

"Rogers wants to become a damned historical figure, the creator of a miracle cure. The Salk vaccine would look like a cough drop compared to what his drug would do. You damn well better not weaken on me, Tom."

The majority leader coolly suppressed a desire to stomp the arrogant egomaniac into the rug. "I am not weakening, Stanley. I just wish it didn't have to be Harley."

"Well, it is! His drug can never see the light of day. We need unanimous support from your party, up front, to give backbone to those squeamish FDA prigs. A couple of them are already waffling."

"Fred Pembroke assures me the FDA will stamp it *not approvable* and send it into the purgatory of your dreams," Kelly said smoothly. "And don't worry about Dalton either; she'll come around. She may be pure as the driven snow, but her husband was no saint. We can use that if . . . We'll be FDA's firewall, Stanley," Kelly said assuringly.

And for emphasis, Kelly leaned forward in his chair. "Tutoxtamen will get buried in bureaucracy."

# 3

My weekday mornings for the past three months had consisted of seeing my husband Jerry off to work and caring for my infant son Tyler. Today, my maternity leave was behind me, but my concentration on readying myself to go back to work was nonexistent. In all my previous years as a newspaper reporter, I'd never had domestic responsibilities. Now I was beginning the life of a working mother.

In our three-plus years of marriage, Jerry and I either had lived on his Catalina 350 sailboat, *Scalawag*, docked in Washington's southeast marina or in my one bedroom apartment in the Cleveland Park section of the nation's capital. Last fall, with Tyler's birth imminent, we'd purchased a house in suburban Arlington, Virginia, which gave us a short walk to the Clarendon Metrorail station.

We were still furnishing the house, but lived comfortably, and I'd thoroughly enjoyed my first three months of motherhood. Even with all of that, right now I felt like I was in an alien land. Today, I would not be playing with Tyler, taking him for a stroll, doing laundry, giving him baths, or cleaning up after him. No, this was the day I would be turning him over to the care of a nanny.

I went to the top of the stairs and called down to Jerry. "Did you tell Anna to be here at 8:30?"

"Yes, Laura," my husband answered in a most placating tone. "It's the same time it was the last time you asked." He answered from the dining room, where I was sure he was playing with Tyler.

"Smart-ass," I muttered under my breath and returned to our bedroom to finish getting ready.

Jerry insisted he drive me in this morning. It wasn't as if I hadn't made this trip before. In fact, I used Metro when I took Tyler to the paper, just before Christmas, to show off my then one-month-old son. It was an easy commute, which had been one of our geographical criteria when home-shopping, for which we'd paid a healthy real estate premium.

I checked myself over in our floor-length mirror on the inside of our closet door. I had decided for today that I'd wear my navy blue skirt suit. Normally, I dressed casual. After a quick examination, I thought I looked fine, even if I was five pounds heavier than the last time I'd worn it.

I picked up my purse and checked its contents. No cell phone! A spike of adrenaline shot through me as I began a frantic search, then stopped almost as fast. It was in the kitchen sitting in its charger—the same spot I put it every day. I heard Jerry's voice. Anna must have arrived. I checked the clock radio on the nightstand: 8:23. I liked that she was early. I went downstairs and found Jerry with Tyler in his arms, talking slowly to Anna. Jerry was wearing his Tyler apron.

Anna wasn't brand new to me. She had come to the house for short visits over the past two weeks, so she and Tyler could bond and I could get to know her. It was an easy way to acquaint her with where things were and what Tyler liked. I liked Anna. I was just being my normal apprehensive self, scared to death.

I had just turned thirty-seven when Tyler was born, and he could be the only child I bear. In my life before Jerry, I rarely dated and had no interest in marriage. Then Max Walsh, captain of homicide for the Metropolitan Police Department (MPD), introduced us.

I know that seems unusual, our relationship with Max—I, a newspaper reporter and Jerry, a defense attorney. Not the type of people cops normally befriended.

I'd gotten to know Max from covering homicides in Washington. When I'd joined the *Washington Daily Star*, I'd already been a beat reporter in other cities for ten years and knew my way around murder investigations. Max and I had soon formed a professional rapport. We would even brown-bag-it occasionally in a park close to the newspaper.

About a year or so later, he introduced me to Jerry. I've never forgiven him for taking so long. I fell head-over-heels in love. It was a sort of destiny thing. Max stood up for us at the wedding and was Tyler's godfather.

"Good morning," I said cheerily, when I reached the first floor.

"Good morning," Anna said haltingly, with a smile. Her English was so-

so, but we'd worked out some short phrases and words for her to use if she needed to call my cell, which would be the way we'd communicate: cell to cell. She wouldn't answer the house phone.

His eyes bright and happy, Tyler squirmed in Jerry's arms as I approached him. *That's right young fella, you just keep remembering I'm your mama.* I took him carefully, holding him out so that some misdirected food morsel on his bib didn't transfer to my dark jacket. I gave him a big smooch, then handed him over to Anna.

"Don't forget your cell phone, hon." Jerry knew my mind and knew it was going off in a myriad of directions. In fact, he had sat me down last night for a little "chat."

*"I noticed over the weekend a definite change in you. You're fretting. Tyler couldn't be in better hands with Anna. You . . . what makes you, you . . . your diligence and caring . . . your brilliance and flakiness, sometimes simultaneously, is what separates you from everybody else. I'm in awe of your talent as a writer and a mother. Editor Lassiter evidenced your professionalism by nominating you for a Pulitzer. Going to work tomorrow is not a worrisome situation."* He had then escorted me upstairs and made love to me. I returned my mind to the present. "Remember, Anna, call me anytime. Okay?"

Anna smiled. "Si, eh, yes."

With one apprehension taken care of, I shifted my concerns over to what Avery Lassiter, my editor, might have in store for me. She'd told me last week that I wouldn't be getting any beat assignments. I suspected that may have been somebody else's decision because she knew I liked being a beat reporter, and that I'd go back to it in a minute, regardless of any celebrity I'd gained from breaking last year's serial killer case.

Jerry nudged me and handed me my cell phone. "It's time."

**4**

Two men sat in a parked black SUV with heavily tinted glass inside the FDA's parking garage in Rockville, Maryland. It was well past quitting time. A cell phone rang and the passenger answered it.

"Yeah." He listened and then punched off. Without saying a word, he nodded to the driver who started the engine and drove up three levels.

"There," the driver said, "the silver sedan . . . those are the plates we're looking for."

"Okay. Pull up there," the passenger said, indicating an empty bay straight ahead at the ninety-degree corner of the ramp. "This'll give us a perfect line of sight to where people come out from the elevator."

The SUV's darkened windows made it almost impossible to see inside. The driver backed it into the bay, about twenty-five yards from the silver sedan. Within minutes, a woman and two men in business attire emerged from the elevator.

"There's Hank and our mark," the driver said. "Hope the woman's not with the mark."

After a few steps, she went to her right and down the ramp. Only the mark and Hank were walking up the ramp. Hank quickly glanced toward the woman to be sure she wouldn't blow his mission. All was clear. He picked up his pace in the direction of his prey. The unsuspecting man pulled out his keys, and the rear lights of his sedan flashed on as his car unlocked. Hank was only a few steps behind him.

As the mark reached his parking slot, the SUV's passenger slid out and moved rapidly toward him. He and Hank were on their man in an instant. The SUV moved behind the sedan.

The driver of the SUV put it in park and moved quickly around the back, opening the right side door as his cohorts shoved the now limp body into the rear seat. The driver then handed Hank a plastic coverall, shoe covers, and gloves to put on before he got in the mark's car.

Hank knew the drill and rapidly stepped into and zipped up the coveralls, affixed the shoe covers, and moved to the kidnapped man's car.

"Hey, Hank, the gloves. If the car don't blow up on impact . . ."

"Yeah, yeah," Hank mumbled, but did as told, and the SUV driver got back behind the steering wheel. His partner, already in the back, pulled his door closed. Hank, fully covered, got in the car, while the SUV slowly moved away and down the ramp.

Hank backed out onto the ramp as a woman appeared from the elevator lobby, but her attention was in her purse. He pulled forward and followed the SUV out of the garage.

# 5

The Christmas holidays were a distant memory for me. Tyler was nearly fourteen weeks old, and I had been back at work for a whole week. I longed for the balmy days of spring as I walked all bundled up in subfreezing temperatures toward Wilson Boulevard and Clarendon's restaurant row. The blustery winds added to the harsh reality that this was the third Saturday in February.

I had selected an Italian restaurant run by Greeks and sandwiched between two Asian eateries a block from Clarendon Metro station.

I'd talked to Max a couple of times by phone since being back at work, but hadn't seen him, mostly because Lassiter had yet to send me out on a homicide. His job as MPD homicide captain was keeping him too busy for a drop-by lunch during the week. That was why we were having a Saturday lunch in Virginia. Recent snow falls had made parking on the street impossible, so Max was taking Metro and I was walking.

Jerry could get the SUV out of our driveway, so he had made plans for the day with Tyler. They were driving to Bethesda, Maryland, where Jerry's two teenage sons lived with their mom, his ex-wife Beth. The boys wanted to spend some time with their new half-brother.

I had my concerns, but Jerry didn't. He assured me that at three months, Tyler wouldn't be hurt by or even remember the trip. Beth was amenable, looking forward to it actually, and Jerry promised that no harm would come to our child. His dark humor aside, I grudgingly agreed.

Max was not officially on duty during the day on Saturdays, although realistically he was never off. As captain of homicide, he needed to be ready for what Saturday nights might bring. Still, I know he kept his fingers crossed for uneventful Saturdays, where he could restock his refrigerator and maybe even get in a nap. Some Saturday night cases could run well into Sunday mornings.

Nearly fifty, Max probably had hoped for better things from life, like raising his daughter. His bright and stylish wife, eight years his junior, had changed all that. She'd worked her way up in middle management at a bank and met a man who was moving up even higher . . . to a New York City bank.

Fed up with being a cop's wife, she'd filed for divorce. That had been just after Jerry and I married. Taking their then seventeen-year-old daughter with her, she moved to New York and married the banker.

I'd only seen Max sparingly since going on maternity leave last September. He'd visited Tyler and me in November at the hospital each day, and he'd joined us at our Christmas party. I know people found my relationship with an older, African-American cop odd. His being Tyler's godfather surprised people—like my folks—even more, but most people quickly adjusted their thinking once they met him.

A bear of a man, he could be intimidating. To us reporters, he could also be cryptic and tight-lipped, giving up nothing before he had all the facts . . . and maybe not even then. To my surprise, one day early on—at our first lunch in the park, in fact—he'd mentioned something about my past. He'd checked me out and learned about the police corruption case I had broken during my reporting days in a city down south. That was the beginning of our deepening friendship.

The little bit of my face that was exposed to the elements felt frozen as I trudged on sidewalks that had not been cleared, and I felt a little pooped when I reached the restaurant. Max was already inside; we greeted with a hug. Once seated, I scanned the nearly full room. There were booths down one wall and tables tightly spread around. It probably accommodated forty-five to fifty diners. I liked that the interior lighting was soft. It made for a nice ambience on a cold day. A neighbor had recommended the place.

"This is comfortable," I said, turning my attention to Max.

"It does have a pleasing warmth to it," he said, looking over his menu.

As I picked up my menu, I glimpsed a couple in the rear corner booth. A salt-and-pepper-haired man wearing large, dark-rimmed glasses and a red-checkered flannel shirt looked familiar. He was sitting on the inside of the bench seat, a young woman with long, light-brown hair next to him.

"Hmmm," I involuntarily uttered aloud. The man's face, his complete demeanor, showed tenseness. His eyes were brooding, like a parent chastising a child in public, but not wanting to make a scene.

"Hmmm?" Max questioned, breaking my trance. He was looking at me over his bifocals and menu. "What has you so curious? Not that you're not always curious."

"Don't look now, but in the far corner booth across from us is an oldish guy, who looks very familiar, having an intense moment with a young lovely."

"Since when, in this town, have you been drawn to older men being intense with young ladies?"

"I wouldn't be if we were in a DC bar at night. However, being that we're in suburban Virginia on a Saturday afternoon, I am."

He grinned. "Could this be a *tomorrow* headline?"

Our server appeared at that moment, blocking my view. We ordered coffee, and Max, true to form, ordered steak. He could not order it rare, so he settled for medium, which was well-done to him. I requested a grilled chicken salad with Caesar dressing on the side.

Max ordered onion rings as an appetizer, and the server departed. "Your Christmas party was very enjoyable. I was going to call . . ."

The server brought our coffee.

"I'm so glad your daughter could be there," I said. "She's become quite a looker."

"Yes, well-coiffed and dressed as only her stepfather can afford."

"She seemed very attentive to her big, teddy-bear daddy. How does she like you being Tyler's godfather?"

"She thinks it's *cooool.*"

"Sounds like Jerry's boys . . . *cooool.*"

We chatted amiably until the server arrived with the onion rings and my grilled chicken salad, saying Max's steak would be ready shortly. He topped off our coffees and left.

Max had a swallow. "You, eh, over the holidays?"

I caught the unspoken meaning to his question, but didn't respond right away.

"Did Mr. Tyler hold up well after his days on stage with your parents?" Max prompted.

"With all the attention, all the holding and cooing he got, he came out of it quite well. I was afraid he would want more of the same constantly, and

I'd be the only one around to give it to him. Fortunately, he settled into his previous patterns." I reached for an onion ring.

"I enjoyed meeting your parents. And if I may say so without getting my head chopped off, I found your father a very interesting guy."

I peered at him over an onion ring as if I would attack, but then lightened up. "Yes, he is. I never saw that part of him growing up."

"Maybe he never expressed himself in a way that allowed for that." Max picked up the last onion ring and held it up in a last-chance gesture.

"It's all yours," I said graciously.

He took it in one bite and looked at me softly, tilting his head questioningly.

"Okay. I was guilty back then, too, focusing only on myself," I said. Max had a way of drawing me out without verbally asking. "Dad and I never had the opportunity to become close."

The server appeared with Max's steak. We both reordered coffee, this time decaf for me, and fell into eating. There wasn't a whole lot I wanted to say about my youth. I peeked at the corner booth while digging into my salad. "Things seem to have relaxed down at the corner ring."

Max couldn't resist and turned to glimpse in that direction. "He does look familiar. I know we're in a low-traffic area for Washington big shots, but doesn't he know that snoopy reporters are everyplace?" He grinned and raised his eyebrows.

"Thank you very much," I smirked. "I wish I had my camera."

"Personally, I'd rather talk about young Mr. Tyler Fields."

"He's a wonderful, playful, happy guy. And believe me, I count my blessings."

"I'm looking forward to the christening."

I had fallen way behind Max in the eating department and I concentrated on that, but my mind went back to Mom, Dad, and their four-day visit over Christmas. Their first-ever trip to see me—anywhere.

"You look like you're off someplace. May I ask where?"

"Christmas." I sipped on my coffee.

"Ah. Not with the couple in the corner?"

"No." I looked in that direction. They were just leaving.

Max looked at the departing couple. "Do you know him now?"

"Only as someone familiar."

"If I said Senate majority leader, would that—"

"Oh my God. Kelly! He definitely looks different out of a suit."

"It's the plaid shirt and black-rimmed glasses."

I picked up my purse. "I promised Jerry I'd call when we finished. Your godson will want to eat soon."

Max shook his head. "I can't get over Beth wanting to see Tyler."

"It was her idea as much as the boys'. This was a good time for them. Evenings were out. You know how bad traffic is during rush hour on the American Legion Bridge and going out 270. When Jerry and I first dated, she didn't want the boys near me . . . us. It got a little better after we married. Besides, the boys really love going out on *Scalawag*."

"Ah yes. When single, you were, eh, living in sin."

"I forgot that. I enjoy the boys, and they me, especially . . ." I let that hang.

"Since you became a celebrity."

"I was the stepmother they never wanted."

"Can't blame them for that, but life doesn't always work out the way we want. They're coming around. I saw that at your Christmas party." He abruptly changed subjects. "Have you and Ms. Lassiter discussed the type of assignments you're going to have?"

"She's given me a couple of research projects right now. No street stuff, although I told her I was okay with that. I'd get to see you more," I teased and went back to finishing my salad.

"I would think with your new stature they might have other things for you to do."

"I find nothing wrong with me showing up at one of your crime scenes. If I remember correctly, I increased the percentage of solved crimes in the District last year," I said with a smirk.

"Yes, well it helped that you were on the right track and could cross jurisdictional lines that I couldn't. Plus, we all realized it was safer staying out of your way."

I extended a hand across the table and squeezed one of his, saying earnestly. "You made me know I was still very much a part of that investigation, even when others didn't."

"I think I worried more about you losing your baby or your life." He rested his free hand on mine. "I'm just hoping we won't be confronted with anything remotely like that in the future." He gave my hand a gentle squeeze.

I nodded my understanding. "I've got to call Jer." I took the cell phone from my bag and punched in Jerry's number. I glanced around the mostly empty restaurant and wondered about Senator Kelly and the young woman. The glasses and flannel shirt were a good disguise without looking like one.

"Hi," Jerry said.

"Hi. We're just finishing up. What's happening?"

T he Senate bells signaled an upcoming vote. Senators and staff left meeting rooms and offices and headed for the Senate subway that connected the three Senate office buildings to the Capitol.

Forty-two-year-old Gavin Crawford was his state's junior senator—twenty-five years younger than his senior senator, who definitely thought of Crawford as young and junior. However, now beginning his second six-year term, he was no rookie.

Crawford and his family lived in McLean, a close-in Virginia suburb. His kids ranged from preschool to a high school junior. All five kept the family minivan constantly on the road.

He had met his wife Mariel in a university art class during his senior year. She'd been a sophomore. They'd married the spring that Mariel had graduated, even though he'd still had another year in law school.

"Hey, Gav," a middle-aged man called out to him, as they arrived simultaneously at the subway. "Harry in good shape for tomorrow's game?"

"Hi, Fred," Crawford replied as he slid into the seat beside Senator Fred Pembroke. "Yeah, we did some one-on-one last night. He should be ready."

"Harry's a damn fine point guard and a dead-on three-point shooter. Tell him for me, I wish him the best," Pembroke said.

---

Senator Roanne McAllister Dalton waited on the subway platform for the Senate train to arrive from the Hart Building. Dalton's offices were in Dirksen, the middle of the three Senate office buildings, with Russell being the third and oldest. She had initially come to the Senate by appointment, filling out the last ten months of her deceased husband's second term—her father's idea.

Rufus McAllister, a former two-term governor, was very much the power behind the throne in their state. Dalton had been against taking the appointment. In fact, after H.T.'s death, she hadn't even wanted to return to Washington to close up their condo.

"It will be a boon to your career. It's a piece of cake," her father had told her.

She'd ultimately given in. Being a former beauty queen and the wife of a two-term senator, she'd been instantly added to Washington hostesses' must-invite list. Heretofore, those invitations had read *Senator H.T. Dalton and wife.* Three months after taking H.T.'s seat, the once-reluctant PhD and associate professor of history had experienced a change of heart. She'd announced her candidacy to stand for election on her own right.

An amazed Rufus McAllister had been elated.

The subway's arrival interrupted her thoughts. She saw Senators Crawford and Pembroke in the front car, but chose to sit in the back. She wanted to talk with Crawford, but wanted more to avoid Pembroke. Once the subway reached the Capitol, she debarked and walked leisurely up the wide, marble stairs to the Senate chamber.

———

Senator Pembroke hurried away as Senator Crawford cut through the President's Room adjacent to the chamber. He liked the high-ceiling room with its frescoes and arabesques overhead and around the walls. Diarist Mary Clemmer Ames had written about them: *"There is not one quiet hue on which the tired sight may rest."* He wished he had time to sketch one of Brumidi's pug-nosed cupids, but when? *Oh well,* he sighed and entered the Senate chamber.

He chose to avoid the Cloakroom. Each of the two major political parties had one—the Cloakroom was an inner sanctum free of outsiders. It was the place senators could drop their public faces, where arm-twisting was an Olympic event and compromise the liniment of disagreements. When Lyndon Johnson was majority leader, he was known to lounge on a chaise in there and give audience to the pleadings of his lowly flock.

———

Crawford hoped the vote would come up quickly. He'd vote *yea* and head back to the office. He wanted to be home in time for the twins' swim practice.

"Senator Crawford," a female page said, approaching him at his desk. "Senator Kelly would like to see you in the Cloakroom after he votes."

He smiled. "Thank you, Maci." He wondered what Kelly wanted and hoped it wouldn't take long. He began to sit, but saw Senator Dalton approaching.

"Gavin," she half whispered, "have a minute?"

"Senator Dalton," he said formally.

"You must be feeling pretty good about this education bill."

"Very. The big job now will be to get the administration to pressure all the states to get on board with it."

"I'm sure they will. They don't want free money withheld from them."

"True," he said. "That was a major point of contention in committee, to get that added. Now, it could well become the enforcer that gets it fully implemented."

She smiled, lighting up her pretty face. Mariel was good-looking and all, but Roanne Dalton was beautiful. "So how are things?" he asked.

"I've wanted to talk to you, get your advice. I'm concerned about the leader wanting unanimous support of the FDA's imminent disapproval of the cancer drug."

"The side-effects issue?" Crawford interrupted.

The Senate president announced that the voting would start. The call of the roll commenced.

"Yes. I don't understand why we're involved at all. Besides, the clinical trials showed an overall survival advantage."

"Wasn't there something about it not clearing all the phases . . . ?" He let that hang.

She explained. "Fred said there were anomalies in the double-blind tests on patients who have tried other sources of therapy or medication. I understood there were some minor problems, but not with the drug itself, only in combination with people being treated for other diseases. I've read where that's not uncommon with drugs that are approved. It's been noted, but left up to the patient's doctor to work out, if they can. On people without that complication, the results of this drug were miraculous. Now Fred says the FDA believes they were hiding—"

"I must admit," he interrupted, "I haven't been paying a lot of attention

. . . I mean, if there are clear advantages between those who used the miracle drug and those who didn't—" He interrupted himself. "Is there something here I'm not aware of?"

"I don't believe so," she replied softly.

"I tend to go with the leadership on issues. I'll check it out. I'm meeting with Tom after the roll call; maybe I can find—"

"Senator Crawford," called the clerk.

Crawford turned toward the dais. "Yea." He turned back to Dalton, who had on a different face. He glanced in the direction she was looking and saw Kelly engrossed in conversation with Pembroke.

"I'll get back to you later," she said, and walked up the aisle.

*What was that all about?* Crawford sat at his desk. He had not been keeping up with the new drug. He'd ask Gordon about it, hoping his AA would know.

Following Kelly's vote, Crawford sought out the majority leader in the Cloakroom.

Kelly dispensed with the niceties. He gave Crawford a broad-brush background, hitting hard on his concerns. It was a drug that Kelly didn't name, but it fit into what Dalton had said.

Pembroke had joined them.

Kelly went on saying that the party needed unanimous support and that one senator was preventing that. "I'd like you to speak to this senator, Gavin, on behalf of the party."

*What happened to the whip?* Crawford thought. Pembroke nodded in affirmation to the various points Kelly was making. Crawford's and Pembroke's families were friends. Their second homes were locally in McLean, and they traveled in the same circles. A few times in heavy snow, he and Pembroke had carpooled, using Pembroke's four-wheel-drive SUV. Crawford's little hybrid was overly challenged in that type of weather.

Kelly was saying, "We have to be extremely careful with this. We don't want the FDA to rush approval on a so-called miracle drug only to find it is plagued with severe side effects."

"What about clinical trials?" Crawford asked.

"That's just it," Pembroke jumped in. "We aren't sure about the validity of the testing."

Crawford realized that this had to be about the drug Dalton had mentioned. "What does the pharmaceutical say?"

"We need to support the FDA, have everyone on board," Tom responded, ignoring Crawford's question.

*That was a quick non-answer,* he thought. "What about our friends across the aisle?"

"They feel there are more critical issues facing us right now and don't want to get into a pissing match over one drug."

Crawford didn't think that sounded like them.

Kelly went on. "We have bigger fish to fry, such as prescription costs and Medicare discounts. We have a lot on our plate and don't need any distractions."

Crawford nodded. "I've always been in favor of *too much* testing over not enough."

Kelly stood. "Good. Glad you see it that way."

Crawford and Pembroke rose.

"Who is it you want me to talk with?" Crawford asked.

"Dalton," Kelly replied. "Thanks, Gavin." He extended his hand and gave a nod to Pembroke. "Thanks to both of you." He turned away and caught the eye of another senator.

Crawford looked at Pembroke. "I'm . . . eh . . . does Tom think I have an in with Roanne?"

"No. Actually, he sees it the other way. She looks to you as an ally. You know, she seems to have rubbed some folks the wrong way."

"I wasn't aware of that. She's new, but I thought she had lots of friends."

"Mostly H.T.'s friends, who accommodate her."

"Oh," was all Crawford decided to say. He didn't particularly agree with Pembroke's assessment, but it wasn't worth challenging. "So . . . eh . . . what exactly is her position?"

"She's not following the party line. It's very straightforward. FDA says there are serious side effects. After those major recalls awhile back, Tom doesn't want a distraction caused by an unproven drug. We have too much going with the pharmas already."

*This seemed out-of-step with the way Tom operated,* Crawford thought. *For some reason, he didn't want the whip handling it. He felt uncomfortable about this . . . it put him in a bit of a bind. He liked Dalton, but he also liked the progress he had been making in the caucus. Maybe this was a leadership test. Free discussion had never been a problem amongst the colleagues. However, Kelly wanted unanimity and had chosen him to get it.*

Pembroke interrupted his thoughts. "There's stuff whipping around in

Appropriations and in Finance, aside from all the issues with Medicare and the cost of prescription drugs."

"Yeah, it's piling up. Okay. Has anyone lobbied Roanne about this, prior to me?"

"We don't know what ties she has, or H.T. had, with the pharmaceutical company applying for approval, if any."

Another non-answer. "What's the name of this drug and the company?"

"It's called Tutoxtamen and the pharma is Rogers, up in New Jersey."

# 7

T he large hotel ballroom was set up auditorium-style, with a raised
dais at one end, on which sat a podium and four straight-back chairs.

A banner behind the dais announced: *Rogers Pharmaceuticals,
Inc.'s Annual Stockholders Meeting.*

Harley S. Rogers, eighty-three-year-old founder, chairman, and CEO
of Rogers Pharmaceuticals, Inc., was ramrod in stature and leadership
with a strong timbre to his voice. He normally stayed behind the scenes,
leaving his son Sherman, president and COO of Rogers, to be the public
face. Harley was absorbed with the product side.

And today the product was his miracle drug, Tutoxtamen. *That damned
FDA fabricated findings saying there were side effects,* Harley rued, standing
in the wings waiting to go on. All the test results had been astoundingly
positive. Expectations verged on the stupendous. Stockholders, the public,
and the media were ecstatic.

The FDA had leaked there were side-effect problems, and his company's
stock had fallen precipitously, over forty percent and now teetering—
dipping and rising on every whisper of news. Harley estimated he'd lost
fifty percent of his net worth.

A scientist first, Harley Rogers had always hoped he'd discover a miracle
drug that would rid the world of one of its horrible diseases. He had that
now in Tutoxtamen.

Nevertheless, it seemed as though the pharmas had convinced the FDA
there was a problem. That was why *he* was coming forward today. The old
soldier needed to take the stage and tell everyone his drug worked. He'd
illustrate his remarks with hundreds of success stories.

Placebo tests, double-blind procedures performed on over two thousand people of all ages in and out of the United States, proved Tutox, as it was familiarly called, was effective in ninety percent of the people using it—an astounding and unheard of result.

Sherman Rogers joined his father. "How you holding up, Dad?"

Harley flinched. "What? Oh, Sherman. I was engrossed . . ."

"It'll go fine. You've been through worse."

"It would be a lot worse if it hadn't been for you, son."

"I'm glad you feel comfortable now with what we'll be doing," Sherman said softly, patting his father's shoulder.

Three years earlier, a medical trade publication had gotten its hands on an internal report describing some of the remarkable results from Tutoxtamen's early tests and published them. That's when the pharma lobby came a'callin'. They were adamantly opposed to the development of a potential miracle drug and threatened Harley with a *not approvable* by the FDA—unless he cut back to only one of the cancers.

Strategic planning had always been one of Harley's long suits. He had learned early in life to expect the unexpected, to keep his options open and his perimeters strong. He and Sherman had spent many long days scoping out a plan to circumvent the pharmas, while making it look like his company was complying with the one-disease approach.

Harley had immediately contacted a German pharmaceutical firm with whom he'd had previous associations, and had paid them to conduct parallel testing on Tutox phases I, II, III, and any other tests the Europeans would require. Harley felt positive the Germans would receive full approval—the caveat being how far-reaching and influential the pharma lobby could be.

"I never dreamt I would ever go against my country."

"You're not, Dad. It's not our country that's giving us trouble. It's a few senators and our own pharmaceutical lobbyists. I wish we didn't have to do this either. But I want you to take your proper place in history, right up there with Curie, Pasteur, and Salk."

Harley became lost in his thoughts. Presidential candidates argued over costs and cures ad nauseam in debates. The public usually went with what was expedient. A recent flu vaccine shortage brought out flimflam operators offering the vaccine at five to ten times the normal price, and the public rushed to use it. They heard *vaccine* and didn't ask if it had ever been tested. The pharmas never said a word. Some companies made a killing on that.

Sherman squeezed his father's shoulder lightly. "Come on, Dad. They're ready." Harley nodded. Maybe floggings in the town square should be reinstituted for the con artists who preyed on the public. The death penalty would be too good for them.

He felt Sherman's reassuring hand and became aware that his vice chairman, Robert Storer, stood at the microphone, extolling Harley and RPI. Harley stood a little taller and fixed his eyes straight ahead.

". . . and now please join me in a salute to the genius behind Rogers Pharmaceuticals's great success, our founder and chairman of the board, Harley Rogers." Harley walked steadily out onto the platform and directly to Bob Storer. They met and shook hands, then Storer stepped back, giving Harley the stage. The applause was deafening. Harley stood to the side of the podium looking out over the thousand or so people who filled every seat and stood along the walls. Bright lights suddenly came on for the television cameras, preventing him from seeing into the hall any longer.

Harley could not tell his stockholders the full truth, something he always held dear. He would fire salvos at Congress and the FDA. One truth was the government's failure to act, to save lives. He had been a warrior once, but since WWII, he had been a scientist. Still, there was no *back down* in him. He'd paint the FDA as the bad guys. He didn't enjoy it, but he was desperate to save his company. As the applause faded, he wondered if he could change some attitudes.

# 8

On the second Sunday in March, Tyler Jerome Fields was baptized. Mom and Dad flew in Saturday morning. Our small invitee list also included Max; Marsha Hines, a part-timer in Jerry's law office while in her final year at Georgetown Law; and Mary Granger, my news assistant.

Jerry and I had found a church reminiscent of the one my parents attended. It had a very traditional look. Tyler, nearly four months old, certainly didn't understand a baptism, but he loved the attention.

Jerry's mother was too ill to attend, and he had decided not to invite his sons. Even though he'd had a nice time taking Tyler to see them and their mother, he and the boys agreed it was probably better that they not go. Beth would have to drive, and well . . .

The church's outstanding choir and the very personal touch the minister gave to the baptism—showing off Tyler to the congregation—gave me chills of joy. Mom, Dad, Max, Jerry, and I stood around the baptismal font and watched as Tyler put on his little show, moving his arms and legs and grinning. It was a very special moment.

The fact of my celebrity had not escaped the church leaders. "That's the reason the church was filled to overflowing," one of them told me. I heard one person say, "Easter came early." We all went to their coffee hour and met many church members. One couple was from Wisconsin. A man sought out Max, whom he had known for some twenty years, and they fell into a long conversation.

My parents held close to me. Tyler was asleep in the nursery. I fretted to Jerry that we were getting close to his feeding time. One of the parishioners overheard me and offered to find a private room, if I would like. I went off to get Tyler. Overall, it was a warm and lovely experience. Mom remarked how it was very much like home—people were so friendly.

After lunch in a nearby restaurant, we all went back to the house, except Mary. She had things to do at home. Our little group was very compatible. Jerry, Max, and Dad spent a good part of the afternoon together, probably telling stories about me. Marsha said it was a touch of home for her, being with our family.

Late in the afternoon, after Max drove Marsha back into Washington, we all did our own thing for a while. When Tyler was awake, he was mostly in a grandparent's arms. Jerry and I felt very fortunate. So many good things had happened recently. Memories of bad times had receded.

I'd been back to work three weeks. Lassiter had me working on a couple of background pieces that involved local government issues, which comfortably eased me back in, since the majority of my time at the *Star* had been spent at City Hall.

I was entering into a completely new experience at the paper, what with my nomination for the Pulitzer and a long layoff. I knew, human nature being what it was, my attitude would be scrutinized and magnified by my peers, putting me in a very strange atmosphere.

Well, I would just have to learn how to breathe it in.

9

Senator Dalton was surprised when Michael told her that Senator Crawford had requested a meeting with her. "Did he say why?"

He shook his head. "Gordon, his AA, only asked if you had some time today. You don't have a lunch."

Crawford met Dalton at the rear of the Dirksen Senate Office Building at 11:30.

"Glad we could get together," he said, extending his hand. Hers was warm and soft. "It's such a beautiful day; how about Union Station?"

"Wonderful. I haven't been there in years."

"There's a restaurant off the concourse," he said, taking out his cell phone. "I'll have Gordon call them."

"Sounds like you've done this before," she chided.

"Yes, it's very clandestine," he half whispered, punching in Gordon's number.

"Are we hiding away in some back room?" she asked conspiratorially.

"Actually, we go through a secret door used back in the Civil War, then down two flights of stairs to—"

"Where listening and viewing devices cannot penetrate?" she said, continuing the game.

"Oh darn, you've heard of it."

They laughed. The repartee relaxed him. Gordon answered the call.

Once situated in the restaurant, Dalton and Crawford quickly got the preliminaries out of the way with the server. In the five-minute walk, they'd talked about family—mostly his, as she was a widow and childless. He hadn't known where she lived until she mentioned settling into the

Crystal City condo she and H.T. had bought ten years ago. "It was hard the first month, but then I found some good restaurants."

"Oh? You never ate out when you were here with H.T.?"

"We did, but not a lot. After I knew we wouldn't be having children, I wanted to do something for myself and not just sit around Washington. I chose to go home and get my graduate degree. I was teaching at the university when H.T. was killed."

"But you, eh . . . I remember seeing you."

"Yes, you did. In fact, I've met your wife Mariel on at least two occasions. Such a lovely and unusual name."

"I'm sure she would have mentioned that if I'd told her I was meeting with you," he said boyishly. "Her given name is Mary Loretta."

Dalton liked this self-effacing man. He was not caught up in himself like so many others. The server appeared with their iced teas and took their meal order.

"How are things going now that you're into your second year?" he asked.

"You can't count my first year. I was only a guest then. But when I chose to run in the primaries, things began to happen. Mostly *don't run.*"

"I remember hearing tidbits of that in the Cloakroom."

"Everyone feared I'd lose. I don't know if you saw my results, but I won the primary in a landslide and then the election with sixty-one percent of the vote. I think my colleagues forgot my father was a former two-term governor and that I . . . well, let's say I was fairly well known. Also, I'd worked in campaigns all my life . . ."

"And," Gavin added, "you had a PhD in history and an associate professorship at the university. A mighty strong resume."

She smiled. "What route did you take to get here?"

"I had two terms in our state legislature. I pushed for some reform that got me some good press. I thought taking a run in the primaries would get me more statewide notoriety, and I could air out some of my ideas for a future campaign. I was thinking governor. Then surprise of surprises, I won the primary and the election."

"And now you're in your second term."

He nodded. "What got you on HELP?"

"My interest in health and education. It was the only one on my list that I did get."

*Yeah,* Gavin thought, *and Tom Kelly's still kicking himself over that one.*

"I've always had an interest in health issues," she continued. "I'm sickened with the high cost of medical care for seniors and the rising cost of prescription drugs."

He agreed. "It seems like we make little if any progress in those areas." "We need to create a federal formulary on drugs," she said bluntly.

Her candor surprised him. "Unfortunately, our hands were tied, or rather we tied our hands on that one," he said. "To get even a modicum of cooperation from the pharmaceutical companies, Congress had to promise no requirements for discounts."

"What's tied can be untied. I don't believe these programs can be remodeled like an old house," Roanne went on. "They must be torn down and built anew, from the ground up. Look at what Lyndon Johnson tried to do back in the '60s. A picture of Johnson taken from the front page of our hometown paper during his presidential campaign in '64 shows him visiting an old couple sitting in broken down chairs on a dilapidated porch in front of a falling down, termite-infested shack.

"My father had that page laminated and framed. It hangs in his den at home. A small plaque on the frame underneath says, *The Ultimate Politician.* I've often wondered whatever happened to those folks after the news media left."

Gavin sat rapt at her outpouring and was glad for a break when the server brought lunch.

After the server left, Roanne picked up where she left off. "The citizenry is fed a lot of hogwash at election time and sent into a frenzy, all for the sake of their vote. I've watched that in amazement for many years. With all the hot air, I don't think the general population is any better off today than they were ten or twenty years ago."

She paused to take a bite. He jumped in. "Maybe thirty. We have bills before us now that are not unlike bills a generation ago."

She looked up from her eating. "This pharmaceutical issue is a good example. The Senate is so concerned with protection, they're forgetting about prevention. Take the new cancer drug—why is everyone in such a big stew?"

Gavin was shocked, then relieved, that she'd brought up the very issue he wanted to discuss.

She continued, "I had my staff go over Rogers Pharmaceuticals's reports. Each phase showed amazing results. That drug's cure rate was over ninety percent. Yet our chairman of HELP wants it ditched, saying there are too many irregularities, too many questions about the testing. I don't see that."

Gavin went from grateful at not having to bring it up to downcast. This wasn't the time to defend Tom Kelly's position. He'd have to come up with another tack. He also wasn't up on the drug's history, and she certainly had abundant knowledge of it.

Roanne felt a little sorry for Gavin, a genuinely nice man. She and Michael had speculated he might have been asked to talk to her about Tutoxtamen, because the decision was imminent and Kelly wanted no cracks in the majority caucus.

Gavin then interrupted her thoughts. "I think the whole drug issue is a mixed bag of contradictions. We have those who are pro-cure at any cost, and we have those who are pro-caution because of costs."

She smiled. He continued.

"Some do not want the drug because it will put a lot of other cancer-drug producers out of business, and others want the drug because of the great good it will be for humanity. The advocates of those differing positions are extremely adamant in support of their position. The pharma lobby is willing to sacrifice one member pharmaceutical for the sake of the many, regardless of the value of one over the other."

She appreciated his gentle explanation of what he was really trying to say: *Do what the party wants.*

He was on a roll. "I have to admit I back-burnered Tutoxtamen when I heard it was going to be rejected. Now I'm told the caucus is concerned. There are other pharmaceutical issues in committee, and Tom wants the Tutoxtamen situation disposed of."

"I don't understand why. I've asked to talk to him."

"You are a person of great convictions, Roanne. We've all had them. Please, if you are ever to have a political future in the United States Senate, understand that party unity comes before personal desires. If the opposition sees a crack in our unanimity, they'll jump all over it and that, I can assure you, will bring out the attack dogs."

She understood his point. She had heard H.T. on the subject more than once. It was why it took so long for anything to get done in Congress.

"We all need to pick our fights carefully," he said. "I like and respect you, and I don't for one minute suggest you change your point of view."

That surprised her—because that's what she thought this was all about. Then he said: "Only that you change your vote."

**10**

"Michael, I don't want you to be disappointed in me," Senator Dalton said softly, while the two sat in her office. "Senator Crawford is an honorable man."

"It's whose honor he honors, is all I'm saying," he responded sourly. "This is all pure crap, if you'll excuse my expression, ma'am. There is nothing wrong with the Rogers's drug. It's all a sham. The drug is superb, but for some reason, Senator Kelly's—" He stopped. "Sorry."

"Don't curb your passion on my part. Do we know that Rogers didn't phony up the reports?"

"Independent firms do the majority of the tests. A German company also tested the drug. There were three, sometimes four, different groups testing. Not one was off from the others by as much as three percent. Everything says the drug is what it has been touted to be. People could start receiving the cure in weeks. Rogers is ready."

She rose and walked to a window overlooking C Street and Union Station. Bad thoughts flashed through her mind. She remembered the bribing of judges in the beauty contests and the devious tactics by some of the parents. Could this be happening in the United States Senate?

Crawford's advice to be patient resounded in her head. The Senate leadership had too many ways of squashing an upstart senator. What she needed was an independent investigator. Her father immediately came to mind. The former governor had plenty of connections. Even though she wanted to be her own person, she also knew calling him might be the wisest thing to do.

Capitol Hill was unlike any place she had ever known—much got done by what was *understood*, not by what was said. There were two faces to everything.

"Will there be anything more?" Michael was standing by her desk.

She turned back to face him. "Oh, I didn't mean for our meeting to be over. I just needed a moment to think." She walked to him. "I will play their game for now. Meanwhile, you and I will keep digging. Are you friendly with Senator Crawford's AA?"

"Somewhat," he said unenthusiastically.

"Is there a way we could find out through him what the senator really thinks of me. I feel he's a friend, but we need to be absolutely sure how politically secure I am with him."

Michael's face brightened. "I think my friend Nancy . . . she and Gordon know each other. In fact, one time . . . well, he was interested in her. I'll work it out."

"I must sound desperate, but I've never been alone like this," she said, concerned. "I've always had a great support group. We need to know what's being whispered. How easily, if a crack appeared in the Kelly armor, could some of my colleagues be swayed?"

Michael looked more pleased. This was right down his conspiratorial alley.

"I'll talk to Nancy and Tyrell. It's dumbfounding how loose-lipped staff can be. Get them together, they blabber their heads off. I'd never learn anything without those gossip sessions," he said cavalierly. "This'll be like a fox in a henhouse."

She laughed. She liked that he was a game player. "Get me Senator Crawford. I'll let him tell the majority leader."

The game was on. Now, if she could only find someone who could dig more deeply and professionally into all of this.

**11**

That evening in a downtown Washington, DC, hotel, Stanley Horowitz had just ushered Tom Kelly into the posh suite the pharma used for entertaining.

"Let's sit over here." The pharma chief indicated two love seats facing each other. "I heard Dalton changed her mind. Crawford turned out to be a good choice." Horowitz went to a small bar. "Still bourbon on the rocks?"

"That'll be fine," Kelly said, as he sat down, exhaling like a weary traveler.

"What does Crawford know?" the trim, expensively dressed pharma asked, while he tonged ice cubes into a tumbler.

"We made it all about party unity, Stanley. We didn't have to tell him anything."

"That was a gutsy call," Horowitz said, as he poured bourbon over the cubes.

"Roanne is not stupid," the Senate majority leader said. "I imagine her experiences in those beauty pageants, where politics are probably dirtier than on the Hill, taught her a few things."

They laughed. Horowitz handed Kelly his drink and then sat opposite the senator. "Yeah, we'll keep her reined in. Test her on small things, see what she does."

"I don't know where I'd be without you, Stanley," Kelly said sarcastically. He downed a swallow of his savory drink. "Our mantra is strong: party unity over personal desires."

The pharmaceutical lobbyist smiled and picked up his brandy snifter, swirling the liquid under his nose before taking a sip.

Kelly continued, "Watching your lobbyists dancing around this has been fascinating. They don't know which way to go with Rogers."

"It's difficult when you have to go after one of your own. Don't underestimate Harley Rogers. World War II types like him have plenty of moxie. They've got an inner strength that doesn't exist in the baby boomers. Tough breeds know how to pull a 'Teddy Roosevelt.' Don't get cocky. Caged rats can still be dangerous," the pharma spat.

"What's to worry? He's right where you want him. Their stock's in the tank."

"The important thing is getting the FDA's *not approvable* so we can forget about this damn drug. Just remember, we don't manufacture cures; we only manufacture dependencies."

"Fred assures me it's a done deal. They had a little blip when one of their key people working on the Tutoxtamen approval was killed; his car ran off the road. Virginia state police reported he had a high alcohol count. For some reason, that caused the Administrative Committee not to meet for ten days. I understand everybody is in sync now, and they will make their announcement any day. Then we'll get to work on prescription discounts—your little trade-off for Rogers."

The feisty pharma grunted. "We've got our protests all lined up."

"Don't overdo it," Kelly said anxiously. "We don't want this to drag out."

"The public doesn't think for itself. It lets its representatives in Congress do that for them. People know you gotta spend money to make money. All manufacturers invest in research and development. It is an absolute essential, which costs."

Kelly loved to push the arrogant pharma's buttons. "Yeah well, the truth's getting out about who really pays for most of your pharmaceutical R&D."

"Fortunately, the public ignores those book-writing malcontents. No university getting huge grants from the government is going to sanction negativity like that. They'd lose their financing."

"The Internet's blasting holes in our control of what gets said," Kelly complained. "We've always had protesters, but they were easily dismissed before. There's too much media out there. They never shut up. I know. I see the emails."

Horowitz acted shocked. "Don't tell me you read that bullshit."

"I only read what my AA or the leadership chief of staff puts in front of me, which is bad enough, and those only scratch the surface, from what they tell me."

"Remember another old mantra: *If we don't get YOUR money to spend on OUR research and development, you will die*," the little man chirped.

"Yeah well, slogans and mantras be damned, we need to turn to the issue of price reform on your drugs."

The lobbyist paced the room. "Aren't you awestruck by how many years we've been able to play political football with drug costs for the elderly—and with Medicare and Medicaid? The public is really dumb about it, which of course plays directly into our hands. You argue on the Hill, but nothing gets done. However, when something does happen, it ends up favoring us."

Kelly smiled. "Yeah, that Medicare prescription drug benefit bill a few years back even surprised me. Your pharmaceuticals lit up the stock market. What a bonanza."

Horowitz nodded. "I do have to admit it was a huge windfall. It's fascinating what you all get done when you really try."

"One thing we can't do is negotiate drug discounts or create a government formulary. That puts the ball squarely in your court," Kelly said. "This is your opportunity to come out smelling like a fresh bouquet of roses, demonstrating your good will and giving us your discount prescription plan."

"What more can we do?" Horowitz said magnanimously. "The Feds are very nicely financing our R&D with billions in grants to the biomeds, nonprofit labs, and universities. With all that generosity, it's the least we can do. We certainly don't want the public to get off their partisan asses and join together against us. We'll throw them some bones. Three of our healthiest companies with their own cancer drug will take the lead.

"After you have your hearings, we'll buckle under. Each of our companies selected will march out their plan to help the elderly and the infirmed. That'll keep you as the majority party. Maybe even propel you into the White House."

Kelly smiled. "We'll take the wind right out of the opposition's bellicose sails." The two men sat back, held up their respective glasses, and saluted each other.

**12**

"Hello," I said, answering the house phone, while balancing an almost-sleeping Tyler in my arms. This was a home day for me, and I'd given Anna the day off. I had just finished feeding my son, and he cozily snuggled with a soft, light-blue blanket as I held him in the crook of my arm, holding the cordless phone in my free hand.

"Ms. Wolfe?" an unfamiliar male voice asked.

"Yes," I answered cautiously, while shifting Tyler to make sure he stayed snug. "This is Laura Wolfe."

"I am Nelson Probst with Mrs. Osterman's office," he said, with a slight hint of a question at the end, as though saying *you know who Mrs. Osterman is, don't you?* I knew. Lillian Hatfield Osterman is publisher and majority owner of the *Washington Daily Star.*

I played it straight. "Yes, Mr. Probst."

"Nelson, please. Would you hold a moment for Mrs. Osterman?" he said aloofly.

"Certainly." I moved a few steps to Tyler's port-a-bed and made the difficult maneuver of balancing the phone between my neck and shoulder while putting him down, almost losing the phone in the process. I glanced down at Tyler, who was fast asleep. He was peaceful. I wasn't.

What would the publisher want with me? We'd met a couple of times in her office in the months following the serial killings. Could this be a late welcome-back call? I doubted the publisher did that. A female voice interrupted my thoughts.

"Hello, Laura?"

"Yes. Hello, Mrs. Osterman." I couldn't call her by her first name. Certainly couldn't say "Hi, Lil."

"How is your son?" She had the soft, smooth, alto voice of a well-bred woman.

"Tyler? Oh, I, eh, just put him down," I stammered at her personal question. "He's doing very well."

"Excellent. I am delighted to hear that. Laura, I have wonderfully good news. You have been awarded the Pulitzer Prize in journalism for investigative reporting. Congratulations."

To say I was shocked would be a major understatement. My eyes teared. As much as I had thought about it and wanted it, it was overwhelming to hear my publisher utter the words: *You have been awarded the Pulitzer Prize in journalism for investigative reporting.*

"Laura?"

"I . . . I'm here," I stammered. "I'm just . . . I . . . well, thank you."

"No. It is we who thank you, Laura. I wanted to be the one to tell you. It is well deserved. Needless to say, it will be on the news tonight, and we will announce it on page one with your picture in the morning," the self-satisfied voice intoned.

I found the sofa and plopped down. Tears were running down my cheeks.

"The official announcement from Columbia University's School of Journalism will be made shortly. Do you have anyone there to help? It may get very busy for you."

The publisher's concern brought me back. I needed to call Anna. "We have a nanny—"

"Good," Osterman cut in. "Well, we will coordinate with Editor Lassiter. There will be an official presentation in a few weeks, a luncheon in your honor. You will find Nelson very accommodating about procedure."

"Yes, I'm sure. I'm a little overwhelmed."

"I'm sure you are, my dear."

I was sure her syrupy tone was well-meaning, but she was still the same Lillian Osterman who told Lassiter to *get your reporter under control or fire her.* I had been a beat reporter digging up dirt inside the White House, and people had complained, namely Gerty, our senior White House correspondent.

"Mrs. Osterman, I need to call my husband."

"Certainly. I fully understand. When will you be back in the office?"

"Tomorrow. Today, if you'd like," I sputtered. Anytime.

"Yes, well, at the earliest." She sounded perturbed.

"Shall I call Mr. Probst?" Then I remembered she would be calling Lassiter.

"No need," she said politely. "We will call Avery. There will be many things . . ." Her voice trailed off.

"Yes, of course. Does she know?"

"Yes."

I was finally regaining my composure. "I will call her right after I talk with my husband."

"Yes. We look forward to seeing you. And again, congratulations."

"Thank you. Your call is very special to me."

"Yes, well, you are the special one, Laura. I'll let you go."

Finally. "Thank you. Goodbye."

"Goodbye."

I punched in Jerry's private line as I went to the kitchen for a tissue. He answered on the second ring and gave me his code line that said he was in a meeting. I still blurted out the news. He burst out with excitement. I heard him explain to those in his office what had happened. I could feel his electricity.

"I'll wrap up here quickly," he said, letting those present hear him. "I'll be home within the hour."

I asked him to call Anna. I then called my assistant, Mary. She wanted to know who had called me and how I had been told. Little things like that meant a lot to the woman's sense of order. I called Lassiter. As controlled as my editor always was, I could hear in her tone that she was excited.

Next, I called Max, but got Delia, the officer who was Max's right arm. "He's somewhere in the building," she told me.

My excitement must have been obvious.

"Is this an emergency?"

Delia knew of the close relationship between Max and me. "I have wonderful news to share with him."

"I'll find him and have him call you. And whatever it is, I'm glad for you."

"Thanks, Delia. I won an award for writing, the Pulitzer, and I want to tell Max before the announcement is made public, which could be at any moment."

"I've heard of that award. It's heavy stuff, ain't it?"

"The heaviest. Have him call my cell phone." I felt out of breath.

"I'll find him if I have to set off an alarm, and I won't tell him," she promised.

I went to the kitchen for a bottle of water and downed it completely. I took three long, deep breaths, and during the last one, my cell phone rang. It was Lassiter.

"Mr. Probst called again about your meeting with the publisher. I think you should come in right after lunch."

"I will." We chatted a few minutes, an eternity for my scrappy boss. When Max called, we had a wonderful, reminiscence-filled talk.

Jerry arrived a few minutes later.

"Lassiter wants me in early this afternoon," I told Jerry as he walked in the kitchen. "Mrs. Osterman is eager to see me, and tomorrow the blush would be off for them. You know how it is with yesterday's newspaper."

"Fine. I'll drive."

We hugged. "I'd appreciate that," I said, my arms still around him.

"I'll drop you off tomorrow too," he said, rubbing my back. "With your picture on the front page, public transportation is not the mode you should take."

"Oh yeah. Things *will* change now, won't they?" I said, still holding him. Then my body began to shake, and I let the emotional tears flow.

He held me until I relaxed, then got me some tissues.

"Let's have a little lunch," I suggested in an unsteady voice.

"I'll take care of that. You rest. Anna will be here any minute. I'll explain what's going on. You're going to need all your energy for this afternoon."

"Lassiter was genuinely happy for me."

"Of course she was. She nominated you, didn't she?"

"I know, it's, well, you know . . ."

Anna came in and was concerned over my tearful state.

"I'm fine, Anna. It's good news."

She nodded, but still looked concerned.

"I'm going to take a shower. I put Tyler down forty-five minutes ago, Anna."

A little after 1:00, Jerry and I walked into a whirlwind of people, and a mini newsroom celebration erupted. I was so thankful Jerry was with me. We finally made it to Lassiter's office. Max was there. We hugged. Jerry had called him. He had a congratulatory card from the chief, who had also called Lassiter. My editor introduced me to Mr. Probst.

She and I talked briefly, then Mr. Probst ushered Jerry and me to the publisher's plush office. It was a memorable, gentle time. Mrs. Osterman and Managing Editor Barton Williams were gracious. We had tea and chatted.

It was over in about an hour, and Jerry and I were on our way home.

"I felt like I'd been in the presence of royalty," I reveled.

He smiled. "It was a very special time."

# 13

Senator Dalton sat in her office drinking her morning coffee and reading the *Washington Daily Star*'s front-page story about its Pulitzer Prize–winning reporter, Laura Wolfe. Roanne remembered the gruesome stories about a serial killer slaying pregnant women and stealing their fetuses. One victim had worked for Vice President Grayson. She buzzed Michael and asked him to come in.

When he entered, she held up the paper, front page facing him. "Have you read this?" she asked, pointing to Laura's picture.

"Not yet."

"She's quite the investigator. She went against the flow, survived two suspicious accidents, and withstood heavy criticism over her persistence to dig deeply into the life of one victim who had worked for the vice president."

"I remember. Seemed there was a sexual scandal or something."

"It appears this Laura Wolfe was right in her speculations. She led the FBI to the killer and has just been awarded the Pulitzer for investigative journalism."

Michael was ambivalent.

"She battled the odds," Roanne said pointedly. "She went up against the powerful and was undaunted by various attacks made on her person and her name . . ." She let that hang. Come on, *Michael*, she urged to herself, *don't make me spell this out.* "Replace sexual misconduct with political misconduct . . ."

Slowly his expression showed some comprehension. "Are you thinking . . . but what does she know about the Senate?"

"What did she know about the White House?"

"May I?" he asked, indicating the paper, which she passed to him.

His eyes scanned the front page, and he moved to the inside page, where the story continued. Roanne watched him, envying his photographic memory.

"Oh, I see she uncovered some fraud in a city government and turned the tables on some cops in—"

She smiled. "Exactly. She often put her career—"

"And life, it seems," he interrupted.

"Well, we don't want that."

"We?"

"She may be the perfect answer to our problem—to investigate the fall of Tutoxtamen. We've got plenty to get her started."

"Yeah, but she's a beat reporter for the Metro section. She was assigned—"

Roanne pressed him. "I know, but maybe we can entice her with more than just the 'unapproval' of a drug. Perhaps we can get her thinking that there is something much bigger happening."

"But what? We don't even know."

"Because we can't ask the questions. Or at least I can't."

He nodded. "So how do we get her interested?"

"You call her and set up a meeting with me. Somewhere quiet. My condo, for instance."

"Isn't she going to be busy with this Pulitzer thing for a while?"

"I'm a United States senator. Ms. Wolfe has a very curious mind . . ."

He nodded and went back to reading the article.

"Tell her we have suspicions about some possible illegal activity," Roanne prompted her AA. "Tell her it's beyond partisan politics. Tell her it's something that affects millions of Americans. Tell her there's a possible collusion between the pharmaceutical lobbyists and some senators.

"Give her until tomorrow—or until you can put together a good synopsis on Rogers, the testing results, and the FDA's reasons for turning down Tutoxtamen. Don't use any names, other than mine, of course. If she balks, tell her she'll get all the names if she decides to take this on."

# 14

**J**erry dropped me off at the paper, as promised. With my picture above the fold on page one, my anonymity on metro would have been short-lived. I remembered Max saying I'd probably start using my car to commute. He was right, but I don't think he had fame in mind.

Mary was not at her desk. I wrote her a note requesting a parking pass for the company garage. Cards and flowers filled my cubicle. Suddenly, Mary was alongside me. "Ms. Lassiter awaits both of us." We went to the editor's office.

"It seems like every local news outlet—radio, TV, print, cable channels, and C-SPAN—want a piece of our Pulitzer award winner," Lassiter said. "Mary, you're her gatekeeper today. Van will move your other reporters elsewhere."

Van Peoples was Lassiter's assignment editor.

"Van's talked with the TV folks. We'll be using the executive conference room, and they'll do their one-on-ones there. Each gets ten minutes. Van will ask everyone to sit in, to help save some time. He also suggested the conference room be set up sports-style, similar to post-game interviews in pro football and golf. Laura, you'll sit in the center with Mrs. Osterman on one side and Barton and me on the other."

I appreciated not having to stand. I could see this was a big day for the *Star* as well as for me. No one from the paper had ever won this particular Pulitzer.

"Van will be with you during the one-on-ones."

Unlike after the serial-killing story and all the fuss over me then, Jerry reminded me that I was the story this time. He encouraged me by saying,

"Act grateful. Remember, what you did was a big deal. Winning the award is a big deal. Some humility is called for." I agreed.

The news conference part lasted a little over forty-five minutes.

It drained me, and I asked for a short break. I went to the restroom and washed my face with cold water. I took some deep breaths and called Jerry, who answered immediately.

"How'd it go?"

I laughed. "Very well."

"I haven't been able to work. I went out for a walk."

"Sweetheart, I was fine." I took a small hairbrush from my bag.

"What's your schedule?"

"I've got TV one-on-ones next. Van will be with me." I placed my phone on the counter, putting it on speaker so I could brush my hair and touch up my makeup while we talked.

"How many, do you think?"

"Half dozen or so. There's not a lot more I can say that I haven't already said."

"Yeah well, you know reporters; they've got to ask the same question three, four—"

"Hey! I'm a reporter, too, you know," I said, leaning closer to the phone for added emphasis.

"Yeah, but you get it right the first time."

"Flattery will get you everywhere, Mr. Fields," I said, putting my things back in my bag. I adjusted my dark-blue jacket over my pale-blue shirt. I looked very much the executive, unlike my normal harried, nothing-in-place look.

"I'm having lunch in the Executive Dining Room with Barton Williams and Lassiter. I'll call you after that. Love you."

"Love you."

The interviews all went well. Most took less than the allotted time. They mostly wanted to know my feelings about being pregnant while tracking a serial killer who was killing pregnant women and to know about my relationships with the White House interns. The lunch was delightful. I felt that some of the extra attention from Barton was his way of saying he was sorry for almost having me fired.

Back at my desk, Mary had sorted out messages, cards, and hard copies of emails and faxes. She handed me some pink message slips. "I thought you might want to reply to these. There are only two."

"Max and who else?" I said, taking them.

"A friend, if I remember correctly."

I looked. "Oh my gosh!" I exclaimed, looking at the second slip. "Kat Turner. You're right; we did part friends."

"Well, I'll leave you to the rest. I have . . ." she paused, grinning. "I forgot. I don't have anybody else to assist today."

The newsroom had celebrated my scoop, breaking the serial killer story. Maybe this second celebration was a little like winning two Oscars in a row. It was great for the recipient, but others might be saying "enough is enough." There was still the luncheon Mrs. Osterman mentioned, but I thought I'd better get out on the beat and get my hands dirty. Although never *one of the gang*, I felt I had better act like one.

Mary interrupted my musing. I was still standing, staring down at my desk.

"Too daunting a task?" she asked.

"I'll be glad when the celebrating is over and I can get back to work. After today, we need to downplay all this and let me mess up my office."

"No more decorations, I promise."

I smiled. "You're like a kid."

"Maybe it's more like my having kids; I know what pleases them."

"Well, you certainly please me. Let's go through all this together, if you have the time."

"I'm all yours," she smiled. "This really is a big day."

We sorted out the messages: friends, insiders, outsiders, and ones we didn't know. Mary placed each group into a file folder, giving it a name.

I called Jerry and filled him in.

"You sound a little weary," he said, concerned.

"Can you pick me up before four?"

"I'll call you when I'm in the car."

I called Max and told him about the media bash.

"I'll be sure to watch as many channels tonight as I can."

I matched his tease. "What, you're not going to tape them?"

"Please, I'm not a teenager. I don't know how to run one of those tape machine things."

We laughed. It felt good.

"Oh, I almost forgot. One of my callers was Kat Turner."

"My, my. That is very special. Tell her I hope she is doing well."

I picked up the message slips, which now numbered five. One puzzled me. It was from a Michael Horne, administrative assistant to Senator Roanne Dalton. He wanted to congratulate me on the Pulitzer and to know if I could meet with the senator in the next couple of days.

A senator wanted to talk with me. I dialed his number.

After my call, I went immediately to Lassiter's office.

"He didn't tell me a lot. He's bringing me some papers tomorrow. He said it involved the pharmaceutical industry and one company in particular."

"He's coming here?"

"Delivering it personally."

"And he's Senator Dalton's AA?"

"That's what he said."

"I'll have Van check him out, see if he's who he says he is."

"He's definitely in the senator's office."

"Fine. Let's see what he's got." Her tone reflected her desire for our meeting to be over.

"Right," I said, standing.

"If it's got a local twist, we might be allowed to keep it here. We don't do Capitol Hill."

"We didn't do the White House either," I chirped, smiling cockily.

"How you coming along on that ballpark story?"

*Whoops.* I got carried away. "I'm on it."

As I left Lassiter's office, I felt things were finally getting back to normal.

# 15

I returned to my desk, properly chastised. I'd gotten too friendly, and Lassiter put a quick button on it. I didn't feel put upon. It was time to be reporter and editor.

I returned three of the four remaining calls, which were from media types. Before I got to Kat, I called my father, filling him in on my day, alerting him to the TV coverage. We'd had a nice chat last night. He'd reprinted the *Star*'s story on my award in his own paper, adding a couple of local touches.

We had a good laugh over that, and it felt so good. In fact, I couldn't remember when we had ever laughed over anything together. Our conversation had buoyed me. How wonderful it was to be able to share what I was doing with him.

Reconciling with my mother and father, having Tyler, and winning the Pulitzer all in less than a year was more than I had ever dreamt possible. Any one of them was huge, but all three: *Wow!* In addition, I had Jerry, a wonderful friend in Max, and a great job.

I thought of Janet Rausch's family in Iowa and the families of the other two murder victims. How had the Pulitzer story affected them? Janet's killing had brought down some self-absorbed people who had toyed with people's lives.

Then there was Kat Turner, a physical and mental victim in the saga. I'd saved her return call for last because I knew it would be the most emotional. I dialed.

"Kat Turner," she answered in her soft alto voice.

"Laura Wolfe."

"Laura! My gosh. Thanks for calling back."

"Hey, thanks for calling me."

"Congratulations. Wow! Our local paper carried your story on the first page," said the former vice presidential staffer, or intern, as they were familiarly called.

"How you doing?"

"Wonderfully. Scott and I are adjusting to married life. I've finished with my rehab."

"Fantastic." There had been a time when I wondered if Kat would ever fully recover.

"I go back for a checkup next month. I'm almost walking without a limp."

The car that had sideswiped us both had almost killed Kat. The driver, Milo Bannini—who worked for George Manchester, the Atlanta entrepreneur who was a major supporter of Vice President Grayson—had crashed into a telephone pole and died. If Max hadn't yelled, I wouldn't have escaped between parked cars. Unfortunately Kat, who had been a half step behind me, had been slammed into a parked car and come very close to dying.

Max had fired at the escaping vehicle hitting both it and the driver, causing the car to go out of control. At first we thought it had been an attempt on my life, but it turned out to be unrelated to anything about me or my job. Manchester had been interrogated, but he'd had no idea why his life-long friend and employee would do such a thing. Alcohol and drugs had not been involved. It was still a mystery.

"You must heal well . . . or was it your mother's soup?"

"A little of both," Kat laughed. "So, your life must be very busy. How's Tyler? Do you see Marsha?"

Marsha had been Janet Rausch's roommate, and Kat had been Janet's closest friend, working together in the VP's office. "Marsha was at Tyler's christening. She's working part-time in Jerry's office and finishing up at Georgetown Law."

"Tell her I said hi. Now, tell me about Tyler."

"He's growing, eats like a horse. We're blessed; he's a good, healthy, happy kid. We moved last fall into a house in Clarendon that has a back yard. We have an extra bedroom just waiting for visitors."

"I don't know," Kat said uncertainly.

"It's there, if you change your mind. We'd love to see you both."

"Too many horrible memories. I don't have nightmares, but I do wake up some nights and see Janet's face staring down at me."

I felt a chill. I offered, "What has helped me recover are all the changes in my life. Tyler, the new home, a great relationship now with my folks . . ."

"A Pulitzer!" Kat said brightly.

We talked awhile longer. For all her not wanting to return to Washington, Kat seemed to be holding onto the call. I finally ended it when we began repeating stuff.

We promised to stay in touch, and I hoped that would be true.

# 16

I got a solid night's sleep. Jerry, Tyler, and I enjoyed our morning. I drove in with my new parking permit affixed to my windshield. Mary said her request for that permit had sailed through. Driving my peppy little convertible into the garage was, as Yogi Berra once said, *déjà vu all over again*.

Jerry usually drove it these days so I could use his SUV to accommodate Tyler's car seat. We had considered trading the convertible in, but now that I was back at work, we decided there would be plenty of time to "mom-up" to a minivan.

Mary greeted me with a message that Michael Horne would like to see me.

"Anytime between 11:00 and 2:00 is good," I said.

"What are you up to?" she asked, alluding to my self-invented shorthand notes on the pad on my desk.

"I've pulled up stuff on FDA and its assorted subgroups."

"Did you find anything about the cost of drugs?" Mary asked. "That's real bad."

"Somehow I don't think that's what Mr. Horne has on his mind."

I logged in and surfed the paper's archives, rummaging through drug approvals. It was a lot of dull reading. Tiring of that, I swung over to articles on the new baseball team and the proposed construction of a new ballpark. I hard-copied half a dozen new stories and set up a file. I called a contact in City Hall and asked for copies of all City Council discussions or actions pertaining to the ballpark. The arduous part was researching these people, looking for connections. I felt a gurgle in my stomach and checked the time. It was a little after noon.

I told Mary I was heading to the cafeteria. A few minutes after I settled down to eat a grilled chicken salad, my cell phone rang. It was Mary. "What's up?"

"Mr. Horne is probably rounding the corner, as we speak," she said.

"Doesn't give us much notice, does he? I'll be there in ten minutes."

I entered the newsroom and headed for Mary's desk. A medium-sized man with dirty-blond, curly—no, tousled—hair stood by Mary's desk holding a thin, black briefcase.

"Mr. Horne," I said, walking up behind him.

He twirled to greet me. "Ms. Wolfe." It was a statement.

"I put another chair in your cubicle," Mary said flatly.

"Thank you, Mary. Mr. Horne," I said, motioning in the direction of my desk. "Let's go to my cubicle. It's small, but homey." For all his casual, thrown-together look, I sensed tenseness in him. He sat in the chair that Mary had provided and placed his briefcase on his lap. He unlatched its two hasps and removed a file folder, thinly filled.

"You will find the information in this folder is devoid of people or company names. Everything in here has been retyped on plain bond paper. I assure you that, other than the identities, we have not edited or characterized the sensitive information these pages contain," Michael Horne said firmly, as he handed me the folder and removed another.

"I have a duplicate of what I just gave you. If you like, I can wait while you browse it, maybe answer any—"

"I appreciate that. However," I said softly and non-threateningly, "I would prefer to take this home and read it at my own leisure."

"No. No, that's fine." He sounded relieved.

I smiled. "I'm so used to working on my own, I have built-in study habits."

"Believe me, I understand." He slid his folder back in and snapped the hasps. "The senator would very much like to meet with you privately. She suggests her place in Crystal City tomorrow night, if that fits your schedule."

I noticed he held my gaze easily. There was no come-on in him. He portrayed earnestness without acting pushy.

"We've been struggling with this issue," he said, "but when we addressed our leadership, we were rebuffed. If you've followed anything on this subject, you may identify a senator or two, maybe even a particular

company. If you choose to go forward, we will provide you with everything."
He flashed me a self-effacing smile.

I studied him as he spoke. He was around my age. His attire, to me,
represented a disguise. He wore earth colors, not the dark suit so typical
in Washington.

"I will read this at home this afternoon. I work short days here right
now."

"Yes. I saw in the news reports that you recently gave birth to a boy.
Congratulations. I hope our suggestion for an evening meeting isn't an
inconvenience."

"No, if we can make it about 7:00. We like to get my son's last feeding
in around 10:00." I was going to say breastfeeding, but some men are
squeamish about that.

"That should be fine." He stood and handed me his business card. I rose.

He said, "Thank you for seeing me so quickly. We feel time is working
against us. My home number is on the back of the card. Please feel free to
call me. I should be home after 7:00."

I gave him my card, and said, "I will be working from home tomorrow.
This has my cell number. We can confirm tomorrow evening's meeting
more easily this way. I'll walk you out."

When I returned to my desk, I buzzed Mary.

"Mr. Horne has gone. I have some reading to do. If there are no cries for
my body or soul, I'm going home. The last couple of days are catching up
to me."

"I think that's an excellent idea. Is your fax machine working?"

"You know, I'm not sure. The copier and printer part work. I guess it
does. We have a dedicated line for the computer. Let me get that for you.
You can give it a try."

"Before you go, call Mr. Probst. They've had a couple of network
requests."

"As long as they're not for today or tomorrow. I want to coast into a
restful weekend."

"You're sounding too sensible—are you sure you are you?"

"I'll call Mr. Probst, check in with the boss, and then check out with
you."

"I'm in awe," Mary said.

**17**

"Tyler, he do good. Eat good," Anna told me. "He sleep now."

I nodded. "I have some reading, for work," I said, holding up the manila envelope.

"Okay," Anna said, and went to the kitchen.

I sat down with Horne's envelope and extracted about a dozen or so letter-sized pages. I curled up in the corner of the sofa and scanned the first page, and then the second, of Michael's synopsis. It became immediately clear there were multiple issues.

Dalton and Horne speculated that heavy pressure was being put on the FDA to disapprove Tutoxtamen, a drug that early testing showed to be a potential miracle cancer-cure drug. There were questions about senatorial ethics. Horne speculated pharmaceutical lobbyists were buying Senate cooperation to get this drug rejected. Why would they want that? I thought they lobbied *for* their members, not against them.

Also included were pages on drug pricing, formularies, and Medicare.

The brief spelled out staggering results the cancer drug had on humans and, before that, on animals. The drug had received outstanding grades. Horne had put a lot into synthesizing what must have been copious pages. I'd have to thank him.

A familiar itch began creeping up my spine. If these tests were true, and that's a huge *if*, then why were nonscientific senators so against the drug? According to what I was reading, the FDA hadn't questioned the test results until recently. What was to be gained or lost here? Who would benefit financially? Who might not? The old saying *follow the money* was not to be ignored. I tried reading more, but I couldn't concentrate. My mind was on fire with the multiple issues. Whose ox was being gored?

Was something really wrong with the drug? I would need an unbiased expert. The closest I'd ever been to the drug industry was getting a prescription filled. Jerry needed to look at this. He might see some legal issues or know how the FDA works.

I didn't normally have the time or opportunity to discuss my work with Jerry until after I'd written the story. The rare times we could kick things around, I enjoyed it. He was an excellent sounding board, agree or not. He certainly had helped during the serial killings. Jerry was also good at pulling me out when I got in deep and when I couldn't see the forest for the trees.

I heard Tyler. Anna must have gotten him up. I looked at my watch, I'd been at it for nearly two-and-a-half hours, and it was nearing Anna's time to leave. I heard Tyler again. It sounded like he was talking to Anna. I heard her soft voice, but not her words. I wondered if she was teaching him Spanish.

There would have been a time, not too long ago, when I would have resented any domestic activity getting in the way of my work. No distractions. Now after four months of maternity leave with Tyler, I almost looked at it the other way around.

# 18

I arrived in the office at 9:30. I had talked with Michael Horne from home last night, asking him about Senate procedures, something Jerry said I should find out. I was also curious about what, if any, paper trail existed that might document the side effects the FDA had purported and who had tracked the testing.

I knew little of how the Senate conducted themselves. It appeared to me things went on there in a very aloof manner, a world unto itself. Where were the checks and balances? The Senate advises and consents on the executive branch. Was there a similar system in place to do the same on Congress? If so, how did it work?

Congress appeared immune to scrutiny, except for the criminal activity of a member. An analogy that popped into my mind was that of trying to prove a cop committed an illegal act with no one to corroborate it. The police have an internal affairs office. Was there something similar for senators? I'd heard of an ethics committee, but senators ran that.

The Senate appeared to have oversight on everything, making them dangerously powerful and open to all sorts of opportunities. Maybe Michael Horne and Senator Roanne Dalton had a legitimate concern.

I called Lassiter's assistant and asked to see my editor following the staff meeting.

Jerry had brought up what a drug failure could do to a company's worth, which had made me wonder whether the company might have built up their drug's potential, after which insiders may have sold their holdings at the inflated price. He said he'd look into it, once we had the company's name.

I pushed my mind onto Horne. He had provided a lot of ammunition, but no gun to fire it. His basic concern was with senators, pharmaceutical companies, and lobbyists possibly defrauding the American people. That would constitute a conspiracy and bring in the FBI. I felt at least one of those senators would have to be powerful, able to push things through and rally legions to him, or her.

I felt antsy; Lassiter's meeting was running long. I called Horne's cell.

"This is Michael."

"Hi, this is Laura Wolfe. I'll meet with the senator. I'm waiting to see my editor—"

"Editor?"

"Look, I can't go probing around," I fibbed, "without official backing. Just so you know, I've gotten in trouble when I didn't follow that directive." And that was true.

"I understand," he said, but sounded unsure.

He was difficult to read.

My intercom buzzed. "Ms. Lassiter is available," Mary said.

"I'm on my way," I told Mary. "Michael, I've got to go. And don't worry."

**19**

"That pretty much sums it up," I told Lassiter.

"Sounds like a lot of mishmash to me. What do we know—?" She stopped and pushed a button on her intercom. "Van?"

There was a momentary pause. "Yes ma'am."

"Did you get anything back on Michael Horne?"

"There's not much on him, but he is who he says he is. He majored in political science at the University of Pennsylvania and got a master's degree in business at Wharton. He's worked for Senator Dalton almost six years."

I jumped in. "That means he worked for H.T. Dalton and stayed on when his wife . . . Van, was he H.T.'s AA?"

"I don't remember . . . oh, here it is. He became AA last spring."

"That's after Roanne Dalton was appointed to her husband's seat."

Van continued. "I have a whole bunch of stuff on Mrs. Senator Dalton. Did you know she was a beauty queen, made the top five in Miss America?"

"Thank you, Van, get that all to me," Lassiter said flatly.

"Will do."

Lassiter turned back to me. "All right. Looks like Horne has some credentials. We'll start a file—without naming names, just a pharmaceutical piece. It'll make a nice project for our newly hired copy people."

"Senator Dalton wants to meet with me privately."

"Go for it. Meanwhile, I have to pass this by Barton, make sure we're not stepping on any journalistic toes up on the Hill." She held up Michael's file folder. "Are these your only copies?"

"Yes."

She handed them to me. "Make a set for me. I'll get back to you after I've talked with Barton. And get me the name of the pharmaceutical company."

That ended our session. I went straight to the copy machine and ran off the pages, hoping Mary wouldn't show up. It would hurt her feelings, my not asking her to do this, but I thought it worth the risk. Fortunately, no one showed up.

Back at my desk, I called Horne and told him to set up my meeting with his senator.

"There are no votes scheduled for this afternoon, so she could make it a little earlier than 7:00, if you like."

"I have to go home first in any case. I need to call my husband. It'll really depend more on his schedule. I don't think I could make it before 6:30."

I called Jerry's private line, but he didn't answer. I dialed the office number.

"Mr. Fields's office," Sophie said softly.

"Hi, Sophie. It's Laura. Is he in?"

"He's not in right now, but he is expected back by 3:00."

"Ask him to call me right after you talk with him."

"We will not hear anything before then."

"Okay. Thank you."

"You are welcome." The line went dead.

I hung up. Sophie was super-efficient and super-literal. Jerry says she was dynamite in her job and a whiz at editing. She'd drive me crazy if I had to work with her on a daily basis. I buzzed Van and asked for copies of what he had on Horne and the Daltons. He'd get them to me.

"Have them put on my desk please, not Mary's."

I went to the cafeteria for a salad. Copies of Van's research were on my desk when I returned. I read all of them, including copies of newspaper articles about Roanne McAllister's beauty-pageant escapades, H.T.'s crash, Roanne McAllister Dalton's appointment to the Senate, and her primary and general election wins.

She and Michael were both well educated. I saw no blips on the screen— very clean. Van noted he found no connections between Dalton, Horne, or any pharmaceutical company. There was some pharma Political Action Committee (PAC) money that had been donated to both Dalton campaigns, but nothing leaped out as unusual.

Jerry called before 3:00. I gave him the short version. He'd be home by 5:00.

"I was talking with Ralph Morgan today on another matter and asked him about any contacts he might have had with the pharmaceuticals," Jerry said. "He'd had some for then-Senator Rick Grayson, but not after Grayson became the Veep. I didn't mention anything about Dalton, only that you were working on PAC stuff in preparation for the impending battle in the Senate over discount drugs and Medicare."

"Anything he has will help, will give me a comparison to what Dalton and Horne tell me."

I called Anna and told her I'd be home by 4:00. Everything there was good. I called Horne to say I'd aim for 6:30. He said the senator would be home by 6:00. He then gave me instructions on which garage to use, which numbers to punch in, and the rest. Dalton's condominium building was right off Jefferson Davis Highway in Crystal City, a mile from the Potomac River.

My intercom buzzed. Lassiter wanted to see me.

My editor started talking as soon as I entered her office. "Barton has given us the green light. We're to keep him in the loop. He'll let his Senate correspondent, Claire Rowley, in on it. Nobody else has a need to know. Rowley will give you a tour once you've cleared their security check and you get new credentials, which should only take a couple of days. Your normal press badge won't suffice."

"My meeting is on with Senator Dalton tonight."

She nodded. "Remember, we have people to do the digging. You don't have to do it all yourself," she admonished.

"Yeah, I do forget that. I'll be glad for the help."

Lassiter gave me a glance that seemed to question whether to believe me or not.

"I will," I insisted.

She gave me her half smile, Harrison Ford-style. "I'm glad, but seeing is believing."

# 20

I wrote out questions I wanted to ask Senator Dalton. I felt a little unsure of myself. I was used to criminal cases. This one was outside my comfort zone. Then it hit me. "That's what I'm missing," I said aloud. I called Max's cell and caught him leaving a dry cleaner's on Georgia Avenue north of Howard University, where a murder and robbery had taken place the previous night.

"Hayes and I are wrapping up," my favorite homicide captain said. "What's up?"

"I'm getting into an area I'm not familiar with . . . the senator I told you about . . ."

"Dalton?"

"Right. I'm meeting her tonight. It looks like I will be spending time on Capitol Hill."

"Why don't we grab a cup of coffee? You have the time?"

"I want to be home by 4:00, 4:30. Jerry will be there at 5:00. My meeting is at 6:30 in Dalton's Crystal City condo."

"I'll be there in fifteen with the coffee. We can walk across to the park."

Max arrived very nearly on the button. He parked, and we walked across to the nearly vacant, one square-block patch of green grass with blooming spring flowers and trees.

"I feel a little out of my league," I said, as we sat on a bench.

"This is not unlike what you have experienced in the past, except that you are not working with clues and evidence."

"Right. I'm in uncharted waters. PAC money and under-the-table deals that can be explained away six ways from Sunday."

"Don't get too far out in front of yourself. I haven't read what you have, but I daresay there's little if any hard evidence for you to chew on."

"Exactly. It's all speculation."

"Hearsay? Or someone's interpretation?"

I took a sip of my coffee. "Both."

"Do you believe Senator Dalton, or is it that you want to believe her?"

"I don't know."

"Go back to the beginning."

"I'm not sure where that is."

"Try this, somebody comes to me and says so-and-so is planning to have Mr. X killed," Max encouraged, trying to get me started on a train of thought.

"Dalton's AA comes to me," I said, warming up to an explanation, "representing her, and tells me that she believes some senators are colluding with the pharmaceutical lobbyists over some drug under consideration by the FDA."

"Very good. Now, the senator tells you what she suspects, but gives you no facts to back up that allegation, so look at her credibility. What motivates her to tell you this?"

"For one, Senator Dalton is politically powerless, and it would be political suicide for her to go up against her leadership."

"You've been there, done that. Last year, you took on some pretty powerful folks."

"Yes, but that was because I saw the potential for abuse, an antagonistic relationship."

"Bingo. You have two sides here you can play off each other, right?"

I nodded, "Pro-drug, anti-drug. What motivates both sides? We need to carefully observe attitudes and keep close tabs on their actions."

"And what reasons they give. Dalton has given you a lot of information, written and spoken, opposing the overwhelming majority of her party. Who has what to gain?"

"Right. I see where there may be ethical problems, money passing hands."

"Okay, why? I would judge it to be something very big, something a freshman senator can't take on alone. She needs outside help and calls you."

I sat back and took a deep breath, blowing it out.

Max said, "She doesn't have the goods to carry it off alone. That's where you come in. Be aware that in a politically partisan hot bed like the Senate, each party draws a line in the sand, regardless of the right or the wrong. It then becomes the party's way or no way."

"But this is intra-party. It's unlike a partisan battle, where neither view may be true. There will be a right *and* a wrong here."

"That makes it more explosive. Getting in between those forces is like when we walk into a domestic fight and get turned on by both," he said emphatically.

"How would I be in the middle? Wouldn't I be the friend to one and enemy to the other?"

"Your only hope here is that Senator Dalton has solid enough facts to get you started. One advantage she may have is her newness in the Senate, not sullied. She is too clean to be besmirched or threatened, and she can't be blackmailed."

"Never compromised? That's got to be scary for the big guys. They won't be able to play intimidation games."

"She has her father, a former two-term governor. He's a power she could call on in a pinch. However, she's no slouch—she impressively went out and got herself elected, against everyone's wishes."

He surprised me. "How do you know all that?" I asked.

"Her AA, Mr. Michael Horne, was the victim of a mugging in January. We were involved early on . . . a possible homicide. He was transported to emergency unconscious. His ID told us where he worked, and Capitol police told us the rest. They notified the senator, who frankly, I was not familiar with, so we did a background check. When you told me about her, I had Delia pull up what we had, which you are welcome to."

"Any skeletons?"

"She's about as clean as a person can be and still be mortal."

**21**

**T**yler's wanting to play made it doubly hard for me to get out of the house by 6:00. This would be the first time since my son was born that my work overflowed into my time with him. Jerry nearly had to push me out of the house.

Horne's directions were excellent. I was in the garage and on the elevator in no time. The elevator doors opened onto a recessed area off a main hall. The décor spoke quality, but at the same time, comfort—tastefully upscale with textured wallpaper in muted colors, chair rails, and plush carpet. The lighting was muted without being dull.

I pressed Senator Dalton's bell, which resulted in a distant chiming sound, suggesting a well-insulated door. I stood in front of the peephole. A female voice came through a speaker I had not seen. "Yes?"

"Laura Wolfe," I looked around the doorframe, but could not locate a speaker. I wondered if there was also video. I got no response, but then the door opened.

"Ms. Wolfe. Roanne Dalton," she said, extending a hand. "Come in, please."

If I hesitated, it was barely a second. I was prepared for a pretty woman, but . . . I recovered. "Thank you." I shook her hand.

"Please, to your right," she said graciously.

I walked through the two-door wide archway into an elegantly decorated living room. Drapes were closed on what I imagined were large windows or a patio door leading onto a balcony. I guessed that the furniture was French provincial or some eighteenth- or nineteenth-century period. I was not up on furniture. We had *early eclectic* at home.

She was at my side. "I thought we'd sit there." She indicated a mid-room sofa, coffee table, and twin, flanking upholstered chairs. They looked much more like they were for show than sitting. I aimed for one of the chairs and placed my briefcase-like bag alongside it.

"I didn't put anything out for us, but I do have a small selection to choose from."

"Water is fine, thank you."

She started in the direction from which we had just come. "Come on, we'll get it together."

"You have a very attractive place."

"I'll take you on the nickel tour, if you'd like." She disappeared through the foyer.

I followed into a short hall, which emptied into a very white, immaculate kitchen. It looked like it had never been used. Tyler would have changed that fast. Recessed fluorescent lights behind translucent panels gave the feeling of daylight without shadows. The senator had a formality about her, accompanied by an easy demeanor. She made me feel immediately impressed, but comfortable.

Dalton wore a scoop-necked, short-sleeved, peach cashmere pullover; a strand of pearls; a medium-grey, knee-length skirt; and low heels—sort of preppy. The outfit accentuated her good figure without being showy. She looked in great shape and made me feel frumpy. However, I didn't hate her for it.

She removed two tumblers from a cabinet. "I don't do much cooking. No fun doing it for one," she said, placing the first glass into the ice-and-water dispenser in the refrigerator door.

"I know the feeling. When I lived alone, I was more of a snacker."

"That's an easy habit to get into." She clanked ice cubes into both glasses, filled them with water, and handed one to me. "I gather you might not care for a snack."

I shook my head. "Pregnancy and a strict, motherly news assistant weaned me off that."

"Well, shall we?" she asked politely, gesturing toward the living room.

We headed to the living room, the tour forgotten. I sat in what proved to be a very comfortable, sturdy chair. She sat at the end of the sofa nearest me and slid two coasters into place for our glasses. I set mine down and took out my steno pad and Horne's folder.

I set them on the table. "You put a lot of work into these papers."

"This is and has been a subject of great interest to Michael."

I got the impression she wanted me to know she had not initiated this.

She continued, "He's been concerned for some time about the pressure from the pharmaceutical lobbyists. After I was elected, I sat down with Michael and had him explain it to me in detail. I assume you are familiar with my background."

"Yes."

"I honestly didn't get into the flow of everything until after I decided to run for the seat. I was only supposed to come here and fill out H.T.'s term—my father's idea."

"He's a former governor?"

She nodded. "He thought my filling out H.T.'s term would be good for my career. I've wondered whether I should be called doctor senator or senator doctor."

"Hmmm, it could become more complicated when you go back to teaching . . . you'd have professor to add to that mix," I quipped.

We laughed congenially.

"My mother prefers I be referred to as senator, replacing the sobriquet, *former beauty queen*—a term used too often in papers around the state."

The senator said all of that without any pretentiousness. She was, after all, a very beautiful woman who happened to have been a beauty queen, but who now had two graduate degrees, a university teaching career, and a seat in the United States Senate.

I wasn't in her league in looks or education, but we both were working girls and strongly influenced by our fathers. The difference there being she had accepted hers and I had fled from mine. Now, she was a senator and I, a Pulitzer-winning reporter. We both had celebrity, regardless of rank. The winner of the Congressional Medal of Honor was saluted by generals and admirals. I had that sort of parity with her. She had the position, and I had the honor.

"I appreciate you seeing me, Laura. May I call you Laura? Please call me Roanne, or Ro, if you prefer."

"Laura's fine, but because of our current relationship, I'd prefer addressing you as senator."

She smiled. "Ah, the wall of objectivity best not be bridged. Well, how shall we proceed?"

"I'd like you to relate exactly what occurred between you and your Senate leadership, and what relationship, if any, you have had with the unnamed pharmaceutical company in the papers Michael Horne gave me."

"Yes. The pharmaceutical is Rogers. Their founder and chair, Harley Rogers, developed the drug Tutoxtamen. I have had no contact with Mr. Rogers or his company, and I don't believe H.T. had either. I had asked my financial advisor to review both of our portfolios—H.T.'s back to when he became senator. He never owned any Rogers stock."

That was as straightforward as it gets.

"Michael felt you would ask that," she said unassumingly.

"That's fine." I sat ready with my pad in hand.

Senator Dalton spent the next twenty minutes going over everything that had happened relating to Rogers, including her conversation with fellow senator Crawford, a new name to me. By the time she had finished, both our glasses were empty and I had nearly twenty pages of notes. I needed to excuse myself, and she pointed the way to the guest bathroom.

When I reappeared, she had refilled our glasses. "Would you care for anything else?"

"No thanks." We resumed our conversation.

"Would you begin with your concerns about ethics, illegalities?"

The senator looked down for a moment, collecting her thoughts. At that same moment, a thought popped into my head, and I interrupted before she responded.

"Excuse me, senator. Have you discussed any of this with members of the Ethics Committee?"

"No," she said bluntly.

Her emphasis made it sound like she had no plans to do so either. "Please, continue."

"I was approached after I won the primary by a pharmaceutical lobbyist at a Fourth of July party here in Washington. They were introducing themselves to me. No proffers were made. I'm sure they assumed my politics were the same as H.T.'s.

"They are a very powerful lobby. The drug industry is in a unique position to help or exploit American citizens. They have something we all want when suffering an illness or in severe pain. They advertise and market their products so suavely, telling us they have all the answers for what ails us."

She paused to take a drink, which gave me a chance to catch up with my notes. I had been writing furiously, even in my shorthand.

"They know this and we pay for it, big time. They are experts in rationalization, and without government protection, our citizens are in jeopardy. This becomes more desperate in a recession, when people are out of work and/or lose their medical benefits. State budgets drop to where they can't keep up financially. With no enforceable controls in place to curb drug prices, we bow to the pressure of the pharmaceutical lobby and do nothing.

"It takes a concerted effort always to have the votes go in one's favor, and that is where I believe illegal activities germinate. Deals are made, and who suffers while they profit? The seniors, the unemployed, the unemployable, the part-timers, and the families who are devastated with life-threatening diseases."

The senator leaned slightly closer to me. "The drug industry relies on complexities, where no one is willing or able to put a finger on the solution. Watchdog groups storm the gates but are rebuffed and ridiculed. Congress pays them lip service at best, unless it's a partisan issue. The protesters don't have the money to compete with the drug companies."

She smirked when she said that and saw my puzzled look. "I'm sorry. I was struck by a funny thought." She paused and then decided to tell me. "I don't think Congress or the entire federal government has the money either. It would take extraordinary financing to compete with the pharmas . . . protestors would have to hire very expensive, professional lobbyists and back them up with TV and print ads."

"Let's go back to illegal activities. Do you believe actual payoffs were involved?"

"Nothing I can prove. What I meant was that some of my fellow lawmakers are sympathetic to the pharmas' cause."

She paused, appearing to reflect on something. I wrote feverishly. She continued. "On second thought, to your question, yes, I do believe some colleagues have been bought off. Those who don't play the lobbyists' games at all, who rebuff them are, well . . ."

She let that hang, and took a sip of water. She then continued.

"Did you know there are more pharmaceutical lobbyists on Capitol Hill than there are of us, including both houses of Congress? Back on the Fourth, while I involuntarily listened to that pharmaceutical lobbyist, it was difficult to maintain a polite demeanor when he coolly and so very sincerely told me how put-upon they were, how misunderstood they were . . . well, that nearly turned my stomach."

# 22

I couldn't go to bed when I got home after my visit with Dalton. She had pushed a bunch of my buttons. My hair was on fire. I couldn't cope with millions of people dying to satisfy the corrupt personal gains of a few senators and lobbyists.

I wasn't so naïve to think this sort of thing didn't go on. I'd seen corruption in each of the cities where I had worked. However, this was different. This was the Senate of the United States, which magnified the greed. I hadn't asked for and she hadn't offered any names.

I'd know soon enough, once I got into that environment. Dalton had mentioned Senator Gavin Crawford. He'd spoken to her about her opposition to her leadership's stance as it supported the FDA's denial of the new drug. Dalton considered him a friend, not one involved in the cabal.

The virtual island that is Capitol Hill is surrounded by the streets where I plied my daily beat—in the same town, but worlds apart. I don't have a "Max" up there. It's a world of subtleties and nuances. Their muggings aren't done with a knife, a club, or a gun. They're done passive-aggressively with manipulation and bribery.

It was nearly 2:00 when Jerry dragged me off to bed.

# 23

I felt lethargic after Jerry woke me around 7:30 a.m. He had been up with Tyler since 6:00. Our five-month-old was playing in his highchair when I arrived in the kitchen. I welcomed a much-needed cup of hot coffee. Jerry went up for a shower. He had a meeting at 9:00.

I played with and talked to Tyler, who was having the time of his life slapping his little toys around the tray and onto the floor. Tyler thought the whole thing was a game. He squirmed and flapped his arms, his bright blue eyes shining with delight. I checked his diaper and, finding it dry, put him in his playpen.

I warmed my coffee and sat in sight of my active son, who was now attempting to put a square block into a round hole. The same thing I was trying to do. I looked through the paper. I was in the business section, which I rarely paid any attention to, when Jerry came down. I rushed upstairs— my turn. I was back in the kitchen by 8:20 and found Tyler in his father's lap. Jerry had a small, non-shedding, waterproof blanket protecting him, just in case. The two boys were jabbering away. How blessed we were to have such a healthy, happy son.

Jerry set Tyler down in his playpen, which Tyler mildly compained about. It didn't last long. He quickly discovered a toy. Jerry took his suit jacket off the back of a kitchen chair, gave me a light kiss, and went out the door.

Anna came a few minutes early, and as usual Tyler was excited to see her. I wondered which he would learn to say first: *Mama* or *Anna*. She and I went over a few items, I hugged and kissed Tyler goodbye, and passed him over to his adoring nanny.

# 24

Michael had found Gordon Pederson—Senator Crawford's AA—easier to get along with than he had anticipated. Gordon was open to dining with Nancy, Tyrell, and Michael at a little café on the Hill. Michael had chosen it because he'd found out that Gordon enjoyed the place.

Michael liked what Senator Dalton stood for and felt trusted by her. She genuinely sought his counsel and built him up to staff by deferring to him on those issues that were his bailiwick. He had no plans to leave his job.

Being in intimate discussions with a beautiful woman might be difficult for a heterosexual male. Even he felt her allure at times. His relationship with Nancy was very much the same way. They shared many secrets. He was a male friend she could turn to when things went bad in one of her relationships. Nancy's big worry each time she fell out of love was that she would wake up, be over forty and single, and panic. She also had constant anxieties about her career. He, Nancy, and Tyrell had shared many a laugh. They had a tight relationship, which is what made Nancy the perfect ally to loosen the tongue of Crawford's AA.

Michael smiled at that thought.

# 25

I arrived at the paper at 9:30 hoping to see Lassiter right away, but she was "elsewhere in the building," her news assistant told me.

I waved to Van, who was in his office on the phone, and then swung by Mary's desk. No one home. I felt like going out and coming back in. Instead, I went to my desk and read over my Dalton notes. I was blessed with clear handwriting and a self-invented shorthand. After a short review, I began typing. I bulleted notes on a pad, my crib sheet for when I talked with Lassiter.

My intercom buzzed. It was Mary. "Editor Lassiter can see you now." I collected my stuff and headed for her office. I was surprised to find Barton Williams there.

"Close the door behind you," Lassiter said. That startled me, and I hesitated. "Not to worry." She motioned for me to close it and sit.

I did as asked. I noticed the blinds on the windows facing into the office had been drawn and wondered what was going on. Barton stood, waiting for me to sit. He had a puzzled look on his face. "Good to see you again so soon, Laura."

Lassiter, knowing how my mind works, spoke, "If Laura seems a little concerned, Barton, it's because I have a policy of never closing my door unless I'm firing someone."

There was a momentary pause while a herd of snails crossed the room, then a burst of laughter from Barton. "That's certainly not going to happen."

Lassiter took control. "This is about you covering the Senate."

I sat next to Barton, who was winding down. Why did I do these things to myself? Of course, I wasn't being fired. Why would I even think that? Why do I think the worst?

Barton said. "I understand you met privately with Senator Dalton last evening."

"Yes. At her apartment."

I became aware of something different in the room. When Barton was present, Lassiter usually sat out in the room, in the copse of chairs away from her desk. However, today she was sitting behind her desk. This told me she was the lead editor in this discussion, if not in true rank.

Lassiter began, "Our sending you up on the Hill is not like sending any reporter. Your new celebrity will attract attention and questions, like . . . why?"

"Yes," Barton said, shifting in his chair to face me. "In your normal beat, you wouldn't be regarded differently, except for a comment about your award."

He appeared uncomfortable, which was uncharacteristic for him. "Going up on the Hill . . . well, that's new territory for you. Your presence will create speculation about why you are there."

"We don't know," Lassiter jumped in, "exactly how Capitol Hill reporters will react, but having a Metro reporter with a Pulitzer in her crib might make some wonder."

My mind raced, but I kept my mouth shut.

"Yes," continued Barton. "We've been scratching our heads, so to speak, and have come up with what we hope will mollify the situation."

Mollify?

"We are reassigning you," Barton said assertively.

He paused and looked at Lassiter. I held my breath.

"We are changing your title to Feature Writer," Lassiter said.

I was stunned and then anxious. I didn't want to leave Lassiter. Not yet anyway.

"But," my editor went on, leaning into her desk, "you won't be physically moving. You will stay where you are."

"Yes," Barton added quickly. "You will continue to report to Editor Lassiter. I will be kept in the loop to ease our congressional reporters' minds, if that need arises. You know how people talk."

That showed how blind I could be. To me, this was just another assignment, different location. I never thought about my celebrity.

He went on. "We have no idea where this Rogers thing is going. We have not gotten far enough into this to understand Senator Dalton's position. After what happened last year, you know, with what you uncovered and all, we don't want to raise any flags that we're looking into the private lives of some senators."

He chuckled a little too nervously, I thought.

"That's why the title Feature Writer," Lassiter said, emphasizing the title. "Using your considerable knowledge of the DC government, your assignment will be to look into the relationship between the DC government and the federal government. See how the current system works, and what might be needed to improve it."

"I'd love to do that story," I blurted.

"Yes, it will be considered a local story. I have spoken with Claire Rowley, our senior congressional correspondent, and asked her to show you around, which she is happy to do. You won't need to stay in contact with her after that."

My head was spinning. Both editors were being very careful to explain away my presence on the Hill. Instead of hiding me or sending me to spy school, they've given me a useful cover. I might even do some real work on it, if or when things heat up.

"Laura," Lassiter said, jolting me out of my thoughts, "to complete the cover, you may have to spend a little time on the House side, go to some committee hearings. I know it will be dull, but then when you ease into FDA stuff, you can cut that off entirely. You may find schmoozing with other reporters a help. I'm sure some would like to socialize with you anyway."

Lassiter knew how independent I was, that I wasn't a mixer.

"Use your best judgment," she said indifferently.

I wondered if Barton thought investigating Senator Dalton's allegations was a good idea, but sending me up on Capitol Hill wasn't.

"I suggest," he said, "you stay away from the pharmaceutical lobbyists. Use this as a breaking-in time, getting background for your cover."

Lassiter cut in. "Schmooze like you did when you first went to City Hall, the council meetings, events that included the mayor, that sort of thing."

"We may be more worried about this than is warranted," Barton half mumbled.

I wished this meeting would come to a fast conclusion.

"You could even joke about the DC/Fed thing as being next to impossible," he chuckled, "and that you were probably assigned to it while the paper decided what to do with you."

I didn't like any of that—neither the whole idea of "mixing" nor Barton's giggle.

He went on. "You have just won a most prestigious award, Laura. It is natural that some may feel a little envy. That is really their problem. Only Avery, Van, and I will know the true purpose of your mission."

I saw Lassiter chomping at the bit for this meeting to end. I decided to help and stood. "When do I start?"

Barton automatically stood.

Lassiter smiled. "Now."

# 26

I had barely gotten out of the shower, getting ready for my first visit to Capitol Hill, when Jerry called up to me.

"Laura, put on WTOP."

Why would I want an all-news radio station? Besides, I liked my easy jazz station. But . . . Jerry was not into idle prattle.

"Hurry, it's almost the top of the hour."

"Okay," I called back to him. I switched stations, catching the tail end of the weather report, followed by a musical jingle, call letters, and finally the news anchor's voice.

"The FDA announced late last night that Rogers Pharmaceuticals's drug Tutoxtamen, touted to be a miracle cure for most cancers, has been denied approval. Reaction opposing the decision has been swift and vociferous. In a late night release, Senate Minority Leader Olin Davis called the decision capricious and without merit. Senate Majority Leader Thomas Kelly has not been available for comment."

*Well, I thought, whether Senator Dalton likes it or not, she is a member of the majority and will be questioned about it. How would she answer that, seeing she supported the leader?*

"Pretty heavy stuff," Jerry said, standing in the bedroom doorway. "A piece I heard while you were in the shower said there were scientific concerns about potential side effects and that Rogers would have to—"

"I know," I interrupted, "do more testing."

"That means a couple of years."

I continued dressing. "More like many years. It's known as FDA's purgatory. What time you going in?"

"Early. 8:30. I'll call Anna."

He knew I'd want to leave early, too. "You're a sweetheart."

When I joined Jerry and Tyler in the kitchen, Jerry was watching the *Today Show*. The male host was just switching to a female reporter on split screen with him. She was outside Rogers Pharmaceuticals in New Jersey.

"We've been told that Sherman Rogers, president and CEO of Rogers Pharmaceuticals, is returning from a family trip in Naples, Florida, and will be making a statement later this morning. People coming into work did not want to talk to us. One woman appeared to have tears in her eyes . . ."

Jerry turned off the set. "The tears thing was a nice touch," he quipped.

"I guess. Except we don't know why she was crying. Could have been dust in her eye."

"Ah, never take anything at face value. You're right." He grinned. "The reasons we attribute to things without knowing the backstory are astounding."

I agreed. "That's where the trouble usually begins."

"Well, that's not something you have been guilty of, my love."

He'd heard me too many times on that subject.

"Why, thank you, Mr. Fields."

"So, what do you think?"

"About the woman?" I teased.

He shook his head and waited, so I got back on point.

"It was inevitable. They were probably waiting for Dalton to fall into line."

"What's your next move?"

"Talk to Sherman or Harley Rogers. I'm inclined to believe there's a lot more behind the FDA's decision than just a suspicion of side effects. Michael Horne and Senator Dalton have provided me with very positive test results, but I'll need to see Rogers's results and get independent corroboration, if that's possible. Testers may all be under the pharmas' thumb."

"My time is up here, my love. Looks like you are into another story you can sink your teeth into," Jerry said in an overacted grimace.

"I don't know. These politicians and lobbyists are slicker than a greased watermelon."

# 27

I paced the long corridor outside the Senate chamber waiting for Senator Dalton. On my way here on Metro, Michael had called and asked if I could meet with the senator at 11:00. I was at the far end of the great hall in my pacing when Dalton emerged, coming out of the chamber or the Cloakroom, looking trim and well turned out as usual. "Senator," I called, as I rushed toward her.

She turned as I made my way through a small group of men, half of whom had turned to look back at the former beauty queen, causing me to have to avoid their wayward paths. I was sure their minds were certainly as wayward.

"Good morning, Laura." She extended her hand.

I took it. "Senator."

"I apologize for my tardiness, I was waiting to see the leader. I wanted us to meet here because things are hectic in my office and we'd be interrupted every other minute."

"This is fine," I replied. She was always so gracious.

"Come," she said, indicating the wide stairway. "We'll go down over here." She asked about Tyler and how balancing being a mother and resuming my career was working out.

"I couldn't do it without Jerry, that's for sure."

She changed subjects, pointing out the gorgeous Brumidi handrails and art.

Down on the next level, she ushered me into a small anteroom. "We'll go in here. The sergeant at arms was gracious to arrange it for our use. It's secluded."

She closed the door. "Let's sit." She indicated two leather, straight-back chairs in the sparsely furnished room, its walls made of stone. "As I mentioned, I met with the leader. I'm no longer held to my promise regarding Tutoxtamen."

"Is that—"

"You may think that a little hasty, but I have my reasons. Senator Kelly certainly pointed out the pitfalls, but I need to be independent. I'll take whatever comes. This is too important to let slide."

"From what little I know about the FDA, they've issued Tutox the death penalty."

"It would seem that way, however . . ."

"I saw hundreds of people demonstrating on the west lawn of the Capitol as I walked here from Union Station."

She sighed. "There are probably hundreds more in Rockville lined up at 5600 Fishers Lane in front of FDA. They'll make for nice pictures on the television newscasts, but as much as I wished otherwise, they won't change anything."

I decided my fertile imagination might muddy up the waters, so I waited.

"But there are things we can do."

I caught the we, but again waited.

"After today, meetings between us will have to be more discreet. I prefer you work with Michael. You'll find him very capable and more knowledgeable than I."

"That's fine," I said, happy with now having an official foot in the door.

"There are some things happening with Rogers . . . namely with the son Sherman. A letter Michael had received a few months back was unfortunately never opened, because he had put it in his briefcase that the mugger had stolen.

"It, or a copy—Michael remembered it as being identically addressed— recently showed up with no attribution as to the writer. Michael has friends all over . . . an interesting network. In fact, a friend of a friend of his works for Rogers Pharmaceuticals in New Jersey. Anyway, the letter hinted there were some hush-hush things going on at the Rogers processing plant."

"Did Michael's friend say what sort—?"

"It had something to do with technicians. It may be nothing. We're—"

"Would Michael be available to take a trip to New Jersey?"

Her face brightened. "Yes."

*Hmmm.* Her quick answer and expression gave me the feeling she and Michael may have already talked about doing this.

"When did you learn of this hush-hush stuff?" I asked.

"This morning."

"May Michael share it with me?"

"Absolutely," she said eagerly. "I'd like for you two to work together. I will see what I can find out through my senatorial contacts, if I have any."

"What about the two New Jersey senators?"

"No help there. The only senator I can talk with is Crawford. Unfortunately, he is not from my state. He's friendly, and I sincerely feel he has my best interests at heart."

I wondered if he were a bachelor or wishing he were one.

"So we go it alone?" I asked.

Roanne smiled. "We do . . . for now."

# 28

A zillion thoughts occupied my mind as I taxied it back to my office. I called Michael on the way. Dalton had already filled him in, and he was working on the arrangements, including my alias—Laura Wood, a researcher for the senator.

That reminded me of the time when Max got me into an FBI meeting on the serial killer investigation as a civilian employee of MPD, assisting him. He'll get a kick out of me now being an aide to a senator.

Michael already had two dates that matched Mr. Rogers's schedule. "I assured him that Senator Dalton wanted to get to the truth and put Tutoxtamen back on track. Mr. Rogers said he respected that and thought of the senator as a friend."

"And are we at liberty to explain how we can help?"

"Maybe. First, we want to be assured by him that there are no real problems with the drug, and secondly, what he will do in either case. Call me after you talk with your husband."

Earlier, Lassiter and I had discussed how we might be up against a mountain without any climbing gear. Kelly had known, from the FDA or the pharmas, that a *not approvable* was coming down against the drug. That sounded like insider information, and people have gotten into big trouble over things like that, if caught. I called Jerry. He had no problem with either of Michael's choices for travel dates. I selected the earlier: two days from now. I called Michael.

The inner workings of the Senate were a mystery to me. Like what committee had oversight over the FDA? Who can call a hearing? They always have hearings. Where was the opposition party in all of this? Could there be a hearing if the majority party didn't want one?

As my cab neared the *Star*, a thought hit me. Why not go find out? I could do that tomorrow. I could call Michael. No. I'll do this on my own.

"*Washington Daily Star*," the driver announced. "That'll be $6.50."

I gave him eight and got out. He said, "Thanks miss. Have a nice day."

He had to be one of the few cabbies in Washington who spoke English. Most never say anything, just point at the meter. "You too," I said, closing the door.

I went straight to Mary's desk and told her of my pending trip.

"Michael sounds as suspicious as you," my news assistant said.

"I like to think of it as being cautious," I said in a mock huff. "This is not the first time I've gone undercover."

"Yes, but previously you had Captain Walsh watching your back."

"This won't be dangerous," I insisted.

"I hope you're right."

I went to my desk and called Jerry.

"Go get 'em, tiger. Now, to important matters. What time you getting home?"

"Around 5:00."

"How about I order dinner and pick it up? It's warm enough to dine on the deck with our son. This way you won't have to slave over a hot stove," my adorable husband said.

"I love it when you plan dinner. It's a delicious idea."

"Okay. I'll aim for around 5:30. Maybe we can go for a neighborhood jaunt afterward."

"You are certainly full of nice ideas," I said, looking at our family portrait on my desk and getting a warm and fuzzy feeling.

"I have a feeling the future may become a little busy."

"If it does, it will be because we're on to something."

"That's what I mean. It sounds like there may be a lot of under-the-table stuff going on. Don't forget Ralph. He was in the Senate with Grayson. I'm sure he had some dealings with the pharmas."

"Do you think . . . ?"

"I don't *think*, I *know*," Jerry said emphatically.

And I knew he did.

# 29

Senator Dalton sat in the Cloakroom reading, awaiting an upcoming vote. There were clusters of senators conversing in the narrow, L-shaped room, but she sat alone.

"Hello," she heard a cheery male voice say.

Not thinking it was for her, she didn't look up. Then a body plopped into the chair next to hers.

"Good morning, Senator Dalton," Gavin Crawford said.

"Senator. My apologies, I was light-years away."

"No doubt," he said, leaning forward in a confidential manner, "there are many places nicer to be than this."

"How did you know I was thinking of home?"

"It's good to go . . . home. I do it as often as possible. It helps to clear the mind."

"You have two real homes. Here I live a solitary life in a local high-rise in Virginia, and I no longer have my own abode back home. After my election I sold the house H.T. and I had lived in and moved in with my parents," she said wistfully.

He smiled. "Well, our house is always available for company."

"Be careful what you offer. I'm afraid, though, my current absorption is over my telling our leader that I would no longer be his parrot."

"I've never heard of party loyalty being likened to a parrot before. A helpful hint: Once an issue is resolved, we are free to speak our minds within these walls."

"I guess I've now added to my pariah reputation unnecessarily, but I can't go around being something I'm not." There was a pause. She changed subjects. "Have you seen the demonstrations against the FDA? I hear the talk shows have been rife with scientists, doctors, health experts. There's a great rage over Tutoxtamen's death sentence."

"That's Washington and the tabloid mentality of the press."

"I don't think all journalists are like that."

He shrugged. "Maybe not, even though it seems that way."

"Gavin, you said I could talk to you. Does that mean in confidence? And no, I'm not planning the overthrow of the Senate leadership, as much as I'd like to."

He let out a low chuckle. "You have it."

"Michael told me the crowds in Rockville were growing."

"FDA Director Miles will make an announcement as to the rationale of their decision. Unless someone comes up with irrefutable evidence to the contrary, nothing will change it."

"Of course, that makes perfect sense. But I won't give up."

"So," his inflection indicated a change of subject, "how would you like to come out to our house Saturday for a bar-b-que? Fred and Sally Pembroke are coming over. It'll be very casual."

"I would love to, but I must ask for a rain check. When this vote is over, I'm out of here. I'm flying home for a long weekend. But thank you, Gavin, and thank Mariel."

# 30

R oanne hugged her father. "It's so good to be home."

"It's great to see you, Ro," Rufus said. "You have any luggage?"

"Only what I've got right here."

"I wish your mother would learn to travel light like you." He had a deep-country tone.

"I have a closet full of clothes here and in Virginia," she said, taking his arm.

"Yeah well, I guess that does make a difference. Let's go."

Father and daughter walked down the concourse, passing gates and rushing people. The five-foot-ten wiry Rufus was barely an inch taller than his daughter. Roanne looked around and suddenly realized that they were still inside security. "How did you get in here without a ticket?"

"Antrell Williams is head of security for the airport. You remember him? He was the big black guy who was head of my security detail. I recommended him for the job."

She shook her head and squeezed his arm. They reached security, walked around the incoming gate, and veered off toward the exit. A couple of guards gave him a casual salute and said, "Governor."

He smiled and waved back. She'd forgotten it was always that way for him. She feigned a pout. "Should I be hurt they didn't say *senator*?"

"They probably would have whistled if I hadn't been with you. There's Johnny."

The big man standing next to a black Town Car tipped the cap he always wore when chauffeuring the governor. "Miss Roanne," he said in his gentle basso voice.

"It's good to see you, Johnny." She gave the gentle giant a hug. He was family, more so in many ways than her siblings.

"The whole shooting match will join us Saturday afternoon at the Club for the prime rib," Rufus said, referring to his son, other daughter, and their families.

Roanne thought of Gavin and the bar-b-que she'd be missing.

After a light supper with her parents, she joined Rufus in his large and very comfortable study. Her mother would join them later. Once they got comfortable, she told the perceptive politician about Rogers and Kelly. He said he had been following developments.

"Have you been talking to Harold Raines?" she asked. Raines was their state's senior senator.

"Now, don't get in a hissy fit. Harry clerked for me when I was on the circuit court, before I ran for attorney general. I'm not doing anything behind your back or asking him to do anything for you. He told me about the pharmaceutical's pressure to ditch Tutoxtamen. I knew about your opposition and was glad you acquiesced."

"I went with the party, but I'm my own person and want to get Tutoxtamen a fair hearing. I know you hate being on the outside looking in."

"There are things I can do, Ro. I know people. Some of your fellow senators were governors when I was. There's not one of our party's congressmen who hasn't worked for me at one time or another."

"Let's get back to Harry," she said seriously.

"I only asked him to keep me up on what was happening, nothing more."

She didn't know whether to be angry or grateful. She opted for the latter. "Harry's stayed away from me during these last few weeks just about as much as all the others."

"I had nothing to do with that. I only wanted information," he said defensively.

"Well then, you don't know everything, because he doesn't."

Rufus leaned back in his chair and squinted. "It got anything to do with Harley Rogers?"

She had learned not to be surprised by her father, but she couldn't hide it this time. "It does."

"Thought so. Harley is a fine man, Ro. I'm glad you're trying to help him out."

His comment told her he knew the drug manufacturer. "Okay, out with it."
"What?"

"Tell me how you know Mr. Rogers," she said firmly.

"Oh that." He smiled. "I like it when you figure things out for yourself. Damn, I wish your mother hadn't forbidden me to smoke cigars, I could sorely use one about now."

She smiled and fixed her eyes on him. "What have you done?"

"After you told me about Michael and an aide going to see Harley, I called him. He might not have known Senator Dalton was my daughter . . . you know, that you had been married to H.T. Dalton. Harley and I haven't always been on the same page politically, but we respect each other."

"Please don't tell me he worked for you too."

He grinned. "The other way around—I worked for him."

"When? You've never worked outside of this state that I ever heard."

"Except for WWII."

"He was a Ranger?"

"He was the boss Ranger. Look, Ro, if you pursue this thing, and I'm not saying you shouldn't, you'll need help. Now, what're your folks gonna accomplish visiting Harley?"

It was her time to grin. "Actually, only Michael works for me."

He flashed a 'what-are-you-up-to' look on his face.

"The second person is a reporter."

Rufus rocked forward, almost coming of his chair. "A reporter?"

"A Pulitzer Prize–winning reporter superb in investigative work."

"A reporter, Ro? That's playing with fire," Rufus said, shaken.

"Dad, I've spent hours with her—"

"Her?"

She interrupted. "There are female reporters."

"I know that," he spat. "Who does she work for?"

"The *Washington Daily Star.*"

"Aw geez, Ro. Are you sure you wanna do that?"

"Look Dad, there's practically no one in the Senate I feel I can trust. Michael has uncovered what looks like some unethical activity between a few senators with the pharmas and the FDA. That is why I initially opposed the leader's call for unanimity. You and I are alone in this, and we need an objective investigator."

"But what if she uses what she finds out and puts it in her paper?"

"She won't. We went over all this before she signed on to help. Of course, she'll get a story out of this, but right now, she's in for the long haul . . . investigating and collecting information."

"Does Rogers know he'll be talking to a reporter?"

"She's going under an alias . . . a research assistant working for me."

He looked at his daughter "You think all this up?"

"Michael, Laura, and I did."

"Laura? That her real name?"

Ro nodded.

"You going to tell me her real last name?"

"What are you going to do with it if I do?"

Her father enjoyed this game.

"Look her up, see how good a writer she is."

"You're in for a lot of reading. She's the one who solved the serial killer case in DC last year."

His face lit up. "Aha! Now I can find her all by myself."

"Wolfe. Her name is Laura Wolfe."

# 31

Michael and I met at Union Station and took the 6:30 morning Metroliner to Newark, New Jersey.

He provided me with more papers on the FDA than I could ever get through in a day, much less in a three-hour train ride. I did my best to scan and highlight.

In Newark, we were met by a man holding a small sign with Michael's alias, *Mr. Howard*, on it. We soon were out of the city in our mini limo and into heavily wooded, hilly terrain. Michael and I both read during the half-hour trip to Morris Plains. I had no idea what nuggets we might mine, but Michael was confident we'd learn something.

We were politely ushered into a very comfortable room along the lines of a large paneled library in an opulent mansion: plush leather, mahogany desks and trim, oriental rugs, a mounted animal's head, and Renaissance paintings. It was a man's room, solid and visceral.

The soft lighting highlighted the very large windows that looked out over the campus-like grounds, resplendent with great sweeps of lawn, copses of trees, and a pond with a fountain in the middle. It was regal and serene.

A door opened and two men entered, one elderly, the other middle-aged. Both were dapper and in excellent physical shape. The younger was in a dark suit, while the older wore a dark blue blazer and grey slacks. The door was closed behind them.

"Mr. Horne, Ms. Wood, so good of you to make the trip. I am Harley Rogers, and this is my son and company president, Sherman."

We did the handshakes and salutations. I'd already forgotten about the aliases. Michael was Horne inside and howard in the outside world.

"Please, let us sit over here, where we can take advantage of the view. Sherman won't be with us long, but he wanted to meet you. It has not been often, if ever," and he looked at Sherman, "that we've had someone from the United States Senate, other than our own two, visit us."

Michael took the lead. "Senator Dalton sends her regards and asked me to convey to you her deepest respect for you and your company."

"You are the senator's administrative assistant?" Sherman asked.

Michael nodded.

"And Ms. Wood?" the son asked.

"Administrative aide in charge of research," Michael said.

Harley nodded. "Ah, research."

I took up the baton. "Yes, and I'm afraid I'm all FDA'd out."

The senior Rogers chuckled. "This is your first experience with an FDA case?"

"Yes sir."

Harley smiled. "Well, we'll see if we can enlighten you and lighten your reading load at the same time."

I returned his smile. "I'd appreciate that, sir."

"Well," Sherman said. "I have some things to see about in the lab."

"Would that something be Tutoxtamen, sir?" I asked.

The younger Rogers gave me a forced smile. "We produce many drugs here. As much as we wished Tutox was among them today, we still have a large operation to run."

"Yes sir," Michael jumped in with what I perceived as a little anxiety. "We appreciate meeting you and look forward to visiting in the future."

"I'm planning to join you at lunch. But if I don't make it, please give my regards to Senator Dalton." He extended his hand to Michael. "Thank you for coming and caring, Mr. Horne." He looked at me. "Ms. Wood."

He didn't extend his hand to me. He nodded to his father and left.

"Come now, please let's sit," Harley offered. "We have light refreshments. I hope you'll be staying for lunch. I'd like the time to show you around our facility."

"That would be very nice, sir," Michael said.

The octogenarian took a large chair, Michael and I shared the large sofa. I took out my notebook. Michael maintained his stature as the senator's number one.

Harley spoke first. "You needn't worry about your senator's prior actions regarding me. There was nothing else she could do, then. With your presence here today, I am assured of her position regarding Tutox and am grateful for her support. Although I don't know how a minority of senators could be effective facing the powerful pharmaceutical juggernaut."

Michael looked pleased. "I will convey your kind comments to the senator."

"What we need, sir," I piped up, "is assurance that there really are no deadly side effects to Tutox and how we can corroborate what you tell us. We don't doubt your veracity, but we need irrefutable proof if we are to curry support from other senators."

There was a deafening silence. I didn't know how what I'd just said affected Michael, but I'd been in this position before. If I'm not up front at the very beginning, the rest could all be a huge waste of time.

"I don't, for a minute, doubt your reasons, Ms. Wood. In fact, I admire your gumption. We can corroborate everything we tell you. Several independent groups have worked with us on phases I, II, and III. We even went beyond the FDA's requirements, studying many more people with other diseases, using our drug in combination with other drugs."

Michael jumped in. "Were these reports given to the FDA?"

Harley leaned forward. "Phases I, II, and III were provided to the FDA over a year ago, but we continued testing, ironically, against the same negative side effects they have used against us: the problems with heart patients. We went out and explored new populations to use with Tutox in combinations with other drugs to see if they compromised the primary curing qualities of our drug."

He eased back in his seat. "Will there be heart patients that may not be able to take Tutox? Unfortunately, yes. Nevertheless, we are working with those anomalies and hope to come up with an answer. It may be possible that the heart treatment can be altered, allowing a patient to take Tutox. However, that's all up to the patient's doctor," Harley said caringly.

"What was the FDA's reason for not approving Tutox, in your opinion," I asked.

"You know their official reason?" Harley asked.

"Side effects," Michael jumped in. "A combination of safety issues. You were given the designation of 'not approvable' because additional studies needed to be conducted on more different people for a longer period of time."

He nodded at Michael. "You've done your homework, son. I admire that."

Michael blushed, but recovered. "Your opinion of that matter, sir?"

"The FDA will choose their language carefully, citing many intangibles that will force us into more studies. Even after we prove Tutox is everything, if not more, we say it is, quality control issues will then have to demonstrate Tutox still contains the same curing elements that were in the earlier tests.

"If in the upcoming process, we discover something new to add, not because there is anything wrong with Tutox, which there isn't, but because we have discovered something new and better, we couldn't . . . we're not allowed to. The tiniest modification to the drug would require testing to start from the very beginning."

I was completely engrossed with this elderly man's acumen.

"We have to play the game very carefully. We've received the FDA's action letter. CDER will give us an opportunity to meet with the agency officials to discuss the so-called deficiencies." Harley sat back.

"CDER?" I asked.

"Center for Drug Evaluation and Research," he answered. "The FDA had fully reviewed our NDA, eh, New Drug Application. It included all animal and human data, analysis of that data, as well as information about how the drug behaves in the body, as I mentioned earlier."

I nodded that I understood. "I've read that some new drugs for life-threatening illnesses like cancer are given accelerated approval that would allow, say Tutox, to be approved before some measures required for approval were available."

"Surrogate endpoints," Harley clarified. "But we didn't seek that. We wanted all the details—the measurements of how a patient feels, functions, their chance of survival—everything on the table. We're considerably beyond phase III in our studies."

"Someone in the FDA said that they thought all the information they needed had been provided and that the real problem seemed to be with clinical trials."

"Balderdash! We went overboard to detail every phase of safety and effectiveness, and the studies of different populations . . . everything imaginable."

"Then how can they justify their *not approvable* classification?"

"They don't have to. They could move fast on this, but they won't. They'll take two to three years. I may not live long enough to see the miracles this drug can perform."

"You believe that Tutox will eventually be approved?"

"There are no guarantees that it will."

That rang out like a death warrant, but the vibes I was receiving from Harley Rogers were not those of a defeated man. Michael had listened emotionless in rapt attention. I couldn't read his true feelings. Could Harley have an ace up his sleeve? Faking out his enemy, while secretly . . . no, that was too conspiratorial.

He suddenly stood, taking us by surprise. "How about a tour of the grounds and the labs before we have lunch?"

We both rose. "That would be very nice," Michael said distractedly.

I couldn't understand why Harley wasn't outraged. He had the well-known reputation of being a fighter. There was more here than met the eye, and I was beginning to think that my earlier feelings were not as conspiratorial as I thought.

I'll have to dig deeper into Rogers Pharmaceuticals and its founder.

# 32

"**I** found it strange Rogers didn't ask us any questions about the senator," I said to Michael, as the Metroliner train to Washington was pulling out of Newark station.

"Why?"

"Because we were representing her. I did think he overreacted when I walked toward what appeared to be another lab."

"Maybe some secret . . ."

"Maybe. He sure rushed us through the rest of the tour."

I took out my notepad.

"It could be another miracle drug," he said offhandedly.

I didn't care for his aloofness. "I'm no threat. I don't know a bacterium from a virus."

Michael uncharacteristically slouched. "Where do we go from here?"

"How 'bout neither Rogers appearing traumatized by their drug being turned down."

"What? How can you say that?" he said intensely, sitting up and turning to me. "They certainly have no love for the FDA."

Finally, he was out of his lethargy.

"I'm talking about attitude," I explained. "Harley Rogers talked angry, but didn't act angry."

"So?" Michael snapped at me, clearly irritated.

"What? You think I'm being skeptical? I'm looking for ideas here. Give and take. I do it with my husband and Max Walsh all the time."

Michael turned sharply to me. "Walsh? The homicide captain? You are friends with a homicide cop?"

"Very much so." It dawned on me that Michael knew little or nothing about me.

He went on. "After I was mugged, I was interviewed by a homicide detective."

"That was probably Hayes. But Max knows all about your case."

Michael was on the edge of his seat. "He told you?"

"When you were found, no one knew your exact condition. You were lucky that a neighbor saw the mugging and called it in. Max answered the call along with the Capitol Hill police. He saw that you worked for Senator Dalton, whom he didn't know. He looked up both of your bios."

Michael frowned. "Is that good or bad?"

"Not bad. He's just very thorough. If you had been killed, you would have been his case. He followed up anyway. He found it odd that you'd been mugged at your front door. It's rare there's a homicide or vandalism in that neighborhood."

"That's amazing. I wouldn't have—"

"Little things are important. They sometimes create big things," I said easily.

"Like with Rogers. I'm impressed with your observations. I saw and heard the same things you did, but you came away with a very different picture than I did."

"I look at people's attitudes, their reactions and body language, and their eyes. They all tell a story."

"Did you learn that in journalism school or just pick it up?"

"I wish they had taught it. I learned it on my own. I'm always learning."

The train slowed for Trenton. Michael said he was going to the dining car and asked if I wanted anything.

"A Diet Pepsi and a bag of peanuts would be great." I reached for my bag.

"That won't be necessary; it's on me." He went up the aisle.

I took out my cell and called Jerry's private line. He didn't answer. I called Anna's cell. She told me, "Tyler, he nap, not too hungry, some, eh fussy." Anna had picked up *fussy* from me. She said she liked the word because "it say much."

A guy who had gotten on the train wanted Michael's seat. He acted as though he didn't believe me when I said it was occupied. Maybe his disbelief was because I was passing the wonderful opportunity of his company. His ego sealed it when he asked me whose seat it was. I gave him my sternest look. "Believe me, it's occupied." He reluctantly moved on.

Michael returned. The Diet Pepsi and peanuts hit the spot. "You know, Michael, there's nothing like a bag of salted nuts . . . and a soda," I quickly added. "I was up in your neighborhood yesterday," I said, wanting to get back to business.

"Oh? For anything in particular?"

"Yes and no. I wanted to familiarize myself with the Senate office buildings. I was also curious about what Senate committee had oversight of the FDA."

He looked put out. "I could have helped with that."

"I know, but I'm used to nosing around, ferreting out my own information. Plus I wanted to browse."

"Not much to see," he said flatly.

"For you, but for me the meeting rooms like SD430—"

"That's in Dirksen, our building."

"I know. I walked past your office. I discovered that different committees include Health, but it was in the committee office of Health, Education, Labor, and Pensions that I got my first good lead."

"Senator Pembroke's committee."

"They sent me over to Hart—"

"Health Policy."

"Right. A pleasant woman there—"

"Nancy Morris."

"Mid-thirties, long, light-brown hair?"

"That's her. We're good friends."

I must have blanched at his remark.

"What, I can't have women friends?"

"Of course not." Then realizing he might not catch on to my wry sense of humor. "What do you take me for? Of course."

Nancy Morris. I had recognized her as the same woman I'd seen in the Clarendon restaurant with Kelly. That put her in both camps.

"Where is Pembroke on the Tutoxtamen thing?"

"Right in the middle. Being chairman of HELP, he's been Kelly's point man on locking down FDA's *not approvable* of the drug."

"And Nancy?" I wanted to learn more about this woman.

"She's the top aide to the committee's chief of staff."

"Should I know him?"

"You wouldn't want to. He's a real asshole."

His frankness startled me. "Will Senator Pembroke chair meetings concerning Rogers Pharmaceuticals?"

"No, that's all FDA. That reminds me, I need to call in."

His abruptness puzzled me. I shrugged it off and began looking at my Rogers notes. Michael stayed in his seat talking quietly on the phone. The train slowed for north Philadelphia. I wondered about Nancy's role in all of this.

Michael finished his calls.

"Michael, how good a friend is Nancy?"

"A good one. We get together after work a couple of times a week. She also uses my shoulder to cry on after one of her romances goes sour."

"Does that happen often?"

"Only a couple of times a year," he said with a wry smile.

I chuckled. "That doesn't sound very stable."

"That's not unusual on the Hill. It's like we want it, but after a while it becomes a drag. Some become partners, but most move on. Also people come and go a lot."

I looked at him questioningly without asking.

He read my look. "I'm between right now. He wasn't from the Hill and I'm not looking. Being an AA is a lot of work. A new relationship would be too much of a distraction."

"I hear you. I had a couple of serious relationships. Both ended poorly. One guy wanted me to quit reporting and get an office job."

He laughed. "I bet that slammed the door."

"In his face. Tell me about Nancy. By the way, she doesn't know I'm a reporter, just a writer doing research on Senate oversight committees. She referred me to their press office."

"Right. Because her office does investigations, she's not permitted to talk with writers."

"The guy there was busy and must stay busy. The woman I talked with suggested I leave him a voice mail and gave me his direct dial. He never called back. The next day I sent him an email with four questions on it."

"You'll get used to *busy* on the Hill. I think people are more intent on out-busying each other than doing a good job. I can talk to Nancy . . ."

"No. I think it best she not know that you and I know each other. Besides, I got a very nice reply, each question answered."

He grunted. "You did better than most."

We sat quietly as the train rolled on toward Washington.

"Did the senator tell you about Senator Crawford?" Michael asked, breaking the momentary silence.

"About him giving her advice?"

"Yeah, but what we needed to know was if it is safe to confide in him, so I asked Nancy to help. She's currently between loves. A year ago, Gordon, who is Senator Crawford's AA, showed some interest in her, but she was otherwise involved. Anyway, she sounded Gordon out about his senator, making it appear as if she was asking for Senator Pembroke." He leaned back, looking very self-satisfied.

"And . . . ?"

"Yeah. First, Crawford and Pembroke are friendly. They both have homes in McLean, and their wives socialize. Pembroke's kids are out of high school. Crawford's five are preschool into high school."

This concerned me. "Doesn't that preclude any help for Senator Dalton?"

"You would think so, but things on the Hill are never as they appear. Nancy is committee staff, so it's not her senator against mine."

I laid my head back on the comfortable seat's headrest. "I think it best she not run into us together."

"That is a good idea. Nancy remembers everybody. She'd most likely ask you how you were coming on your research of Senate oversight committees."

"That kind of memory makes her a good spy." I suddenly felt a wave of fatigue. "I'm going to catch a few winks. I enjoyed the conversation."

"Me too."

# 33

I awoke from my nap as the train was slowing. I stared out the window, thinking of Harley Rogers. I felt at a loss—no smoking gun. That made me think of Max. I called him.

"To what do I owe this honor," Max said in his mellifluous bass-baritone. "How are you?"

"Better now. How is my godson?"

"Growing, well, and happy. Do you have a minute?"

"Where are you? I hear train sounds. Are you on Metro?"

"Amtrak's Metroliner. We're pulling into Wilmington."

Michael tapped my arm. "Baltimore. You slept through Wilmington."

"I was just corrected. Baltimore. I've been on an out-of-town assignment."

"What time do you get in?"

"Eh, 6:09, then I'm hopping Metro for home. Senator Dalton's AA, Michael Horne, and I were in New Jersey visiting Rogers Pharmaceuticals, the manufacturer of Tutoxtamen, the cancer drug that the FDA has rejected. I'm an undercover aide to the senator."

"You've been covert before, if I remember."

"I'd love for this one to prove as fruitful," I said, remembering again last year's story. "Can we get together? I need a good speculation session."

"Why don't I pick you up in front of the station?"

"You sure? I mean, I'd love to see—"

"My day is over here. I should be there before you arrive. I'll call if I'm running late."

"Fine, see you then," I said, clicking off, and then punching in Jerry's number. I looked at Michael. "Excuse me again, Michael, I need to call my husband."

"This is Jerry."

"Hi there."

"Hey. Where are you?"

I gave him my location and told him about Max meeting me at the station.

"I can pick up some Chinese food. That's a sure bet with Max."

His thoughtfulness gave me a tender feeling. "That's perfect."

"I'll make sure we have some cold ones. Oops, gotta go. Sophie needs me."

I turned in my seat to Michael. "There's something I'd like you to do."

He perked up. "Sure."

"Your friend at Rogers, can he snoop around . . . look for any unusual goings on?"

"He's cool. He'll be glad to help."

"At no cost to you, I hope," I said concerned.

"None whatsoever," Michael said confidently.

# 34

**M**ichael and I parted company in front of Union Station. He headed for 1st Street NW and the Dirksen Senate Office Building. I spotted Max leaning against his unmarked Crown Victoria chatting with one of MPD's uniformed cops. It was muggy, but not as insufferable as Washington can get in the summer.

When I got close enough not to have to shout, I said, "Anyplace a gal can get a ride around here?" The cop that Max was talking with gave me a sharp look.

Max pushed off his car and turned to me. I put my arms out and gave him a big hug. He returned it and then held me out at arm's length.

"I do believe you are taking care of yourself." He chuckled. "Laura, this is Officer Travolta."

"No relation to the famous one," the officer said shyly. He touched the brim of his hat with his index finger in a casual salute.

"This little lady solves the tough cases we can't," Max said with one arm still around me.

"Me, MPD, and the FBI." I gave Max a friendly nudge.

The officer smiled uneasily at my familiarity. "Well, I better get back to my rounds."

Max turned to me. "You'd best get in the car before you melt."

We buckled up, and Max maneuvered his unmarked cruiser through the maze in front of Union Station and headed for Constitution Avenue. I took a drink from a cold bottle of water I'd picked up in the station.

It felt so natural, driving in Max's comfortable car. We passed the National Gallery of Art's two buildings and passed other museums on the left and government buildings on the right. As we crossed 15th Street, everything opened up with the Mall grounds and the Washington Monument on our left and the grassy expanse of the Ellipse and the White House to the right.

There was a softball game on the Ellipse where the White House *Execs* played their games. They would largely be a new team of players this year. Janet Rausch, the murdered intern, had played on last year's team along with Kat Turner.

"Conjure up old memories?" Max asked, looking past me at the field.

I nodded, my lips pressed hard together.

"A lot of people got hurt because of one man's lust," he said disgustedly. "But enough of old, ugly thoughts. What new ones would you like to discuss?"

"One that may kill hundreds of thousands of innocent people." I stared straight ahead, as Max drove west on a heavily wooded avenue. "I honestly don't have a clue how to stop it."

"You feel as though you're backed up against a wall with a bright light in your eyes?"

I nodded. "There's no hard evidence to chew on, Max. The Senate's a never-never land. Tutoxtamen may never be approved. Yet the man most affected by this acts like they called off his fox hunt, rather than being angry that his miracle drug was given a death sentence."

"A little thing you've picked up from your observation of him?"

"Truthfully, if Michael hadn't explained the value of the little things, I might not have had the same concentration."

"I highly doubt that. Little things are ingrained in your soul. You don't have to work to remember them. You can't help but absorb them."

I smiled. "That's part of why I called you. Oh, Jerry's getting Chinese. Please stay."

"You sure, after your long day?—Forget I asked. I want to see my godson."

"Jerry and Tyler are either at or returning from the restaurant right this minute."

We were passing the Lincoln Memorial where Constitution became a ramp to the Teddy Roosevelt Bridge. "Jerry's in charge of the food, and you'll be in charge of Tyler. I have it by good authority that some brews are cooling in the fridge. You two will have time to talk and play with our little one while I shower and change."

He half grunted, half laughed. "You give me the tough stuff."

"You won't be able to get your godson into any bad habits in that amount of time," I teased.

"Prepare me. What is he into these days?"

"People's undivided attention. He is very curious."

"Gets that from his mother. I have forgotten what that age is like. Are you and Jer spending any time on *Scalawag?*"

"We are. In fact, he went down last Saturday and gave her a once over."

We drove in silence as we crossed the Potomac and exited onto the George Washington Memorial Parkway. I looked upriver at Georgetown and the hills beyond.

"Back to my serious problem, I'm having a tough time with this one," I said quietly.

"What about your lists? You always make lists. What do you know? What do you suspect? Is there a suspect or—?"

"Only the politicians, but that's pure speculation."

"Ah yes, those lovely, loosely gathered thoughts."

"Which usually connect to make up a story," I said grandiosely.

"Right, while we poor cops have to struggle for clues and evidence."

"That's what I'm missing. No crime site. No trace evidence. Only the act itself."

"That's about where we were last year when we found an unidentifiable body, and then you showed up and identified her."

"Sheer luck, which I could use right now. If there's a trail, I haven't found it."

"You're too used to being a beat reporter, collecting hard facts. You're dealing with senators who have fought to get where they are. Many may have even been involved in a shady deal or two, done things hidden from the public. It may have been when they first ran for an office, be it dogcatcher, council, state, or whatever. They've had their share of mixing it up. They have strong egos, and their clashes over the years have hardened them. There is not a weak sister in the bunch. They've had their fights, and they've learned the art of compromise."

He stopped as though overtaken by other thoughts. I mulled over his words.

"That's why they have all that sweet talk like: *honorable, gentleman, gentlelady, esteemed colleague, my good friend,* you name it. On the Senate floor, they act like the *Stepford Wives,* and behind the scenes, like *Jack the Ripper.* They're a bunch of actors who know how to put on a show for C-SPAN." His voice had hardened.

I was puzzled at his diatribe. "What senator crossed you?"

"None. I hear them and read about them. My point is they are a different species in a made-up world. They walk around and look normal, smile for the cameras, crack jokes with their constituents, but up there, in their castle . . . well, they're just different."

"So, I have to get inside and find out why their water flows upstream?"

"Yup. They don't like change or inquisitive reporters. It's why new senators are rarely heard from. Senator Dalton has some celebrity, but that's only good for them if they can use her to their advantage. She was forced to compromise her principles and didn't like having to do it. She called you. She smells rotten meat and knows she can't do anything alone.

"Computer chips may not be put into a new senator's brain, but I wouldn't put it past the leadership to try if they thought they could get away with it. Away from the Hill, these mafioso of legislation become bearable. Most have a good sense of humor that ingratiates them to their adoring public. Your Senator Dalton is struggling against the current. I wish her well."

I felt like I had just been given a sociology lesson.

"This is not like last year when my beat included the White House."

"I suggest you look at this the same way," he replied tightly, "even with no corpse. Although knowing you, I am sure you are intuitively."

*Ingrained in my soul,* I thought. Spout Run loomed up ahead. We began the run up the hill to Lee Highway into my neighborhood. Max turned onto my street and a couple of blocks later into our driveway, parking right behind my little red convertible.

We found my two boys in the kitchen. I kissed and hugged Jerry and rushed to Tyler, who was clearly letting me know it was his turn. Jerry and Max greeted as good buddies do. After a few minutes of bonding, I turned my seven-month-old over to Max with a squeal of protest by Tyler.

"He'll stop as soon as I'm gone." I headed for the stairs. Before I reached the top, Tyler's squeals had turned to happy gurgling.

My shower did wonders for me. When I got back downstairs, I found the three on the back deck. I fished a cold bottle of water from the fridge and joined them. Tyler was still in Max's arms, and Jerry was setting the table. The containers of food occupied the center of our round picnic table. Tyler's high chair was already in place.

"Looks cozy," I said, pushing the screen door open.

My voice alerted Tyler to my presence, and he began to gyrate and struggle in Max's arms. "I think I'm history," he said, handing up my son. "Jer was explaining your plans for the backyard. I like your hot tub."

I received the blond-haired bundle of energy and got a squeal of delight and a playful slap on my face with a pudgy little hand.

"Come on, let's get at this stuff while it's still hot," Jerry urged.

I put Tyler in his high chair. He fussed, but I directed his attention to the food on his tray, which he happily began to bat at. After some urgings, he picked some up and aimed for his mouth, missing more often than not. Fortunately, Jerry had remembered to put a plastic mat under Tyler's chair. We attacked our mixture of sweet-and-sour pork, moo-shu chicken, and Mongolian beef mixed in with more rice than an army could eat.

After dinner, I took Tyler up to clean and dress him, and then brought him back down for a round of goodnights.

"Is this the same kid who was here earlier?" Max said, taking Tyler and giving him a smooch. Tyler was relaxed with Max and gurgled his delight. Jerry and Tyler played noses. Max promised to stay as I relieved Jerry of our son and hustled him up to bed.

Max and Jerry were lounging on the deck with fresh drinks when I joined them. Once settled, I filled them in on my visit to New Jersey. Some of it Max had already heard, but I knew from past experience he never minded hearing stuff a second time. There might be some subtle difference that could give more texture to the story. Even in the telling, I thought of things I hadn't covered earlier.

Jerry asked, "Why would Rogers put on a face for you? For what purpose?"

"I don't know enough to know. Max, you remember our lunch when we saw Senator Kelly and the young woman with long, light-brown hair?"

"Yes."

"Well, she comes under Senator Pembroke, who chairs the Health, Education, Labor, and Pension Committee. She works for the Health Policy Committee, its investigative arm. Pembroke was Kelly's point man in rallying party members to support the FDA's rejection of Tutoxtamen. Pembroke and Senator Crawford are friends. They live in McLean, and their wives socialize."

I explained Michael's covert actions using Nancy Morris to cozy up to Crawford's AA. "It's so convoluted. I get weary just thinking about it."

"I told you, it's a different world up there," Max chortled.

I nodded. "Michael and the Hill staff are a conspiratorial bunch. They've formed a sort of underground, totally beneath the radar."

Jerry chimed in. "Ralph Morgan may know Pembroke."

"Isn't that the lawyer who worked for the vice president?"

"He joined us last fall, finally fed up with government lawyering and being lied to."

"You knew him from college?"

"Law school. We were roommates."

"You see, Miss Laura? You do have contacts."

"Before you go taking up any of Ralph's time," Jerry jumped in, "remember he works on billable hours. He's no longer salaried like he was at the White House."

Our evening ended with promises all around that we would get together in a week or two. I missed seeing Max. He and Jerry had already talked about a weekend down on the Potomac. They said they'd even include Tyler and me. Life was good.

# 35

I awoke feeling refreshed. Last night had been like old times. It became even more perfect when Jerry and I had made love. I had so much passion, maybe my desire to belong. He must have sensed that because we'd played for a long time. The nice thing was that my lover didn't have to be at work early, which prolonged our lounging after being awakened by our little tyke.

Jerry had cleaned Tyler up and brought him in with us, much like on weekends, and we almost overdid the playing. We had to hustle to be dressed when Anna arrived.

Jerry drove me to work.

"I like that we're getting back with Max," I commented.

"Yeah, with you not on the crime beat, he hasn't been on *Scalawag* since last summer. In September, we were busy with house-hunting and then getting ready for the baby." He gave me his special, loving look. "You want to go on *Scalawag* this weekend?"

"That would be nice," I replied in a sultry voice.

"Oh? That nice, huh? Well then . . ."

"Yes. That nice. Maybe Max could come by on Sunday, get him back in the habit."

"Right. And we have to be there for that to happen."

I smiled my sweetest at his flirtation as our drive swung us down onto E Street going east, away from the Kennedy Center and into the downtown business district.

"What journalistic caper will you be involved with today?"

"Organizing. Will you ask Ralph about Pembroke? If he's amenable, maybe . . ."

"Not a problem."

"Thanks." I patted his leg for extra emphasis. It was nice to ride in with him. We arrived at my building much too soon.

I got off the elevator and went directly to Mary's desk.

"Nothing came in for you yesterday. I can't get used to you not flying in and out of here with three or four things in the air at once."

"I can't either. I'll be in the library researching Rogers Pharmaceuticals and the old man. Who's our Health editor?"

"I'll find out," she said perfunctorily.

I went to my desk and cogitated about what Max had told me: I had to treat this the same as I would a beat assignment. My intercom buzzing interrupted my thoughts.

It was Mary. "Sarah, spelled with an *h*, Metzger is the Health section editor," Mary reported, and then gave me Metzger's telephone extension and email.

I called Metzger immediately.

"This is Sarah," a deep, mature voice answered.

"Hi. I'm Laura Wolfe."

There was a moment of silence.

"Our Laura Wolfe?" Metzger asked surprised.

"Over in Metro, yeah," I said nonchalantly.

She didn't reply. I jumped in.

"I'm interested in pharmaceutical companies and wondered if you did anything on the recent FDA turndown of the cancer drug Tutoxtamen?"

"That's not our bag. We do health issues," she said, with an accent on *issues*. "Soft stuff. An occasional surgeon general piece, but no breaking news."

"Right. I'm looking into Rogers Pharmaceuticals and its founder Harley Rogers."

Another pause. "Seems . . . yes . . . we did a story on the old man and his vision for a miracle drug. We had much more than we could ever use with the limited space we have once a week."

"Would you still have the raw stuff?"

"Yeah, but it was by phone and only a few quotes. We drew mostly from watchdog writers, like a former editor with the *New England Journal of*

*Medicine,* a university professor or two . . . we could have done a series with all that."

"Watchdog writers. Reporters?" I asked, feeling like that was an explorable area.

"Authors. The ones with the books raking the drug companies over the coals, mostly on retail costs. They complain about import laws, the seniors rip-off, that sort of thing," Metzger said disinterestedly.

"Any good ones . . . writers, I mean?"

"Oh sure. I can give you some names if that would help."

She had no idea of the gold mine on which she sat. "It would," I said, curbing my excitement.

"I'll put something together and email it to you."

Watchdog writers. I bet one of them would have an opinion on Tutox. I wrote "Watchdogs" on a five-by-seven card and pinned it to my board. As usual, when I go looking for one thing, a bevy of new things pops up.

Mary buzzed again. "Ms. Lassiter would like to see you."

"Thanks. Metzger has some good stuff for me." I picked up my pad and headed for Lassiter's office. I did the ritual knock and walk in. "You wanted to see me?"

"Have a seat. Barton called yesterday while you were in Jersey, asking me how things were developing."

I felt a sudden spike of anxiety. Here I was finally getting somewhere, and Barton probably wants to ditch it.

"I told him you were pursuing leads, the usual stuff."

I waited. Upset at my paranoia.

"Barton talked with the Style editor. He would like you to do a profile on Senator Dalton, from childhood to the Senate. You'll work with Style's editor, Lori Chow. She's written pieces on celebrities and can help with the format. They'll work with you."

"Is there a deadline?"

"This summer. You'll have to make a trip to her hometown, meet with her folks, and get background, that sort of thing. This will add to your cover, explain your presence on the Hill."

I was amazed, ready to burst. "It's perfect."

"I figured you'd like it. You won't have to sit and watch the grass grow.

There will be two photo sessions. One in her Senate office, the other back home. Chow will set it up."

I tingled inside. "This is great, boss. Thanks."

"It was Barton's idea, and a good one. This'll get you on the inside, instead of having to skulk around. How's it going?"

"The trip was okay. A little weird. Neither of the Rogers men acted like they'd just been given a death penalty by the FDA. We were mostly with Harley. Sherman joined us for lunch."

Lassiter leaned back in her chair. "They feed you well?"

"A little rich for my diet, but I didn't go hungry. My impressions didn't jibe with what I expected. But maybe I'm digging too hard to find anything."

"That's possible, but keep at it and get on the Style piece."

I wanted to keep on talking. I couldn't help myself. "Michael Horne has a friend who works at Rogers. He's asked this person to keep his eyes open and to call him with anything unusual, out of place. We don't—"

"You put him up to it?"

"I did. Well, I mean, we don't have anything. You never know. We'll see. I talked with Sarah Metzger, the editor—"

"I know her." Lassiter's tone was saying *wrap it up.*

"I'm getting names of pharmaceutical watchdog writers that they have used."

"Sounds good."

This was over.

"Let's hope," I said, standing.

"The Style story will get your juices going."

Lassiter reached for some papers, and I returned to my desk and called Michael.

"This is Michael."

"Laura. Guess what I've been asked to do by the paper?"

"Accuse Kelly of corruption?" he said, playing the game.

"Good try. No. I've been asked to do a profile piece for the Style section on Senator Dalton."

"For real?"

"Style's editor wants me to go to Dalton's hometown, interview her parents and friends. Plus this means I'll be able to come and go from your office openly; it's a perfect cover."

"It couldn't come at a better time for her."

"The Style editor, or someone she assigns, will call you to set up a photo session in the senator's office and will follow her around for a day. They'll hire a local news photographer to do the shoot at her parents'. Is she around?"

"Actually, she's at her parents' now . . . flew out yesterday. She'll be back late Sunday or Monday morning."

"Could you schedule in some time on Monday afternoon? We'd like to set up my visit for Wednesday to meet her parents and siblings, get the lay of the land, and do the location photo shoot on Thursday."

"Monday afternoon ought to work." He paused. "Eh, she might prefer you go light on her brother and sister. They get along, but there are lingering bad times from her pageant days. She was always the star in her father's eye."

"How about you get me the details: who they are, years married, kids, occupations, where they live. If the editor uses it, it will only be as generic background."

"I'll put together a chronology of her life with dates and places. Same with the family."

"I'd like to use her office for my interview of her. Remember, this is all overt. Maybe it'll quiet the suspicious voices in that wary castle you call Capitol Hill."

He chuckled. "You're catching on."

# 36

I busied myself with packing for our five-mile drive to the Washington marina where *Scalawag* awaited us. The day and weekend were going to be hot and sunny. Ralph and Elaine Morgan were joining us around one in the afternoon on Saturday. Max said he'd be by on Sunday.

I felt things were getting back to normal. My mind flicked to Sarah Metzger, who had not sent me that list of watchdog authors. It wasn't critical right now, but it could give me a little better insight into the pharmas and maybe even the FDA.

Jerry and Tyler interrupted my thoughts as they came in from the deck. "Hey, slowpoke, we'll never get on the water at this rate."

"And who says I'm the one who's causing this alleged delay? What do you think all this is?" I asked, pointing at two coolers and a large shopping bag filled to the brim.

Tyler squirmed and squealed, reaching for me. "Okay, but only for a moment."

Jerry handed me our wiggling bundle of joy. "Eh, while you're not doing anything, would you fetch Tyler's and my bag from the bedroom?"

He went upstairs. I put Tyler in his high chair and cut up a banana for him to mush around. He squealed with delight as he whacked a slice off the tray. He grabbed a second piece and pushed it into his mouth by sliding it across his cheek first. I wondered what process he used to make the selection . . . which slice went where.

Jerry came down with a travel bag in each hand. "I'll put these in the car."

"I'll get Tyler clean. Both coolers are ready."

To lighten our transition from house to boat, we used a collapsible two-wheel dolly to ferry stuff from the SUV onto *Scalawag*. On an earlier day trip, we had put duplicate stuff like a port-a-crib, toys, and sundries on board.

The short trip was smooth. Tyler nodded right off and slept the whole way.

Once on board and with Tyler happily in his crib, Jerry set about readying the boat for our sail. I went below and cleaned the head and galley, made a food list, and walked to the fish market adjacent to the marina.

After I stowed my purchases, I put Tyler in his onboard car seat and took him and my computer aft by the helm. Jerry had installed onboard Wi-Fi after we were married. I didn't need the enticement to spend time on *Scalawag*, but it did allow me to stay current with my work.

I found an email with several attachments from Michael and pulled it up. They were all about Rufus McAllister and the life and times of the McAllister family.

Jerry was in the salon of our thirty-five-foot sloop when Ralph and Elaine arrived. I had met her before but didn't really know her. Our visitors fussed over Tyler, who was curious and quiet with these new people. After a little socializing, Jerry took Elaine on a tour. She went without question, most likely prepared for my wanting to talk with her husband. Tyler was content, so he stayed with me.

Ralph and I hadn't spoken privately since our lunch a year earlier at the Powtomack Restaurant, downstream of Reagan National Airport. Ralph was about the same age as Jerry, but looked older—more facial lines and considerably heavier.

"Jerry told you Senator Roanne Dalton brought me into the Tutoxtamen thing, right?"

He nodded.

I kept my scenario superficial, while giving him the chronology of events.

"So Dalton believes Kelly put the heat on his caucus to support something only he and Pembroke knew about in advance—the FDA's *non-approval* of the drug?" Ralph asked.

"According to Dalton's AA, Michael Horne, the pharmas are tight with Kelly and some senior senators. Kelly made the party's unanimous support of the FDA's decision obligatory. Horne insists some senators are engaged in illegal and unethical activity."

"Horne. I remember him. He worked for H.T., right?"

"Yes, H.T.'s AA at the time had died in that same crash. Had you ever dealt with Senator Pembroke?"

"I knew him. He and Grayson sat on a couple of committees together."

"Would one have been the Health, Education, Labor, and Pension?"

"Yeah, it was."

"Pembroke is now that committee's chair. What were your impressions of him?"

He looked at me strangely. "You going after him for something?"

I was a bit taken aback by that. "Should I?"

He shrugged. "He's a likable guy. Has a grown-up family. He was in his second term when I knew him. He hung with Kelly, something I found strange. Kelly's a cutthroat politician. Fred's always . . ." He let it go with a *you know* expression.

"Do you know Senator Gavin Crawford?"

"I've heard the name but never met him. He new?"

"Beginning his second term. He and Pembroke are friends, neighbors in McLean."

"Is he another one you're worried about?" he asked flippantly.

Ralph's potshots were getting tiresome. Maybe he thought he was being witty, but he was rubbing me the wrong way. "No, he has befriended Dalton professionally." I added that to stop another remark. I needed to move on. "How do senators interact with the FDA?"

He reacted as though I'd thrown him a fastball, when he expected a slider. He took a long pull on his beer. "Officially, they don't, except in hearings. The pharma lobbyists use their considerable influence over both the Senate and the FDA. They manage things."

That piqued my interest. "How so?"

"The pharmas finance a lot of research and quietly dictate. I'm not referring to the thousands of scientists and associates who do their work very well. Besides, the pharmas only need to target a few key people, influence the hiring of special government employees . . ."

"Special . . . who are they?"

"They're called an Advisory Committee. It's something that was established in 1972 throughout the federal government."

I felt we were getting close to something new and important. "Could the pharmas influence who's hired?"

"I would say they do. The committee members are paid a fee."

"Could such a committee advise the FDA to turn down a drug that they might under other circumstances have approved?"

"There is not a doubt in my mind they could," Ralph said firmly.

# 37

As I entered the newsroom, I had a feeling that this Monday would be full of good opportunities. I found Mary busy on the phone and went directly to my desk where I found a message slip indicating Michael Horne had called earlier. I called him.

"Good morning," he said enthusiastically. "Senator Dalton flew in last night. How's 1:30?"

"Great."

"The senator is thinking of asking for a hearing on Tutoxtamen. Unfortunately, Senator Pembroke would have to pass on that. I was just about to call Nancy for some guidance."

"Could Senator Dalton talk to the minority party's ranking member?"

"That would only add to the alienation our party members have for her. I'd rather see her get turned down by Pembroke than do that."

"Okay," I said unperturbed. "I'll see you at 1:30."

I called Lori Chow and brought her up-to-date. She had a photographer in Dalton's hometown on standby, and the McAllisters were available Wednesday and Thursday. I suggested I fly out Wednesday morning, meet them, and scope out the house.

That met Chow's approval. Because I had already asked to be part of the shoot in the Capitol, Chow would set that up for next week. I called Sarah Metzger to ask if someone could sort through the watchdog authors' interviews and pull out some quotes . . . or give me the whole story if they liked.

"I have some interns around who can be put on that," the Health editor said.

"Having the luxury of others doing the sifting will save me a lot of time."

"You're easy to work with," she said cheerily.

"Maybe you could tell that to my editor."

"Lassiter? I'd rather walk the plank," she said bluntly.

I had to stifle a laugh. Lassiter's stern reputation was certainly widespread. The truth was they had no idea how fair and loyal my editor was. I guessed that part never got out. "Her darts don't always hit live targets."

"You seem to have survived, even thrived, if I may say so."

"I run fast and am a better dart player."

Metzger laughed. "It's all in what you're used to, I guess."

We hung up, and I read for a while.

Michael called. "Nancy said flat out it would be political suicide to make a request of Pembroke, shutting that door. Switching to good news, Tyrell, by pure luck, fell in with a group Friday night at The Goose that included a male aide on the majority leader's staff."

"Oh?"

"He turned out to be one of the Hill's shit-for-brains people. He's married but chases the skirts and talks too much. He became interested in a couple of women at a far table and wanted to hit on one, but needed a buddy to take the other. Tyrell went along."

"What a guy. I hope the other one wasn't a dog." I laughed. I couldn't help myself. It sounded so funny. "Did they score?"

"Why, Ms. Wolfe, you surprise me."

"I'm just one of the guys," I quipped.

"Somehow I doubt that. Anyway, this guy's big into impressing the women, boasting he had an important job on Senator Kelly's staff. Ty thought we might like to talk to him."

"And the punch line?" I never cared for shaggy-dog stories.

"The guy hangs out with heavy-hitters from the pharmas, who all praise him and Kelly for going the extra mile to help out their industry."

I was experiencing the Capitol Hill underground at work for the first time.

"Tyrell fanned the guy's ego, but even in his fog, he talked mostly fluff. Tyrell thinks he's ripe for expert plucking. The two couples are meeting tomorrow night. Ty once worked for a federal prosecutor and is going to play detective. He looked up the guy and found that he had actually done some interesting work."

This might lead to something sometime, but I needed to switch subjects.

"Are you sitting in on my interview?"

There was a slight pause. I must have caught him off guard.

"Of course, I always protect my senator from prying reporters," he bantered.

"Keep that thought; I'm a bad one. Very devious."

That prompted a good laugh. We wrapped things up, and my journalistic mind wondered if I could be getting too chummy with people I might have to report on. Did I need to be more circumspect? As much as I liked the senator and Michael, they were also part of the story. I would have to keep my guard up and my senses clear.

# 38

My interview with Dalton went smoothly. It reminded me of our first meeting in her condo. She exhibited strong confidence, with warmth and congeniality, and spoke in full sentences. Many people jump around, don't finish sentences, or interrupt themselves. The exact thing I do when I'm pumped up.

"I refrained from telling you homespun stories because you'll get an earful of those from my father."

"I consider myself forewarned."

"How do you think the interview went?" the senator asked.

"Swimmingly. Do you have time to discuss Rogers?"

"I mentioned Tyrell to the senator," Michael interjected.

Dalton showed concern. "That's a ticklish one."

"And best left up to Tyrell and me, not involving you, ma'am."

"I have something you both should know," the senator said. "My father knows Harley Rogers. He served under him in the Rangers during WWII."

I shook my head. "My, what a small world."

"That was a total surprise to me. Dad also knows a lot more about what's going on here than I thought. Our state's senior senator, Harold Raines, and two congressmen have each worked for my father at one time or another."

"This is going to make my meeting with him even more interesting."

"A word of advice. Let my father take the lead. Knowing you as I do, you should find it very easy to go with the flow. He loves company, showing off the ranch and telling stories. It's his way of sizing up a person. Let the Rogers thing come out naturally. If, as I suspect, he becomes impressed with you, he will open up."

I felt my face flush and my adrenaline surge.

"I must have commented to him during one of our phone conversations that you two were going to New Jersey to meet Rogers, because he called Harley to pave the way, telling him that the current Senator Dalton was his daughter."

I looked at Michael. "That accounts for Harley's demeanor when we were there."

# 39

I flew to Dalton's hometown on Wednesday morning, as planned. As I cleared the gangway, a large man dressed in a black suit and a starched white shirt was holding up a small sign with "Wolfe" on it. I introduced myself.

He did the same. "I'm Johnny. Governor sent me." He took my carry-on. "Do you have luggage?"

"No." I wondered how he had gotten all the way to the gate with security being so stringent. We went down an escalator and out through the automatic sliding glass doors to a highly polished black sedan.

An airport security officer near it waved and said, "Hi, Johnny," as we walked to it. Once we were on our way, Johnny said, "Governor and Mrs. McAllister are at the country club and would like you to join them for lunch."

"Thank you." I was entering into a new world. I'd never eaten at a country club.

"I'll see to your check-in at the hotel, if you'd like. I believe the governor would like you to spend the afternoon with him."

"That would be fine, but just my carry-on . . . I'll keep my computer bag with me."

"Yes ma'am."

I saw a few high-rises off in the distance. We skirted that area, driving through a light commercial district that slowly transitioned into scruffy residential. A mile or two later, the homes became significantly upgraded, the yards manicured, and the streets lined with huge, old trees that formed a canopy across the two-lane road.

We pulled into a private roadway. The name *Swale Hollow Country Club* was on the white brick pillars bracketing the drive. The tree-lined road took us up a slight incline, and I saw pieces of the golf course through gaps in the foliage. Johnny stopped in front of a four-story structure replete with large pillars. Johnny escorted me through the spacious lobby to a terrace that overlooked a swimming pool to the left and a large putting green to the right. As we neared a café-like area, a trim elderly man with white combed-back hair stood. He was dressed in white slacks and a blue blazer with an open-collared, lightly striped, white shirt.

"Ah, Johnny. Thank you. Be back in an hour and a half."

"Yes sir. I'll get Ms. Wolfe checked in."

"Excellent. Ms. Wolfe, it is a pleasure. I'm Rufus McAllister." He turned to his wife, who was now standing.

"Call me Laura, please."

"Sara Jane, this is Laura Wolfe."

"Mrs. McAllister." I accepted her extended hand.

"Laura, such a beautiful name. Welcome."

I asked if my taking notes would bother them.

Mrs. McAllister smiled. "Certainly not, especially for such a good cause."

Rufus was a good storyteller and regaled me with some background about his senator daughter. Mrs. McAllister barely made a comment.

After our meal, the governor announced, "I'm going to show Laura around."

Mrs. M and I stood. She smiled graciously. "I have things to tend to. We'll meet later."

It was his party. She had made her requisite appearance and now slipped away right on cue. Rufus, who insisted we be on a first-name basis, took out his cell. "We're ready to go, Johnny," and clicked off. "I'd like to show you Ro's town, show you where she 'hung out.'"

I seriously doubted Roanne McAllister had ever *hung out*, in a kid's sense of the word. However, Rufus was the ringmaster, and I, the little kid with the pink cotton candy. He talked about his daughter's growing up, the pageants, her education, and marriage to H.T. Dalton. I took notes. He would interrupt his narrative each time we approached some memorable landmark, in his mind, in the life of his little girl.

"Okay, Johnny, let's go home." We'd been driving around for nearly two hours.

"Yes sir."

This was Rufus McAllister country, and I had the feeling I was getting more of that than the life and times of Roanne Elizabeth McAllister Dalton. But it was all background and part of what I had to do.

"Well," Rufus said self-satisfied, "that ought to give you something to fill the pages of your newspaper."

"Probably no more than a couple of paragraphs." I couldn't resist that, but I hastened to add. "It's valuable background."

He grunted. "Background."

"Editors," I replied. "The story is the senator. You've given me all the public stuff . . . how about Roanne, the daughter. What did she do? What did you do with her?"

"She was always so pretty. Startlingly beautiful," he said wistfully.

I thought I was losing him, but then he came around.

"She played with dolls, the normal stuff, until she was about four. That's when the modeling and the pageants started. After that, it was all about clothes, hairdos, and makeup—not my kind of thing. She's had her own bank account since the age of five and an investment portfolio since she was eight, with a financial advisor to go along with it. Of course, her mother was in charge of all that."

He said that as if he was reading someone else's bio. Detached. He paused and looked out the car's side window. He became pensive, not the outgoing warrior of the political wars. We drove in silence. I waited.

"Seems she never had much of a childhood, what with me in politics and running a business. Her brother Rusty was born a little before Ro's fourth birthday. That's about when Ro's beauty pageants began. Regina, Reggie, came along two-and-a-half years later. Sadie—that's my wife Sara Jane— had her hands full with Ro's goings and comings, so we hired a full-time nanny for the younger two."

I heard sorrow in his voice.

"I'm afraid the two younger ones developed a resentment toward Ro, but that didn't come out until they were both in their teens, when Ro went off to college. They sort of teamed up on their mama. I thought Sadie was going to have a nervous breakdown. To ease things up, I sent Rusty off to military school. Over time, that proved to make things worse."

"It was always Ro, no matter what you did?"

"Yeah. Sadie was all wrapped up in Ro's winning the state and then going for the national crown. She lost there because she hadn't developed a real good talent. She was more beautiful than any of the rest . . ." His voice faded.

"I've seen the pictures. You're right. Yet, she came in third."

"It was the only time—ever—she wasn't first. I thought it would destroy her. However, I didn't know the stuff Ro was made of. She took one on the chin and walked away smiling. Not one complaint. She said it was time to get her degree."

"I see a lot of quiet strength in her."

"Oh, she has that. I didn't want her to run for the Senate—just to fill out H.T.'s time, then come back home and teach at the university, like she always wanted. I figured the title of senator would just give her a little more prestige. I held out hope she might marry again and maybe, well . . . but that may not happen."

"You have grandchildren, don't you?"

"Yeah, but none of them . . . my kids won't let their kids go into politics. I'm glad I get to see them when I do. Rusty and Reggie are tighter now than they ever were putting up a strong front against Ro, who loves them both. The shame is it's not Ro's fault. It's ours. Mine and Sadie's."

I wondered if he was sharing this to explain away the rift. I liked that he trusted me enough to tell me. Of course, the old codger could be playing me. He suddenly shifted his body to an upright position, coming out of his reflectiveness, as one who suddenly awakens. He looked at me and rested his hand on my leg. Not the thing to do, but I held my reaction.

"Now," he said in a hushed confidential way, "none of that is for publication." He removed his hand.

I relaxed. "Never thought it was."

He snorted a laugh. "You sure you're a newspaper reporter?"

"I know boundaries. Besides, this is a fluff piece about the senator, not an investigation. Oh, and I was warned off her siblings by her AA, Michael Horne."

He reflected and then said very quietly, "I'd give anything for it not to be like that."

I needed to change the subject and the mood. "What's your feeling about the issues surrounding the cancer drug?"

He looked at me, a twinkle in his eye. "You're okay, you know that?"

I smiled and waited. A reply wasn't necessary. The senator had suggested I not bring up that subject, but I sensed the timing was right; the old trooper was about to get back in the saddle.

"I got contacts in DC. People tell me what's going on. Ro handled herself real well, changing her position like she did."

"You didn't have anything to do with that?"

"Not one damn thing," he said emphatically, almost daring me to challenge him.

I waited.

"When she's here, we talk. She'll ask, but she's in charge of what she does."

Even though we were sitting only inches apart, he shifted himself, turning more toward me, and leaned in to confide . . . without putting his hand on my leg this time.

"I don't know you, but I am curious why a Pulitzer Prize–winning reporter is a long way from her beat talking to a senator's father about dolls and pageants."

He was a man of surprises, and I was caught off guard momentarily. To allow for some recovery time, I shifted my body toward him and smiled. His eyes were bright and challenging, blazing into me.

"It's a cover," I whispered. "The fluff piece will be written, and your daughter will have a major story, but that's not my real assignment." I waited for a reaction. He was wily, but his eyes questioned me.

"My managing editor came up with the idea to explain my presence in Senator Dalton's offices and my times with the senator in the Capitol. My real assignment is to learn about Tutoxtamen, the reason why she contacted me. I'm not alone. I'm backed by my paper, unlike my travails trying to put together last year's serial killing case."

He leaned back but kept his eyes on me. "Seems we are both sharing secrets," he said in his folksy manner. "You are definitely on Ro's side."

"Absolutely. She has a strong issue but can't go it alone. With Michael's help, we're beginning to put a scenario together. It's the pharmaceutical lobby and a few senators we're interested in. We're looking to turn up the heat and see who yells ouch."

"How can you be going after the pharmas? Rogers is a pharmaceutical company, and they're getting their ears pinned back."

"It's been known to have one member sacrificed for the betterment of all, right?"

"But why?"

"There's a lot of locker room speculation, but no clear-cut answer. I'll say this, neither Harley nor Sherman Rogers acts like they've been given the death sentence."

"So you don't know," Rufus said flatly, then snorted another laugh. "I'm liking you more by the minute," he said, slapping my thigh, as men do to each other.

It was okay. I guessed now I was one of the guys.

# 40

T he McAllister home sat behind manicured grounds atop a small rise, well back from the road. A half-dozen pillars fronted the mansion and reached to the third floor; a second floor balcony sat over the imposing front portico. The façade was white brick. I viewed some smaller buildings to the rear of the side-loading garage. One looked like a cottage, and then a large barn-like structure with double garage doors, and two one-story rambler-type buildings.

Senator Dalton had mentioned that her father took the saying *"A man's home is his castle"* literally.

"We keep horses," Rufus said. "Everybody in the family rides. It's the main way I get to see Rusty, Reggie, and the grandkids. My sister and her husband are visiting. Sadie's mother and father, both in their early nineties, are coming next week and staying a month. The old guy still plays golf. We'll go out a few times."

The governor had gained wealth, prominence, property, and the envy of many. Yet, he said all that without feeling—it just came out like a rambling of facts. With everything he had, he did not have the family he wished for.

Mrs. M met us as we entered through the kitchen and fussed over me. Rufus excused himself, while she showed me around the house. It was all very impressive. She wished I could stay with them, but I told her that the paper preferred my staying on my own, that it was better this way. She told me she understood, and I believed she did.

She showed me her daughter's room. "It's so wonderful when Ro stays with us. She was just here last weekend. Time goes by so fast, I can barely keep track."

I found her delivery to be an airy affectation, as if everything was a chore or to be tolerated. She walked me to an adjacent bedroom.

"You may use this room to relax and freshen up. We will have cocktails at 6:00." She left, closing the door, like a parent would do after saying goodnight to a child.

I wanted to take advantage of the fifty minutes I had, taking off my shoes and plopping down on the quilt-covered, queen-sized bed. The oversized pillows forced me into too much of an upright position, so I removed them. I missed being at home and called Anna.

She was staying an extra two hours while I was away. I caught her in the process of giving Tyler a bath. He had finished his dinner, which meant to me that he'd smeared a lot over his face and in his hair. Anna assured me "things go good." I thanked her and called Jerry.

"How's it going?" He had caller ID on his private office phone line.

"I'm sprawled out in the lap of luxury, my dear, in the McAllister's mansion."

"Don't get too used to it."

"The reality is that you and I are much better off."

He laughed. "What's happening?"

"Well," I said, retrieving one of the pillows to prop up on, "I was treated to a lovely lunch by Mr. and Mrs. McAllister at their country club, and then the former governor took me on a chauffeur-driven tour of where Roanne McAllister Dalton grew up. I'll tell you about that when I see you."

"You're staying there? I thought—"

"I'm checked into a hotel. I'll go there after supper. The chauffeur checked me in during lunch. We have a photo shoot here tomorrow, so Rufus is going to walk me around the grounds later, see what appeals to me."

"Rufus?"

"The governor insists on that. He's a down-home aristocrat."

"Quite a combination."

"I checked in with Anna. Tyler's bathing."

"I'll get there by 6:00. Ralph told me they enjoyed the visit Saturday and that he would be looking into some things for you. He thinks those senators have overstepped their bounds and may have left a wake behind them."

"I appreciate in advance everything he can do. Give our little boy a hug from me."

"I'll give him a couple. Enjoy yourself."

"Love you."

"Love you."

I slid the pillow away and stretched out. My mind wandered all over with no one thing capturing my thoughts. I set my travel alarm to go off at 5:50 and took a nap.

When I walked onto the terrace that overlooked an extensive pasture, I found the McAllisters and another couple sitting at an umbrella-shaded patio table. Two horses were grazing at a nearby pasture fence adjacent to the barn.

"Ah, Laura," Rufus said, standing. "Please." He gestured to the chair he was holding out for me. "Frank, Jane, this is Laura Wolfe, a friend of Ro's."

I had wondered how he was going to handle who I was. We greeted all around, and I sat. The conversation was general, but when the sister asked me a personal question, Rufus jumped in with an answer and quickly diverted the conversation to another subject. Following dinner, he excused the two of us, saying he wanted to show me the horses. We walked out through the kitchen and into the side yard, out of view from everyone else.

"I apologize for my sister, she's a bit of a snoop," he said earnestly.

"I thought you handled it like an expert fencer parrying an opponent's thrust." I used the metaphor to infer he had done a courteous thing.

"You're too kind," he said, bowing his head.

We both laughed.

"Come on," he said, taking my arm. "You have family?"

We began walking. "I bet you already know the answer to that."

"Me . . . why?" Then he grinned. "Yeah, I do. I like to know who I'm dealing with."

"That's fair. Did I pass muster?" I liked this man. I wasn't fooled into feeling he was a touchy-feely kind of a guy. I was sure he'd laid some leather on some skin. Right now, he was showing me his warm side. I hoped he and Jerry would have the chance to meet one day.

"I have a wonderful husband and a beautiful eight-month-old son, whom I am missing. This is the first night I have not been there to kiss him goodnight."

"Keep those feelings," he said ruefully. "Nothing's worth losing that."

"I have no intentions of letting anything change that, I assure you."

He looked me in the eye. "I believe you. Come on, you can see where you want to set us up for tomorrow."

I held back, and he stopped. "What?" he asked concerned.

"A question, Governor. You've been around the horn and taken the measure of a lot of people." I had his attention. "Do you think Tom Kelly could forsake principle and a career for money?"

My question caught him off guard, which is why I chose this moment in time to ask it.

"I have no first-hand knowledge of the man," he said cautiously.

"You don't need it." I knew his answer was a stall. He'd gotten my meaning.

"Yes, and that's what scares the bejesus out of me, for Ro. If he's that cold and calculating, then he's capable of going to any means to meet his end. Men like that—and believe me I was no saint, but I drew the line—they have no compunctions about doing what's needed to get their way."

Our walk took us to the pasture fence. It was three rows of long wooden rails painted white. I took a deep breath, as if enjoying the fresh air, and then took the plunge. "I don't know if you know who Harley Rogers is. He—"

"He the one who created the drug that's got Kelly and the pharmas in a hissy-fit?"

I suppressed a laugh. "He is. Michael Horne and I visited him in New Jersey recently. He's a fit old man, in his mid-eighties. His son Sherman runs the place, handles the day-to-day."

I paused looking out over the pasture and the two horses still grazing near the barn. Rufus leaned on the fence looking in the same direction, but more toward the horizon where the sun would soon set. I placed a hand on the rail and continued, "I found Harley to be a complex person. He suffered a huge defeat with his miracle drug that could bankrupt him, yet he neither acted down nor showed he was particularly worried."

I waited for him to reply. He held his pose looking off in the distance. I didn't think his mind was on the scenery. He let his foot slide off the rail and looked me straight in the eye. "Men take defeat in a variety of ways. Some act nonchalant, which maybe keeps them from committing suicide. Some suck it up, come up off the canvas, and struggle to get to the bell. Some plan for the eventuality of defeat and take measures to shore things up and keep everything from caving in. Some plan ways of circumventing bad news with something already on the back burner that could turn defeat into victory."

He returned to leaning on the fence, looking out over the pasture.

Somewhere on Rufus's menu was Harley. I felt he was scratching, unsure of how much I knew. On the other hand, he could be telling me without telling me and wants to see if I could pick it out. I liked his metaphors, but decided not to take the bait.

Harley's movements of people and equipment could have the trappings of a military maneuver. Rufus had corroborated for me that Harley had a plan, or that he had already implemented one.

And that would be up to me to uncover.

# 41

I woke refreshed at 6:30 in my hotel room, showered and dressed, went down for a light breakfast, and read the local paper. When I returned to my room, I called Jerry.

"I'm pretty sure Harley has an ace up his sleeve. Rufus knows, but is not talking. He gave me a little parable, with four choices, one I'm sure fits Harley. Dalton told me her father likes playing games, to see how smart the other person is."

Jerry laughed. "He doesn't know who he's going against, if he's taking you on."

I love my husband. "It's time. Give my boy a hug . . . tell him his mom loves him."

"He already knows, but I will tell him anyway. Love you."

"Love you."

Johnny was waiting, parked right outside the hotel's front door. We chatted comfortably while he drove along a scenic road to the McAllister's. "The governor sure has been enjoying your visit. He's looking forward to the picture-taking," the likable man, who had a friendly child-like demeanor, said.

We arrived in twenty minutes. The photo crew was already busy at work. The photographer told me he had visited a week earlier to get familiar with the grounds. All of his ideas sounded fine to me. The only request I made was that he get pictures of the governor astride his horse. The photographer understood.

The shoot went well. The photographer and Lori Chow had agreed that for the space she could give it, the house was the only place they'd shoot.

I enjoyed watching. Mrs. M was atwitter. I noticed fresh flowers in the living room and large foyer. We got Rufus on his horse. Both were up for the occasion.

At our food break, we all were treated to a gracious and plentiful lunch. Afterward, there were two inside photo sessions. It was over by 3:00. At one point, I had a little time with Mrs. M. That was a trip. She was vapid and noncommittal. Even with my prompting, she skirted all talk about Reggie and Rusty, except for flowery remarks about their lovely homes and beautiful children.

When the crew had gone, I discovered that Rufus had as well. I walked around the estate for about an hour, freshened up in my room, and went down for cocktails and another scrumptious supper. It was just the three of us. Mrs. M was more engaging this time. They both talked about the senator. The memories were golden.

The McAllisters were marvelous hosts. I had checked in with Lori earlier. The photographer had emailed her the pictures, and she was delighted. Because there was now no need for me to stay on for a supplemental morning shoot, I was able to move tomorrow's flight from early afternoon to 11 a.m. Johnny drove me to the hotel, and Rufus came along.

As I got out, he thanked me for coming and for what I was doing for Ro. "Johnny will pick you up at 9:00 tomorrow."

"Thank you for your hospitality and wonderful conversation, Rufus. I can honestly say I enjoyed my entire time."

I didn't see him the next morning, but that didn't surprise me. We'd said our goodbyes. Johnny was sweet and gracious. We talked a little at the beginning of the drive to the airport, but fell into silence for the rest of the ride. When I alighted, with Johnny holding the door, he handed me a white, card-size envelope.

"This is from the governor, ma'am. He asked if you would please wait until you are in the air before you open it," he said precisely and politely.

Why wait I wondered? "Thank you, Johnny. Tell him I will do as he asks."

"Yes ma'am."

Johnny retrieved my carry-on from the trunk, gave it to a skycap, and returned to me.

"I was going to carry that on, Johnny."

"Yes ma'am. I just asked the man to see you through security, make sure everything goes okay. You'll have your bag. He will take good care of you. I already took care of him."

With that, he tipped his cap and went to the limo.

The skycap was waiting for me. "If you'll have your ticket and ID out, we can get you right through, ma'am."

We were in Rufus McAllister country. Although the line at the security gate wasn't very long, one word from my escort and we were moved over to the first-class gate. I had well over an hour before my plane and browsed a sundries shop, buying a book entitled *Fix-Up Tips For Your Home*.

Once my carry-on was in the overhead and my computer bag under the seat, I sat back and flipped through the in-flight magazine, stopping to scan a story on Georgetown in DC. They had most things right except about Metrorail, where they had revised history. A quote from a merchant complained that they should have gotten a Metro station, saying they were overlooked for political reasons back when the system was planned.

The writer didn't editorialize or give the real reason. The truth was that, back in the 1950s or 1960s when Metrorail routes and stations were being planned, the Georgetown residents and merchants overwhelmingly turned down having a Metro stop in their community. They didn't want undesirables having such easy access to their precious village.

It was not Metrorail's or the planners' fault. It didn't take many years after Metro was running deep into the suburbs that Georgetownians realized their mistake. Now riders have to walk five to twelve blocks from the Foggy Bottom station; trek back across the Potomac River on Key Bridge from the Rosslyn, Virginia, station; or clog the roads with their cars.

History revisionists drive me crazy. I stuffed the magazine into the seat pocket, like it was the publisher's fault. I took Rufus's letter from my bag. The plane was sparsely filled, and I had no row mates. I put up the arm rest between seats, checked my seat belt, and laid my head back, closing my eyes. I'm always a little anxious during takeoff.

Once we were airborne, I looked at the envelope. I stared at my first name on the face of it, and then opened it.

*Dear Laura:*

*Thanks for being a good friend to Ro. You will find she will be a good friend in return. I've given a lot of thought to what I'm going to tell you. Ro doesn't know this, but my association with Harley began with a phone call from him well before Ro was a senator. My call to him before your visit to New Jersey is as you know it to be.*

*Harley is going offshore to manufacture his drug and will*

*distribute it through a German pharmaceutical company. That's all I know.*

*He called me a couple of years ago about security companies. He ended up using an outfit I believe is thorough and trustworthy. That's all he wanted from me. Please convey this to Ro for me?*

*I know she will think I'm involved because of her, putting in my two cents. But I assure you I am not. My hope is that with you telling her, she can rest assured I am not meddling in her affairs. I don't want her thinking that my talking with Harley was because I thought she needed help. That's not true.*

*The only call I made to Harley was, as I have said, to tell him that the Senator Dalton who was sending two people up to talk to him was my daughter.*

*I didn't ask for anything. I only wanted him to know that. I love my daughter, Laura, and I am immensely proud of all she is doing and will accomplish. In no way do I think she can't do it without my help. Shoot, she'll do it a whole lot better without me.*

*Much thanks. You're good people.*

*RMcA*

My eyes teared before I finished. I wiped them away. Family relationships are so complex. Roanne was the only one of his children he stood a chance with, and he feared one misstep on his part could cause him to lose her.

I thought of the years that were lost between my parents and me. Thank God for my Mom, who took the chance of being rebuffed by me—again—when she wrote me a month after I had broken the serial-killing story. That was how she'd known I was pregnant, because Dad had run excerpts of my exclusive breaking story and subsequent pieces by me in the *Star*.

I had shown Jerry the letter from Mom. He was noncommittal, only saying it was nice, but offering no advice. It took me a week to get around to writing her back. That began my recovery with my parents. I put Rufus's letter away and blew my nose. My concern now was how to go around Michael to talk with the senator alone.

As soon as I was on the ground, I called Michael's cell. He answered after the first ring. I gave him a rundown on my meeting with the governor and concluded with, "I think he's inserted himself into the Rogers's project; however, I don't think the senator needs to know that now."

"I agree."

"Did she ever call Harley Rogers?" I remembered he was going to suggest she might make that call.

There was silence on his end.

"Michael?"

"Shit," he said, half under his breath. "I forgot to tell her."

Actually, that was good, because that told me the senator didn't know what Harley had told her father.

"Hold on a sec, Michael." I was out on the sidewalk and found the taxi stand. "North Arlington," I told the dispatcher. He put up three fingers meaning I was third up in the Virginia line.

"Okay, Michael, I'm back. If the senator wants—"

"Your editor called me . . ."

A bolt of adrenaline shot through me.

". . . to schedule the shoot," he finished.

Not Lassiter, Chow.

"Lady!" The dispatcher called. "You're next." He pointed to a cab just pulling up.

"Hold on, Michael, I'm getting into a cab," which I did. "Clarendon."

The driver grunted and pulled away from the curb. "Okay, Michael, I'm back."

"We suggested next Wednesday to your editor."

"Time?"

"Nine, in our office. Then we'll go from there."

That sounded fine, as I relaxed in the comfortable leather seat of the cab. "Things getting busy on the Hill?"

"Sort of," he said offhandedly.

He wasn't being his talkative self. "How'd Tyrell make out?"

"Well, both ways, from what he said."

I laughed. "The perks of spydom."

"I guess."

He was in a funky mood. "Michael, what's wrong?"

He didn't answer, so I waited.

"It's the guy," he said very quietly. "Tyrell says he's in over his head; they own him."

"They?"

"The pharmas."

I hated having to drag it out of him. "Own him?"

"He's in deep. Let me back up. After their respective dates last week, Tyrell waited a day, then called the guy. Tyrell's reason was to see if they could get together, without dates, get to know each other better. The guy agreed, and they had lunch.

"I'll give you the short story. The guy's up to his eyeballs in trouble. Being close to the leader, he constantly received gifts, trips, cash . . . . He had become a high-roller, Tyrell said. The guy even broke down when telling him. His wife and two-year-old daughter had left him and gone to her parents in Michigan, and they might not come back."

"She knows about his philandering?"

"I don't know what she knows, except that she did complain about all the gifts he brought home and his spending money that she didn't think they had," Michael said disgustedly.

"Yeah, the pharmas bought him hook, line, and sinker," I said softly, in case the driver knew English.

"He's very vulnerable."

"Can we turn him?" I whispered.

"We'll probably have to threaten him with exposure."

A pang of concern shot through me.

"We have no other option, Laura. We have an opportunity to get inside the Kelly slash pharma camp," Michael said strongly.

I didn't like dragging innocents into . . . yet Michael was right. Besides, this was in his backyard. He could go it alone and probably would.

"Our intention . . ."

Our? Did that mean Dalton was in on this?

". . . is to garner information . . . names, places, that sort of thing. We'll set up a dinner, something that's part of the guy's normal social routine."

"His goose is cooked regardless of which way he goes," I suggested.

"I guess. Maybe we can orchestrate a way for him to get another job, be fired, something to keep the wrath of the pharmas from coming down on him. Try and get him off the hook, give him a way to set things straight with his wife."

Michael is a major conspirator.

"How many scenarios have you developed?"

"Well, I'll talk to Nancy—"

"Oh, they'd make a pair," I said sarcastically.

"Nancy is a solid citizen. If you saw her work, you'd see what I mean."

"I'm sorry," I said, catching his tone. "I didn't—"

"It's my fault for divulging her private—"

"No. That's me. When I know people, I tend to joke around. Let's get back to your plan," I said, hoping to right the ship.

"Okay," he said calmly. "I thought you, me, Nancy, and the guy could have dinner. We'd start out with Tyrell, but a prearranged phone call will call him away. Then we'd be two couples—"

It sounded like he had interrupted himself, so I waited.

"Laura, would you do that?"

"Sounds safe enough. I can be a member of your staff, like in New Jersey. You sure about Nancy? They may know each other. She works for Pembroke."

"Ouch. Maybe using Nancy isn't such a good idea. Besides, I momentarily forgot, she's working on Gordon. How about you, me, and Tyrell having dinner with the guy?"

I'd forgotten about Nancy and Gordon too. "Sure. Maybe have the senator—"

"What?" came his sharp response. "She won't agree . . . I won't let her. That's not her style. You said so yourself."

"It wouldn't be asking her to go against her principles."

"I can't allow that," he said assertively.

I found his objection a little hollow considering what was at stake. However, I agreed to it being Michael, Tyrell, and me. Then I broached the sensitive issue of wanting to talk with the senator, even though we would be getting together Monday.

He told me he'd check with her and get back to me, adding that I shouldn't worry about the potential mole. "The guy wants a new start."

We said our goodbyes. I told the driver to stay on the Parkway and exit at Spout Run. I sat back in the seat, eager to talk to Roanne Dalton. My cell phone rang.

# 42

I talked with Roanne during my cab ride home. She was enthusiastic to hear about my trip. I made my case about seeing each other in person without telling her I had something for her. She suggested FDR's Memorial in West Potomac Park. We agreed on a time.

Anna and Tyler welcomed me home, and I held and hugged my very excited little boy. Jerry came in at 5:30, and the three of us enjoyed our reunion, albeit a short one. I told Jerry about the note and that I was meeting Roanne at 6:30, a ten-minute jaunt across Memorial Bridge and into West Potomac Park. Jerry was okay with that and said he'd feed Tyler. We'd pack up and go to *Scalawag* after I got back.

The drive was as quick as I had expected. I parked and began walking toward the outdoor Roosevelt Memorial when I saw the senator standing alongside a cab in the drop-off area. I waved, and she waved back.

"Hi," I said happily. "Thanks for doing this."

"If you wanted to see me privately, it was the least I could do," she said lightly. "Why don't we walk through the memorial and down to one of the benches along the Tidal Basin?"

We went through the open gallery passing polished granite walls with quotes from the WWII president. Water cascades fell into catch basins giving life to an otherwise colorless ambiance. "I have heard that it takes an out-of-town person to get a local out to see the sights."

She smiled. "Ah, you've not been here either?"

"Right."

"We can walk around, play tourist if you like."

"I like your first suggestion better," I said casually.

We found a path through trees to the edge of the water and took a bench facing the gorgeous Jefferson Memorial across a portion of the basin. It seemed majestic, only a few hundred yards away.

"When H.T. was on the Hill, and I was here during cherry blossom time, I would walk along the basin. It's a rare beauty . . . the trees and the setting."

"I've driven by," I said sheepishly.

"You have to get out more, girl."

"I get out . . . just to less engaging places."

She smiled. The soft breeze off the water reduced the mugginess. "Well, what do you have for me? Was my father a good boy?"

I had obsessed about how I would handle this and decided she should read Rufus's note to me. "Your father was great. He asked me to give you a message in a note he addressed to me. I think you should read the whole thing, even though that was not his intent."

Her face was expressionless except for her eyes that had narrowed slightly. I took the note out of my bag and handed it to her. "I'm, eh, going to take a short walk."

Roanne accepted the note, and I walked off in the direction of the memorial. After about fifty yards or so, I stopped and turned. She had already read it. The note was in her lap, and she was dabbing her eyes. Seeing her like that, my eyes teared, and I turned away using a finger to wipe off a tear running down my cheek. I sniffed. I'd forgotten to reload my purse. I turned back and found her walking toward me. I started back to her, and we met. She spoke first.

"When this whole mess is over with, I would like for us to spend some time together. I hardly know you, but right now I feel that you are the best friend I have ever had."

I was stunned. Only a stride apart, she extended her arms and closed the gap to give me a hug. I returned it in kind.

"Thank you," she whispered.

She backed out of our hold, sniffled and laughed lightly.

I felt overwhelmed and changed the subject. "Jerry and I need to get you out on *Scalawag* and show you a good time."

She frowned. "Oh?"

"It's our sailboat, a thirty-five-foot gorgeous sloop in the marina." I half-turned and pointed. "It's on the other side of the 14th Street Bridge and the Interstate. Jerry was living on it when we met."

"Oh?"

"When his wife divorced him, he moved aboard. He was a defense attorney with an office near police headquarters. He's now a partner in a different firm doing corporate law." I told her all that because I didn't want her to think Jerry was a bum.

"And you are there now, with the baby?"

"No. We bought a house in the Clarendon section of Arlington."

"I've eaten in that area. We're Metrorail neighbors."

I chuckled and she joined me, while wiping her eyes and blowing her nose.

She held up Rufus's note. "Your suspicions about Rogers were correct. Where do we go from here?"

"I asked Michael earlier if we three could get together Monday. I'll break your father's news about Harley to both of you at—"

"I can tell him."

"Yes, but that would break a trust between Michael and me. I could have told him, and he would have told you, of course. But I felt you needed to see the letter first, privately." I hoped she didn't take offense to my plan.

"Of course. Michael did ask me about Monday. I have some time late morning. Then what?"

I mentioned that Michael's friend at Rogers could become more talkative when he heard what we now know.

"I'm going to research General Aviation's airline records of private passenger and cargo planes departing from Newark Airport the past few months."

We began walking back through the memorial, and I asked if I could give her a lift.

"My cab's waiting," she said, shaking her head and offered Rufus's note to me.

"Oh no," I said. "It may have been written to me, but it's yours. I was just the messenger."

She looked at me softly. "Heaven sent."

# 43

I stayed home Monday morning and tried to work on the Style piece, but I couldn't concentrate. Tutoxtamen and Rufus's note were demanding too much attention in my brain.

For a diversion, I refilled my coffee and went out onto the deck. I pushed my mind to think about the blissful weekend Jerry, Tyler, and I had enjoyed sailing down the Potomac to St. Mary's, Maryland. We anchored in its inlet and stayed on the boat the entire time. We discussed my trip to the McAllisters, my impressions of Rufus, his note, and Roanne's reaction to me after she read it.

Roanne's family relationships led us to examining our blended families, especially my relationship with my parents. Jerry and I had tried to visit them shortly after our marriage, but it had never been the right time for my father. Then I received the handwritten note from my mother. After that, we graduated to email, and the frequency of our correspondence increased, culminating in my visit to them last September, about six weeks before Tyler was born.

Jerry's time with his sons Scot, 17, a rising senior, and Colin, 15, had slacked off last summer and fall. Our Christmas party was the first time I'd seen his boys in over a year. Although Jerry hadn't been making his weekly trips out to Maryland, he did talk to them regularly. He said the visits he did make were around a game or event that involved his sons. Occasionally, he'd take them to lunch or dinner. All very artificial. He was only a visitor. They hadn't stayed overnight on *Scalawag* since the summer before last. We returned to our marina Sunday evening.

My cell phone's ring brought me back to reality. It was Michael. Our meeting was on for 11:00.

I took Metro and emerged from the Union Station stop and ended up walking behind an excited group of tourists heading for the Capitol. They were enthralled at seeing the dome through the trees. It was an interesting contrast to how I had recently been feeling about the place.

I went in the C Street entrance of Dirksen. Senator Dalton's third floor office was halfway down the corridor. A young woman at the front desk greeted me.

"Good morning, Ms. Wolfe. I'll tell Mr. Horne you are here."

Michael appeared, thanked the receptionist, and led me to his office. He glanced at the buttons on his phone. "Oh, she's off now." He pressed one. "Senator, Laura Wolfe is here . . . right." He hung up. "She's ready." We went in. It was obvious Michael had no knowledge of my Friday evening meeting with his senator.

Roanne greeted me with an extended hand. "It's wonderful to have you come here, openly." We laughed lightly. "Let's sit over here where you interviewed me." It was a casually arranged setting around a large coffee table. I could feel we were different people to each other.

"Are all the senators' offices the same?" I asked.

"Yeah, all government-issue," Michael joked.

"Our personal accoutrements, of which I have few, are the only difference," said the senator.

Michael asked me, "Would you care for some coffee?"

"Actually, I would."

"Senator?"

"Water please, Michael."

Roanne sat in the chair next to me. We looked at each other and smiled. She waited for Michael to close the door.

"I had a long talk with my father over the weekend. I would have rather hopped on a plane. I had no idea there had been a wall between us. He knew it existed because of the way I acted around him. I had unconsciously put up a barrier . . ." Tears formed in her eyes. "Oh dear, Michael will wonder . . ." She wiped them away with a very available tissue. She smiled shyly. "I best stay off that subject."

I returned her smile. There wasn't anything for me to say.

She continued. "After Michael returns and you tell us about Harley Rogers, I will tell you about the call I was on when you arrived."

Michael arrived a moment later with our drinks.

I told them about Harley, his plans, and Rufus's present relationship with him. I suggested to Michael it might be a good time to garner more information from his friend at Rogers.

"I'll call him. He . . . you're right, this might open him up."

I nodded.

The senator said, "I believe my father's call to Mr. Rogers, telling him who I was, drew their old friendship back together, prompting Mr. Rogers to discuss his plans with Dad as they would have done sixty years ago. Two warriors slipping back into their old jargon."

That wasn't exactly how it happened, but I saw no point in correcting her.

# 44

"The call I was on when you arrived was from Senator Alfred Szymanski," Roanne told me after Michael had gone off to call his Rogers's contact.

I wasn't sure . . . "Szymanski, isn't he—"

"The opposition? Yes, he's the ranking member on HELP."

I waited. What was this all about?

"They have developed a bill to override one adopted by the Senate a few years ago. Are you familiar with Howard/Wasserman?"

"It pretty well gave the farm to the pharmas," I said, pleased that I knew.

"Namely, preventing the government from creating formularies. Senator Szymanski needs a cosponsor from our side of the aisle. He asked if I would consider being that person."

That concerned me. "Wouldn't you be digging a bigger hole?"

"I'm number fifty-two out of fifty-two now. However, I believe three of my colleagues, namely Gavin Crawford, Jean Witherspoon, and my state's senior senator, Harold Raines, would consider supporting a meaningful drug bill, other than the flimsy one our party is proposing. Al has unanimous support in his caucus. That's forty-eight votes. I'd be forty-nine. Gavin, Jean, and maybe Harold would be more than enough to push it over the top. Maybe others would—"

"Wouldn't it get filibustered?"

"Tom could try, but the press would be all over him. Al's proposal will be very popular, especially with the moderates. Fred's proposal is window dressing. Besides, it's time I acted."

She said that with a *so there* tone. I had liked this woman from the first, and my admiration was growing daily. I may be an outsider, but one with a wonderful front-row seat.

"Because I'm a reporter, when can I do something with this . . . or have my paper . . . ?"

"I will be attending a closed meeting later today with Al and his colleagues. The only one I'm concerned about is Michael—this might rattle his partisan bones. Although, I don't think he's particularly happy with our leadership these days."

"This would shove Tutoxtamen off the front page."

"Wouldn't that be a good thing?" she asked. "I imagine Harley Rogers's strategy is to stay under the radar. If he's quiet, the pharmas might even leave him alone. And I would think even an organization their size can only be stretched so far."

Michael came back in, grinning, highly energized. "Rogers is definitely developing an offshore manufacturing plant. According to Robert, it is somewhere in the Caribbean. Maybe Puerto Rico. He knows six people who have flown there recently."

"Puerto Rico is just like being in the United States. That wouldn't be offshore. They may as well go to Alabama or Idaho. My guess is it's somewhere our government has no reciprocity agreements. Wily old Harley has an ace up his sleeve."

Michael appeared a little bewildered. "So Rogers sets up a place to make the drug, but where will he market it?"

I shook my head. "*He* doesn't, Michael. He has someone else to do that for him."

He puzzled over that and then got it. "The Germans," he said excitedly. "They worked on phase-testings and clinical trials coinciding with Rogers's testing. I bet they did it for European approval, too."

"Harley Rogers is an ingenious man," Roanne said respectfully.

"And the Caribbean is a big place," I added.

# 45

O n my way back to the office, I stopped at the public library and looked up what it takes to build a drug-processing plant. I later scoured maps of the Caribbean.

Roanne continued to impress me. Her cosponsoring of the Szymanski bill would be good for the people. It would certainly drive Senator Kelly and the pharmas up the wall. I could picture pharma lobbyists in Washington sprinting to their respective senators' offices.

I stopped walking and wrote a note to call Senator Pembroke's press secretary after their bill was announced to ask for an interview. I didn't expect I'd get a positive response, but his knowing I called would hopefully create a little anxiety in their camp. Not exactly Journalism 101, but what was the harm. I'd certainly do the interview if he granted it.

During my seven-block walk to the paper, Michael called. I was at a street corner, so I stepped to the corner of a building to be out of the way of pedestrians going four different ways and found I was standing next to a plaque: *National Press Club.*

Michael said, "Tyrell and I are having drinks tonight with the guy from Kelly's staff. Want to join us?"

"Where and what time?" I asked.

"Around six, the Hill Retreat at D and—"

"I know the place. Let me check with Jerry. I'll call you back." I called Jerry.

"What's up," he asked cheerily.

"I'm conflicted." I told him about the meeting.

"You knew these things were bound to happen. What would you have done if this were last year?" he asked, knowing how to push my buttons.

"I know you don't mind because you'll have our son all to yourself," I said, half teasing.

"You can tuck him in when you get home. Are you outdoors?"

"I stopped at the King Library and decided to walk back to the paper."

"Call me later when you're on the way home."

I crossed the street and then called Mary.

"Ms. Lassiter is looking for you."

I picked up my pace and was in the office in ten minutes. I waved at Mary and went straight to my editor's office. I knocked and entered. She wanted an update. I gave it to her right up to having drinks that evening with a possible informant.

"What do you have on Rogers in Puerto Rico?" she asked.

That was old news to me, but I should have included it. "A three-year-old press release on Google said Rogers had opened a clinic for seniors in honor of a longtime employee who was born there. The employee had been killed in a car accident. Rogers personally funds the clinic, and Harley and Sherman take periodic trips there. Do we have somebody in Puerto Rico, a stringer at least?"

"I'll check on it." Lassiter said reaching for the phone.

I was out of there.

# 46

I reached the Hill Retreat at 5:50 and found Michael sipping a beer. I joined him and ordered a diet Pepsi.

"You driving?" he asked, as the waiter left with my order.

I shook my head. "Just not drinking. I'm wearing a wire. I want this guy on tape. We have a reporter in Puerto Rico checking out the clinic."

"Good on both accounts."

"The senator filled me in on Szymanski's bill. How do you feel about it?"

He smiled. "Recently, my ties to the majority leader have become strained. I'm all for it. She asked if I'd feel out the Hill underground."

"Where is Senator Crawford on this?"

"I'll see what Nancy—"

"Nancy?"

He frowned and reminded me, "She's cozying up to Gordon Pederson, Crawford's AA."

"Right. I forgot." My mind flashed back to my February lunch with Max when I saw Nancy and Kelly sharing a table. *When do I bring that up?* Michael had never mentioned a Kelly/Nancy liaison. "Fill me in on Tyrell's guy," I said.

"Before I tell you that, I need to say one thing about Ty that you wouldn't know. He won't be talking like the Yale man he is with this guy. He uses street lingo. I don't know why." He then went on to tell me more about our important guest.

Tyrell and the guy arrived about ten after. I finally got a name: Mort Stroble, big, good-looking with a friendly face. Michael introduced me as Laura Wood, a researcher for Senator Dalton. I wondered if Tyrell, a handsome black man in his early thirties, knew who I really was. Both

Mort and Tyrell looked athletic and were sharply dressed. The waiter got the drinks order, and I listened to some Hill talk.

Mort, I guess because he couldn't help himself, was softly hitting on me with sly comments. I didn't want to spoil his fun, so I went with the flow. He stepped lightly: maybe he didn't know about Michael and could think we were a twosome. He was just a guy who couldn't pass up hitting on a female, available or not.

Once he leaned in too close for my comfort, so I hit him with a question. "You like working for Senator Kelly?"

"What? Oh yeah . . . we're close."

The waiter brought the second round of drinks. There was a lot of back and forth as Michael began drawing Mort out, using flattery as his primary approach. A third round of drinks arrived, and Michael began homing in.

"I never saw a problem with the money," Mort said. "I mean, they had some things for me to do away from the office, like run an errand, if you know what I mean." He was loose and trying to be cool.

"Yeah, dude, I know what you say," Tyrell said, using his street lingo. "It like, you know, they got stuff like they do, they try to hide." He was also dropping the "g" on his gerunds.

"Yeah, you know what I'm saying," Mort said appreciatively. "I mean, a lot of money gets spread around. The leader says they gotta move it. He tapped me. The man trusts me."

Michael and Tyrell were working him well.

"And could he?" Michael asked.

His question surprised me.

"Oh yeah. He gave me a little something every time. It added up."

True to form, Michael knew what he was doing.

"Yeah, I been there. How much you get?" Tyrell asked.

"Ho, ho, ho," Mort chortled in a lofty way. "You think you got more than me?"

"I don't know, man. I'm just saying, I got a couple of Cs; it depended."

"That all? Wow, you work cheap. I got five minimum. One time he got real generous, gave me a grand."

Tyrell gave a low whistle. "Whew! You the man. Where you go, make the deal?"

"Mostly in the southwest. The wire transfers, you know, they're on the quiet. I get a receipt and give it to the senator. I did it for a couple of other senators, you know, when the big man asked me."

"Those other senators never asked you themselves?" Michael prodded.

"Naw. I worked for the big guy. It was a favor he was doing for them. I helped." Seeing his bottle was empty, he signaled to the waiter.

Michael stayed on him. "Did you give them their transfer receipt?"

"No names, just a lotta numbers. Naw, I give 'em all to my senator. I didn't know who they were for by name. They were just a number to me."

"Yeah," Tyrell said. "I'm good with numbers, had 'em memorized by when I got back."

Mort hooted. "I'm good at numbers too."

"Looks like I missed the boat. My senator's pretty straight," Michael threw off.

"What about you, sweetie," Mort said, looking at me. He couldn't remember my name.

"I'm too new to be given that kind of responsibility," I said, proud of my quick response.

Michael winked at me.

"Yeah, you gotta be around a while."

"You say you good at numbers?" Tyrell challenged Mort. "You ever get yours down?"

Mort had to think about that. "They had, like, two numbers. I think one was the account, the other a routing number or something."

"Yeah, I dig. Mine was ten . . . no, nine numbers, the other . . . the longer one was like fifteen or something."

"The last time, eh, my top number had, eh, four zeros, three sixes, an eight, and a nine," Mort said proudly.

"Wow, that's good man. I never thought—"

"The other had four ones," he said boisterously, "one of each other except a three. It had two eights." Self-satisfied, he slugged down his beer.

"Man, you good. Look, I know we all got jobs, so put it on us man, so we see what we gotta do. Ain't fair, you being in, you know, what you in." Tyrell turned to Michael and me. "Am I right?"

We nodded. "Right," Michael added. "You have no one to turn to, right?" Michael whispered confidentially to Mort.

He nodded limply. "This has me in deep shit. My wife and kid, you know, I can't . . ."

He began to lose it, sniffling and using his napkin to blow his nose. Mort spilled out his heart. It was all over.

I whispered to Michael. "Have to make a pit stop."

When I came back, Mort was in better spirits. As I neared the table, Michael stood and said, "We're calling it a night."

I nodded. We said our good nights. Michael and I went out together, followed by Tyrell and Mort. They headed up D Street toward the Capitol. Michael graciously walked me to Union Station and told me that the only thing I'd missed taping was Mort saying that Pembroke was one of the other senators, which surprised me.

"I thought he was a straight-shooter, good family man. Aren't he and Senator Crawford friends? You don't think Crawford is—"

"No," he interrupted firmly. "Senator Crawford is a lot like Senator Dalton, not particularly friendly with Kelly or his cronies, with the exception of Pembroke, of course."

"You know your senator . . . she'd be devastated if Crawford was in deep with Kelly."

"Oh absolutely," he said. "It would blow our cosponsorship with Szymanski right out of the water."

"Could Nancy—" I stopped myself, sorry I'd mentioned her name.

Michael jumped into the void. "I don't think Nancy should be included in any of this. We're friends and all, but she is very tied to Pembroke, even to Kelly."

"Tied?" I pushed.

"She wants to work her way up in the party, build a career, and maybe get a high-level job at the National Committee. Senator Dalton is not popular with those folks."

"Then, I gather Nancy doesn't know about what Tyler is doing concerning Mort."

"Not at all," he said sharply.

I thought back to Nancy's Saturday lunch in Clarendon with Senator Kelly. Maybe that was only about her career.

# 47

I waited until after Anna arrived and Jerry and I were heading downtown for work in his SUV before telling him about my previous evening's activities. He had been asleep when I got home, and we both liked to concentrate on our son in the morning. I played the more incriminating part of the Mort tape to him, which he agreed was damning testimony but would need independent corroboration to make it stick in court.

I called Michael as soon as I got in. Jerry had suggested we try the Alley Pub on Seventh, a couple blocks from the Verizon Center, for our next rendezvous with Mort.

"It's not a Hill hangout, Michael. It's also a decent place for the senator."

We needed Roanne to demonstrate to Mort that we had the clout to help him.

"The senator wants to change her look . . . clothes, hair, makeup," Michael said shyly.

I thought she'd do something like that. "Who's making sure Mort gets there?"

"Tyrell's got Mort, but he won't stay. When the senator and I get outside the restaurant, I'll call his cell. When he picks up, I will disconnect. He will continue his fake conversation until we walk in. He'll then apologize that he has to leave. As to the senator, eh, she can't change at the office; she'd be seen leaving. Security would certainly notice. She prefers not going across the river to her condo." He cleared his throat.

Then it hit me; she was going to use his place to change. Probably would be the first time a woman had ever set foot in his apartment. I almost laughed at my thought. "Fine. I'll get there early and secure an out-of-the-way table."

"Oh. What kind of a crowd? I've never been there," he asked.

"Office workers mostly. Maybe some tourists, suburban white-collar types. Jerry and I used to eat there before a Wizards or Caps game." Like a couple of years ago, I mused.

"You sure it's safe for the senator?"

"As long as she doesn't dress like a hooker." As soon as I said it, I regretted it. "I'm sorry, Michael. It's my weird sense of humor."

"I'm getting used to it," he said magnanimously. "Will you be wearing the wire again?"

"Yes. See you later."

I put a call into Senator Pembroke's office, just for fun, and was told they'd have to get back to me. I then called Sarah Metzger, who had nothing new on the watchdog writers.

"They're an elusive lot," she told me in her dry tone. "Even if one of these writers comes through, you've got to know their point of view is slanted. They may know of what they speak, but they have such angst against the pharmaceutical companies . . . you won't know what's true or not true, unless you've got something to compare it with."

"Thanks, you may have saved me a lot of time. I'm not interested in something I can't use. Is anyone unimpeachable?"

"I doubt it."

I appreciated her candor. I'd leave those writers alone for now. We had good irons in the fire with Mort, Rufus, Harley, and Michael's New Jersey friend. I called Lori Chow.

After our greetings, she said. "I'm waiting on Mr. Williams for a go-to-print date."

I guessed that Barton was waiting on the Szymanski/Dalton bill.

"Okay, thanks," I said, about to hang up.

Lori quickly added, "I want to thank you for doing such a good job. There wasn't anything we had to change or question. Very solid and entertaining. The governor must be quite a character."

"He is. But underneath all his folksiness, there is still a very powerful man."

"Sounds a little like the senator."

"Oh?"

"Yes, you showed her to be very much like what you just said of her father, if you, let's say, changed folksiness to savoir-faire," she said affably.

I had not consciously made that comparison, but obviously it had subliminally come out in the article. I should go back and reread it.

I said, "I see her as bright with a quiet confidence cloaked in social graces. The more I get to know her, the more I admire her. She's decisive, made of stern stuff." After saying that, I wondered if I had gotten all that in my article.

"That's what I like about your style. You don't come out and say it directly, but show it in the things she does: a strong individual under the beauty."

I felt a wave of relief go through me. "She's all that, for sure."

"Maybe we could get you to do another feature for us down the line."

"Thank you."

"Thank you, Laura."

Lori was certainly a lot different from Lassiter.

I cleared my desk and got out my newly acquired map of the Caribbean. There were independent archipelagos with large populated islands and small unpopulated or sparsely populated ones. I went online. There was no detail on the satellite islands, except where I read that one was . . . *a great bird sanctuary and had a gorgeous coral reef for divers in the crystal clear waters.* I saw nothing about human habitat.

A little after five, I took a walk around the newsroom. Most everyone was busy with last-minute deadlines, doing rewrites, or research. I got a Diet Pepsi from a vending machine and returned to my desk.

At 6:00, I called Jerry, who was trying to get Tyler to walk on his own.

"He's still a little young for that."

"He thinks dropping back onto his diaper-cushioned butt is fun. He gives me a big laugh and then reaches for my hand and squeaks with joy. He's going to wear me out."

"I'm sure you can distract him. Teach him chess."

"I already tried that."

"Oh you poor, forlorn, little boy. I shouldn't be late. It'll really come down to what Roanne thinks she can do for our man. Maybe she could ship him out to her Dad's ranch, put him to work in the barn. Rufus would straighten him out."

I heard a squeal from Tyler.

"There's probably a lot of truth to that," Jerry said.

"Give our little boy a hug for me. Love you."

"Love you. Call when you're leaving."

# 48

I found a table off to the side, away from the bar that was the centerpiece of the Alley Pub. I told the waiter there would be five of us, and he accordingly brought the water. I looked over the notes I'd made from the Mort tape until Tyrell and Mort arrived. I turned on my tape recorder.

Unfortunately, Mort decided to sit right next to me. Not to worry—when he saw Roanne, I'd be history. The two ordered beers. Mort seemed anxious, looking around. When the beers arrived, he slugged half of his down in one gulp.

That got him started. He touched my arm when making a point. He bragged about games he saw at the Verizon Center. He mostly sat in a skybox—a plush corporate suite where clients and politicians were entertained. I wondered how the senators filed that on their gifts-and-entertainment form, if they filed such a thing at all.

Tyrell's cell phone rang. He answered and then stood up, moving away from the table. A moment later, Michael and a very different-looking Roanne came in. She had dressed young, her hair not beautifully coiffed, but in the popular unkempt look many young women went for. Her skirt line was above the knees, and she'd gone heavy on the mascara and blush.

There was no look of the sophisticated senator, but she still turned heads. The heavy makeup took away from her natural beauty, going more for the flashy look. The men at the bar took her in from head to toe. It made me feel very plain. Mort had no clue who she was. Michael introduced her as "Betty."

"Hey, man," Tyrell said to Mort. "I got a call; the man needs me. Cool?"

"Yeah, fine," Mort said, barely taking his eyes off the new female arrival.

"You in good hands, my man. Mike, Betty, Laura, you all take care." He left.

We closed ranks. I got up and moved to the chair with its back to the bar. I now had Michael to my left and Betty to my right. Mort was now across from me and giving full attention to the great-looking chick on his left. The waiter took the drink orders.

Betty was showing deep cleavage, and I thought Mort was going to fall in. She was into the game and enjoying her disguise. Mort's hits on Betty were easily diverted by her bringing Michael or me into the conversation, frustrating Mort. Michael suggested we order our food.

The interruption by the waiter appeared to calm Mort's libido. Michael wanted to get into why we were all together. We ladies agreed, and Mort reluctantly acquiesced. Then Michael spoiled Mort's fun and told him who Betty really was. Even this hotshot lady's man got embarrassed, realizing what his libido had just done to him. He stammered out an apology, but the senator stopped him.

"Please, Mort," she said graciously, "I enjoyed the attention. It's been a long time."

"Thank you, ma'am."

"Please, call me Betty. We have important things to talk about and I don't want titles to get in the way," she said gently. "I want to see what it is we can do for you."

"I appreciate that, ma—Betty."

Michael stepped in. "As you and Ty discussed, this is a quid pro quo. Right?"

"Right."

"Mort, why don't you tell me what work you do for Senator Kelly," she said oozing charm. "We all know the routine of the Hill, but what are your interactions? I take it you do a lot with the pharmaceutical lobbyists."

"Yeah, that's my biggest job. I'm the senator's go-between with most of them, except for Mr. Horowitz, who deals directly with the leader and sometimes with Senator Pembroke."

Horowitz. A new name added to the game.

Betty honed in on him. "Have you ever been part of those times?"

"Some . . . not often."

She gave Mort a friendly smile. "Tell us about those discussions."

He melted. "They talk about some heavy stuff, like how they needed to stop that new drug, Tutox-a-something. Mr. Horowitz . . . he's a very intense person . . . was always saying how disastrous it would be for other pharmaceuticals who had cancer drugs on the market . . ."

"Disastrous? How?"

"He didn't say, but the leader knew. Mr. Horowitz could get real hot and Senator Kelly would have to calm him down. One time, Senator Pembroke brought you up, ma'am. They all talked about how they needed full agreement with what the FDA was gonna do."

"And what was he going to have the FDA do?"

"Well, ma'am . . ."

I suppressed a smile. Somebody in Mort's past must have taught him some manners. Except now after he calls them *ma'am*, he wants to paw them.

The senator asked who Horowitz dealt with at the FDA.

"A doctor, Edward Kelso. That's the only name I remember," he said weakly.

Our dinners arrived, and Mort ordered another beer. We settled into eating, then Michael took over, asking Mort about the private parties the pharmas threw . . . and the favors. He jumped all over that.

"Those guys always had some good-lookers with them in case a senator wanted a little action. Oh, yeah, they always did stuff for us. We got invites to all sorts of places, and they always had women there too."

We'd been at this for nearly forty minutes.

"Were they available for you as well as the senators?" Michael asked.

"Yeah, you know, there might be one or two lookers left over. They were very willing, being they already got paid."

A look of surprise suddenly flashed across his face, and he looked at Betty. I thought this could be a revelation of some kind.

"But there wasn't a one who could hold a candle to you," he said invitingly.

He was immersed in his addiction. She smiled and took a bite of food.

"Mort," Michael said firmly, getting his attention, "the pharmas provided women and gifts only to Kelly and Pembroke?"

Michael wanted a clear statement from Mort for my tape. Mort rubbed his chin with his fingers, thinking. He slugged down a swallow of beer, smacked his lips, and leaned into Michael.

"There were others, like the whip, when Senator Pembroke wasn't there."

"Pembroke didn't take part in the fun?" Michael asked, straightforwardly.

"He didn't enjoy it. He never did anything with them. But he liked the money."

How damning was that?

Michael nodded. "Yeah. To each his own."

"Did the pharmas and senators ever talk business at these affairs?" Betty asked.

"Oh yeah, they kicked a lot a shit around." Mort was back into the swing of things. "They talked about how after that cancer drug got ditched, they'd play around with giving discounts on a few drugs to the old people . . . you know, that sort a thing."

Mort clearly was not into the details.

Betty followed up. "Did you ever see any money change hands?"

Mort thought about that. "Yeah some, but a lot of it was trips and gifts. They'd take us out to dinner or we'd play golf . . ."

He drifted off. I needed a little more about the gifts. "You mentioned the other night that these gifts had caught your wife's attention, and she had questioned you about them."

"Yeah, she's very straight, you know, honest. She thought what I was doing . . . taking things . . . that's what got us into fighting. I shoulda known. I shoulda listened to her."

Tears began running down Mort's cheeks. I passed a couple of tissues to Michael who handed them to Mort. I felt sorry for the guy. He'd lived high and was now dropping fast. He wiped away the tears but remained emotional.

"What can you do for me? If I stay here, I'm going to get in deeper."

"You could even go to jail," I added.

"I know," he whimpered. "I've thought about that. It might be my only way out."

"Hopefully, you can avoid that," Betty said. "We will find a safe place for you. Were you given cash to deposit in offshore accounts?"

"Yeah, it couldn't go from them to . . ."

"Them?" I asked.

"Sorry, I meant from Mr. Horowitz's bank to the senators'. Somebody could trace it back. The place I went, well, they kinda move around. Sometime it's in the southwest. I've gone to Virginia and Maryland, like Tyrell said. They move it around."

"So," Michael joined in, "did anyone else do the same as you, you know, like when you might not have been available?"

"Nah." He sniffled and wiped his nose. "Senator Kelly didn't spread that type a thing around. You know, they got some other things . . . I'm not . . ." he sniffled, again. "They got other lobbyists, you know, people like that . . . other companies . . . you know, I hear things." He looked down at his plate and wiped his nose. He was running out of gas.

"How soon would you like to make your move?" Betty asked caringly.

"I guess soon. Where will I go? They could find—"

"We'll work that out. We'll get you away as soon as we can. You can say you have a family problem, put in for leave."

"I don't think her folks want any part of me," he mumbled.

"How about your parents . . . or somebody else?"

He shook his head. "Let me think . . . I'll call my wife, I'll tell her I'm giving it up . . . we love each . . . I know I don't act like I love her, but I do. I swear. I love my wife and daughter, I just . . ."

I looked at Betty and Michael; they nodded. Michael signaled to the waiter. "Michael will get this," she said and then whispered to me. "Why don't we wait outside?"

I collected my stuff. The waiter took Michael's credit card.

"We'll be right outside, Michael," Betty said.

She preceded me and had just reached the door when a loud burst of yelling occurred near the bar. I turned to see two men in business attire in a shoving match. *A little too much to drink,* I thought. There were yells. Suddenly, one man went reeling backward, to where we had just been seated, knocking into other patrons. The two instigators tumbled to the floor and disappeared from my sight amid people screaming.

I felt a tug on my arm. I turned, thinking it was Roanne, but it was another woman who held up a badge. She moved to stand between the fracas and me.

"I'm with B&G Protective Services. Please move to the outside, away from the fighting."

I looked a Roanne quizzically.

"Please, Senator Dalton," the B&G agent said intensely, "I'll explain outside."

Her knowing Roanne startled both of us, but we did as she asked. As we reached the door, a male wearing the same uniform intercepted us.

The female agent said, "The two men, dark suits, at the bar. It was a staged fight."

"I'll see what I can do."

"Our two male friends are still in there," I blurted.

A woman screamed from inside the bar, "He's bleeding!"

I couldn't see Michael or Mort in the melee. Outside, the agent moved us across the street. People were pushing behind us to get out. Once across the street, one man caught the female agent's attention. "He's one of fighters," she said, taking out a camera.

She turned in the direction of a large man in a dark suit pushing his way through a stream of cursing customers.

The agent snapped a picture just before the man turned away from us. Another suited man followed, unceremoniously picking his way through the growing crowd. The agent continued taking pictures as the second man ran off, leaving shocked people in his wake.

I got out my cell phone and called Jerry. A moment later, the male security agent came out of the restaurant escorting a very distraught Michael to us.

"Mort, oh God, he's been stabbed. He's, he's . . ." Michael choked.

"Mort?" I asked.

"He's dead, throat cut," the security man said.

I was dumbfounded. Then I heard Jerry's voice and realized I had sent the call. "Jerry, I'm okay, but Mort was just killed in a bar fight."

"Where are you now?" he asked, fear in his voice.

"Outside the Alley Pub with the senator, Michael, and two security people, who materialized out of nowhere. We were leaving the restaurant when a fight broke out. Mort stayed with Michael, who was paying the bill. A woman flashed a badge . . ."

"Who are they?"

I looked at the male. "Where'd you come from?"

"We're B&G Protective Services hired to watch over the senator. I'm Jeff Maxwell. Sandi Fisher is with the senator."

"You hear that, Jerry? They're B&G Protective Services."

"Yeah, but . . ."

"Hold on." I looked at Roanne, about to ask—

"My father," she said. "That's all I know."

Agent Maxwell interjected. "We need to get the senator out of sight . . . the car," he said, pointing up the street. Agent Fisher gently took Roanne's arm. Michael trailed them with the male agent. I stopped while talking to Jerry.

I asked. "Can you—?"

"I've already called Anna. She'll be here any minute."

I felt relieved; he was coming to get me.

"Are you covering the action?" he asked.

"No. I was going to call, but I didn't want to have to explain my presence to the assignment editor. I'm sure somebody's on the way."

"Then shouldn't you get out of sight? Every reporter there will know you."

He was right. I started after my group, as I said to him, "Thanks, my street instincts were kicking in. I was beginning to think like a beat reporter. But I do need to call Max."

"I'll get there as soon as I can and check in with Max once I'm on my way," Jerry said.

I walked toward the B&G security car while punching in Max's number. I wondered how Roanne was taking the fact that her father had hired a security company to tail her.

# 49

**M**ichael and I stood alongside the car with Jeff, talking. Roanne sat in the back seat of B&G's sedan with Sandi Fisher. I saw Max arrive and go into the restaurant. Moments later he called, wanting to know where we were. As we were talking, he came out and headed my way. I was sure my involvement did not make him happy.

"I'm not a member of the working press on this, somebody else from the *Star* will be handling this," I quickly assured him.

"I only have a moment. Jer called, and I told him what to do when he arrived. Is your group here?"

I nodded. "Senator Dalton's in the back seat of the sedan with the female agent."

Before I could introduce him, Max moved toward the two men. "Max Walsh." He shook Jeff's hand. "Which service are you with, Agent?"

Max was smooth as a politician. I'd already told him who they were.

"B&G Protective Services, sir. I'm Jeff Maxwell."

"Gary Graves's outfit?"

"Yes sir," the agent replied.

I introduced Michael, and Max shook his hand, then he turned back to Maxwell. "You bring the senator here?"

"Ah, no sir."

I saw a questioning look on Max's face. "They were hired to follow the senator by her father," I explained.

Max asked Maxwell some questions and got a timeline of events as observed by the two agents. He then turned to me. "Agent Fisher was inside and met you as you and the senator were leaving, identifying herself when the ruckus broke out, right?"

"Yes, and when Maxwell came in, Fisher moved us outside."

"I'll check on Hayes and be back shortly. Why don't you get in the car and stay out of sight. A half dozen of your friends might be very interested in why you're here."

I smiled and nodded. My men certainly have my well-being at heart.

"Agent Maxwell, will you please keep anyone from getting close to your car?"

"Yes sir."

Max turned back toward the restaurant, and I got into the front passenger's seat. Roanne asked me what was happening, so I filled her in, concluding that Captain Walsh would withhold all of our names, especially Mort's, until MPD contacts Senator Kelly.

"Why Kelly?"

"Protocol. A courtesy when it comes to congressional or White House personnel."

"Oh, I didn't realize they contacted the majority leader first. I would have thought they'd call the Capitol police."

The area in front of the restaurant had been blocked off, and traffic was being diverted. I watched through the security car's windshield for any headlights not turning at the barricade, keeping my eye out for Jerry. After many turning off, one came straight to the barricade. It looked like Jerry's SUV.

"I'll be right back." I got out and ran the half block. I saw a uniformed officer approach Jerry, listen, and then gesture to where he should park. I waited until he parked.

"You all right?" he asked, as we hugged.

"Fine. Better now," I said, giving him another big squeeze to hide my shaking.

He held me. "Where's Max?"

"Inside. Come on, the senator, Michael, and two protective service agents are up the street." We distanced ourselves from the restaurant. "The two agents are Sandi Fisher and Jeff Maxwell. Sandi saw the fight break out. I thought Michael and Mort were right behind us, but the brawling cut them off."

We were nearing the B&G car as I wrapped up my scenario of events. As we reached the sedan, Roanne emerged. I introduced Jerry to Michael and Jeff, who were standing alongside the car, and then to the senator.

She smiled and extended her hand to him. "Mr. Fields."

He took her hand. "Senator, I understand you were working undercover tonight."

She laughed. We all did, sort of.

After Max and Detective Hayes interviewed us, we were all released.

Jerry and I headed home. A day that had started out so promising with so many good leads had ended up in tragedy.

B&G Protective Services were taking Michael to his apartment and then Senator Dalton to her car. Fisher would ride with the senator to Crystal City with Maxwell following. They planned to sweep her condo—just as a precaution.

"The B&G agents proved extremely observant in their descriptions to Max," I said, beginning to relax, as we drove through light traffic.

"Yeah. They sure were."

"They had made those two guys right away . . . as not fitting in."

"And here you are on the inside of another big story . . . or have I already said that?"

"You have, dear, but that's all right. My tape of Mort, can that be used in court?"

He grinned. "We'll see. But you certainly can use it to scare some people."

# 50

I sought out Lassiter as soon as I got to the office. Despite last night's hyped up activity, I had slept much better than I expected. Lassiter was in her office, and I gave her a rundown of what had really happened—which wasn't in the paper.

She nodded. "I thought Buzz's story was short on the details."

"Captain Walsh didn't give much to the media. MPD's withholding stuff, like the staged fight. He has my tape. I hate to sound callous, but we didn't get to Mort any too soon."

Lassiter agreed, and I went back to my desk. I had an uneasy feeling I was becoming involved again with people who used assassination to settle their problems. I called Max.

"I like your writing style better than Mr. Wilder's."

"He didn't have much to go on, but thanks. Anything on the photos, my tape?"

He told me they had positively identified one perp from the B&G photos and fingerprints on a bar glass. "Unfortunately, they don't have home addresses."

"I'm concerned that one or both could identify me."

"I doubt it. They were focused on Stroble. From what I heard on your tape, he was in deep. Obviously, too much so to keep around. Didn't you say your back was to the bar?"

I felt relief flowing through me. "Yes."

Max said that they were pros all the way. He thought if they went looking for anybody it would be Michael. "He may need some protection and—oops, Delia's paging me. Don't worry. I have gotten more on these perps than I usually get on professional hits. I'll have Delia send that tape over to you. Have a good day."

"Thanks, Max." I hit speed dial for Jerry. He answered almost immediately.

"Max ID'd one guy. He doesn't think they knew who I was."

"I don't like the ominous feeling of this, my dear," he said in his bad Groucho Marx impression, "but for a small fee I can give—"

"You're crazy, you know that?"

"Only about you," he said, continuing his bad Groucho.

"My, my. Am I missing something here?"

"Hmmm, we'll have to give that close scrutiny," he said suggestively.

"I thought I was the one whose juices were flowing."

"Yes. That's the close scrutiny I was thinking about."

"I've got work to do. I'm a busy reporter," I said, trying not to get too excited.

"Tsk-tsk."

"Enough please." He knew exactly what I needed. "You are a treasure, you know that?"

"No. You'll have to tell me more about that."

"Don't you have a case . . . or a client?"

"I'm afraid so. Love you."

"Love you too." I hung up.

"You are so lucky." It was Mary standing behind me.

"I know. What's up?" I said, trying to stay on an even keel.

"Ms. Lassiter awaits you."

Barton Williams was with Lassiter. He stood to greet me. I sat in the chair next to him.

"Fill Barton in."

I began with my first Stroble meeting and concluded with, "MPD has definitely ID'd one of the hit men." I shifted to what we suspected Rogers Pharmaceuticals had up its sleeve. Both editors were overwhelmed by the breadth of activities.

"All this started with a junior senator not wanting to go along with her party's leadership on dumping a drug," Lassiter said sarcastically.

"Having me write the Style piece on Senator Dalton got me to meet her father and learn some about Rogers Pharmaceuticals's plans."

"Yes," Barton said, shifting in his chair. "You had also, if I remember correctly, encouraged Senator Dalton's AA to engage some of his friends in a little private sleuthing. And do I gather correctly that Stroble was a result of those efforts?"

"He was. The tape I made could become the heart of the case along with Mort's murder. In death, he may become the important person he wanted to be in life. He gave us a terrific inside view of how the pharmas, namely Stanley Horowitz, have gotten a vise-like grip on the United States Senate."

Barton blanched. "Horowitz? I know him. I've run across him at fundraisers."

"He may be making Senator Kelly and other senators wealthy men."

Barton looked uncomfortable. "Yes. Well, our Puerto Rican reporter hasn't found anything helpful."

"In a passive way, he may have. Because no Rogers's technicians were at the clinic, I'm convinced Puerto Rico is a jumping off place to some rock in the Caribbean."

Barton was studying me. "When will the Szymanski/Dalton bill be introduced?"

"Within days. Senator Dalton is sure three members of her party will join with her and the opposition, giving them a majority."

"According to Claire Rowley, Senator Pembroke's bill is weak and creating some rumblings."

"That's the discontent Senator Dalton is counting on."

"Yes. We see vulnerability there." He outlined a series of critical articles he was planning on the Congress's handling of pharmaceuticals in general. "We've lined up the paper's top medical, congressional, business, and health writers, who will be under Associate Managing Editor Riley Harris. I want it to be a hard-hitting series."

Management was putting the *Star*'s prestige on the line. Each reporter was well-versed in his or her respective niche. Barton planned to begin the series following the cosponsored bill's announcement and Roanne's Style piece. I was to concentrate on Rogers and Dalton.

"You and Claire can share your information," he concluded hesitantly.

There was a time when the idea of me giving up any of my private information would have torn at my insides. However, I didn't think I would be writing stories using Claire's background. I conceded with, "Claire's insights will be useful to Senator Dalton—that's her beat. I'll share what I have, but prefer to remain covert on details concerning Kelly, Pembroke, and Tutoxtamen."

My editors looked shocked. Lassiter recovered first.

"That might work, Barton, I think that might work very well."

"Yes, eh, I think it will. Yes," the managing editor agreed offhandedly.

# 51

"**W**hat the hell happened to Mort Stroble last night?" Fred Pembroke raged, as he burst into the majority leader's office.

Tom Kelly did not appreciate the senator's lack of consideration. "Calm down, Fred. MPD Homicide Captain Max Walsh called me a little after ten last night. I called Capitol Police Chief Dan Harbesham and asked him to help us track down Stroble's family."

Kelly then explained to Pembroke how he and his chief of staff, Charlie Frost, had worked with Harbesham to locate Stroble's wife, Kyre, who was at her parents' home in Michigan.

"Charlie placed the call. The father-in-law was not happy being disturbed late at night." Kelly had never had to make such a call in all his twenty-five years in the Senate.

He continued, "I then got on the line and explained that I need to talk with Kyre, which was a very trying but short conversation. She broke down, and her father came back on calmer this time and I gave him the meager details, assuring him we were doing everything possible to apprehend the killer. Then Charlie got the Strobles on the phone for me. It was not a fun time.

"Afterward, Charlie and I had a couple of stiff drinks while scoping out what needed to be done and who would do what. Charlie's our point man with MPD."

During Kelly's soliloquy, Pembroke had sat. "How could this happen?" he asked weakly.

Kelly leaned forward, forearms on his desk. "The police don't know much. There was a fight, two drunks, something. They suspect Mort got caught between them and took a knife meant for someone else."

"Were they Blacks?"

"No. Two white guys in business suits who didn't stick around. Mort was having dinner with three others. They had all gotten up to leave when the fight started."

"Do you think this had anything to do with . . . ?" Pembroke said, slouching back in his chair rubbing his face.

"I don't know any more than you," Kelly said solicitously. "It is what it is."

Pembroke slowly rose and slouched out.

Kelly put in his third call to Stanley Horowitz, who had not returned his previous two.

**52**

S enator Dalton sat behind her office desk, studying the bill she was about to cosponsor. Michael jauntily came in.

"My, your disposition has brightened."

He sat opposite her. "When I got home last night, I called Tyrell and Nancy to tell them about Mort. I got Tyrell. He blamed himself immediately, so I spent a half hour in a psychotherapy session with him. I didn't get Nancy, so I left her a message. She called me back at 6:30 this morning. She hadn't heard."

Roanne shifted restlessly in her chair, wishing Michael would get to the point.

"Nancy and Gordon had dinner last night. Senator Crawford's feelings about you are very positive. He was not happy when Senator Kelly asked him to talk to you about Tutoxtamen, because he likes and admires you. How about that?" He was jubilant.

"Yes. I desperately needed something to lift my spirits. I have been having a difficult time concentrating on Al's bill."

"Senator Crawford doesn't care much for Kelly, but likes Senator Pembroke, who he feels is caught in the middle doing Kelly's bidding."

"Do you get the feeling Gavin will support our bill?"

"That is not something I'd ask Nancy. She's too close to the leadership."

"Of course; I wasn't thinking. Have you heard from Laura?"

"No. She and her husband are certainly friendly with Captain Walsh. I thought the story in the *Star* was bland, devoid of facts. Somehow, she protected you."

"Laura is a good person to be with. She certainly knows her way around and shows great poise. I called my father, but not to complain. I saw his wisdom and experience at work last night." She looked softly at her AA. "Michael, he and I are concerned about you."

That startled him. "Me?"

"We've learned some damning information, and you have already been attacked once. It is not unreasonable to think . . . you walk to and from work, which makes you very vulnerable. We think you should have protection until—"

"I could always sleep on the sofa," he said flippantly, indicating the large, leather, overstuffed sofa along a sidewall.

"That may do in a pinch, but I was thinking more about utilizing B&G."

"Secret Service stuff, huh?"

"Michael, they may have been watching Mort for a while and know who you are. If they know that, they may be able to figure out I was one of the women with you in spite of my youthful 'babe' makeover." She finally saw a glimmer of understanding in him.

"Can I think about this a little?"

"Yes, but tonight you will either sleep here or be escorted home." She was trying to be both firm and caring at the same time.

"Okay," he said, nodding in agreement.

"Good. Let's move onto pending items. I'd like to meet with Senator Crawford today. Please see if that's possible?"

"Certainly."

She watched him leave. He had a rumpled look and could be hard to read at times, but he was strong underneath it all. She went back to reading Szymanski's bill. It seemed like only minutes had passed when her intercom buzzed. "Yes."

"Senator Crawford is on line three, Senator."

"Thank you."

She punched button three. "Gavin?" No answer. He hadn't picked up. A few seconds later he did. "Senator?"

"Gavin, thank you for taking my call."

"Happy to. That was terrible stuff last night about Mort Stroble. I talked to Fred, who is very broken up. He knew Mort quite well."

She had to bite her lip not to respond. "Yes, Michael did too. I'd only met him once." *Unfortunately that was last night*, she ruminated to herself.

"I may have met him. I don't remember."

*That makes you all the better man*, she thought. "Gavin, can you give me some private time today? And yes, I may ask you to do something for me."

"Oh, ho," he laughed lightly. "Touché."

"I have to warn you, it could be job-threatening."

"Well, you have piqued my interest. I can't do lunch. How is 2:00?"

"Would here be agreeable?"

"Ah, so you don't mind staff seeing us together, eh?" he said wryly.

"You're good for my image, which needs improving," she said, enjoying the banter.

# 53

I sat in Max's office at MPD headquarters on Indiana Avenue NW having metroed directly there from home. I was tense. "It can't be anything else, Max. They followed Mort to the Alley Pub last night. Maybe they've been tailing him for a while."

"I don't disagree it was murder, thanks to B&G. We have a positive ID on the one perp, who conveniently has a criminal record, but nothing where he'd used a knife."

"Is the knife traceable?"

"Very."

My heart jumped. Another break. Then I saw his grin. I'd been had.

"A restaurant steak knife with no prints. I have asked Gary Graves to make his two agents available for some more questioning."

"Gloves?"

He stopped me again. "Let us wait and not put any thoughts in—"

"I won't talk to them until you say I can."

"It would be better that way. You know, you are definitely a much different person than a year ago—more compliant."

"A few things have happened to me since then."

He grinned. "Well, it's all for the better and less stressful on me."

"Did I . . . you never . . . was I . . . ?"

He put his hand up to stop me. "You are always energetic and imaginative."

He was being kind. I was probably a pain in his butt. "How'd you ever put up with me?"

"Because I knew if Jerry married you, you couldn't be all that bad."

I was losing this tête-á-tête badly, and he was piling up points. "You introduced us," I countered, trying to regain my aplomb.

"Could we change the subject please?" he asked, faking a plea. "Mr. Michael Horne and Mr. Tyrell Ward are coming in separately later this morning."

"They're good guys, Max, and they're friends with Nancy Morris, the young woman we saw in the restaurant in Clarendon with Senator Kelly."

"I appreciate your championing them. I'm satisfied about how the meal was set up, but we'll still need Horne's cell phone to confirm his call to Ward."

"Will there be any restrictions from you on what they do?"

Max looked concerned. "You and they need to be careful; tread softly up there."

"Does it feel to you like we've been here before?"

"Unfortunately, yes. But last year, you were after one killer. This time there could be a gang of them."

We finished up, and I headed for Metro and a three-stop ride to the office. I'd barely taken a seat in the train when my cell rang. It was Michael.

"Laura, the senator would like to talk with you . . . in person."

I changed trains at the next stop and went to Capitol Hill.

"Laura, thank you for coming so quickly. Michael said you were on Metro going the other way. How's your time?"

"I'm fine."

"Good. Ah, as it's nearly lunch, may I treat you to a meal in the Senate dining room? We can ride over on our private mini subway to the Capitol."

I had the feeling this was not a spur of the moment thing. "Oh?" I looked at her questioningly.

"Okay. There is someone waiting there for us."

I grinned. "A mysterious person. How could I possibly turn you down? What hath murder wrought?"

"A lot of interest and maybe some cooperation."

We headed for the elevator chatting amiably. I enjoyed how comfortable she was with me. We took the Senate subway to the Capitol. This was going to be quite a week for her, with the cosponsored bill being presented tomorrow, followed by her Style profile the following day. Senator Roanne Elizabeth McAllister Dalton was coming out.

We entered the dining room and weaved between tables. I saw a familiar gentleman with white hair and a permanent tan rising to greet us. Senator Dalton preceded me and hugged her father. I came next, but we only shook hands. Talk about a power move. "Governor."

He had a glint in his eye. "Ms. Wolfe." He had inserted himself where he ached to be.

The senator and I sat, Rufus McAllister followed. "Where's Michael?" I asked.

Roanne was still smiling. "Hopefully returning from police headquarters."

Rufus turned to me sporting a wily grin. "You are one astute young lady, *Laura*."

"Why, thank you, *Rufus*."

He emitted a low laugh.

"Dad's here because he has something to discuss and intends to become a part of our *war room*."

I enjoyed their being so relaxed with each other.

"Yup. Ro and I are doing a little horse trading. I want to thank you, Laura. I honestly had not intended for Ro to see the note I wrote to you. But I'm more than pleased she did."

I nodded. The waiter arrived to take our orders. Rufus and Roanne ordered the Senate dining room's famous navy bean soup and prodded me to do the same. I gathered that this was to be a social hour before we got to the serious stuff.

Michael arrived as I was enjoying the soup. He ordered an entrée and then told us about being interviewed by Max, which had gone very well. When the subject got around to the presentation of the cosponsored drug bill, I learned that Rufus would be in the Senate gallery. Ro asked if I would please be her guest in the balcony instead of sitting in the press gallery.

That surprised me, but the offer of not having to mix in with a gaggle of Capitol Hill correspondents was too tempting to refuse. "Yes, I would like that very much."

"Tomorrow's going to be a great step in Ro's career," Rufus said. "Can you believe I never wanted her to run for the office?" he chortled.

I was right in thinking the real action was yet to come. I was invited to be at Roanne's apartment for a catered meal at 6:00. This was to be a strategy session. The combination of Mort's murder and the cosponsored bill was going to take a huge swipe at the power structure in the Senate.

Following lunch, Rufus went off to see Harold Raines, their state's senior senator and his former law clerk. I felt a little arm-twisting was about to take place.

I looked at Roanne. "I need to speak with you."

She paused. "Something wrong?"

"No, but there may be areas we move into that might need legal advice," I answered quietly. "Could we walk out, I wouldn't want . . . I'm told the congressional underground has ears most everywhere."

"Certainly."

Once in the great corridor, I softly resumed. "Jerry was a criminal defense attorney before moving over to corporate law. I think we may be entering into areas where a little legal advice may be useful. Jerry's very trustworthy."

She smiled. "I wouldn't doubt that for a minute."

"He's a great sounding board for me, and God knows I need one."

She laughed lightly. She and I were almost the same height, she maybe being an inch taller. She looked at me, slightly cocking her head. "It must be wonderful to be in love with a man who is also such a good friend."

That choked me. I cleared my throat. "More than I can tell you." I sensed a little sorrow in her and wanted to touch her arm reassuringly but held back.

Roanne smiled. "I saw how he moved around last night. He observes well and stays out of the way, even though he and Captain Walsh are close friends."

"We both know we're not the show. He is a great listener and remembers everything."

"I'm sure it will be fine. I can't see where Michael would have a problem with it. I'll ask my father, too. It's his confidentiality with the Rogers information I'm thinking about."

I rode back with her to Dirksen and then walked to Union Station.

At the paper, I stopped at my desk long enough to drop off my bag and to pick up my research files on the various Capitol Hill involvement I was encountering and went to Lassiter's office. I brought her up to speed with what was swirling around up there. She confirmed that the Style piece would run the day after tomorrow, following the introduction of the Szymanski/Dalton bill, and asked that I write a sidebar for Style, two or three inches, mentioning the bill.

I went to my cubicle and called Max. He had talked with Reed Davis, the special agent in charge of the FBI's Washington field office, and another participant from last year's case.

"Which means what?" I asked.

"We're using their computers and manpower to track the perp. He was definitely brought up here to do a job. He left Miami two days before . . ."

"That would be the day Michael, Tyrell, and I had drinks with Mort."

"Yes. He flew back to Miami the night of the killing."

"Sounds like a hit man to me."

"Let's not get ahead of ourselves," he chided.

I was pumped. When he used that expression, it meant my instincts were right on, but there were no facts to support them.

"Because the Capitol Police don't like MPD cops wandering around in their buildings, we find it easier to involve the Justice Department—"

"Is that another reason for bringing Reed into this?"

"It helps more when we have already involved them. Mr. Horne and Mr. Ward were completely open about their covert operation on the late Mr. Stroble. Along with your corroboration, the picture is very clear as to what we are dealing with."

# 54

**M**ichael escorted Senator Crawford into Roanne's office. "Can I get you anything, sir?"

"No thanks, Michael."

Michael went out and closed the door.

"Let's sit in the comfortable chairs," Roanne said. She grabbed a bottle of water off her desk, and they sat.

"Thank you for your time, Gavin. I have given considerable thought to what I'm about to say. I've discussed it thoroughly with Michael, and he's promised he won't quit over it."

"My, you pique my interest. You're not planning a coup are you?"

She laughed. "I hadn't thought of that, but . . . I have strong concerns about Tutoxtamen and the outrageous cost of prescription drugs."

"I believe you mentioned both to me over a lovely lunch."

Gavin's very engaging, she thought. "I have been asked by Al Szymanski to cosponsor his extensive and thorough drug bill, doing away with Howard/ Wasserman. I've spent hours with Al and three of his colleagues and find the bill to be comprehensive and very workable."

Gavin's expression had not changed, and he had made no effort to interrupt.

She continued, "It also speaks to controlling the costs on drugs initially developed by government-supported organizations."

"In other words, rewrite how the pharmaceutical industry does business."

"Would that we could. I realize this will meet with an explosion of opposition, but somebody has to take the first step and who is lower on the rung than I? The pharmas are the tail wagging the dog, and this dog wants to bite back." She felt flushed and took a drink.

"Is this your way of asking me to be your pallbearer?" he asked seriously, before breaking into a big grin. "This isn't fair, you realize that, don't you? You can always go back and teach history in a nice, plushy university. I'd have to learn how to work for a living."

She felt warmed by his free and easy style. "True, I have little to lose. But I'm not interested in losing. That happened to me once, and I didn't like it. I want to win this even more than I did my first pageant's crown."

"My, you must be serious. So, I'd make it fifty votes. You counting on the vice president?"

"No. There are two others. Harold Raines and Jean Witherspoon."

"They've agreed?"

"Jean and I have had casual conversations over the plight of seniors and the poor. She told me she admired my stand against the leadership over Tutoxtamen. Harold is on the cusp, but he used to work for my father, comprende?"

"Plus two makes it fifty-two. That's a safe margin. Anyone else?"

"According to the *Washington Daily Star*'s Senior Congressional Reporter—"

"Claire?"

"Yes, you know her?"

"She did a piece on me two years ago. She was looking into earmarking. I got my piece tacked onto the late September HHS budget. I had a plan to entice developers into building some low-cost housing units for low- or no-income seniors. We based the rental schedule on the Section Eight HUD rent reimbursements. I got $37 million.

"The deal required my state to match the federal grant with money and/or in-kind real estate owned by the state, counties, or municipalities, which all had to be convenient to shopping. No small task.

"We began our first construction a little over a year ago, and hopefully the building work won't stop as teams of negotiators all around the state work with the local authorities to procure land for more units. Habitat for Humanity took over one project, with us supplying all the materials. That savings in labor stretched our dollars.

"Former President Jimmy Carter and his wife spent a week there, as did hundreds of volunteers who rotated in and out. A cadre of professionals has been able to provide much of the construction supervision while training House Captains to fill in where needed. I'll tell you this, those buildings are solidly built . . . lots of nails." He smiled. "That's an inside Habitat joke."

"This is astonishing. Everybody should be doing it," Dalton said awestruck.

He nodded. "When we finish, we're projecting we'll have over 9,000 units of 600-square-foot apartments . . . a bedroom, kitchen, bath, and living room . . . in a low-rise campus setting. Each senior community will have 300 units or so. The local jurisdictions will be responsible for the common building: a place for residents to commune, play cards, dance, a sort of clubhouse. Local Social Services will interview applicants, who must have been a full-time resident of the state for two years and a continuous member of the community where they apply for one year. Newcomers go to the bottom of the list.

"We don't want to be flooded with people from other states, as happened when new homeless shelters were built. We have a large population of poor senior citizens, and they come first. Some people back home want to up the restrictions to five and three years, respectively."

Roanne Dalton was in total admiration of what she'd just heard. Afraid she was gaping, she took a long drink from her water bottle, and then asked, "I'm sorry, was that a yes or a no?"

"Did I go off topic?" He laughed. "It's a yes, and I'll begin convincing a few of our waffling colleagues. We could easily top sixty and nuke the thing through."

She was overwhelmed with emotion. He made it sound so simple.

# 55

I hadn't yet reached Jerry, so I called Anna to make sure she would be available for tonight. Her English and my limited Spanish were both improving. We communicated a lot better in person than on the phone, but we worked it out. An absolute dear, I believed her to be a wonderful mother to her two grade-school daughters.

I sat down and began scoping out what Mort had given us. The tape might not get played in court with all the technicalities, but it would give Max and the FBI a good picture of what he'd done for Kelly, Pembroke, and the others. I put a third call into Pembroke, telling the phone-answerer that Mort Stroble was the subject of my call. She said they'd get back to me.

I called Claire Rowley. After the preliminaries, I got right to it. "I'm interested in Senator Pembroke."

"Pembroke?" came her startled reply. "He's an easy-going, open sort. He stays out of the public eye as much as he can. He's a respected third-term senator, a family man, kids in college . . . why Pembroke?"

"It's the Tutoxtamen thing. He fought alongside Kelly for party unanimity in supporting the FDA's *not approvable* decision."

"I hate to bust your bubble, but the senators weren't involved in that. They only supported the FDA's decision for further testing of possible side effects."

I'd been here before. The newsperson closest to the action not acknowledging there could possibly be something wrong on their beat. However, I decided to let it go.

"That's why I'm calling you, Claire. You know these people. Is there some sort of compromise brewing between the pharmas and the Senate?

Tutoxtamen goes down the tubes, and now they're willing to negotiate a few discounts." I hoped I sounded incredulous.

"That's been going on, the talking, for a long time."

I could tell by her tone that my minor mea culpa had its effect.

"Do you have any insight into Kelly and Pembroke, other than leader to chairman?"

"Not really. They are very different types—Kelly bombastic, Pembroke soft."

I almost said opposites attract, but refrained. "Did you know Mort Stroble?"

She let out a guffaw. "Any woman that got within sniffing distance had a Mort experience."

"He ever lust after you?"

She was still giggling. "You kidding? I'm thirty pounds and twenty years out of his hit zone." She sounded like she was enjoying this or thinking me naïve. Either way, she had a sense of humor.

"Do you think that's what got him into trouble at the Pub? Maybe an irate husband? I understand from my crime beat buddies he was sitting with two women and a man."

"That's a very probable scenario."

"You ever interview Pembroke?"

"Not formally, just questions on the run."

"What about Kelly?"

"No. His home-state papers put out the stories on him. We get them from the wire services. I don't believe we've ever run one of them.

"My father has run a small town paper for nearly forty years. I could never imagine him taking some third-hand story when the subject was available live. My years on the street haven't prepared me for this sort of drawing-room journalism."

"I hear you," she said, sounding bored.

I thanked her for her time and hung up. Mary buzzed me immediately after my phone light went out. "Mr. Horne would like you to call him."

I punched in his number.

"The senator got the go-ahead for your husband," he offered immediately.

"Great. See you then." While calling Jerry, I wondered whether Michael approved.

"Hi. What's up?" He sounded unusually down.

"You don't sound like your day is going very well," I replied softly.

"I've had better."

"Well, maybe I can pick you up. I'm inviting you out for dinner." I hoped I sounded cheery without sounding soupy.

"What's the . . . did I forget something?" he asked, concerned.

"You never forget anything. No. It has something to do with the Caribbean."

He didn't respond. I imagined he was trying to pull his mind out of whatever had him in a funk. He normally shifted from his stuff to mine fairly easily. Finally he said, "We planning a trip?"

"Noooo. We're promised an evening of engaging Rufus conversation. And maybe a discussion about an island or two."

"The Gov—that should be fun." He was sounding more up. "What time?"

"At 6:00. I've already talked with Anna, so we are all right there."

# 56

I had a little playtime with Tyler waiting for Anna, and then showered and dressed. When Jerry came in, I gave him a big hug. I knew he appreciated it by the way he gave his body to me.

"I'm sorry you had a tough day," I said, still holding him.

He gave me a peck on my forehead. "A recalcitrant client."

"I hope my call interruption didn't make things worse."

He squeezed me. "To the contrary, you brought me back from the brink." He hugged me harder. "Does the governor being here . . . are things moving along?"

"We'll see. I suggested a good legal brain could be very helpful."

"Oh?" he asked gently, pushing back from me to look into my eyes. "We've never done this before . . . a team. Do I see a Nick and Nora Charles in the future?"

A chill of excitement went through me. "You better get ready. We need to go."

We arrived at Roanne Dalton's door at 6:05. She hadn't changed, but Rufus was wearing slacks and a polo shirt with his country club's logo prominently displayed. Michael had removed his jacket and tie.

"Dad, this is Jerry Fields."

"Glad to meet you, Jer." Rufus gave my husband a hearty handshake. A little testosterone test. Jerry's no slouch, having done a lot of manual work in his life, and sports a strong grip.

"Governor."

"Can we make it Rufus and Ro, at least for tonight?"

I looked at Michael for a reaction. He liked formalities, but he didn't react.

I jumped in. "It's not always easy, when you have a working relationship. I promise to think casual, even if it doesn't always come out that way."

Rufus smiled and shrugged *what the heck.* "I understand."

Roanne announced the food was ready in the kitchen. "Pick out your drink?"

Jerry and Rufus got a beer. Ro and Michael wine. I had water. We spent the next half hour consuming a light repast, while being regaled by Rufus. I could see in his manner he loved being back in the game. I liked that Michael was relaxing and enjoying himself.

Ro finally broke in. "Before you get all *storied* out Dad, let's hear about Harley Rogers."

"All right. For starters, Harley is not one to be caught unawares. He knew way back that the FDA would capitulate to the pharmas, and if he didn't come up with a plan to save his drug, he'd be out of luck. Now, along with being an inventor, strategic planning has always been one of Harley's long suits.

"Three years back, a medical trade journal published pirated results of early Tutox testing that touted remarkable findings, far better than other cancer drugs had at that same stage in their development. The pharma lobby then approached him about the drug. Its potential was daily gossip, and Rogers's stock price was inching up. Not ones to beg, those rustlers just flat made him an offer: concentrate on a cure for only one of the cancers, and they'd make it worth his while."

I hoped this background was leading someplace. All I was getting so far was that Rufus had been involved with Harley Rogers longer than he'd originally owned up to.

"Harley and Sherman said to hell with the pharmas privately, but to delay any immediate pressure from them, Harley publicly went along. He set up some scientists to work on the single cure, as a subterfuge for the pharmas, while at the same time, hidden away from outsiders, he continued to develop the real Tutoxtamen.

"Harley was well schooled in the art of diversion and disinformation, and he allowed things to leak out about the singular drug. I believe it was around then when Sherman began working on a plan to manufacture Tutox outside of the good old US of A."

I couldn't resist sticking in my two cents. "So they used Puerto Rico as a jumping off point, while making people think they were going to the clinic they built outside San Juan."

Rufus looked at me quizzically. "You learn that on your own?"

I nodded. "It was easy. Sherman went there and came back from there, and no airline showed he ever took a flight anywhere else. But he did."

Rufus shook his head. "She's a good one, Ro. You're right, Laura. Another former Ranger had his own air charter service in the Caribbean following WWII, which is now run by one of his sons. Their little airline goes to all the islands, except Cuba and Haiti. They file flight plans that get changed, it's very casual, and they don't publish a manifest. Sherman became an expert of disguises. No casual observer would have known the passenger was Sherman."

"The Rogers's corporate jet never went beyond Puerto Rico?" Jerry asked.

"Right. Sherman found a poor island group that was ripe for his proposal. I can't say more about that, but you get the picture."

I wanted to know more. "So, Harley's people and equipment are on an island. Does it have a name?"

"I'm not at liberty to say more, Laura. But I will tell you that Sherman worked out a deal on an island, and that's when Harley called me. He needed help with security. He wanted a combat outfit like what we were in the Rangers. He worried he might have to fight off an invasion some day. I thought Harley's age had finally caught up with him, you know," and he gave the typical finger move that people use to describe a whacko.

"How long ago was that?" I asked.

"Two-and-a-half years ago, before H.T. was killed and Ro went to the Senate. There wasn't anything political in what I did. I was helping out an old friend, that's all. I knew Gary Graves of B&G through a mutual friend, that's why I used them to watch over Ro. His people aren't Delta or Rangers, but he recommended an outfit that does stuff for the Department of Defense. I've visited Harley's island a couple of times. It's a sweet arrangement with all sorts of geography working in their favor. Johnny and I are going there in a few days. With the type of detection devices available to us, shoot, nobody'll be able to get near them without—"

"You think Harley believes—" Laura began.

"He knows these cutthroats, Laura," Rufus responded before she could finish. "Look at what happened to Stroble. And oh yes, I do believe the pharmas were behind that boy's death."

"So do I, gov—uh, Rufus," I concurred.

His face lit up with a big smile. "I would have bet you did, Laura. I'd bet you even know more than you're saying." Ro's eyebrows went up. "Is that true, Laura?"

The old boy surprised me, but I couldn't go covert. "Okay, there's a lot of trust in this room. MPD knows the identity of one of the two suspects. He's a hit man who flew in from Miami two days before the killing, the evening Michael and I had drinks with Tyrell and Mort."

I saw Michael's eyes widened to saucers.

"But how . . . I mean that was purely social," he stammered.

"I know. But maybe the pharmas were already watching Mort because of his extramarital activities. Maybe they worried about loose, drunken lips," I suggested.

"Dad told me the cover story for the construction is that the island's new facility needs privacy while researching oceanic life, to improve the world's understanding of how undersea life can benefit mankind. Rogers's name is no place to be seen or heard."

"Right, I forgot about that," Rufus said, moving back in. "This place is an investment in Rogers's future."

# 57

The next day, I sat in the Senate gallery eagerly waiting for the Szymanski/Dalton bill to be announced. The chamber was sparsely filled, creating an *I couldn't care less* attitude on the floor.

Senators and staff were quietly disinterested. Rufus sat one section over from me with two men I didn't recognize. The three were smiling and whispering. This had to be a very special day for the old politician. His gorgeous and famous beauty-queen daughter, now a United States senator, was about to turn her party into a bucket of snarly, poisonous snakes.

On the floor, the minority leader yielded his time to Szymanski, who took the podium. There was a constant, low hum of people talking quietly. Some minority party senators knew what was coming; only four from the majority party were in on it.

Szymanski opened with the normal niceties of Senate decorum and then invited Senator Dalton to join him. That was an attention-getter. When she stood alongside him, he announced their cosponsored bill. Dalton spoke for about thirty seconds on how proud she was to be a part of a landmark bill and then returned to her desk. After the shock, a rumble came up from the majority members. Szymanski asked that his entire bill be entered into the Congressional Record, without objection, and then began spelling out the highlights of its contents.

Senator Kelly wasn't on the floor. A senator asked if the *Gentleman*— Szymanski, in other words—would yield. Meaning he wanted to take the floor, but Szymanski denied the request.

Within a minute, Kelly barged into the chamber from the Cloakroom and tried with all the power of his office to have the Senate president stop the proceedings.

I wondered if the title of "president" confuses some. The vice president of the United States *is* the president of the Senate ex officio. However, he is rarely there, unless needed to break a tie vote. There is a president pro tempore, the most senior senator in the majority party, who is next in line, but the rank-and-file senators of that party commonly hold the gavel. All who do so are referred to as *Mister or Madam President.*

Even though the majority leader carries a lot of weight, Senator Harold Raines continually called for the chamber and Kelly to come to order. This was not how it normally worked on a Senate floor that was now quickly filling as senators clamored into the chamber. It had all the signs of a good old knock-down, drag-out brawl. The room was electric.

Raines called for no more outbursts or requests for the *Gentleman* to yield, as none would be granted. That spurred more shouts. I honestly thought Kelly might rush Szymanski.

How Raines came to be sitting in the president's seat at this particular time might forever remain a mystery. The noise did not abate, and Raines called for the sergeant at arms, additionally demanding, "The senators will please observe proper decorum, or I will have them removed." That got their attention, and the chamber fell silent. Raines then asked Szymanski to continue.

I glanced over at Rufus. He and his friends had big grins on their faces. What had he done? I looked at Roanne, who sat at her desk demurely watching her cosponsor, a no-fly zone around her.

By this time, my colleagues of the fourth estate had jammed into the press gallery. I imagined C-SPAN would be mostly focused on Szymanski. It would be interesting to see how much of the chaos they show. This might not be a historic moment in the Senate, but it was a *hysteric* one.

I wondered what Claire Rowley would write about this uproar and what, if any, political slant she may give it. She hadn't seen the beginning, so I guessed she would review the video to get the exact chronology. I just hoped she'd be objective, but then she had to deal with these folks on a daily basis.

Szymanski continued with his presentation to a now relatively quiet Senate floor. Many of the majority members had vacated the chamber. The press gallery, too, had begun to thin out. Those reporters would soon have hard copies of the bill. Right now, though, it was time for them to seek out members for interviews.

When Szymanski concluded his presentation, he yielded back to the minority leader. He stepped away, accompanied by rising cheers with every step he took. It was quite a sight. When the gavel finally pounded, it wasn't Raines but Gavin Crawford in the Senate president's chair. Kelly and his entourage were nowhere to be seen. Kelly's bluster and futile attempts to take over the proceedings had to be on tape. Certainly his voice would be. I left the chamber and sought out Rufus. I found him saying goodbye to his gallery companions.

He and I went to the President's Room adjacent to the Senate floor to wait for Roanne. He was beaming and muttering platitudes . . . a proud father, who had somehow convinced a three-term senator to face down his own party. I had no doubt about his part in that.

Rufus handed a note to a Senate page and asked that it be delivered to Senator Dalton. She appeared soon after, accompanied by Michael and Raines. Because the room was available to others besides senators, Roanne had asked the sergeant at arms for a private room.

Knowing there would be a crush of press and maybe a disgruntled senator or two, she had also requested that security be present. Two officers led us through a considerable gaggle of people. Someone shouted a derisive question; another swore at Roanne, which caught the attention of the security escort; and an officer ahead of me spoke into his collar microphone.

We reached a room off the corridor similar to the one that Roanne and I had met in not too long ago. This was exciting stuff, but Ro showed exhaustion. Rufus clapped Raines on the back.

"Harry, you done good. I bet you picked up enough extra support to stop them from *filiblustering*."

I knew he meant the *bluster* part.

"I thought Tom was going to drag me off," Raines said.

Rufus shook his head. "He knows he's in trouble."

Raines remained fretful. "I expect I'll get some flack over it."

"Harold, we all appreciate what you did and what you are willing to do," Roanne said.

"How many you think we can pull in?" Rufus asked, now fully engaged.

"You sure about Crawford and Witherspoon, Ro?" Raines asked.

"They're solid and all we need."

I finally spoke up. "Maybe we could get to a TV and see what's brewing."

# 58

I t wasn't Katrina, a tsunami, or 9/11, but the cable news stations were scrambling to cover the epic Senate battle, and camera men and TV producers were wildly searching out senators to interview. This was an intraparty battle not seen in years.

We left the Capitol and rode over to Dirksen, with an escort, and took the Senators Only elevator to the third floor. Ro insisted the escort stay with Raines who was going on to the Hart Building.

Rufus and I sat in Roanne's office while she and Michael attended to things. An aide escorted a woman into the room and introduced her to the former governor. She was Senator Jean Witherspoon, a fiftyish, slightly plump lady from the Great Plains. Her short, brunette hairstyle gave her an outdoorsy look. Rufus took right to her, and they sat and chatted like old friends.

I decided not to join in with them. Roanne and Michael were using Michael's office for their work, so I looked for a room with a TV and watched C-SPAN's umpteenth showing of Kelly's neck arteries about to burst.

I was thinking of doing something else when Michael asked me to join him, which I gladly did. We went into his office, where Roanne stood with Senator Szymanski.

"Al, this is Laura Wolfe. Laura, Al Szymanski."

He extended his hand. "Ms. Wolfe, I am proud to make your acquaintance."

"Senator," I said cordially.

"Laura's been my beacon through the bulk of the Tutoxtamen mess, Al. She is a reporter above reproach."

I knew we had some slackers in the media, but we're mostly an honest, hard-working group. However, I smiled at her compliment.

"I followed that serial-killer thing closely," he said. "You were almost killed."

"By about a second, actually," I said, and immediately wished I hadn't when I saw Roanne's shocked expression.

"You never said—" she started.

"It's not something I dwell on or talk about."

Szymanski bored ahead. "Weren't you pregnant . . . didn't that ever make you . . . ?"

"In the heat of the chase, it was the killer we wanted."

"That was weird the way . . . you know who . . ."

I interrupted him, trying to keep my tone neutral. "I prefer not talking about it, sir. It was sickening and sad. So many people, other than those killed, were irreparably damaged."

"Yes, yes, I guess there were, well . . ." He looked to Roanne.

She said to me, "It looks like we'll have sixty votes, and Al will also have a majority on the committee. He wants to move fast. Can you see any reason why we shouldn't?"

I was startled by the question. Two senators . . . but she must be asking because of what Rogers was doing, and we were keeping that quiet. "I think the timing couldn't be better. Especially as my Style piece on you is coming out tomorrow."

Szymanski looked surprised. "Style piece?"

I jumped in. "We worked on it last month, but then when you made your offer to Senator Dalton, we decided to hold off running it until the partnership and the bill were announced.

Today's notoriety makes it good for her and good for your bill." *My God, I'm getting political*, I thought. "Your bill should be very popular . . . it's bipartisan . . . yeah, go for it."

Both senators smiled appreciatively.

"This has all the signs of a good boxing match, Senator. You've knocked the opponent down once, and you're going right after him, before he can get his legs back."

I could see Szymanski liked my simile and smiled.

"Damn, Ro, you're right; she's solid."

Whatever that meant. I thought he was going to slap his leg and let out a hoot. He had some rough edges, but I doubted he was anyone to take lightly. I'd have to look up his bio.

# 59

Senator Fred Pembroke, Majority Whip Marv Hatcher, Appropriations Chairman Wallace Clarence, and Finance Chairman Maurice Jarvis along with several staff, including Nancy Morris, were in Majority Leader Tom Kelly's office, awaiting his arrival.

The mood was somber.

"How could this happen?" Pembroke groaned.

"We're the majority party for God's sake," the whip said. "One of our own . . ."

"Raines got bought out by Dalton's old man," Senator Clarence said acrimoniously.

Nods and verbal agreements rolled through the room.

"Dalton and Raines only give Szymanski a fifty-fifty split," Senator Hatcher growled.

"Our problem," Pembroke offered, "is we're too damn complacent."

The door loudly burst open, and Kelly rushed in. "Sorry I'm late. I've been on with the White House. The president wanted an explanation," he said, moving to behind his desk, "and frankly, I didn't have one. Anyone have any ideas?" he asked in a demanding tone.

Hatcher spoke up. "We knew Al was shopping his bill, trying to get a cosponsor, but we thought he was shut out."

"Nancy," Kelly asked sharply, "you are friends with Dalton's AA. Did he tell you they'd been approached?"

"No sir. I haven't talked to Michael since the morning after Mort—"

"All right," Kelly spat, "where do we go from here?" His piercing eyes challenged each senator. "Are there more turncoats?"

Nobody answered.

"Okay. Marv, talk to everyone. Fred, talk to everyone on—"

Pembroke interrupted. "Nobody talks to Dalton outside of small talk or a perfunctory greeting. Crawford, at your request, Tom was . . . but he'd never . . . he's a straight shooter."

"Yeah, but who's he shooting for?" the whip blurted.

"All right then, you talk to him, Marv. You find out," Pembroke shot back.

Kelly extended his arms with palms down. "Let's keep it calm." He gave his whip an ease-it-up gesture. He looked at staff grouped together in a corner. "You folks spread out; use that underground network of yours." He turned back to the senators. "This is not one of our finest hours."

"It's a disgrace," Senator Jarvis bellowed.

"Okay, we took a black eye," Kelly said, "but we're still on our feet. We have the traditions and the rules. We'll overcome this."

"The trouble is," Clarence moaned, "we have nothing on her. We can't just pick up the phone and say—"

"Forget about her," Kelly demanded. He looked at the staff. "Why don't you all head out. See what . . . well, you know."

Staff filed out, nodding and muttering amongst themselves.

Once they were gone, Kelly addressed the four senators.

"Who can get to Harold? How much will it cost us to drag him back in?"

# 60

I was still with Roanne in her office along with Senators Szymanski and Witherspoon. Rufus and Michael had gone off somewhere. It was getting late, and I was being pulled between staying and leaving, when my cell phone vibrated. I didn't recognize the number. It wasn't one in my address book.

"Excuse me," I said, moving away from the group. "Hello?"

"Laura?"

It was Lassiter. She rarely called me.

"Yes."

"Where are you?"

"In Senator Dalton's office with two other senators."

"We have a reporter in Frankfurt, Germany, working on a series about our wounded warriors still hospitalized there. He called Barton fifteen minutes ago. He picked up a rumor that a civilian German hospital has a drug which is curing the hell out of a lot of people."

I raised my voice. "A cancer drug? Where specifically?" I caught the senators' attention.

"He didn't say cancer. It's in some small hospital on the outskirts of the city. Travis, the reporter, overheard a couple of nurses jawing about it."

I was pumped. Could this be Rogers's doing? "Has he checked it out?"

"He's working on it, but Barton wants you to talk to him. Travis is expecting your call. Here's his satellite number."

"Hold on," I grabbed my pad and a pen. "Shoot."

She gave me the number.

"I'll call and then head back to the paper." When I clicked off, the three senators were staring at me.

"My editor," I said, moving toward Roanne. "Our reporter in Frankfurt, Germany, has heard that a local hospital is treating patients with a miracle drug."

They looked at each other with eyebrows raised and eyes wide: *Could it be?*

"What I'm going to say is deep background. It must stay in this room," I was firm and hopefully polite. After all, I was talking to United States senators. I looked to Roanne.

"Absolutely," she agreed. "Al, Jean, this may be a huge break, but it must stay in this room."

Both nodded. "That's fine," Szymanski added.

Assured, I went on. "The reporter overheard medical staff talking about a new drug that was doing astounding things in a local hospital. Our managing editor wants me to talk with the reporter immediately. He didn't say cancer drug, though. May I use your phone?"

"Certainly. Do you need privacy?"

"No." We went behind her desk, and she punched a button on her phone console.

"This is an outside line, direct dial."

"This won't take long." I tapped in the number.

"Travis," a male voice answered.

"Laura Wolfe. Barton asked me—"

"He told me."

"Okay. Have you found the hospital?"

"Yeah. I got the impression it was hot. I've got the hospital name, address, and directions."

"You're my kind of guy. Can you go there tonight?"

"I can find it, but it'll be after eleven here."

"Fine, I don't mean to tell you—"

"I don't take it that way. Is this something you're working on?"

"If it's what I think it is, it will be everybody's story. I'll fill you in later. I'm with three US senators right now. We've been discussing a drug and—"

"They're involved?" He sounded surprised.

"Yes. Look, this is your story. I only have to be in on it because it may be important to what we're doing here. Capisce?"

"Gotcha. Where should I call—?"

"Call the paper. I'm going straight there."

We signed off. The senators waited. I felt like I'd been sprinting and took a couple of deep breaths as I walked around the large desk to where my bag was.

"Okay. Travis has located the hospital and is going there now. He heard no mention of cancer. I'll be with our managing editor and others. Travis will call me there."

"Laura, could it be Rogers?"

I smiled at her. "Is the Capitol Dome white?"

"He's amazing! That's why—"

"Excuse me," I cut her off softly and looked at the two other senators. "I need a word with Senator Dalton."

"Al, you and Jean wait here," Roanne said. "Laura and I will use Michael's office."

Once in there, I whispered, "This is tricky. You and I know Rogers has an offshore operation, but they don't. We need to keep it that way. Please impress on the senators that patience is critical. We'll know if it's cancer tonight . . . by tomorrow for sure. Nothing about this will be in tomorrow's edition. We'll wait for Travis to do his interviews first, so we can learn more about these treatments."

Ro smiled. "Today, only we few know. This is exciting. I hope it is Harley Rogers."

"Me too. Either way, it could change the world." I headed for the door.

# 61

Lassiter and I were with Barton Williams and his associate editor, Riley Harris, waiting for Travis Sutter's call. Barton sat behind his antique desk, and we sat across the desk from him, Lassiter between me and Riley.

"You say you don't know if this is the cancer drug, but you're sure the hospital in Germany is Rogers's doing?" Riley asked me.

I knew who Riley was, but had never met him. He came across a little haughty, so I concentrated on staying calm. "Everything points to it being Rogers's miracle cancer drug. A German pharmaceutical company has been independently testing the drug for three years, I believe.

"This could be part of that . . . part of a well-planned strategy designed by Harley Rogers. It won't be called Tutoxtamen in Germany, but if it is what we are hoping it is, you can be sure that Rogers is the supplier."

"Laura's kept us in the pipeline, Riley. She's been anticipating something like this," Lassiter said pointedly.

I appreciated my boss saying that. It's nicer to be backed rather than be backed up. I continued, "This isn't something that just happened. Rogers set these plans in motion at least three years ago, when the pharma lobby offered him a bribe to isolate the drug's effectiveness to a single form of cancer and not the entire disease."

"Three years?" Riley asked, incredulous.

"Old man Rogers knew the slime he was dealing with," Lassiter said tersely.

I almost cracked up. I suspected she didn't like Riley, but he did need some history on Rogers's drug. I told him what else I'd learned, concluding, "When Travis breaks the story, don't be surprised if Senator Kelly rushes to Justice, insisting they search Rogers's entire facility in New Jersey. He'll claim they've been manufacturing and distributing an illegal drug."

"Yes, good thought, Laura," Barton said. "We might want somebody up there, Riley."

The associate editor looked unsettled. "But you don't expect Kelly will be right, do you?"

"I know Rogers is not making Tutoxtamen in New Jersey and that Kelly will get a lot of egg on his face," I said.

"How long has Travis been with the paper?" Lassiter asked Barton.

"Less than two years . . . as a stringer. We moved him up when Wallace retired. He's been researching the conditions of wounded warriors in Army hospitals in Germany, which is why he is in Frankfurt. It's a soft piece on those folks this country tends to forget."

Barton's phone buzzed.

He put the phone on speaker, and his secretary said, "Travis Sutter on line two, sir."

Barton pushed the button for line two.

"Travis, Barton Williams. You're on speaker with Riley, Editor Avery Lassiter, and Laura."

In the proper order of rank, I thought.

"Okay." The connection was remarkably clear.

"It's your dime, Trav," Riley said in a macho tone.

"It was easier than I thought. I drove up and walked right in."

"I take it he speaks German," Lassiter whispered.

"I do. My grandparents came over in the fifties. Mom was their only child. She married an immigrant German. We always spoke German at home."

Lassiter looked chagrined, not realizing her aside could be picked up.

"I saw a nurse, in what we would call an administrator's office. I explained I was looking for my aunt, who had been admitted to a hospital in the Frankfurt area, but the family didn't know where. As it turned out that nurse didn't work in the reception area; she was just dropping off some paperwork relating to her ward. I asked if I might look in the ward where she worked, to see . . . She thought I could, and I did."

I interrupted him. "Laura here, Travis."

"Hey, Laura."

"Did she mention what went on in her ward?"

"Yeah. I first asked if there were differences between the various wards at the hospital. She said there were; for instance, her patients were being given a new drug that was having better-than-expected results."

My heart was pounding. "Did she say for what? Like a cancer treatment?"

"Oh right. Actually, it was cancer!"

"Barton again, Travis. It sounds like you have a good sense of the place. I think it might be best to see it in the light of day, when the patients are up and about."

I teased, "Your lost-aunt cover should prove very effective on the patients, as it was on the nurse."

# 62

I had a restless night sleeping, my mind turbulent with speculations. The world was on the cusp of a major upheaval, one that didn't involve guns, bombs, or politicians' failed promises. The portion of the United States Senate that had been bought off, who followed Kelly down the barrel of a cannon, will now have to face an electorate of millions of cancer victims and their families.

I dragged my tired body down to breakfast. Jerry and Tyler were having a good old time.

"Great piece on Dalton."

I'd completely forgotten about it. I gave both my boys kisses and went straight for the coffee.

"You had a bad night. About the worst I've seen."

"Uh huh. I'm sorry, I should have slept on the sofa. Ugh, I'm not very good company, right now." I plunked down at the table. Tyler wanted me, and Jerry shifted him over. I couldn't help but react positively to my son's enthusiasm. He was a good cure for what ailed me.

"You really liked it?" I asked.

"I did. I also think you need a long, hot shower and a ride into work." He reached for Tyler, "Come here, big guy." Tyler transferred without a complaint.

Jerry was right. The shower, a couple of cups of coffee, a little food, and my two adoring men revived me. I appreciated the ride in, allowing me to recap an amazing day and night. I gave my man a big kiss before I got out.

As I walked through the newsroom, my cell rang. It was Michael. "Hi. What's up?"

"Your story on the senator is great," he said excitedly.

"Thanks." I walked by Mary's desk and gave her a wave.

"Senator Dalton would like to speak with you."

I arrived at my cubicle as she came on the line.

"Laura, I should have had you as my publicist when I ran for Miss America; I would have won in a landslide. I'm flattered by the beautiful way you put the story together. My father called me first thing. He was thrilled."

"It was a pleasure," I said unenthusiastically. I still wasn't functioning on all cylinders. Plus, my background as a beat reporter had not prepared me for a congratulatory call from someone I wrote about.

"How did things go with your reporter in Germany?" she asked.

"It's cancer."

"That is wonderfully good news."

"I'm sorry I didn't call you, but—"

"Please, you don't owe me an explanation. Gavin called to congratulate me on the article. If it is possible, I would like him to hear Mort's tape. He and I are meeting after lunch. I'll reschedule if you can't make it."

She wanted to use her new leverage to go after Kelly and Pembroke. "Sure. I have some meetings this morning, but I'm sure one or two o'clock will be fine. I'll call Michael."

"Thank you, Laura."

I called Max. "I think you are well-suited to be a Style writer. It is also a lot safer."

"I just got off with Senator Dalton. She was very pleased."

"The timing couldn't be better for her."

"How's murder-for-hire going?"

"We're closing in . . . rather, the FBI is. It is only a matter of luck and time."

I felt someone close to me and looked up; it was Mary. She mouthed *boss* and pointed. "I just got word the boss is calling. Talk to you later."

On my way to Lassiter's office, it dawned on me. I hadn't asked Max about Mort's tape.

"Good job on the Dalton piece," Lassiter said.

That meant a lot. "Thanks, boss."

"Barton called. Travis got back inside the clinic. He talked to patients in the cafeteria and on the grounds. They all felt sorry about his lost aunt and poured out their good fortune. He estimated there might be as many as a hundred beds there. The patients he talked to had been there three to four months."

I was pumped, but held down my emotions. "What's the plan?"

"Barton wants the scoop and is going with Travis's exclusive in the morning. What can you put together?"

"It depends on how much we want to say."

"Try the FDA's turndown of the drug and Senator Dalton's opposition to that decision."

I liked that and suggested I make my contribution as background to Travis's lead.

Lassiter's face went blank. "Yeah, that sounds like the way to go."

"I don't think my name needs to be on his story. Why not Claire, instead? I can provide her with what we know. Then I can stay under the radar. After all, I'm a Style writer now. At least that's what the Hill people will think. Claire can concentrate on Kelly's and Pembroke's reactions. Besides, I know much more than we want to write at the moment."

Lassiter stood and came around her desk to where I stood. I couldn't make out her expression and hoped I hadn't misstepped into editorial territory.

"Laura, you've grown up. I'm proud of you."

I felt flustered.

"You've always been a damn good reporter, a little flaky at times, but dedicated. What you just suggested, in my opinion, is the way it should go. You're close to breaking a huge story involving the Rogers drug, senatorial corruption, and other crimes against humanity. Travis's story will shake up the Hill people, but you'll be there to slam the door when the time comes."

If there was anyone I ever wanted to receive an *atta-girl* from, it was Lassiter. She returned to her desk. I took a deep breath and cleared my throat.

"Senator Dalton would like me to play the Mort tape to Senator Crawford this afternoon in her office. I'm only guessing, but I think she wants him to play it to Pembroke."

"Go for it. I'll tell Barton." Lassiter reached for her phone.

I wasn't sure if I could walk out of there without stumbling. But I wasn't weak-kneed; I was exhilarated and virtually floated back to my desk.

# 63

I reached over to my recorder and turned off the Mort tape. Senator Crawford sat staring at it as though the machine had some magical aura.

He asked quietly, "Are you sure Stroble wasn't making that up?" His voice was husky. "I can't believe that Fred . . ."

"Mort was telling the truth, sir. He wanted out. Tyrell Ward had developed a good relationship with Mort and learned all this from him earlier on. That was why we set up our first meeting—Michael, Mort, Tyrell, and me. That's when we learned about the bribe money."

"Fred. Fred. Fred," he said distraught. He rubbed his face and looked at Roanne.

"Mort was in meetings that included lobbyist Stanley Horowitz," she said.

"I know Fred. He's so straight his shirts don't need starch," Crawford said sadly.

"He wasn't involved in the partying. It was just the money," I said delicately.

"I heard what Stroble said," Crawford said sharply. He let out a big sigh. "Sorry, Laura. Fred's such a great family man, always involved . . . they're all in college . . . oh damn," he sat upright, "three kids . . . that's why the money." He slumped in back in his chair, rubbing his face. "He's a friend. What happens now?"

Roanne reached out to reassure him. "I was concerned if Laura had come to you cold, you might have questioned the tape's authenticity. I know it's real because I was there and heard it live. It's been edited to focus on the salient points."

He nodded and stood. I thought he might be leaving, but instead he walked around, rubbing his temples. He drank some water and then looked at me. I braced for a possible onslaught.

"Okay, Laura, what do you propose?"

My mind was ablaze; we had a new ally.

# 64

S enator Crawford carried my tape recorder as Roanne and I walked with him to the Hart Senate Office Building, next door to Dirksen. He went up to Senator Pembroke's office alone, and we browsed the monumental Alexander Calder sculpture—*Mountains and Clouds*—in the nine-story atrium. Calder was famous for his gigantic mobiles designed to move. The cloud portion of this sculpture had moved at varying speeds until it malfunctioned and stopped. There was no money appropriated to fix it.

"I can't imagine the pain Gavin is feeling right now Roanne," she said ruefully.

We ambled through the atrium. "Have you heard from your father?"

She shook her head. I decided to change the subject.

"Johnny's . . . eh . . . interesting."

"Johnny's a dear. He had served four years in prison for drug abuse and distribution, when his public defender wrote Dad about him. Johnny had barely gotten through grade school. He was a big kid and forced to earn his keep. He endured a litany of abuse. I'm thirsty," she said abruptly. "Let's find a vending machine."

"There's a cafeteria along the basement corridor between here and Dirksen."

"You know more about—yes, let's go there."

As we headed for the stairs, she continued on about Johnny.

"Nobody knew how old Johnny was when he was arrested, so they charged him as an adult. His sentence was much too long for a first-time offender. They also sent him to a place they had no business sending him.

"Dad surprised everyone when he went to the jail to see Johnny. They talked for half an hour. He saw a lot of good in Johnny and pardoned him, with the proviso that Johnny live on our ranch until he learned to read and learned a trade. Once he became self-supporting, he would be free to leave. Johnny was scared. To him, Dad was a giant . . . a man to fear. Fortunately, he listened to his public defender's assurances that Dad was someone he could trust."

We reached the cafeteria and selected a drink from the machine.

"Dad set him up in our small bunk house. He told his ranch foreman, Roper, what he wanted. Roper taught Johnny how to use tools and then put him to work using them. Ours was the first real home Johnny had ever known. He'd never even had his own room.

"It took Mom a long time to get used to Johnny being in the house, even though it was always with Dad. Mom's a social princess, or maybe a queen since Dad was a governor. She's great, but very narrow in her points of view. Dad told her Johnny needed some polish and that she should contribute to his overall education. Suffice it to say, Mom had never done anything like that in her life. She was an Edith Wharton socialite of the highest order. Work to her was taking a bath. Nevertheless, she did it. Once she takes on a task, she is diligent. She worked hard to learn and understand Johnny.

"He improved. I would see him during visits home. Dad wanted Johnny to learn how to drive and put Roper on it, but that was a disaster. Roper had no patience. That happened around the time I had come home to work on my doctorate in history. Dad asked me to teach him instead. I was flabbergasted, but forged ahead."

"That had to be . . . I mean you and a healthy young man."

"Yes, I thought about that, but Johnny didn't look at me that way, and believe me, I know *that way*." She made a grotesque, leering expression.

I broke up. Her caricature was priceless.

"About a year and a half after Dad left the governor's office, he had a small car accident, nothing serious, but it was his fault. He felt it was time to see if Johnny could be his chauffeur. I suggested that he get used to riding in the back seat of his Town Car, while having Johnny drive him around places, never more than a mile from the house.

"Dad declared a week later that Johnny was ready for downtown and taking him to the club. That's when a good relationship became closer. Johnny adores Dad, and Dad reciprocates. Johnny's always with or around him, unless Dad has him off doing something, like picking you or me up at the airport."

She looked at her watch. "Oh, to be a fly on Fred's wall."

I was still absorbing Johnny, when my cell phone vibrated. "Excuse me, it's Max. Hi."

"The FBI arrested our alleged killer on a federal warrant a little less than an hour ago in South Beach. They're bringing him directly to Washington."

"Wow. I'm with Senator Dalton . . . may I share this with her?"

"Sure."

"The FBI has arrested one of Mort's killers and is bringing him to DC."

"That's wonderful news. Tell—" She was interrupted by her cell phone.

"Anything on the other guy?" I asked Max, as Roanne answered her call.

"No. We'll see what, if anything, our man gives up."

Roanne placed her hand on my arm, whispering, "Gavin."

"Max, I need to call you back."

"I look forward to it."

"Gavin has just left a very distraught, confused, frightened, but feisty Fred Pembroke. We'll meet him in my office."

I remembered, too late again, that I hadn't told Max I'd played Mort's tape for Crawford, and now Pembroke has heard it, too. I wasn't worried either would make it public, but it did mean more people knew about it.

When we arrived at Roanne's office, I excused myself and went off to call Max. I felt uneasy and worried that I'd done something that could be harmful.

"That was fast," Max said.

I felt my throat tighten and cleared it. I told him what had transpired and that I was about to hear how it went with Pembroke.

"It doesn't appear to me that either will want to go public, so you haven't blundered badly. However, I would keep that tape under wraps. It could be dangerous for you if the wrong people found out where it came from."

**65**

C rawford was with Roanne when I rejoined her. I was still stinging from the ramifications of what Max had just said to me.

"Fred ranted," Crawford said. "He accused Stroble of telling a pack of lies. According to Fred, neither he nor Kelly had a Swiss, Cayman Island, or any other offshore account."

Roanne looked at him softly. "I'm so sorry you had to go through that."

Crawford paced. "I knew he was killing the messenger. He had to vent. Finally, in sheer exhaustion, he collapsed into a chair, mumbling about his wife, children, and his long-term status as a senator. He demanded to know how I got the tape. I said I couldn't say. He wasn't happy with that, but after he mulled things over, he calmed down and apologized for his temper.

"He then said, 'I can't imagine what I ever did to Mort for him to say lies like that about me.'"

That blew my mind.

"What's next?" he asked.

I looked at Roanne and asked, "May I?

She nodded.

"Tomorrow, the *Star* will be running an exclusive report out of Frankfurt, Germany, on a miracle cancer drug."

"Where'd this come from?"

I told him the story.

"Is Rogers aware of this?"

I nodded. "He's the brains behind it. The patients have been in treatment for three and four months . . . long before Tutoxtamen was turned down by the FDA."

# 66

W hen I joined Jerry and Tyler for breakfast, my husband held up the *Star*'s front page. The headline read: MIRACLE CANCER CURE UNCOVERED IN GERMANY!

Travis's interviews and quotes gave a vivid picture of German cancer patients being treated with a powerful, new cancer-curing drug.

Jerry read Travis's story out loud while I ate my breakfast. When he put the paper down, he said, "This ought to stir up a hornet's nest."

*An understatement*, I thought, but still very true.

Jerry took Tyler upstairs for a cleanup, and I reread Travis's piece. I had already planned to stay home and review the journal I'd begun after my first meeting with Roanne Dalton. I wanted to revisit our thinking from early on and compare that to where we were now. Had we skipped over something, a person? I have always found this type of reflection a useful exercise whenever I moved deeply into a case.

Jerry returned with Tyler, who was reaching out for me to hold him. As I took my giggling son, I said to Jerry, "I was thinking about asking Roanne to join us on *Scalawag* this weekend."

"Fine with me. From what I've heard and seen—"

"Down, boy. She's not flaky enough for you." I put Tyler into his crib, got him interested in his toys, and then sat with my husband.

"Can you imagine what must be going on in one hundred Senate offices this morning?" I said, reaching for the last piece of toast. "Want this?"

Jerry declined the toast. "No, I'm watching my figure."

"Ha, ha, ha. Mine is doing very well, thank you."

"You get no complaints from me." He put the Business section down. "Where is Senator Dalton in all of this? Eh, not the toast, Tutoxtamen."

"She wants it approved. She likes Barton's plan of running hard-hitting prescription drug stories. It should gain enthusiasm for her cosponsored bill. Michael will like the pressure they create on Kelly and the pharmas."

"And you?"

"My story on the conspiracy to dump Tutoxtamen is building, as we tie Kelly and Pembroke to Horowitz in bribery, corruption, and Mort's killing." I ate the last morsel of toast and chased it with coffee.

"Travis looking for a lost aunt was a bit of genius," Jerry said. "Something you'd do."

I smiled, puckered my lips, and blew him a kiss. "The beauty is I'm not openly involved. Travis has put a fresh face on it, and my cover is—"

Jerry interrupted. "There won't be enough hotel or hospital beds in all of Germany for the hordes of Americans who will be flying there. Cancer patients with passports are probably making reservations, as we speak, while their doctors are calling the hospital. Do you think the Germans are manufacturing it?"

"No, Rogers is. That was what Rufus sort of told us, and probably why he flew to some island in the Caribbean last night. Rogers Pharmaceuticals probably supplied the Germans from their pre-*not approvable* stock. Harley had the Germans testing Tutox long before the FDA rejected its being manufactured here."

"Do you know if Rogers's new offshore operation is up and running?"

I shook my head.

"I mean, he's going to have to restock awfully fast or . . ."

"Our discovery may not rest well with Rogers," I said. "Although, who knows? This could all be part of his strategy. I'm sure Kelly and the pharmas believe it's Rogers. The question now is what will they do about it?"

**67**

R oanne called late that afternoon. "Nancy told Michael that the HELP staff is under the gun to connect the German hospital with Rogers Pharmaceuticals. Fred wants Justice to investigate Rogers for illegal manufacturing and distribution of the drug."

"How will all this affect your new alliance?" I asked.

"I convinced Al that we should all want to know if it is Rogers."

"That'll rattle some cages. I like your thinking, though."

"And fortunately, it worked perfectly. When Fred convened his committee, Al asked for a minute that Fred begrudgingly granted. Al announced that the minority unanimously supported the chairman. After the shock wore off, Fred was elated, put off the meeting, and asked Al to join him on a call to the attorney general."

"That's awesome," I said enthusiastically. "Have you heard from your father?"

"He and Johnny are taking underwater diving lessons."

"Sounds like they're making a stay out of it."

"Dad's very adventurous, especially when he's away from Mom. It wouldn't surprise me if they stayed a week. It would be great for both of them."

"Speaking of being adventurous, I realize this is short notice, but Jerry and I would like you to join us on *Scalawag* . . . for a day over the weekend." She paused a moment. "Is there a day you prefer over the other?"

# 68

R oanne preferred Saturday. Jerry suggested that we could take a run
down to Mount Vernon. "Give our senator with a PhD in history a
little history."

Roanne arrived at the marina's gate exactly at 10:00. On board, she met
Tyler, and I showed her the galley, head, and salon. Jerry was in seventh
heaven having two women to boss around. Once into the channel, Roanne
went below to change. She had come on board wearing dress-up casual.
She changed into a two-piece bathing suit and a light, long-sleeved, baby-
blue cover-up.

Jerry pointed out all of the navigational and communications equipment,
going over what to do in the event of an emergency. He demonstrated a life
jacket and self-inflating raft in the manner of a flight attendant with an
oxygen mask. Now that we had Tyler, I felt I needed the indoctrination
session too. I had never sailed without Jerry and had never given survival
much of a thought beyond where these items were stowed.

Jerry powered us out onto the Potomac River where we picked up a
light breeze and hoisted the mainsail and headsail, or jib. We set out
downstream. Roanne enjoyed seeing Reagan National Airport from the
water, the coastline of southeast Washington, and the mild confluence
with the Anacostia River.

"This is glorious," she exclaimed, sitting aft with us.

We sailed under the Woodrow Wilson Bridge, the main north/south
traffic artery that carried Interstate 95 travelers on the easterly bypass
around Washington. As we neared Mount Vernon, we hauled in the sail
and converted over to motor.

Ro—she asked us to call her that—and I started below to fix lunch, as

Jerry said, "Once we anchor, Tyler and I will work on the principles of navigation."

As we reached the galley, Ro said, "Your husband has quite a sense of humor."

"What? Oh, the navigation. I admit, at eight months, Tyler's a very inquisitive, energetic child, but not a phenom. At least, I don't think so."

We laughed. "Jerry seems very attentive to Tyler. Does he help out a lot?"

"If I'd let him, he'd hog Tyler—cleaning, feeding, the whole works. He has two teenage boys and sadly admits he never did much of that with them. Beth had been a stay-at-home mother, and he'd been working long hours as a criminal defense attorney."

Ro cut celery sticks while I cleaned the lettuce.

I broke the silence. "I'm living a life I had never dreamt about having before I met Jerry."

Ro nodded and smiled. "I've wondered whether I might ever have a relationship or get married again. It would take a man with extreme patience, understanding, and strong self-esteem to fit into my life."

"Jerry and I clicked immediately. After our first date, I knew I was with a very special man. The first time we made love was right here." I indicated the V-bunk forward. "I didn't want to leave *Scalawag* Sunday night for fear it would all turn out to be a dream.

"That Monday morning was the pits. I normally couldn't wait for Mondays so I could get back to work. Jerry had to go out of town for two days, and I was crazy. *Would he ever call? Would I ever see him again?* He called Monday afternoon and asked if we could have dinner Tuesday. We were both smitten. He lived on board, and I had a one-bedroom apartment in Cleveland Park, just north of the National Zoo. We wintered in the apartment and summered on the water.

"We courted eight months before tying the knot. It could have been sooner, but I put it off. I'd been on my own for seventeen years from when I left home for college. Jerry didn't rush me. He cut down his asking to only once a day."

We giggled.

"H.T. and I started out more old-school. Our wedding night was our first time. We came close several times, but . . . well, I didn't want anything to go wrong. We had a huge June wedding. My mother did everything she could to turn it into a royal ball.

"H.T. had been Dad's attorney general. I helped in his campaign and in Dad's reelection. That's when we met, but we didn't date. I liked him, but my interests then were getting my master's and teaching. In the middle of H.T.'s four-year term as AG, Dad wanted him to run for the US Senate; the incumbent was retiring. He also wanted me to run H.T.'s campaign. We naturally began spending considerable time together."

I joked, "He'd have to have been a monk not to feel something."

She smiled shyly. "The heat of the battle turned up our emotional heat as well. It took great willpower not to jump into bed with him. We agreed to concentrate on the election, and then we'd talk about our future.

"After H.T. won, we announced our engagement and Mom set out to have a coronation. You've seen the country club. It's a perfect setting. It was also another wedge in my relationships with my brother and sister. Neither received the same treatment . . . although under normal circumstances, you'd have thought their weddings lavish."

"You paint a vivid picture. You and H.T., were you . . . good together?"

"I think so; I didn't have anything to compare it with. What relationships I'd had by then were strictly platonic. H.T. and I loved each other. The early years in Washington were like a long honeymoon; a blur of parties, receptions, and dinners, including several at the White House.

"I looked forward to having children, but that didn't happen. After three years, we agreed to be tested. He had the problem. I brought up adoption, but he balked. I believe that took some of the air out of our loving relationship."

"Hey," Jerry yelled, "Tyler and I are famished."

"We're coming." We had been dawdling.

Ro put her hand on my arm. "One other thing. I didn't want to spend my life being only the wife of a senator. H.T. agreed. That's when I went back home to work on my PhD. I also worked for him out of his office in town. I represented him at functions and traveled back here when he asked me to. We still loved each other; we were just not as loving."

We enjoyed our day with Ro and arrived back at the marina by dusk. We watched the setting sun's orange reflections on the Potomac fractured by the 14th Street Bridge before pulling into the channel. Ro changed and left soon after we docked, profuse in her thanks. We invited her back. After putting Tyler down, Jerry and I sat aft listening to music from the yacht club and the happy sounds from boat parties.

My pulse quickened when he reached his hand over and took mine.

# 69

**M**ax came aboard Sunday afternoon—and not empty-handed. His Sunday morning fishing trip with his cousin had produced a good catch, which he would later fry on our electric grill. First, though, he imparted some interesting information.

"Yesterday, Stroble's alleged killer, faced with all our evidence against him, decided not to lawyer-up in exchange for a favorable plea. He gave up the man who had hired him—an employee of Mr. Horowitz's law firm. The FBI is now tapping that person of interest. On the drug front, US Marshals and DEA agents visited the Rogers New Jersey facility on Saturday and are still searching and interviewing today."

I hoped no one had let slip where the manufacturing might be taking place. Max said he hadn't heard this was the case. We had a delightful day topped off with a delicious fish entrée.

My Monday morning was full of warm memories of our weekend. Max's visit had made our weekend extra special. As I walked from the station to the paper, my cell phone rang. It was Max. "Good morning," I answered.

"And to you. I'm pressed for time. Nothing incriminating was found in New Jersey."

"Okay if I tell the managing editor?"

"Keep it in-house." We signed off.

"Good morning, Laura," Barton said, as he came from his office into the reception area to greet me. "Please come in. Coffee?"

"Yes, black."

"Please have a seat." He put in my request and sat behind his desk, across from me.

He began, "We are witnessing a migration. American cancer patients are flying to Frankfurt in droves. We have that from Dulles and Frankfurt airports. We had people check all the airlines servicing Frankfurt . . . flights were rapidly filling up, weeks out."

"According to Travis, the hospital was full."

"Yes. He called me first thing. By the way, he's a real find. It seems the Germans were expecting this and had hundreds of additional beds available in nearby hotels and inns. They also had extra doctors and a second hospital on call."

Barton's secretary brought in our coffee.

"That's quite a logistical undertaking," I said. "Something I'm sure Harley Rogers would be very good at planning. Governor McAllister told me Harley was a superb strategist in World War II—planning ahead and knowing his enemy,"

"Yes. See what you can find out from the Rogers people. We have people here looking to interview cancer hospitals, NIH, for their reactions. Travis will continue to work on the Germans."

"My speculation is . . . do you have a few minutes, sir? I'd like to give you a chronology."

He nodded.

I began with my New Jersey trip, ending with my knowledge of an offshore manufacturing operation. I gave it to him in great detail. What coffee I had in my cup when I finished was cold.

"That is a fascinating story, Laura, and one I hope you are prepared to write. It also proves Senator Dalton's position on Tutoxtamen. I believe you made a similar statement as to its efficacy awhile back. This means that Senators Kelly and Pembroke and others are engaged in a little skullduggery along with Mr. Stanley Horowitz and the pharmaceutical lobby."

I was thrilled.

He continued, "The death of Stroble is another indication that—"

"It's more than that now, sir," I blurted out, startling him. I needed to control that. "Sorry. Captain Walsh has told me off the record that Stroble's alleged hit man is in custody and talking."

"Background?" he asked, perturbed knowing he couldn't print that little morsel.

"Only because they are not arresting the hit man's PI . . . eh, 'person of interest' . . . at this time. The FBI wants to observe him, in hopes he'll lead them to higher-ups. With Senator Dalton and Senator Szymanski tied together in their cosponsored bill, and US Marshals finding nothing in New Jersey, I believe that—"

"Yes," he interrupted, amused. "I can imagine that some people will be a bit stirred up."

The rest of Monday dragged, so I went home mid-afternoon to work on my journal. It would be the source from which I put together the story that Barton expected from me. After I spent a little playtime with Tyler, Anna took him for his afternoon carriage ride, and I began my writing task.

**70**

For whatever reason, I got a good night's sleep and arose with Jerry and Tyler at 6:00, but I didn't interfere with the boys and their routine. I read the *Star* instead, especially Claire Rowley's article on the Senate's bewilderment, a story I thought was pretty much matter-of-fact. I was obvious to me that Claire had reviewed the C-SPAN coverage from the beginning, especially the part she had not seen live. Her piece was reportorial, without editorial comments. She also mentioned that Senator Kelly had called a caucus meeting for today.

I wondered what Kelly's strategy would be? My cell phone rang. The display showed it was someone from the paper. "Good morning," I said cheerfully.

"It's Riley. You were right about Puerto Rico. Two gringos had been sniffing around the clinic asking questions."

"And went away empty-handed, I hope."

"Our stringer, Rias, talked to a nurse he'd met during his earlier visit. She said the gringos thought the clinic was a laboratory, a processing plant."

"Not very clandestine of them was it. Well, now the pharmas and Kelly will know that Puerto Rico is not a destination point."

"Claire says the Hill is in a fury over the German story, and there's double to triple the normal media up there. We've found the same attention at Dulles and Reagan National interviewing passengers taking or trying to get Frankfurt flights."

"This will be bigger than the migration to Lourdes," I quipped. "It's a travesty that Americans have to fly to another country to get an American-invented drug."

"Barton says you two agree it's Rogers's drug."

"It fits."

"Yeah. What's your schedule today?"

"I'll be on Capitol Hill. I've got to go. I'll call you later."

"Who's calling so early?" Jerry asked, coming back down with a clean Tyler.

"Riley. It could have waited. The pharmas checked out Puerto Rico."

My cell rang again. I thought about not answering but saw it was Max.

"To what do I owe this honor," I said brightly.

"I've just come out of a task force meeting with Chief Douglass, FBI Director Cole, Special Agent Davis, the attorney general, and the president's chief of staff."

"Sounds serious."

"Six thirty was the only time the principals could agree on. The FBI's surveillance on the PI picked up a conversation he had with Stanley Horowitz."

"Bingo, as a friend of mine likes to say." Bingo was one of Max's favorite words when revealing a key clue or person.

"You flatter me, but the bad news is that Horowitz appears to have known about Rogers's offshore plans for some time. He and the PI talked in a sort of shorthand, nothing direct, but there is something brewing. The PI then flew to Miami. Have you heard that reservation requests to fly to Frankfurt are off the charts? And I doubt it's for the sausage."

"Yeah and I can imagine the chaos at the airports and with online booking agents."

"The FBI has added Horowitz and Kelly to their surveillance list. You have a good day."

"You too." I clicked off.

Wow. What a surge of activity. Today would be busier than I expected. I went upstairs to get ready for work. An hour and a half later, I walked into Michael's office. Ro was out.

I started right off with my news. "The pharmas visited Rogers's clinic in Puerto Rico. Captain Walsh attended a sunrise meeting with some heavy hitters, including the president's chief of staff. The FBI's phone tap picked up a conversation between the PI and Stanley Horowitz. He already knew Rogers had set up a processing plant."

"Then why check out the Puerto Rican clinic?"

"Maybe they are like us: knowing, but not knowing where."

Michael didn't react as I thought he might. He seemed preoccupied. "What's up?"

He said, "A hysterical Nancy Morris came in here yesterday afternoon. I was stunned by her demeanor, plus she'd never come to my office before. She was uncontrollable. When I asked if I could get her anything, she replied 'a fifth of bourbon might help.' There was no humor in her voice. Then she moaned 'this is the major jilt of my life.'"

According to Michael, Nancy had been in Senator Pembroke's office working on a plan to get the pharmas to allow greater discounts to counteract the Szymanski/Dalton bill when Kelly, his AA Charlie, and his leadership chief of staff barged into the room.

Michael quoted Nancy as saying, *"I'd never seen Tom like that. He berated Senator Pembroke for the party being in this mess. He was so out of control."* Michael added, "Then she really broke down."

"Her God has feet of clay. He showed his ugly side."

Michael nodded. "She said Kelly chased all the staff out, but even in the next room, they could hear him ranting about the cancer drug in Germany and accusing Senator Pembroke of not doing anything about it. She didn't know how long that went on, but when things quieted down, and she couldn't hear their voices anymore, she came over here.

"I told staff Nan wasn't feeling well, and that I'd take her home when she was ready. She fell asleep on the senator's sofa for three hours. I had to alert Jeff, the B&G guy who still drives me, of a deviation in my schedule. When Nan was more composed, I took Jeff and her to dinner. All she wanted was booze, but I insisted she had to eat. It was a real ordeal, and she mumbled stuff neither Jeff nor I needed to know."

"Did she know Mort?"

"Only by reputation. It was after 11:00 when we got her home. We stretched her out on her bed, I turned off her alarm, and we left. When I got home, I found a long message from Tyrell. The gal he had met that first night with Mort? Well, he and she have been dating two, three times a week since. That evening she told Tyrell that Mort's date, Tina, had been asked to spy on Mort, get close to him.

"Tyrell's squeeze doesn't work for the pharmas like Tina, who has been plagued with guilt, worried she might have contributed to Mort's death. Tyrell's girl came clean because he and she were getting it on. I'm sure I'll get more details when I catch up to him later today."

*The Hill underground at work*, I thought. "Sounds like more cracks in the pharmas' armor. There are people who will want to talk to both of those women."

He began to object.

"This is a murder investigation, Michael. Nothing will happen to either, but Tina especially knows things that are valuable for Captain Walsh to know."

After a pause, he said, "Okay, I don't like it, but I'll do it."

"It'll be very much like what you and Tyrell experienced. I suggest you get to Tyrell quickly and have him tell his girlfriend she must absolutely keep this to herself."

"Okay, I'll— "

His office door opened, and Ro walked in.

"Laura, I was hoping I'd find you here. I just left Gavin. He's seeing Fred tonight in the Cloakroom at 6:00."

I looked at Michael. "I think you better add Nancy to your list when you call FBI SAC Reed Davis. He will want to hear about last night's blow up."

Ro showed surprise. "What blow up?"

"Between Kelly and Pembroke," Michael said. He told Ro what he had told me.

"Why the FBI, Laura?"

"It's about corruption and conspiracy. The murder is separate, and it's MPD's. Plus the German pharmaceutical's operation may be a deal-breaker between the pharmas and the senators. They need to look at everything . . . nothing is insignificant."

I switched gears and asked her gently, "Have you been able to reach your father?"

"No. He hasn't returned my last three messages."

I wrote down Reed's and Max's telephone numbers. "Here are the numbers you'll need, Michael." I looked at Ro. "Tyrell; has been dating the girl he picked up at The Goose when he was with Mort. Well, she told Tyrell that Mort's date, Tina, had been assigned to get close to Mort. We need to know who told her to do that."

"Absolutely," Ro said, looking at Michael.

A little sheepishly, he said, "I'll go see Tyrell; it'll be easier that way."

"Laura, I have to go to a meeting with Al. I'll call you if there is a change to the 6:00 meeting. Fred is known for changing things midstream."

# 71

M eetings, telephone calls, and researching a long list of speculations filled my day. It was a relief to get out of the paper and head for Roanne's office.

Michael and I waited for Senators Dalton and Crawford to return from the Senate chamber. When Ro showed after an hour-long wait, she was without Crawford. She said he had stopped to use her restroom. His meeting with Senator Pembroke had been very hard on him. Michael went for a pitcher of water and glasses, returning just ahead of Crawford.

The senator's tie was loosened. He looked drained. We sat around the coffee table and waited as Crawford took a long pull on his water.

"This is the most difficult thing I've ever gone through as a senator." He cleared his throat. "Fred's usually very prompt. I waited fifteen minutes and then checked the Senate chamber, but he wasn't there. So I went back into the Cloakroom.

"He came rushing in around 7:10, barely acknowledging colleagues, and plopped into the chair next to mine. He was definitely not himself.

"He said, 'I'm stepping down as chairman of HELP, Gav. You're the first person to know. It's true, what was on that tape. I took the money.' He impressed on me he had never asked for it. It had started with $2,500 in cash in a brown envelope. No name. Just a note: *For the kids' education.* He remembered talking about having two kids in college and a third about to start, and how he and Sally had scrimped; she'd even taken a part-time job, so they could give the kids the things they'd been promised. He chided himself for being so stupid, because now he had completely failed them and Sally.

"Fred told me the pharmas opened up an offshore account as Mort had said. Over $30,000 the first year. He said Stroble was right; he had never taken part in anything else . . . not the women, nothing. He said it was the euphoria of power . . . the chairmanship, the prestige, and the money . . . they blotted out reality. He asked me about you, Laura."

"Me? Why?"

"He wanted to know if you were a good person. I told him Ro had confidence in you, and that from what little I'd seen, I'd say yes."

I was confused. Why would he ask about me?

"He said the story you wrote about Ro was a good one. He was sorry about how he'd handled you, Ro. He was under pressure from Kelly and Horowitz. He asked that I tell you that."

"Is he planning to leave the Senate?" Ro asked.

"It's possible. He plans to tell Tom about stepping down in a few days. Then he really got me when he said, 'Stroble didn't have to die, Gav,' and then abruptly got up and walked out. I couldn't believe what I had just heard."

"I found Gavin in the Cloakroom," Ro said to me.

"I was stunned and appreciate you giving me my space, Ro. Fred's saying the tape is true implicates Kelly . . . he's guilty, too, you know. Look, folks, Fred's a good friend; this has taken a lot out of me."

"I truly feel sorry for him," Ro said.

"Telling his family will be the hardest part for him. He's a great father, family man. Ironically, that was his undoing. It's tragic."

"I remember H.T. telling me—"

The phone rang, interrupting her. Michael grabbed it and immediately showed shock.

"Senator, it's your father. He—"

"Finally," she said, rising.

"He says they're under attack!"

"Attack?" I said incredulously, jumping to my feet.

Ro took the phone. "Dad?"

Panic flashed across her face. She put the call on speaker, and we heard sounds of gunshots and explosions.

"My God! Who?" she exclaimed.

Crawford was on his feet. "I'll call DOD," he said rushing into Michael's office.

Rufus's voice was weak and overpowered by the sounds. ". . . one of our security men is down; there are a bunch coming at us. Sherman got hit,

Johnny and I are . . ." There was a loud explosion amidst sounds of close-in rifle or machine-gun fire. Then the phone went dead.

I had my address book out looking up Harley Rogers's cell number.

"Dad! Dad! Can you hear me?" Ro yelled. There was no answer. She plopped into her chair, elbows on her knees and her head in her hands.

Michael stood, stunned.

Crawford rushed in. "Michael, punch up line three."

He did.

Crawford said, "Okay, General, I'm in Senator Dalton's office. You're on speaker."

I was punching in Harley's number.

"Senator Dalton, where was your father calling from?" the general asked.

"It's all been so secret," I heard Ro say. "He's in the Caribbean, southern part, I suspect."

"What do you mean, secret?" the unnamed general asked, upset.

"General, let me explain, give you what we know," Crawford said.

Michael comforted Ro, as Crawford explained things to the general. I got a recording. I selected the emergency number and finally got a live voice at the answering service. I told her my name and explained as clearly as I could why it was imperative she find Mr. Rogers or put me through to him. She was hesitant, then adamantly said she couldn't.

"His son is in extreme danger and every second talking to you may be one too many to save him. Call Mr. Rogers and give him my name and the message."

She asked me to wait. After what seemed like an eternity, a male voice came on.

"Ms. Wolfe? This is Harley Rogers." His voice was shaky and husky.

"Your island is under attack. We have—"

"I just heard. How—?"

"Rufus called. I'm with Senator Dalton. We think the governor got hit. He said Sherman had. We heard gun fire, explosions. Where is the island, sir? We have a general on with us and—"

"It's Carmaya, an archipelago off South America. I'll give you the coordinates."

"I'm ready," I said.

He recited the latitude and longitude.

"Senator Crawford," I called, waving the paper as I rushed to him. "This is from Harley Rogers. It's Carmaya, an island archipelago."

The surprised senator took my note and read the information to the general.

I asked Harley, "Please give me a direct line where—"

"I'll give you two."

I had my pad. "Okay."

Ro was still slumped in her chair with Michael beside her. I signed off with Harley and went to her, crouching down. Tears streamed from her eyes, and several wet tissues lay in her lap. I put my hand on her arm and said, "We know the island's location. DOD's got it now. Let's get away from here. I don't know what they can do, but . . ."

"Hopefully, send in the Marines," she said hesitantly, crying.

# 72

I called Jerry. True to form, Ro had food and soft drinks brought in from somewhere. I wished we were in a situation room instead of her office. We were in a cocoon—what we in Senator Dalton's room knew nobody around us knew. Our umbilical of information was our open line to some office in the DOD.

Senator Crawford, who had been on the phone in Michael's office, came in to tell us that some sharp general had ordered a detachment of Marines out of Gitmo, in full battle gear, to get airborne ASAP.

To help us understand the logistics of what a plane full of combat-ready Marines might face in Carmaya, Gavin had requested DOD fax us a recent satellite map of the Carmayan archipelago. I saw it was close to South America, as Harley had said. I teased Ro about the Marines actually getting sent in, but got no reaction.

The Marines' plane had already been airborne about five minutes when Crawford had passed the coordinates to DOD. I found them very proactive even before Crawford announced that they had dispatched their closest ship, a destroyer, to the island.

Senator Crawford's AA, Gordon, had joined us and was working with Michael. He came in to Ro's office and said, "We just got off the phone with the State Department. They've been in contact with Carmaya's president. The Rogers compound is on a small, previously uninhabited island two miles from the main island, in the five-island archipelago."

"Did he send troops to—?"

"He only has a police force. They sent a helicopter, which was shot at, and it hightailed out of there. The pilot said he saw smoke billowing up from a large building."

Some of us sat, some walked around. Time hung heavy on all of us. I was on and off the phone. Michael came in from the mini war room in his office and broke the long, somber mood.

"Everybody, Harley Rogers is on the phone. You're on speaker, sir."

"Senator Dalton, my security chief reported they have repelled the attackers."

A spontaneous cheer went up from all of us.

"Chief Driscoll said four of the attackers are known dead, two are wounded and in custody. He didn't think there were any more. Your father was hit by shrapnel in the shoulder, arm—"

Gasps and "what," "oh no," "how is he?" came from us.

"He seems fine," Harley shouted. "He also has a small scalp wound, but whatever hit him did not penetrate the bone. He is alert, telling people what to do. Old war horses never change."

Ro asked, "When can I talk to him? We can't get through on the numbers you gave us," she shouted. "What about Johnny?"

"I have a satellite connection. I'll have Driscoll get me a phone you can call. Don't worry; your father and the others are being cared for. I have two EMT-trained personnel on the security force. The worst thing is two of my people were killed, and Sherman is in bad shape."

"Oh, I'm so sorry . . . what can we do from here?" Ro said empathetically.

"You already have. I hear the Marines are on their way. I've got to go."

"What about the wounded attackers?" Crawford asked anxiously.

"We have a lead on who they worked for and have given that to DOD. Driscoll is calling me. I'll get back to you as soon as I can."

"Thank you, Mr. Rogers," Ro said to a dead line.

Now we had another wait. It would be hours before the Marines reached Carmaya.

# 73

I saw one of Michael's aides enter Ro's office. "Senator Dalton, Mr. Rogers needs to talk with you."

That got all our attention. Ro had been napping in a high-back easy chair and took a moment to orient herself. Michael came in and went to her. I had been relaxing on one end of the sofa. She slowly rose with Michael's assistance, and he walked her to her desk and put the call on speaker.

"Harley?" she said huskily.

"Senator, we're loading my plane with medical supplies, doctors, nurses—"

"Yes, I'd like to go. How—?"

"I thought you would. We've cleared a flight into Dulles for around 11:30. You can meet us there. We had prepared for this type of event and have pallets full of medical and food supplies ready to go. The trucks are rolling. I'm leaving for Newark airport now."

"How many may I bring with me?"

"A few, eight, ten." The line went dead

Ro called B&G and asked for assistance, namely picking her up. I wanted in and called Jerry at home. Crawford said he, too, would be going and left for his home to get some clothes.

Jeff would drive Michael home and then meet up with the others or drive him directly to Dulles. On the drive home, I called Max and brought him up-to-date regarding Carmaya and our flying down there on the Rogers medical plane. I also filled him in on Crawford's meeting with Pembroke.

"Sounds like you're in for a long night. I'll call Reed. By the way, Michael

Horne called this afternoon about the young women. We will be talking to them."

I next called the paper, leaving messages for Lassiter and Barton about the attack and gave them my particulars.

Harley had called Ro's cell while I was calling the paper.

"A change has been made," she told me as soon as I had gotten off my calls. "Harley is landing at Andrew's Air Force Base, you know, where the president's plane is kept. There had been a snag at Dulles about not being able to handle the refueling needs quickly."

Ro then called Michael and Crawford in rapid succession. While she was on with Crawford, I suggested that he come to our house and leave his car. She agreed and gave me her phone to give him directions. Ro was dropped off first, a reversal of the original plan, because she lives closer to Andrews than I.

Jerry had a bunch of stuff laid out for me. Bless his heart, he tried. I packed. Crawford arrived, and he and Jerry worked out the parking arrangements. The two men were getting along like old school buddies when I got downstairs. I put my overnight bag and computer bag by the front door. I then raced back upstairs to give my sleeping son a kiss. I wanted to pick him up and hug him, but I instead gave him a light kiss on his blond head. I raced back down, gave Jerry a hug and a kiss, promising to bring him back a coconut.

Crawford and I were quickly in the B&G SUV and on our way. We picked up Ro ten minutes later. A travel problem had come up for Michael and me; we didn't have passports. Being a beat reporter and never traveling, I had never needed one. But Ro had already rectified that.

"A State Department official will meet us at Andrews and issue you and Michael temporary diplomatic status. That person will also fly with us to mediate any problems."

"General Towers called," Crawford said. "Two counterterrorism agents out of DOD will be accompanying us. They'll do the forensics on the island."

Ro had called her mother, brother, and sister from her condo. While waiting for the refueling to finish, I called Jerry.

He blurted, "It's on TV from Carmaya. A reporter was on the island for another reason. He reported by phone that government authorities were not allowing anyone on the little island. People along the shoreline of the main island said there had been some explosions."

We lifted off from Andrews twenty minutes after midnight.

# 74

During the first leg of our flight, Harley told us about his arrangements with the Carmayans. Their hospital was a nice building, but it was woefully short-staffed and ill-equipped. That was why he had a surgeon, a triage doctor, three nurses, two orderlies, medical supplies, and equipment on board with us. He knew he would eventually need oncologists, surgeons, and cancer nurses once the word got out that Tutoxtamen was being manufactured on the island.

Harley and the president of the five-island country had worked out a plan where the tiny country would reap a royalty from the sales of Tutox. Harley would also financially support the building of an additional hospital specializing in cancer care.

While we waited in a San Juan terminal for the plane to be serviced, Harley heard from Driscoll that the Marine plane, with two helicopters aboard, had landed and that Sherman and one of his seriously wounded security guards had already been choppered to the main island hospital. The Marines were conducting a sweep of the island.

Crawford asked Harley to instruct Driscoll that no one, including the Marines, should touch any equipment belonging to the attackers. They should tape off all areas where the insurgents had been and post guards to ward off scavengers or sightseers. "Our counterterrorism specialists need to see the area as undisturbed as possible," he added.

We landed a little after dawn and were greeted by a representative of Carmaya's president. He provided us with vans. Two took the medical team and Harley to the hospital, and two drove us to a hotel, where the government had secured our rooms.

We registered, not sure what would be happening next. Three Marines—a major, warrant officer, and master sergeant—briskly entered the hotel. They introduced themselves as Major Joseph DeMarco, Mr. Shaw, and Sergeant Doll.

"Senators," Major DeMarco said, "Mr. Shaw has procured a meeting room for us just off the lobby. He has also provided light refreshments."

"Thank you, Major," Ro said.

The seven of us had slept in varied amounts; it appeared we wouldn't be getting more sleep anytime soon. Led by the three Marines, we made our way to the meeting room. Though sparsely furnished, it would serve our needs. Hot coffee and an impressive spread of food was on a side table.

"Mr. Shaw," the major spoke to the warrant officer.

"Sir?"

"Would you and Sergeant Doll help the senators and the others with their things and inspect each room?"

"Yes sir."

That caught the interest of the two counterterrorism experts. "Major, we'd like to accompany your men. We have some equipment to assist in a sweep."

Major DeMarco grinned. "Absolutely. We don't carry that kind of gear."

Frances Hartman, who was our accompanying State Department representative, excused herself to go off with the Carmayan president's emissary to handle diplomatic issues.

Ro asked, "Major, my father . . .?"

"Yes ma'am, he's on the island and in good spirits. He refused to leave."

Once we had settled at our makeshift conference table, Major DeMarco gave us an update on Rufus and the other wounded. As we listened, we ate from the opulent supply of cold cuts, chicken, vegetables, and fruits on the buffet table. The coffee was hot and strong.

When his recap concluded, Ro said, "Your Mr. Shaw seems a very capable man. This array of food is excellent."

"He is that, ma'am. He's our copter pilot, but had been a supply sergeant earlier on."

"My father was a World War II ranger, fought in Europe under the command of Harley Rogers," Ro said matter-of-factly.

The look of surprise on the major's face was priceless. "Both of them? I can see now . . . certainly understand your father's insistence to remain on the island."

Mr. Shaw returned and gave the major a thumbs-up. "Sergeant Doll and the two agents are still sweeping the rooms, sir."

"Major, what communications will we have to reach home?" Senator Crawford asked.

"I'll have satellite phones for each of you when we chopper over to the island. The general had them flown down on your plane. They're at the airport."

I was impressed. The DOD men must have brought them aboard.

"Thank you. You told us about the people on Rogers's island. Can you give us an overview of what happened?" Crawford asked.

"First, C-2's security . . ."

"C-2?" Gavin interrupted.

"Yes sir. We're on Carmaya. The Rogers people refer to where they are as C-2 and here as C-1." He looked around. There were no additional questions. "C-2's security was a stunner. The attack commenced an hour after dark. Their tight perimeter detection system picked up movement in the cove. They've had 'visitors' before, but this time their electronic sweeps picked up a group with weapons and considerable equipment.

"C-2's security includes a state-of-the-art control center in an underground bunker with dozens of monitors. They had ground-level, night-vision cameras set up to cover a no-man's area all around the compound. It's generally rocky with some low brush and a few trees. Not too many places to hide.

"The problem was that C-2's sensors were too sensitive. When the insurgents were detected moving in from the bluff toward the compound, the advance system set off warning fire. A speaker system blared first in English and then in Spanish for the intruders to stand down. Instead of compliance, the intruders answered with rocket grenades, which caused most of the damage.

"The compound had six security men. Two were in the bunker operating the communications center and the remote weaponry. The others were out at assigned posts. Their electronically controlled, small machine guns were set to sweep about a thirty-degree area. They would rise up, like in a mini-silo, do a six-second sweep, and then go back down. Then another would go up. It made C-2 security look like a small army. I wouldn't have wanted to be traversing that area."

"So," I said, "none of this was planned yesterday."

The major laughed, friendly-like. "No ma'am. The security chief said their grid had been carefully laid out two years ago for the exact purpose it was used."

"Harley is truly amazing. He knew the pharmas would come after him."

"The pharmas, ma'am?" the major asked me.

"We believe the attackers were hired by a very wealthy and powerful group, most likely a lobby organization that represents pharmaceutical companies. Ironically, the attackers did not want a fellow pharmaceutical company, Mr. Rogers's company, to manufacture his product."

"Yes ma'am, but the insurgents, they're with AMOP. That's an organization DOD uses. Are you telling me the insurgents were privately employed?"

"No. That is only something we assume," Crawford said, "but they were sent by somebody."

Major DeMarco nodded. "I understand sir, but it has always been my understanding that AMOP was a private contractor that only worked for DOD."

"That bothers me, doesn't it you?" I asked the major. "I mean, if they're friendly, what are they doing attacking the same American citizens you were sent to rescue?"

Before the major could answer, the Marine sergeant and the two counterterrorism agents came into the room and headed for the coffee and refreshments.

"Ma'am," the major said to me, "we were told the compound was friendly, occupied by American citizens, and our mission was to rescue them," Major DeMarco said, a little put off, "and to put down the attackers, no matter who they were."

"Laura makes a good point, though," Crawford said, jumping in. "You came on the island, secured it, and then discovered that the attackers may have come from DOD—what about that?"

"That's something I've already asked my general, sir," he responded, straight out. "He's looking into that as we speak."

"Mr. Maloney have you had experience with AMOP?" Crawford asked one of the two counterterrorism agents.

"Not deployed, sir," he said, as he joined us at the table. "But we've been in training where they've been represented."

We all stopped eating, as though on cue.

"I hope you are not saying that these people could have been under DOD orders?" Ro asked angrily.

"Ma'am, DOD didn't do this. Why would they?" the major asked flatly.

Crawford responded. "That is the number one question, Major."

"Yes sir. We were deployed code red under direct orders from General Towers. He didn't wait for it to go through the chain of command. Why would we have been shipped out so fast?" Major DeMarco asked firmly.

"There are a lot of elements to DOD," Crawford said. "What do you know about Black Ops? Ever had any dealings with them?"

"No sir. CIA a couple of times in Afghanistan, where we all worked as a team. I have no first-hand experience with Black Ops, or AMOP for that matter."

"The root of this has got to be Tom Kelly," I said. "Who else? Who could be so powerful . . . so willful?"

"Stanley Horowitz," Crawford offered.

"Someone well-placed and with millions that might buy him assassins, but not DOD. Who could possibly act this covertly and unilaterally?" I asked, my voice now rising.

Major DeMarco looked questioningly at me, but before I could explain further, Ro did.

"The people we believe who are behind this attack are with an organization that has a lot to lose if Tutoxtamen goes worldwide."

"Tutoxtamen, ma'am? Excuse me, but what am I missing here?"

"Tutoxtamen is the reason why we are here," Ro said, as always keeping her poised demeanor. "It is a miracle-cure cancer drug produced by Rogers Pharmaceuticals. Unfortunately, there are very powerful people who do not want Harley Rogers to produce it. They went so far as to coerce the FDA to turn down his application to manufacture it. However, Harley was a step ahead of them. That drug is being manufactured on the island you call C-2 and successfully being used in Germany to cure people of their cancer at this very moment."

"The people that turned down the drug are Americans?" Mr. Shaw asked in disbelief.

I answered. "I'm afraid so. This invasion of theirs shows how far they will go."

These sudden revelations quieted the room. I panned the group and saw a tight-jawed look on the major's face. I was going to let it pass, but then

I caught a glazed look in his eyes. Tears? I nudged Ro lightly, indicating with my eyes to look at Major DeMarco sitting across from us.

He became aware of us looking at him and tightened his jaw even more, fighting back what I was sure were tears.

"You said," the major asked precisely, obviously fighting his emotions, "this drug cures all cancers?"

I felt Ro's hand press against my side. She would take this.

"Yes, Major. The facility on C-2 is the only place in the world this wonderful drug is produced, and Germany is the only place it is being distributed."

"This is the cancer drug that was in the news recently?" he asked.

"Yes," Ro replied softly.

"I heard about it at Gitmo. I need to call my mother's doctor," his voice cracked, "I need to know if I could fly her there."

Now understanding the source of the major's grief, Ro rose from her seat saying, "She won't have to, Major." As she reached him, he stood. "Please write out your mother's and her doctor's names and contact information."

I had just experienced an awesome moment.

"Let's take a break," Gavin said, standing.

"Come, Major," Ro said. "I'd like to talk with you. May we take a little walk?"

He nodded, and they slowly went out of the room.

I looked at Michael. "He may be a tough fighting man, but he's a son first."

# 75

After our meal and meeting, we agreed to a thirty-minute break for whatever we wanted to do. I chose to go to my room for a fast shower and a change of clothes. I had brought khaki cargo pants, a light top, and running shoes. I met up with the rest of our party in the lobby, and we left for the airport.

Major DeMarco greeted us at the airport and, as promised, gave each of us a satellite phone. Mr. Shaw and Sergeant Doll issued us small knapsacks that contained bottles of water and rations. The kitchen in the compound had been destroyed. The major told us Harley Rogers would be staying at the hospital; Sherman was not doing well.

The seven of us were on board and barely strapped in when Mr. Shaw announced we were about to lift off. He also told us to put on our headsets: to save our ears and because it would be the only way we could communicate with each other while in flight.

A big roar went up from the props and we lifted off, tilting slightly left, and then turning in that direction, while also gaining altitude. In moments, we were out over crystal clear water. This was my first time in any kind of chopper, and it was a little disquieting at first . . . no wings.

Mr. Shaw announced we would ascend to six hundred feet, would pass over the island, and then do a U-turn and set down in the compound. That gave us an opportunity to see most of the island. From our side of the chopper, we didn't see the destruction until we turned around. We also saw a scattering of Marines and civilians.

"I see Johnny and Dad. Dad's arm's in a sling," Ro said excitedly, pointing.

Sure enough, the large man was standing right alongside Rufus and supporting him. "They look great," I said.

"They look beautiful," she said a little choked up.

I barely felt the landing. Once on the ground, we greeted all around.

"Miss Laura." It was Johnny.

"Johnny, you look good."

"I'm fine. Governor's got some shrapnel in him, but it ain't enough to put him down." He grinned broadly. "I got a couple of scratches, nothing much."

"Nothing, hell!" I heard Rufus say. "When that damn grenade went off and I went down, Johnny covered me with his body. Bullets were whizzing all over the damn place. Johnny got nicked. Then he picked up one of those small machine guns we'd been issued . . . shit, he blew that ass's head right off!" he said, roaring. "Clean as a whistle. That scum was one of only two who got all the way into the compound. Somebody else got the other one."

I looked at Johnny. "You are a good friend, Johnny."

He gave me a young boy's *aw-shucks* look and scuffed his foot in the dirt.

"Governor's sure glad to see Miss Roanne," he said beaming.

"She is real glad to see him too. How are things going here?"

"We started a cleanup, but just around here."

"Laura," Ro called out.

She waved for me to join her. "See you later, Johnny."

"Yes ma'am."

Ro, Gavin, Frances, and Rufus were with a man in a dark blue, tight-fitting uniform.

Rufus introduced me to the military type. "Laura, meet Chief Driscoll."

"Chief," I responded.

Driscoll gave me a very slight nod. "We all together now? We're going down into the bunker," he said bluntly.

What a grave person, I thought. We entered one of the several small buildings and went down a flight of concrete stairs. Driscoll pushed a button and a thick steel door swung open. We went in, and it closed. We were in a room that was roughly twenty by twenty-five feet.

He explained that we were under three feet of steel-reinforced concrete and six feet of earth. "You may have noticed the mound behind the building we just entered."

"This is impressive," Gavin said.

There were twenty-six video monitors on one wall. It looked very much like a military control center we might see in a war movie: a wall filled with monitors and a huge control panel. Johnny appeared on three different screens, views from different angles and distances. He was working alongside two Marines.

"Only two cameras got destroyed in the invasion," Driscoll said proudly.

"Excuse me, Chief," I interjected. "What do you rely on for stateside communications?"

"Satellite, ma'am. It's how we communicate with Mr. Rogers in New Jersey."

"Is that traceable?" Crawford asked.

"It's scrambled."

Ro asked, "What about talking to the hospital?"

"We have a handset in Mr. Rogers's room." He punched in a number, but it didn't answer. He tried again with the same results. "Let me call the hospital line."

It was answered.

"This is Driscoll on C-2; is Mr. Harley Rogers in the area?" He listened, uttered a couple of *unhuhs*, then "Right, will do." He punched off. "The new medical team that came in with you all is operating on Sherman Rogers."

"I didn't realize he was that serious," Ro said.

Rufus took her arm. "Neither did we, sweetheart. Sherman's tough, like his father. He'll pull through."

"You have done an outstanding job here, Chief," Crawford said. "You were expecting a war and you got one."

"Yes sir. Mr. Rogers told us we were here for the long haul and that someday somebody might pay us an uninvited visit."

We went topside. Rufus, for all his bravado, had to take it easy. The Marines, Johnny, and some of Rogers's employees were busy with the cleanup. I guessed the forensic men must have given them the okay.

"Building materials and construction workers are coming tomorrow," Rufus said.

Frances, Ro, and I wandered around the compound, talking to some of the Rogers people. They had experienced a harrowing night. We then walked along a packed-down roadway to the top of a slope that led down to a cove, where a white launch was tied up to a small pier.

"From what Dad told me, this is where they probably came in. Look," Ro pointed, "over there. Gavin and the DOD men."

"Looks like they're scavenging."

"Gavin plans to spend the day with them. Hopefully . . ."

"Senator," a male voice shouted. It was Mr. Shaw. "I'm making a run back to C-1 at 1130 hours. Anybody wanting to go, let me know. Also the President of Carmaya is holding a dinner tonight in honor of your and everyone else's visit."

"A dress-up? I can't . . . didn't bring . . ."

"That's all right, Laura," Ro said through a giggle, "just wear the best thing you brought."

"Yes," Frances Hartman said. "Casual is very acceptable."

I hadn't brought a "best thing." I'd figure it out later. "I'll be going back with you, Mr. Shaw."

"As will I," Frances said.

"I'll stay here with Dad."

"The governor's invited, too, ma'am."

"I'll see that he gets there."

"That might not be so easy," I teased.

Ro grinned. "I've got the Marines."

We all laughed. A welcome relief in our tension-filled day.

# 76

**F**rances had her own car and driver, so she dropped me off at the hospital. I went straightaway to find Harley, who was in the ICU.

"Ah, Laura, things are looking up. Sherman is responding fairly well. We'll know better in a couple of days."

It was lunchtime, and I gently convinced him to join me in the cafeteria. I chose a salad, a bowl of fruit, and iced tea. Harley ordered only iced tea. I told him about Senators Kelly and Pembroke, Stanley Horowitz, and the circumstances surrounding the death of Mort Stroble.

"All of this activity came about because Roanne Dalton got you interested in Tutoxtamen and the FDA's *not approvable* of my miracle drug? You seem to be very far out in front of the curve, Ms. Wolfe."

"I'm second-guessing the hell out of myself, though. It cost Mort his life."

"There is evil in the world, young lady. There was no way you could anticipate mindless cruelty, especially coming from men of stature; men who spout love of God and country; men who swear to uphold the Constitution and protect American citizens. They are the great actors on this stage we call life."

I ate. I sensed he wanted to get some things off his chest.

"I don't know where or when our country went wrong. Maybe from its inception. There were bad actors back then too. Duplicitous men make great speeches, propose great social programs, yet continue to shove the poor and uneducated to be even poorer and less educated. We are keeping people alive longer, but the sick and the elderly become more desolate and isolated. This is creating an immense underclass, to which we only give nominal attention, if any," he said, his despair evident.

"We've developed a drug that can save millions of lives, but for their own personal, evil reasons, selfish men have rejected it. Fortunately, Sherman and I saw that coming and did something about it. Now they come here and try to destroy us and, in the process, kill innocent people, maybe my son. Tom Kelly may not have pulled the trigger, but he encouraged this in all ways possible.

"I'm not faultless. We thought we had a good plan, but two of my people who believed in what we were doing here lost their lives. Others have been wounded." Sorrow draped his words.

I finished my lunch. "I'm going to visit your wounded and take a tour of the island."

"Are you going back on our plane tomorrow?" His voice was faint; he was obviously exhausted.

"Yes. There are people from DOD investigating—"

"DOD?"

"Yes. Two of the men who flew down with us yesterday are counterterrorism experts."

"Oh? Are they going to seek or hide?" he asked dryly.

"Senator Crawford's with them. He's a good guy. I wish you well with your rebuilding."

He looked away from me, his eyes damp. Even with that, I thought he was holding up remarkably well, being eighty-three years old, getting little or no sleep, and with his son's condition still critical.

I decided to switch subjects, trying to sound upbeat. "I understand we're dining with the Carmayan president."

"I appreciate your sacrifice," he said groggily, but with a wry grin and a glint in his eyes. "El Presidente means well. He's done a lot for us. But as I mentioned, our success will mean a lot to him financially. For him to have two United States senators and a Pulitzer-winning writer here . . . well, it's like a royal visit."

I asked if I could do something for him. He said no and for me to go see the island. I left him and went into the wing where the C-2 survivors were recovering. By presidential order, no media were allowed in the hospital or on C-2. No helicopters were allowed over or near C-2 either. I was traveling with diplomatic papers and a badge Frances had supplied.

I found the patients to be in good spirits, considering. One knew of me from having lived in Washington last year. The word spread fast who I was, and they all received me well. Celebrity does have its benefits.

My satellite phone rang, and I excused myself. "Laura Wolfe."

"How you doing down there?" It was Riley. "Barton wants to break this story into two reports. The stringer from Puerto Rico, Hernando Rias, should be landing there around 1:00 p.m. Barton wants you to work on the human-interest aspects and have Rias handle the war aspect."

"Sounds like a plan. I guess I'll need to sneak him onto C-2—"

"What's C-2?"

I explained. "I've been provided a car and driver. I'll meet Rias at the airport."

"Don't get too spoiled down there," he said. The line went dead.

On my trip back in the copter with Frances, I had asked her about transportation. She had gladly arranged a car and driver for me, which I could expect to be at the hospital within an hour or she'd call me. She'd reminded me to carry my diplomatic papers at all times. No media would be allowed in our hotel.

The car was waiting out front as promised, and fortunately, the driver spoke good English. I admit to being one of those Americans who expects everyone to speak my language. I had two years of Spanish in school and avoided foreign languages thereafter. Learning to be a journalist was tough enough.

I explained my plans for the afternoon, after we picked up and delivered Senor Rias. The plane was ten minutes late. I was expecting a recycled reporter, but got a thirtyish, good-looking guy about five-ten and fit. He was very respectful and didn't have a libido demeanor. I wondered what Riley had told him about me.

I filled Rias in on the lay of the land and about the media restrictions. I got him registered and was about to call the Marines when Mr. Shaw and Sergeant Doll entered the lobby. I introduced Rias and explained his presence.

"Because he's one of yours, Ms. Wolfe," the warrant officer nodded, "he can ride out to C-2 on our next run."

"Would you ask Chief Driscoll to show Mr. Rias around and give him a verbal picture of how the fighting went? Hernando, not a word to anyone. I'll be back by 5:00. Eh, Mr. Shaw, would you see that he gets back in the hotel?"

"Yes ma'am."

I thought he was going to salute, his reply was so snappily given. My driver became a tour guide. He chose the perimeter road. The map of the island showed it was about twice the size of the original Washington, DC, roughly two hundred square miles. The trip along the coastline was lovely, and we stopped at vantage points where my guide pointed out places of interest while giving me some island history. The coast was cliffs and rocky beaches on one side and long, flowing, white sandy beaches on the other.

Along the way, I called Riley and told him I'd sent Hernando off with the Marines.

"He's supposed to have something in to me tonight, to run tomorrow."

"The State Department person with us said a TV network complained about my having access and they didn't."

"We got a call, too. We told them you were a friend of the family."

That hit my funny bone and I roared. Riley hadn't impressed me with a sense of humor. My driver almost ran off the road. We finished our tour, and I was back in the hotel early enough to buy a bathing suit and relax in the outside hot tub.

Crawford arrived a few minutes late to the dinner, coming in with the major. He profusely apologized to El Presidente—E.P. as we now referred to him amongst ourselves. E.P. was effusive in his pleasure of having two United States senators on his island. Gavin took his place with Ro at the head table.

Down the table, I sat to Gavin's left, and then Michael, Frances, and Major DeMarco. Across from us, after Ro was Harley, Rufus, and a member of E.P.'s staff. Our terrorism specialists were not present. A few Carmayans sat at a nearby table, looking very official.

The lavish dinner went very well. The food was delicious and plentiful.

Afterward, people spread out into groups. I noticed that E.P. followed Ro everywhere she went. She was aware of it, but gracious, and then she pulled a beautiful maneuver, joining Rufus and Harley and making room for E.P. The two former Rangers regaled him with stories of their exploits. The three got into man-talk, and Ro slipped away.

Michael was telling me about his day on C-2. Frances was sitting with the Carmayans. I saw that Crawford had joined the three men. The cigars were out. I'd lost track of Ro. Michael and I speculated on what might be going on in Washington.

I felt restless and decided to go for a short walk; Michael declined. The evening was pleasant. Most of the tourists appeared to be Europeans. I did know they weren't speaking English. The hotel was beautifully landscaped. I walked past the swimming pool and tennis courts. It was balmy, and I wished Jerry was with me. I hoped to catch Ro before I turned in.

Then it hit me: I had forgotten about Hernando. I rushed to the lobby and called his room. Fortunately, he had called room service for a meal. He came right down, and we went off to the meeting room our group had used earlier. He showed me what he'd written. He had a good account of what took place from Chief Driscoll. We went over his story. Riley was probably biting his nails.

I had Hernando take out names, replacing them with our typical "sources" or "a senior security person" or "government official." He was okay with that. He had covered the action well. I suggested he might mention Sherman Rogers's condition and that the other wounded were recovering in the hospital and would soon be returning to work or going back to the States. He had mentioned that the bodies of Rogers's two employees killed during the assault had already been flown back on a Caribbean charter.

Hernando had included Rogers's rebuilding plans. His story was a keeper. This would let the bad people know they were wanted for murder— and that rebuilding had commenced.

No mention was made of the bunkers and electronic surveillance. You never know when somebody might want to make another run at Rogers's facility. Rias went off to edit and rewrite. He would then fax it to Riley, who I knew would call me if he had questions.

I walked outside and called Jerry. He had just put Tyler down.

"He's about to walk on his own, Babe, you better hurry home."

He was teasing, but I'd hate to miss that first step. "We're flying out midmorning. A cargo plane will be coming in later tomorrow filled with lumber, carpenters, and building materials. I should be home by dinner."

"They're wasting no time, are they?"

"No. Fortunately, the processing equipment was deep underground." I was aimlessly wandering as we talked when I saw Ro walking with the major. I ducked behind some bushes. *Well, well,* I thought. "Look, hon, I've got to get off in case Riley has any questions for me on Hernando's article. Love you."

"Love you, too. I'll meet you at Andrews."

I peeked around the corner, but didn't see Ro and the major. I went into the banquet room and saw them there with Crawford. I strolled toward them.

Ro spotted me. "Oh, there you are. I thought maybe you'd gone to bed."

"After I played editor to our reporter, I went for a walk and checked in at home."

"Well," she almost gushed, "we have a lot to talk about tomorrow. We've also made special arrangements for Joe's mother."

*Joe? My, things are progressing,* I thought.

"Her doctor said she's more able to travel than we thought," Major Joe added. "Mr. Rogers's doctors will treat her here. He's taking personal charge of her care."

I smiled. "How long will you all be here?"

"General wants things shipshape. Maybe a week, a little more."

"You'll get to see your mother?"

"Yes ma'am," was his upbeat reply.

Ro smiled.

O ur morning flight out of Carmaya was moved up to 7:30. With a stop in San Juan for refueling, it was expected that we'd arrive at Andrews around 3:30 in the afternoon.

The *Star* was headline news on the Internet. Rias was getting his fifteen minutes of fame. He was also quoted in interviews he'd done on CNN and Fox. Editor Riley had called me after reading Rias's piece, which he begrudgingly thought was pretty good. "How much of this was you?"

"Very little. I framed it as you asked, making sure he wasn't giving anything away."

"Barton freed the guy to do the interviews on only what he wrote. No speculations. We'll leave that to you," Riley said sarcastically.

I had an adrenaline spike, but he was right. "He's a good man, Riley. The Marine major told me Rias was very businesslike on C-2. He got the blow-by-blow from Rogers's chief of security, who walked him around the island."

"The story's gonna kick ass. Who you going after when you get back?"

"We've got the audio tapes. I'm waiting on MPD."

"I'll tell you one thing, Barton's strategy to use Rias and keep you out of it will pay off. We're saying he's a freelancer, one we'd used before, but that he did this on his own and offered it to us. It keeps you out of it completely."

I agreed Barton's decision was brilliant. "Maybe Rias could do a follow-up with Harley on the company's plans, and then do a piece on Sherman Rogers."

"Don't you think you could get more out of the old man than Rias could?"

He had a point there. "Okay. Rias could do a piece on casualties."

"I like that better. When do we see you?"

"Day after tomorrow. One thing, though. Harley told me he and El Presidente are about to open a Carmayan cancer treatment center, converting a four-hundred-room hotel into a residence for the patients and family members. Harley will open a website on how patients can apply, along with PDF forms for the patient and his or her doctor to complete. The severest cases will be taken first. Carmaya can't handle thousands flocking in; there'd be no place for them.

"The hospital can only dedicate about fifty beds to the sickest. It will be mostly a large outpatient operation. The Germans, on the other hand, can take upwards of twelve hundred right now, and can expand. Harley has oncologists, surgeons, nurses, and volunteers lined up for Carmaya. Two teams flew in with their cargo plane this morning."

"That sounds like an article for tomorrow's paper," he said.

"Fine with me. Where's Claire on this? Does she have a handle on the corruption angle?"

"She'll report on how the Senate is handling revelations with the discovery of the German hospital, meaning you've got the corruption, conspiracy, and the murder. The rest of the media doesn't know about Kelly and Pembroke, so they are all yours. Those tapes of yours are going to seal their fate."

"When MPD and the FBI let me go public with them. In the meantime, Kelly will put the blame on the FDA scientists, while spraying himself with Teflon."

"Yeah, he may deflect, but you've got the right ammo."

"For one, we have that FDA guy, Kelso, who Stroble gave up. Captain Walsh told me that the FBI has him under surveillance. They're also investigating a driving accident that killed one of the top FDA people working on Tutox a few weeks back. Because we know the pharmas won't stop at murder, Kelso could be a target. There's a lot happening, Riley. Maybe when law enforcement is ready to move, we should have our science reporter primed. Maybe I should talk to him or—"

"Her. Grace Herman. She and I've already talked. Yeah, you two should spend some time together ASAP."

"Great. Reed Davis, the FBI SAC, would be her prime contact there. I'd like her to keep me in the loop before—"

"I'll take care of that," Riley interrupted. "Everything on this goes through me."

"Good. The guy could spook if he thought he was a target."

"She's been around," he said sharply.

"I'm sure she's great. Has she ever been involved in a murder investigation?"

He didn't answer. I waited. "I'll talk to her," he said less argumentatively.

"Once the FBI moves in on him—"

"You brief her, and I'll handle the rest."

As gruff as Riley acted, I found him easy after Lassiter.

The steward put out some snacks and drinks after the captain announced our corporate jet had reached cruising altitude. I helped myself to coffee and a bran muffin. Ro, Michael, Gavin, and I convened at the mini conference table. Rufus was staying on C-1 to coordinate the Carmayan hospital staff, the Rogers medical people, and the upcoming expansion.

"Dad'll be chief of operations," Ro said cheerily. "Dad said Johnny's having the time of his life and making friends. Nobody knows his background, and they accept him as he is. Dad's worried he might not get him back."

That was a feel-good story that should never be written. Johnny's past belonged buried.

"Who's going to start?" Ro looked at the three of us.

I opened. "How about what Gavin and his two assistants uncovered?"

Crawford laughed. "That should be the other way around."

"Well, you three did find some interesting stuff, right?"

"Maloney and Trautman are good. I looked over their shoulders. We went through every piece of the invaders' equipment. The biggest trove was in the three rubber rafts."

"The ones that were in the cove?" I asked.

He nodded. "We suspect they were dropped off and that the mother ship remained close for a quick retrieval. We requested DOD do a satellite search for powerboats within a fifty-mile radius of Carmaya. We found a recent satellite map of C-2 in one of the rafts. It showed the compound. I asked Mr. Shaw to check the tourism office about maps of the archipelago. He found none that had any detail. They were crude and not to scale."

I looked at Crawford. "Aren't satellite photos something DOD does?"

"The National Geospatial Intelligence Agency, actually—a subset of DOD. However, their stuff is not for private consumption. There are private companies with satellites, and Major DeMarco has requested that DOD check them out."

I was surprised to hear of professionals making those kinds of mistakes. "For a precision operation that included great detail, it seems awfully sloppy for the map to be so easily found."

"I don't expect they thought they'd lose," Ro said softly.

I smiled. "Highly trained military types are trained not to overlook the small things."

"Do I smell a conspiracy?" Michael asked animatedly.

That created a spontaneous laugh from all.

Crawford went on. "Maloney thought the map should have been destroyed. He was sure the assault team had the layout memorized. He and Trautman are doing a re-creation today. They have two distinct scenarios, but didn't share them with me. We'll get to see them after the fact."

"Okay," I said. "A combat team and satellite maps takes some doing. The Marines on Gitmo didn't have time to get one."

"Right. The attackers planned to be in and out fast," Michael said enthusiastically. "Like a quick extraction . . . that sort of thing."

Ro was intent. "But how did they get to that point so fast?"

Michael replied, "Maybe the pharmas had a spy in Rogers."

I nodded. "Good point. Harley was covert about his plans here and in Germany. However, Captain Walsh told me the FBI has a wire tap on Horowitz and picked up him saying that he knew, not suspected, that Rogers was up to something."

Ro said, "Try this. The attack was planned before the German news came out, which was a huge surprise to the pharmas. Maybe they knew about Carmaya and had already planned to destroy the facility, but were unaware of the German operation. When the *Star* broke the story, their plans were escalated and things were overlooked."

I liked that. "That's highly possible." I felt our group intensity growing. "This, however, is not a cut-and-dry case. We have to check up on everyone."

Ro smiled. "I think your serial-killer investigation proves that point."

I appreciated that. "We need to research Tutox, Kelly, Pembroke, and the others . . . hold on. I just realized I'm always saying Kelly, Pembroke, and the others. Who are the others?"

# 78

We arrived at Andrews a little after 4:00, slowed by a large storm over the Atlantic. It seems Crawford's intelligence on the satellite map and AMOP attracted considerable Pentagon attention. By the time we landed, a meeting had already been scheduled for 10:00 the next morning at the Pentagon. When Ro and Crawford had received that message while we were airborne, they had both insisted I be allowed to attend with them. The reluctant general, after some grumblings, had finally acquiesced.

Jerry was waiting for me at Andrews along with a large passenger van from General Services. We took Ro and Crawford in our car. Michael and five Rogers employees went with the van. Jerry had brought copies of *The New York Times*, *Washington Post*, and *Washington Daily Star*. *The Times* was a little reserved in its reporting; they had no reporter on Carmaya. The *Post* gave a paltry six inches on page one before jumping deep into the A section. Their slant was mostly on Senate reaction. They had not interviewed anyone at the FDA.

The *Star* gave headline treatment to Rias's exclusive story. Riley added a sidebar on the American patients clamoring to get to the German and Carmayan cancer centers. The State Department had asked the media to warn people not to go to Carmaya independently—that Rogers Pharmaceuticals was providing forms on its website for applications. The tiny island of Carmaya could not service hordes of patients, and those disregarding this request would be turned around at the airport and sent home.

Riley promoted that the *Star* would have more in-depth coverage in tomorrow's paper regarding plans for the treatment center and Tutox, as well as more details on the island assault. One would be the piece I had finished on the flight. I'd fax it to Riley as soon I got home. I also posed a question to him: Had there been any comment from the American Cancer Society?

# 79

I got up early the next morning to have time to play with Tyler.

The Washington Daily Star was carrying two major stories on Carmaya: Rias's and mine. Jerry had the Today show on, and they were reporting that Senator Dalton had been in Carmaya because her father had been a casualty in the attack. NBC had wanted to talk with Senator Dalton, but she was not available. That must have been Michael's doing.

Neither Rias's nor my story had anything about Rufus, yet one reporter had found him helping at the hospital. Rufus hadn't gone on camera, but did say that he and Harley Rogers were lifelong friends and that he had been visiting, doing some fishing and diving, and had been with Sherman Rogers at the time of the attack.

Jerry clicked the remote with great dexterity, hitting all the networks. Our articles were a subject of much discussion and speculation. Nobody had tied the US Senate into any of this. Any mentions of Tutoxtamen were relative to the FDA's rejection of the drug and Travis's report about the positive results of the drug in Germany.

The networks and cable news had many different guesses as to what came first: the Germans, Carmayans, or Rogers. That showed how little homework any of the media had done. The FDA's only statement was that it would not be making one because the product and the treatments were outside the United States.

Lassiter called, knowing I would be going directly to the Pentagon. CNN had interviewed Travis, and she had a tape of it. The CNN reporter had tried to tie the German drug to Rogers, but Travis only had knowledge that a German pharmaceutical company was behind the clinic outside Frankfurt. He knew nothing about Rogers Pharmaceuticals in the States.

Lassiter said there had been several requests to interview me. Basically, they wanted to know why I had been in Carmaya. She had turned them all down.

Most media reports assumed that Rogers was involved in the German clinic. Travis had not reported that. However, no reports went so far as to say Rogers was manufacturing and shipping Tutoxtamen to Germany. They assumed that the recently constructed offshore facility, which had been attacked by unknown assailants—unknown to the media at least—was, in all likelihood, a processing plant. Some suspected terrorism, but hadn't a clue about who was behind it. One talking head on Fox wondered why anyone would deliberately want to destroy a drug that every cancer patient could use.

Ro called me at 8:15, asking that I go to the Pentagon's north gate. "Bring your diplomatic papers, if you still—"

"They're in my work bag."

"Good. I talked to Dad. Things are looking up for Sherman."

"That's great. Some TV reporter quoted your dad. He wouldn't go on camera."

"I haven't been watching. Michael and I were in here before 7:00 on other matters."

"We're media hounds in our house. Jerry's been expertly exercising the remote."

I heard her chuckle. "Dad, Major DeMarco, and Chief Driscoll will be in the communications bunker and hooked up to the Pentagon. Driscoll worked the satellite pictures down to the day after Dad arrived in Carmaya."

"We know your Dad's not the mole."

"He said his plane stopped at Bridgetown, Barbados, and then flew on to Carmaya. I know he and Johnny would have never thought about being covert."

"I'm sure," I said. "Let me extrapolate, though. Suppose the pharmas had found the Rogers island by following your father. That was no more than a week before they attacked."

"Coincidently, the day your paper broke the German story," she acknowledged.

"If they had tracked Rufus, they had their own jet and would have landed in Barbados too. We need flight plans of planes taking that same route as your Dad on that same day. The jet might also have had to refuel.

"Is that something you can get from the FAA?" Ro asked. "Somebody from that plane . . . we need Driscoll to interview all Rogers employees, and somebody should talk to the wounded who have already returned to New Jersey. Maybe somebody making like a tourist visited that heretofore uninhabited archipelago, known for its excellent SCUBA diving, a few days before the attack."

"I see why you're so good at what you do. You're saying someone went out to C-2?"

"Yes, and that tells me they most likely rented a boat." My brain was racing, searching for other options. "Another job for the Marines," I said. "Maybe the major could ask Harley about contacting the New Jersey returnees."

"I'll suggest that to him," she answered quickly.

I thought I heard a soft edge of excitement in Ro's voice.

# 80

Ro and a Marine lieutenant colonel met me at the Pentagon's north entrance. My driver's license, the diplomatic papers from Carmaya, and my high-level assistance moved me briskly through security.

We walked around the outer ring made up of five seventy-two–degree turns. We were ushered through a door by the officer. Gavin, Michael, a male two-star Marine general, a female bird colonel, and a man and woman in civilian clothes stood to greet us.

"Senator Dalton, Ms. Wolfe, welcome," the general said, indicating two chairs between Crawford and Michael. Ro indicated I sit next to Crawford. The general sat in the middle across from us. The colonel and two civilians were to his right, the lieutenant colonel to his left.

"There's coffee and some hot water for tea," he said. His nameplate read *Towers*. "Senator, Ms. Wolfe, please meet Colonel Sholander from my staff; Ted Schmitt, FBI counterterrorism; and Cynthia Wright, CIA analyst." We all nodded to each other. "Senator Crawford and Major DeMarco have been in continued contact with me or Colonel Sholander. To say the least, this is a very unusual set of circumstances. However, with a mixture of intelligences we are beginning . . ."

I had a feeling he was going to ramble over stuff we already knew. I speculated that if the two Senators had not been in the thick of this, the incident would not have been taking up any of the DOD's precious time. State would have treated it as a diplomatic issue.

". . . the most disturbing circumstance is that AMOP, a contractor to DOD, is alleged to have been involved. The FBI has new information." The general looked at Agent Schmitt.

"Thank you, General." Schmitt then addressed us. "None of the six insurgents is an American citizen. Interpol has identified two of the dead as being eastern Europeans. Both were known as highly trained mercenaries used for this type of mission. The Carmayan police provided us with photos, fingerprints, and DNA of the perpetrators. Of the two still alive, we have positively ID'd only one."

Colonel Sholander spoke next. "Both of those wounded men remain under Marine guard and will be moved to Gitmo when they are able to travel. Interrogation will begin as soon as we secure interpreters."

General Towers followed. "The president of AMOP came in earlier this morning. He is still undergoing heavy questioning. I was with them before coming here. He swears AMOP did not hire out to anyone, and he emphatically stated that they do not use foreign personnel. They claim all of their people are former American Special Forces operatives from the various branches, now making ten times what they made when they were in the service."

I noticed a bit of disgust in his tone. This type of minutia could go on forever. It's important to the FBI, DIA, CIA, and the Marines, but not to what we needed right now. I took a breath and jumped in.

"Excuse me, General Towers. For the sake of brevity, can we assume AMOP's clean, that there is no DOD complicity, and that these mercenaries were hired and armed by an outside group?"

There was considerable shuffling in chairs, but not from our side of the table. A look on the three faces opposite me showed disdain for my interruption, but none answered. I asked, "Who has the ability, the knowledge, and the experience to be able to put well-equipped, combat-ready men on Carmaya, replete with a recent satellite photo of the island? Not of C-1, but C-2."

Now I saw furrowed brows.

"We," and I indicated my side of the table, "are extremely interested in knowing who was behind the assault. It is of the utmost importance we know who did this."

Agent Schmitt answered. "We have no leads."

"The six were delivered to C-2 after dark, and no one knows how?"

"We assume by boat, but we don't know that," Schmitt said flatly.

"We saw the rafts. Where did they come from?"

I looked at Crawford, who nodded and said, "As you know, General, the DOD's antiterrorism agents, Maloney and Trautman, are making a final re-creation on this matter today. They will be submitting their findings to you, but I'll give you a preview of what will be in their report because some things need immediate attention. The insurgents were dropped off from a mother ship, type undetermined as of now.

"Their equipment included explosives with timing devices. Here's how Maloney and Trautman unofficially have restructured the assault team's intent, collected from items the insurgents brought with them. Their plan was stealth—secure the compound and isolate all the residents away from what was going to be blown up, and then set their explosives and timers.

"Four would evacuate the island immediately upon completing those objectives, join the mother ship, and power out of there, leaving two men and one raft on the island. Those two would remain to ensure everything went as planned, which included guarding their prisoners. Maloney guesstimated that the timers would have been set to go off around three hours after the mother ship had departed."

Everyone across the table was taking notes.

"It is assumed that the mother ship might then have docked in the Carmayan harbor or gone on to nearby Trinidad or South America. On C-2, the explosives would have been placed at each of the five levels of the processing plant, one each in the smaller buildings, and two in the main building. This design came from the marked up satellite maps we found in one of the rafts.

"This is the linchpin. One raft contained two wet suits, tanks, and fins. When it was close to time for the explosives to blow, they would make a rapid departure in this raft. By the time all the bombs had detonated, they would certainly have been in the cove or farther out.

"We figured they were to row as close to the main island as they felt was safe. They'd alert the mother ship, assuming she had been docked in the Carmayan marina, and scuttle the raft, sinking everything. Then they'd board the mother ship, and no one in the marina or on shore would be the wiser." He sat back.

"Harley Rogers," Ro said, "literally and figuratively blew their plan to smithereens, but at the same time brought tragedy to his own people. When C-2 security was alerted to infiltrators, Chief Driscoll put his technology to work. Once he determined the intruders were up to no good, he activated his remote sensors, which set off intermittent bursts of ground fire."

Crawford again. "The invaders withdrew, regrouped, and retrieved heavier weaponry they'd brought as backup and attacked, firing rocket grenades and machine guns. There were hundreds of bullet holes in the buildings."

"General," Ro said, "I believe it's time to contact C-2."

*The general was not in command at the moment, Ro was,* I thought. He picked up a black handset and spoke quietly, then hung up. His demeanor had softened considerably.

"That must be a multimillion-dollar operation they have down there," General Towers commented, "to have two-way video capabilities, robotics . . . they'll be coming up on that screen." He indicated a twenty-foot wide, white screen sliding down into place at one end of the table. Some flashes streaked across it, and then the picture locked in, and there sat Major DeMarco and Chief Driscoll in a two-shot side-by-side.

I glanced at Ro, who was staring at the screen.

"Major DeMarco," the general demanded forcefully.

"Yes sir, General, you're coming in five-by-five."

The camera aimed at us was elevated and at the foot of the table. There was a monitor to show us what it captured of us. Michael and Ro backed up their chairs so that Crawford and I would be clearly in the picture.

Towers spoke. "You know everyone except the two to your left: CIA analyst Wright and FBI Special Agent Schmitt."

"Thank you, sir. Governor McAllister will be with us momentarily."

Ro spoke, "Major DeMarco, Senator Dalton."

"Senator."

As hard as I tried, I couldn't detect anything personal in their salutations.

"Do you have something on boats for us?"

There was a stirring by the government folks.

"Yes ma'am." The major looked off camera. "Oh, Governor McAllister has arrived."

The picture on the screen widened to include Rufus sliding in next to Major DeMarco.

"Ro, you there?" Rufus asked.

"We're all on camera."

"Oh yeah, I see that. Hey, Laura, you were right on the nose about me being tailed."

That created a startled rustling around the table.

"I'm all ears, Rufus."

He laughed. "More brains, if you ask me. Anyhow, a private jet came in about five minutes after us. They must have picked us up in San Juan. We landed in Bridgetown, Barbados, for passengers and fuel. We now know a private jet had landed ahead of us in Barbados and had followed us out by about eight minutes to Carmaya.

"They must have had somebody on the ground, because Johnny and I hit the tarmac and boarded a passenger van waiting on us. As soon as our bags were on board, three minutes tops, we were headed to the marina, where we hopped on Harley's launch and took right off.

"Somehow they tracked us. We've learned that one of the couples working for Harley on C-2 had been taking a walk along the bluff above the north cove, where folks there like to swim. Two men dressed in slacks, short-sleeved shirts, and city shoes came up from the dock. They were cordial and wondered about the fishing and diving, and said they didn't realize people lived on the island.

"Fortunately, Harley had trained his people well, and they told the men they were working for an oceanic research company on potential food supplies for human consumption. The men thought that to be a wonderful project and moved on. The couple didn't see them again. It was about two hours to dark. Chief Driscoll will tell you about the harbor."

"Good morning."

We all replied in kind.

"The harbor master says two men rented a powerboat built for speed and brought it back at dusk. It went out empty and came back empty. He figured they were out joyriding. They stayed at the Hilton. We're checking with retailers to see where they spent any money."

I saw a look of satisfaction on General Towers's face. He may not have wanted to become involved in this low priority operation, but he appeared to appreciate what he was hearing. His comrades around the table seemed to feel the same. "Rufus, Chief Driscoll, that's excellent. What about their jet?"

Driscoll said. "It had refueled and waited for the men to return. They went aboard, but after an hour, they came out and went to the hotel. The plane then took off."

Ro asked, "But both men stayed; the reservation wasn't a ruse?"

"According to the hotel, they both had breakfast there the next morning," Driscoll answered.

Crawford asked, "Where did the plane go?"

Driscoll replied, "San Juan, according to their flight plan."

"Governor, this is General Towers, good to see you so chipper."

"Thank you, General. Harley's folks are taking good care of me."

"Do you have that private jet's tail numbers?"

A look of disgust came over Rufus's face. "Dang. I'll get it for you."

"How long did the two men stay on the island?" I asked.

Driscoll picked up on that. "They checked out the day of the attack. They didn't fly out. They may still be on C-1. We lost track of them."

I knew what that meant. "Maybe they were waiting for their boat to come in."

A look of excitement showed on Rufus's face. "The damn invaders' boat, right?"

"We believe the 'mother ship' was a yacht—a party boat. Great cover," Crawford said. "Chief, do you have anything on what you and I discussed?"

"I came up with three possibilities, Senator. One, a small yacht. A second craft, which left the next morning for Aruba, and was boarded there. It had a crew of three and two elderly couples."

"What's happening with the yacht and the third boat?" I asked.

Rufus answered. "They're both still in the harbor and in El Presidente's hands, Laura."

"How can he prevent them from leaving?"

"He's a resourceful guy. He quarantined the harbor, claiming there'd been report of a citrus virus. Each boat has been or will be boarded and thoroughly gone over. Arriving boats will be sent to a cove five miles south of here to anchor and wait, or move on."

"What's he going to do after the search, send in the Marines?" I asked flippantly.

There was laughter all around, except from General Towers. "Major?"

"Whoa, I was only kidding, General."

"This is being handled as a local government matter, sir," Major DeMarco answered sharply.

"Good. Any ideas about what you all just heard?" Towers asked.

"The Carmayan government could ask for assistance," CIA analyst Wright offered.

"I think that's best. It could then be handled by State," Ro said.

"Maybe we let the party boat go and track it," I said. "I'm sure we have the technical ability to do that, don't we?" I looked at the two civilians across from me.

"That could be arranged," Wright replied.

"Sounds like a winner," Rufus said. "Let me know when to tell El Presidente."

# 81

Our Pentagon meeting wrapped up, and we prepared to leave when word reached General Towers that the yacht was American-owned . . . out of Charleston, South Carolina. I hoped that might be the one. As we were saying our goodbyes, Towers complimented the senators on how focused we all had been. He would report to the SECDEF and proceed accordingly, which means that the Defense Department would confer with the State Department on how to handle the yacht still sitting in Carmaya's harbor.

Ro, Michael, and I rode into DC with Crawford, the only one of us with a vehicle. As we neared the *Star*, I knew I needed to put Carmaya behind me and concentrate on the Senate. We'd been gone less than forty-eight hours, yet it seemed like a month.

"Do we know if Senator Pembroke has resigned the chairmanship?"

"Not that I've heard, Laura," Gavin said.

"I expect the FBI is close to indicting some folks. I know Captain Walsh is anxious to wrap up Mort's case," I said, partly to bring this subject back into everyone's focus.

"I'll be following up with Dad on Carmaya."

Crawford added, "I'll keep up with the DOD."

When they dropped me off, I was feeling a special kinship with my three partners and hoped it was mutual.

Everybody seemed to want a piece of me the moment I walked into the newsroom. I met with Grace Herman and talked with Claire Rowley. I met with Barton and Riley, and saw Lassiter for a minute. When I finally was able to sit at my desk, it was nearly 3:00, and I hadn't talked to Max. I called him.

"Well, how was Treasure Island?"

"This treasure was a pharmaceutical processing plant for Tutoxtamen."

"How was the fishing?"

"Rufus McAllister will have to tell you all about that."

Max grunted. "Don't bother, I couldn't tolerate the long ride down and back."

"The attackers were foreign mercenaries, most likely eastern Europeans, according to CIA and Interpol. It's fairly certain they came from a yacht that is now being held in the Carmayan harbor by the Carmayan government."

"War is getting classier all the time," Max teased.

"What's happening here?"

"It's unglamorous, but steady. The PI is still in Miami, but has had no known contact with H. Don't have anything new on the Hill people."

Horowitz would have layers of intermediaries between him and the PI. "Have you talked with the Mort girl?"

"The young lady is an innocent. Did you know she worked in H's law firm? A female lawyer there was her handler, who we're now observing."

I hadn't known that. "When you talk to Reed, would you ask if he knows a Ted Schmitt, an FBI counterterrorism agent? He was at our morning meeting at the Pentagon. By the way, we'll be on *Scalawag* this weekend."

"I'll call you."

We said our goodbyes. My office phone rang. "Laura Wolfe."

"It's Michael. How's your day going?"

"Too many meetings. Captain Walsh told me Tina is a person of interest, but on the low end. Did you know she worked in Horowitz's firm?"

"No. I called to tell you to put fresh batteries in your tape machine."

"I always have an extra pair, why?"

"Senator Crawford just called us; Senator Pembroke is resigning his chairmanship at the end of the day tomorrow." He let that hang.

"And . . ."

"Senator Pembroke wants to tell his story to you before the dam breaks."

"Wow. When and where?"

"Senator Crawford's office tomorrow at 3:00."

"Any strings?"

"None were mentioned."

"I'll be there." We signed off, and I sat for a moment reflecting on Crawford's comments about his earlier meeting with Pembroke. Then I gathered my notes and headed to Lassiter's office. Even though she was not technically my editor on the Senate story, she was very much involved in Mort's murder. But the truth be known, I wanted her reactions and advice to everything I'd been doing. In my heart, she was still my editor.

"How was the trip?" she asked, as I walked in. "Was it worth the time?"

"Very much." I didn't start with that, though; I told her about Pembroke first.

"You're right in the middle again. Any embargoes?"

"None were mentioned. I'd like to run something by you." I gave her my thoughts on the ramifications of what I saw as coming down in the Senate.

Without comment on my remarks, she said, "We better go see Barton and Riley."

The two men were captivated and pleased at having the exclusive on Pembroke. Resigning a Senate chairmanship is news, but what was contained underneath that decision was very obviously the bigger story.

"Has he been approached by the authorities?" Barton asked.

"Not as of an hour ago when I talked to Captain Walsh."

"Get his mea culpa," Riley said. "Let's see what he says; maybe that'll give us a clue about how to proceed."

Lassiter said, "Developing a headline story is one thing, acting on it is another. Pembroke hasn't been charged by MPD or the FBI. I think Laura should pass this by Captain Walsh."

I smiled to myself. Lassiter knew how I worked, and Riley didn't.

Riley was scowling. "Could he be planning a vanishing act?"

"No," I said. "From what little I know of him, I believe he'll stay and humble himself before his peers and family. I believe he wants to write his own obituary. Get his words out there before others do that for him."

# 82

I was at my desk finishing a light lunch when Max called. He told me Reed Davis had talked to the counterterrorism agent I'd met at the Pentagon. They believed the attack had to have been in the works for several weeks. That said to me that the pharmas had a mole inside Rogers Pharmaceuticals.

"They must have a deep mole inside Rogers to know those plans," I said. "Harley told us he had begun his alternative plan three years ago; at the time the pharmas wanted to broker a deal with him to reduce the cure to focus on a single form of cancer.

"Even though he faked cooperation by establishing a parallel program to produce a single cancer cure drug, he didn't trust the pharmas and had planned accordingly. I don't believe he thought his subterfuge would work for long, but it did buy him some time to set up his offshore processing plant.

"According to Rufus, the offshore plant's construction was a tightly held secret . . . yet the pharmas were ready weeks in advance of the drug's rejection to attack and destroy that processing plant."

Max said, "Well, as you were speaking just now, Delia brought me a message from Reed that the Carmayan government, who had taken charge of the yacht, has now turned it over to our Marines. A destroyer, the *USS Gregory*, will be escorting the yacht to Gitmo. Two civilian males on the yacht were transferred to the destroyer's brig."

"What about the babes?"

"It seems their sunbathing was a distraction for the healthy American males, so they were restricted to below decks on the yacht, clothed."

"Our Carmayan contingent believes those two civilians are the ones who tailed Rufus from Puerto Rico," I said. "However, their involvement in the attack doesn't fit with everything else we now know." I made a note to ask Crawford to be sure the interrogators pursued that.

Max snickered. "It is always disturbing when you have a pat hand you thought was a royal flush, but turns out to be only an ace high flush."

I hated to think Max could be right. "Switching to the home front, Senator Pembroke has requested through Senator Crawford that I take down his side of the story tomorrow at 3:00, before he meets with Senator Kelly at 5:00 to resign the chairmanship of HELP. The Senate officially begins its summer break at the close of business tomorrow, making it unlikely any announcement will be forthcoming until after the weekend. My overriding concern, though, is what Pembroke will tell Kelly, and if he'll play the Mort tape to the majority leader?"

"That would alter dynamics considerably. I best call Reed," Max said, hanging up.

I called Barton's office and asked if I could see him.

When I arrived, Riley was in with Barton. I filled them in, right up to and including Max's call to Reed Davis.

"We'll need someone at Gitmo," Barton told Riley. "Alert Claire to Laura's session with Pembroke. Make sure she understands why it is happening the way it is."

"I doubt either Kelly or Pembroke will go public right away, but could she hang close to the majority leader just in case? We don't have a handle on what Senator Pembroke is going to tell the majority leader . . . namely about the Mort tape."

"Ouch, I see your point," Riley said. "That could be huge."

"What's your guess, Laura?" Barton asked. "Will he or won't he?"

"Won't, sir. I think he'll blame his health." I didn't want to get into a speculation game.

"I'll go to Senator Dalton's office after the interview. Senator Crawford will hang out at the majority leader's office while Pembroke is in with Kelly . . . to be there for whatever happens."

"Thank you, Laura," Barton said, standing.

He seemed pleased.

# 83

A fter Jerry went to work and Anna had Tyler, I began organizing myself for the Pembroke interview. I called Ro's office and was passed through to her immediately.

"Good morning," she said cheerfully.

"Hi. I'm at home until I go to Gavin's office at 3:00. I expect to be finished by 4:30, give or take, and I'll join you after that, if that's still okay. Did Michael mention his and my conversation from yesterday?"

"Yes. I talked to Dad last night. He told me Harley's flying Sherman to a New York City hospital for better care, but Dad's staying in Carmaya. Did you know that the Carmayan government commandeered the yacht, and then turned it over to our Marines?"

I forgot to call her about that. I faked it. "That's good news. Is the major's mother there?"

"Got in early yesterday. They put a medical team on her immediately."

"That's a wonderful thing you and Harley did for—"

"I did very little. Once Harley knew about her, he took over. A private medical air service got her and a nurse to Miami. A charter service then flew them both to Carmaya. The nurse will stay with Mrs. DeMarco for a while."

"That must have been a wonderful reunion between mother and son."

"I'm sure," she said wistfully.

"I'll let you go. See you later." A moment after I hung up, Mary buzzed.

"FBI Agent Davis asked if you would call his cell phone."

"Thanks." I placed the call.

"Special Agent Davis."

"Reed, Laura."

"Hi. Our people at Gitmo, using translators, have interviewed the two wounded mercenaries individually. On the yacht, a man running the operation had shown all of them photographs of Harley and Sherman Rogers, giving them instructions to kill both, even though their primary objective was to just blow up the place."

"Senator Dalton told me two minutes ago that Harley's flying Sherman to a New York City hospital sometime today. Could he be in danger?"

"There is always that possibility. I'll contact our New York field office."

"Back to the yacht, have you learned anything from its crew? Or the women?"

"It gets to Gitmo tomorrow. We'll fly the women to Miami to be interviewed. I doubt they know anything about the boat's mission, only their own. Laura, you're looking at the big picture: Why would the perps want either of the Rogers dead?"

*What a difference a year makes,* I thought. Last year, the FBI had ignored Max's request to include me on an investigation that I had created, but that the FBI had taken over.

"I wish I knew the answer to that."

# 84

"Thank you for doing this, Ms. Wolfe," Senator Pembroke said. "Gavin graciously offered his office, as I wanted this to be as private as possible. I've asked him to sit in."

I nodded. We moved to the upholstered chairs surrounding the round coffee table.

"Please," Pembroke said, indicating where he wanted me to sit.

"I would like for us to sit opposite each other, sir."

"Oh, certainly." We arranged ourselves.

Crawford sat a few feet to the side, and I noticed he had moved his chair back a couple of feet, acknowledging he was a bystander and not a participant.

Pembroke cleared his throat. "I am not being gratuitous when I say you have a reputation for honesty and are a respected journalist, your Pulitzer notwithstanding. The sensationalists will have a field day at my expense and deservedly so, which is why I want to tell you my story ahead of that."

I could think of no response that was appropriate, so I chose instead to arrange my tape deck, pad, and pen. Crawford had mentioned Pembroke was a precise person. My being orderly may seem a small thing, but he'd notice it, and maybe it would put him a little more at ease.

He asked, "Do you have any questions before we begin?"

"No sir." As I was given the option, I didn't want to establish a beginning point.

He looked at Crawford, who nodded slightly, saying in effect: *It's your stage.* Harley's comment in Carmaya about senators—*they are all actors on this stage of life*—flashed through my mind.

Senator Pembroke pulled some stapled sheets of paper from his briefcase and placed them on the coffee table. "This is my bio. It's well detailed, covering my life. This way we won't have to spend time on my history."

"Thank you, Senator. May I?" I reached out to my recorder, indicating I would like to turn it on. The curtain was about to go up.

He fidgeted, gearing himself up. "Certainly." An edge of nervousness cracked his voice.

I turned on the tape and said, "Interview with Senator Fred Pembroke in the office of Senator Gavin Crawford, who is present." I sat back, my note pad on my lap and waited.

He shifted nervously in his seat, and then began by talking about his two daughters and one son. It was a walk down memory lane, a Shakespearean prologue of sorts. He was serious, but occasionally attempted some humor. He nervously attempted to draw Crawford in with a "you remember" and "we were all at," but Crawford remained impassive.

Pembroke cleared his throat several times. His eyes projected sadness and teared easily.

"I didn't want Sally to work after I became a senator, coming over from the House after six years there." He let out a sigh and took a swallow of water. "McLean's a great community, superb Fairfax County schools, great recreational programs, and good neighbors like Gav and Mariel." Small beads of perspiration appeared on his upper lip.

"Life was good." He wiped his lips and forehead, had another drink.

"Our eldest, Freda, selected the University of Virginia, UVA. She loved the school and her grades were great. She made the freshman team in volleyball and swimming." He drained his glass of water and wiped his mouth. "I'm sorry, I know I'm . . . it's just . . . I need to say these things."

His eyes teared, and he sat back grimly, wiping a hand over his face. He sniffled and wiped his nose on a handkerchief. Crawford refilled his friend's glass.

"Two years after Freda, George began at Virginia Tech. He's a wiz in math and science. Heh, those two have always been competitive. He relished going to a big rival school. Blacksburg and Charlottesville are not that far apart either. Boy, do they go at it, but don't ever let anyone get in between them—whew, that would be trouble."

He took a deep breath. I worried that the weight of his personal story might drag him down to where he would stop before he got to the main subject. I cleared my throat. I hoped he'd get into the corruption phase without me having to steer him into it.

"Okay." He sat upright. "It was two and a half years ago. We had the two in college and Sadie, our youngest, about to start. I was at one of those cocktail parties the pharma crowd is always throwing, as Stroble said on that tape. I was in line for the chairmanship of HELP. We'd just won the majority. Tom was building me up to Stan . . ."

Horowitz I wrote on my pad.

". . . about my great family and how expensive having three kids in college at the same time would be. I remember mentioning how tight things were for us. Two days later, a messenger delivered a brown envelope with a big 'Eyes Only' below my name.

"A standard-size envelope was inside with the same admonition. There were twenty-five $100 bills in it." He sniffled and wiped the sweat off his face with the handkerchief he kept at hand. "A simple note, *Please accept this for your kids.* It was in a standard font on plain bond paper. No name. I damn near broke down. Sally and I were struggling to keep things together.

"Looking at that money I didn't know . . . well actually, I was pretty sure, if you know what I mean." He cleared his throat. "I was going to give it back," he blurted intensely. "I was." Then like air escaping a balloon, he deflated and sagged into his chair. "But I didn't." His head drooped.

I waited and was about to ask my first question when he lifted his head. "I received $30,000 over the next six months in an offshore account they'd established for me after the first cash gift. Tom handled all that, as Stroble said. Tom has an account also. So does the whip and some others. When Freda graduated, I got a card of congratulations from a local car dealer saying a benefactor would like to make a down payment on a car for her.

"The general manager took personal care of us. He had been given a $10,000 deposit to go toward the purchase . . . that made the payments much cheaper. Things kept coming my way. Later, I traded George's old car at the same dealership and got him a demo, one of their sporty cars. The money kept coming."

He sat back, looking down at the handkerchief he constantly played with. I hoped he wasn't fading out. He wasn't. "Stan gave, and we gave back," he said, straightening up.

He'd finally completed the circle. Pembroke blew his nose. Half embarrassed, he managed a tight-lipped, grim smile. "The gifts increased, up to $5,000 a month, with . . ." He sat back and looked around Gavin's office with a vacant stare. "I had it all. What could be better? What I feared the most . . . in the beginning . . . was letting my kids down. The cars would have been older. There'd have been fewer new clothes and less electronic gear."

His lips pursed, he was fighting a breakdown. "I didn't trust the love we shared for each other. I had to prove . . . I was a big man in the Senate. I had to show them I was just as big at home. And . . ." He bent over in his chair, his elbows on his knees, his head in his hands. His body heaved emotionally.

I looked at Crawford and indicated I'd heard enough. I didn't need any more. I turned off my recorder and placed everything in my bag. I'd witnessed a *Macbeth*, a *Willy Loman*. I slipped out through an anteroom into the main corridor. I descended the stairs to the street level and left the Russell Senate Office Building on my way to Ro's office in the Dirksen Senate Office Building.

Pembroke had a 5:00 appointment with Majority Leader Tom Kelly.

# 85

**B**efore I went into Dirksen, I stopped on the sidewalk and called Barton's direct line.

"Barton Williams."

"Laura, sir."

"Yes. How'd it go?"

"What I have is pure narrative . . . an American tragedy."

"Yes, but a story nonetheless," he said firmly.

He sounded concerned. I shot back, "Absolutely. I'm going to Senator Dalton's office."

"Thank you, Laura. I'll tell Riley and Claire."

I punched off. This was becoming a sour victory to me. I called Max's private line.

"Ms. Wolfe."

"I have a tape that unimpeachably implicates K and others. It corroborates the content of the M tapes. I'll get you a copy."

"Why don't you give it to me tomorrow?"

"Okay. I have no idea what reason he will give for his resignation."

"We and our friends have teams in place."

I teased smugly, "Gosh. I keep forgetting you actually do things on your own."

"We try."

I went into Dirksen and up to Ro's office. Michael came and got me. I nodded to assure him we had gotten what we needed.

"Senator Dalton has been very anxious," he said. "Senator Szymanski is with her."

We greeted all around, and then Ro took me aside. "Al is up-to-date on

Carmaya and Pembroke's imminent resignation. I've also informed Harold Raines of the same things. He was shocked about Fred and worried he might also resign his Senate seat and reduce our majority to 51-48, or maybe worse because the governor of Fred's state is not from our party."

I updated her on my conversation with Max and that MPD and the FBI were keeping a tight surveillance on their respective persons of interest. "They have more than enough to implicate Senators Kelly and Pembroke in a myriad of things, but nothing yet about who was behind Mort's murder. We are in a waiting mode until the authorities move in. My paper has several reporters standing by. Right now, secrecy is our surest road to success."

She nodded. As we moved to rejoin Szymanski and Michael, I asked, "You mentioned talking to Senator Raines. Is he senior enough to be the one to hold things together in the Senate when the authorities make their move?"

She looked puzzled. "How do you mean?"

We four were standing together.

"Senator Pembroke told me he and Kelly were not the only ones to take money under the table. I see the potential for a catastrophic implosion when most of your leadership is arrested. How will the minority members react? It would be of immeasurable help to the MPD and FBI if this isn't immediately politicized. Is there a method in place where all your colleagues can be reached quickly?"

"Laura makes a good point, Al. We need to curb the attack dogs on both sides."

"On our side, that'll be up to the minority leader, but I'll be—"

Crawford rushed into the room. "Fred's on his way home." He stopped when he saw Al. "Hi, Al.

Ro said, "I've told Al, Gavin."

Crawford relaxed. "Okay. I walked Fred to his car. He was only in with Tom about three minutes. He told me he gave poor health as his reason, saying he didn't believe he could withstand the pressure of the upcoming pharmaceutical battles. He told Tom we'd be better off if Harvey—"

A name Pembroke had mentioned. "Did he play the tape?" I asked anxiously, my heart pounding.

"I asked, and he said no. He did ask Tom to wait until after the weekend . . . for time to tell the family." There would be no Senatorial coup 'd'état this evening. I called Max.

# 86

T om Kelly sat alone in his office, feeling his large, empty room crushing in on him. Where had things gone so wrong? He had cultivated a solid political organization, a strong power base. He wondered if Dalton and Crawford had aligned; they'd gone off to Rogers's island together. It must have been Crawford who convinced the Pentagon to send in the Marines. He sat on the Armed Services Committee.

Harley Rogers had out-foxed everybody. The price of his company's stock had risen fifteen percent solely on the rumor that the German drug could be his.

He wondered what Fred would do now. Pembroke was really a decent guy, but Stan had found his weak spot—wanting to give his kids the best. Stan was a master of playing on the good in people as much as he did the bad, maneuvering them into doing evil to embellish their goodness.

Pembroke's stepping down would actually be a big plus for Stan, who always wanted Frank Harvey to chair HELP. Stan liked Harvey's bulldog approach. That would help to get the committee back in line to block Szymanski and his cosponsored bill with Dalton.

That buoyed him up and made him feel less pessimistic. He stood and walked around the room, thinking. Harvey could also move Kelly's pharmaceutical discount plan through committee. He'd have the guts to push for hearings on possible illegal activities by Rogers and keep his damn cancer drug out of the country.

He picked up his private phone, the one with no extensions, and punched in a number. He let it ring three times and hung up. Then he redialed it, waited four rings, and hung up. He waited. His phone rang.

"Hello," he said dully.

"Is Mabel there?" Meaning, *Is there a problem?*

"There's no Mabel here." Meaning, *I have something urgent.*

"She gave me this number." Meaning, *Where do you want to meet?*

"I don't care if Thomas Jefferson gave it to you." Meaning, *Meet at the Jefferson Memorial.*

"This is the second number I've been given for her. I'm sorry to have troubled you." Meaning, *I'll be there in two hours.* The phone went dead.

Kelly wouldn't have to call his wife about being late, because she'd already gone back home earlier in the week. He changed into running shorts, shoes, a T-shirt, and a *Nationals* baseball cap that had been given to him by the team on opening day. After an hour going over boring paperwork, he went for a snack before heading off to his rendezvous.

He drove into the parking lot south of the monument memorializing the nation's third president and took a pair of large, black rimmed eyeglasses from the glove compartment. Even in his dank mood, he was moved by the classic beauty of the memorial. The brightly lit Washington Monument's reflection on the still waters of the Tidal Basin pointed directly at him. The water was placid with no paddle boats at night.

He jogged down to the water's edge and along the Tidal Basin, passing the front of the memorial. There were a few people sitting on the steps taking in the view and inside getting an up-close look of Jefferson's majestic statue, reading the many Jeffersonian quotes. Kelly jogged easily along the water toward a copse of trees on the far side. A jogger loped past him and went off the walkway at the trees. Kelly arrived there a moment later.

The jogger was waiting in the deep shadows. "What's so urgent?"

"Fred resigned as chairman."

"That wimp. I never knew why you wanted him on your team in the first place," the wiry man spat out.

"Because people like him and because of his outstanding record. Let's not rip up Fred; he's doing enough of that to himself."

"Guilty conscience? What reason did he give you?"

"Tutox, the German clinic, the public furor, the cosponsored bill, your prescription plan . . . maybe one of his kids didn't get straight A's. Take your pick. I thought you'd be happy . . . the timing is a plus. Frank Harvey'll go in there and kick ass."

"What's Pembroke's story going to be?"

"His health." Kelly looked around, but saw no lurkers.

"We've got other problems," the wiry man said tersely, while doing some stretching. "Your pal Crawford is getting too close to the beauty queen. Going down to that island fiasco is gonna make them look like a couple of heroes."

"I don't like them being in tight with Rogers either," Kelly added. "How come you didn't know about his processing plant and the German hospital?"

"Who says I didn't?" the pharma snapped. "How'd the Marines get involved?"

"Crawford, I assume. He's on Armed Services, has good DOD contacts. Remember Reagan and Grenada? Plus the Carmayan government requested assistance and State got involved.

"That German hospital . . . the mood isn't with us, Stan. The expedient thing is for me to hold off a few days before announcing Fred's stepping down. Maybe we can get the FDA to rethink its decision on Tutoxtamen. We have to quell any panic—"

Horowitz erupted, "That drug cannot see the light of day. Why wait to announce your distraught friend's—?"

"Distraught?"

"Yeah. Maybe he should resign from the Senate."

"He can't do that. We'd lose a seat."

"He's our scapegoat. Think, man! Put the focus on him, say you and the party relied on him concerning the drug and that's why you rallied the party to show support of the FDA. We'll cover that by making sure the FDA has sufficient fire power . . . solid reasons why that drug can't come up for reconsideration."

"Fred and Sally will be going away for a few days."

"Yeah? Well, maybe he shouldn't come back!" Horowitz growled and jogged away.

Kelly was chilled by the lobbyist's words. He remembered Mort Stroble.

# 87

With a streak of good weekend weather ahead, we planned on spending it aboard *Scalawag*. Max, normally a Sunday visitor, had asked to come aboard Saturday because on this particular Sunday he was having brunch with his college-aged daughter, which unfortunately included his ex-wife, on one of their infrequent visits to Washington.

As soon as both his feet were on deck, he said, "Reed called me from Miami this morning—they have received no cooperation from the two male civilians taken off the yacht. They maintain they were on a pleasure cruise. From their IDs, we know one's from Chicago, the other from Paterson, New Jersey. They are both in the long-haul trucking business. They claim they are good Americans and don't do business with mercenaries.

"However, the good news is what Reed and a female agent learned from the six party girls. Faced with accessory to murder charges, they all cooperated. They are employed by an escort service in Miami that has ties," he said very slowly, "to a porno operation in Atlanta . . ."

"George Manchester?" I questioned.

Max smiled his best Cheshire cat grin. "The man with known ties to Washington politicians. Two Atlanta-based agents paid Mr. Manchester a visit at his home last evening. Their ruse was an investigation of two women arrested in Miami on drug charges who admitted to working in Atlanta and Washington. And because Mr. M had sworn to the FBI—after last year's brush with the law—that he would forever be cooperative, they knew he wouldn't mind answering a few questions."

My adrenaline was exploding.

"That's a wildly interesting coincidence," Jerry said.

Max nodded. "Manchester quickly proved to be a valuable asset."

This was astounding. "Horowitz?" I asked hopefully.

"It seems that the pharma lobby utilizes Mr. Manchester's escort service on a regular basis in both Miami and Washington."

I was freaking out. "Manchester knows Horowitz?"

"It appears they've had a direct dealing or two, but the escort service is handled through surrogates," Max said in his most deliberate—and for me, agonizing—manner, except his grin was giving him away.

"Do I hear the strains of *It's a Small World?*" Jerry asked. "What else did they pull out of the man from Atlanta?"

Max said Manchester assured the FBI agents he was no longer in that business, but did allow that he knew Mr. Stanley Horowitz professionally. "This ties the women on the yacht to at least the pharmaceutical lobby. Reed said the contract for the women's services was filtered down through several layers. However, we still need another breathing person to fill in the details. The yacht has been searched and found to be clean."

I found that curious. "If there were no incriminating items like weapons, clothing, or personal stuff belonging to the six men, maybe it was all dumped."

Max smiled. "I believe the Marines have some SCUBA equipment and, along with Carmayan divers, are searching the harbor bottom as we speak."

"Okay. I didn't think of it first, but I did think of it," I said.

"Max, you can't be saying that somebody other than our own Miss Marples comes up with these gems?" Jerry asked, trying hard not to burst into laughter.

I slapped Jerry's shoulder and let out a sardonic laugh. "Ha, ha. I get it. But you'll have to admit—"

"Of course, we do," Max interrupted, "I was just curious to see if your being off the street-beat had dulled your thinking."

He and Jerry joined in a guy-type, loud laugh. They loved it when they could tease me. But that's why I feel so lucky . . . having them both in my life. My eyes began to tear, so I jumped up and turned away from them. "Can I get you boys anything?" I said, heading away from them toward the galley.

"I'll take a brew," Jerry answered.

"Make mine water," said Max, who preferred to stay sharp on Saturdays in case he was called to duty. I descended the ladder and got a tissue. I washed my face and went to the ice chest.

I was thrilled we had Horowitz pinned to the yacht. Human life was so cheap to him. It's easy to believe he'd want both Rogers men killed. I pulled a beer and a bottle of water out of the ice chest, while wondering if I should call Ro or Michael. Max believed the pharmas had Mort killed and were behind the processing plant attack. Assassination and annihilation were tools in the pharma lobby's trade. I went topside.

"Here you are, gentlemen."

"Well," Jerry said, "as you're in a giving mood, when do we eat?"

"Oh, I'm so sorry . . . I forgot to bring my sarong and leis, but maybe I can find a luau CD," I said, holding up Jerry's can of beer, making as though I was about to shake it. "May I open your beer, sir?"

"No, no . . . that will be fine." Jerry cowered playfully.

"Consider yourself fortunate I did this much." I turned to go down below.

"Where you going?"

"Check on Tyler and make my lunch." Actually, I had decided to call Ro. As I reached the ladder, I had a thought and twirled around. "Perhaps the two incarcerated men were on an entirely different mission and should be let go. Maybe we could learn more from them that way." I went below and made my call.

"Hello," Ro answered softly.

"It's Laura."

"Good morning. Are you on *Scalawag*?"

"We are, with Max Walsh. I have good news." I filled her in.

"That is great news. Dad mentioned there were some new developments in Carmaya, but wouldn't tell me on the phone. Do you know—?"

"I believe that would be a search of the bottom of the Carmayan harbor for stuff possibly dumped from the party boat, because there was nothing incriminating on board."

"That stinker, not telling me. Thanks. I'll have some fun with this."

"If you're not doing anything, how about coming over?"

"I'm visiting some friends later who are far apart from all this. I need the break."

# 88

I sat in my small home-office alcove Monday morning, incorporating the Pembroke tape into the body of my article. I needed it to be as up-to-date as possible when the FBI and MPD made their move on Kelly or Horowitz.

I took a short break when Anna and Tyler returned from their stroll and played with my son while Anna got a snack and drink for him. The reality of the pharmaceutical conspiracy and my moment with my son could not have been starker. My ringing cell phone jolted me from my bliss. I picked it up. It was Max. Could this be it?

"Good morning," I said cheerily.

"There have been better Mondays," he said darkly.

An ominous shiver ran through me. "What's happened?"

"Sherman Rogers is dead."

"Oh no!" He was in a New York City hospital.

Max explained he had been discovered not breathing when the nurse went in to prepare him for breakfast. "There were no evident signs of foul play, according to NYPD's medical examiner, who is probably conducting an autopsy as I speak. Harley Rogers was livid, saying his son had been murdered."

"Max. The two mercenaries told the FBI that both Rogers were targeted, remember—"

"That's news to me."

"Didn't Reed tell you?"

"No."

"Oh no," I said, kicking myself. "That's my fault. Reed told me." I felt crappy. It hadn't been urgent, but I always tried to keep Max in the loop as he did me. "The FBI was thinking of protecting both of the Rogers men because—"

"I best call Reed." The line went dead.

Now I felt doubly awful. I needed to get busy. I called Barton to tell him about Sherman. However, his secretary told me he couldn't be disturbed. I was on edge, and my intensity must have come out when I told her, "I have to talk to him immediately."

She paused a few seconds. "Just a minute," she said curtly and put me on hold.

I breathed deeply, hoping to reduce my anxiety level.

Barton came on. "Laura?" He was not happy. "What is so—?"

"Sherman Rogers is dead, possibly murdered," I said sharply.

"When? Where?"

I repeated what Max had told me, including that the FBI had said both Rogers had been targeted in the attack. "Sherman wasn't on life support, because the nurses would have known when he straight-lined. He was in recovery. Death was not a concern." I realized I'd not been told all that exactly, but from the pieces, I deduced it.

"What about the old man?"

"He's saying it's murder."

"Anything on Senator Pembroke?"

That startled me. My head was still wrapped up in Sherman's death. "Actually, I have been working on that piece this morning."

"I'll see what we can find out in New York," he said. "Thank you, Laura."

"Ah, Barton. I apologize for my rudeness to your secretary. I didn't handle that very well," I said, putting it as humbly as I could.

"Yes. I'll tell her." He hung up.

I can do the stupidest things. Maybe I should send her some flowers. Lassiter's used to me, but I know better than—

A squeal of joy from Tyler interrupted my thoughts. I found him on the back deck with Anna, playing. Anna looked at me and frowned.

I must have looked over-anxious, judging by her questioning look. "It's about work. A sad thing happened. Everything here . . . *aqui* . . . okay?"

She smiled. "Si . . . yes."

I went back to my writing. The pharmas must have had a big hurt on the Rogers to kill Sherman. I wondered if Pembroke was in any danger because he'd shown what some might construe as weakness. I called

Crawford's office, but he wasn't in. I called his home, and a young, female voice answered. "Hi. I'm Laura Wolfe. Is Senator Crawford home?"

"The real Laura Wolfe?" the little voice squeaked.

"The reporter, yes."

"My father told us all about you. Wow!" she giggled. "I'm sorry, it's just—"

"Not a problem. Is your father home?"

"Oh sure. He's out in the yard. I'll get him." The phone thumped down on a table, and I heard a door squeak open and the girl calling out, saying I was on the phone. I guessed she might be one of the ten-year-old twins. The door slapped closed, like a screen door on a spring. The phone was picked up. "He's coming."

"Thank you."

"Oh sure."

I heard the door, then Crawford saying, "Thank you, sweetheart." He got a giggle in response. "Laura?"

"Sorry to bother you at home. Captain Walsh just called. Sherman Rogers is dead." I gave him the details. "Do you know if Senator Pembroke is still at home?"

"He and Sally left yesterday for Greenbrier, West Virginia, for a couple of days. They had no definite plans after that."

"Can you reach him?"

"I have his private cell phone. Is there . . . have you heard something?"

"There's a good possibility it was a professional hit on Sherman." I explained what Reed and Max had told me. "I'm concerned for the Senator . . . his family."

"Fred?" He asked excitedly.

"If somebody wanted to, they could find him the minute he used his credit card or cell phone."

"I know the FBI . . . police can, but how . . ."

"Don't underestimate . . . their money can buy many things. They thrive on control. A credit card trace would not be a problem," I said resolutely.

"Should I call him?"

"They need to check out of wherever they are, and then they should use only cash and public phones. Tell them to cash a check, if they can. Tell him to buy a phone card and to call you at a prearranged time twice a day."

"This sounds a little cloak-and-dagger . . ."

"Maybe, but it could save their lives."

89

"Editor Lassiter wants you to know," Mary said on the phone, "that the Carmayan government asked the Organization of American States (OAS) for oncologists, internists, surgeons, nurses, and police support. Our president announced that our Marines would remain to complement the one hundred and fifty peacekeepers other countries would be providing.

"Rias reported to Riley that Rogers Pharmaceuticals employees on Carmaya are quite shaken over Sherman Rogers's mysterious death. There's more; I'll fax it to you."

"I can imagine their fear. I'm surprised any are still there."

"Well, as long as they don't come after you . . ." She hung up.

I called Max and hoped he had gotten over my screw-up. He greeted me pleasantly. I told him I'd gone as far as I could on my Pembroke piece.

He asked if I'd heard about the president's order to keep the Marines on Carmaya. "This is becoming an international incident," he said. "Reed told me the German government is installing additional police at that Frankfurt hospital."

"Sherman's death . . . something's out of whack there. He ran the company, but not the drug processing. It feels to me there's another reason why—"

Max interrupted. "Let's look at the usual reasons someone is eliminated. They know too much, screwed up, or backed out."

"Like Mort. Okay, let's say hypothetically, the same people are behind everything bad that's happened. The pharmas are intent on keeping Tutoxtamen off the market at any price. They learned about Carmaya and planned its destruction. But they did not know about the German operation and believed they were betrayed there."

"That narrows down the *bribees*," he said.

"Exactly, except how or where does Sherman Rogers fit that scenario? Rufus McAllister had worked closely with Sherman on C-2 . . . Sherman doesn't make sense."

"It usually doesn't," Max said. "The quiet guy next door who is the good neighbor turns out to be a murdering pedophile or serial killer."

"I understand . . . but that's hard to believe . . . the son would turn against the father."

"True. Didn't you say Senator Crawford and the counterterrorism agents had developed a theory that the invaders might have been planning to take the island without resistance?"

"That was a scenario that seemed to best fit what they were discovering at that time."

"Right, so when the insurgents got fired upon, that went against the plan. The mercenaries felt betrayed and fired rocket grenades and attacked," Max said, tying it up.

"Senator Crawford told us Maloney had speculated it must have smelled like an ambush—because the insurgents were not expecting heavy machine gun fire. They expected little if any resistance. They regrouped without firing a return shot, then rearmed with heavier weaponry that they would have brought with them to use on an as-needed basis.

"The mole might be somebody high up in Rogers—a person the pharmas expected would know everything about C-2. And when the security force on C-2 turned out to be so well-armed, overwhelming the attackers, the pharmas knew they had been betrayed. Killing the son was payback."

"That is a plausible scenario," Max said.

"Maybe Sherman owed the pharmas for something . . . but what? We may have to look back three years, when his father began creating an alternative plan. Maybe Sherman was pressed into a compromising position, something was being held over his head. He went along with the bad guys, except for saying he was heavily fortifying the island."

"Bingo," Max said. "That may not be on the nose, but it's close."

# 90

Ro, Gavin, Michael, and I agreed to meet at Ro's condo at 7:00. I left Jerry in charge of Tyler, or maybe that should be the other way around. I got there a couple of minutes after the hour and found I was the last to arrive. Ro was very upbeat and gave me a hug. Crawford had just arrived, and Michael had driven over with Ro.

Michael had prepared an agenda. My world was so different from theirs. My agendas were ever-changing. The Carmaya attack was item one on Michael's list. I had thought they would've put the Senate corruption first, but I was happy with the order.

Ro asked if I'd begin.

"FBI SAC Reed Davis gave me an update on the yacht, which I'll get to. First, Sherman Rogers's death: Captain Walsh said hospital security and NYPD scoured the hospital's surveillance tapes and found the killer. An outside camera caught him entering the hospital through the rear service area. Another camera showed him inside the hospital, where he entered a room and emerged wearing a hospital orderly's white outfit, pushing a laundry cart.

"He then used the service elevator and was next seen moving down a deserted corridor, then entering Sherman's room, so identified by hospital security. He came out thirty-seven seconds later and retraced his steps back to where he had changed clothes. He reappeared in his street clothes, but went out through the front lobby. Police consider Sherman's death a homicide."

Crawford jumped in. "That's good enough for me. What next?"

"Your attack scenario, senator," Michael said.

"Good. I have something to add to what you just said, Laura. Along with the ambush theory, consider that Maloney had mentioned Sherman as a possible leak. It sounded absurd to me at the time."

"Captain Walsh thinks the FBI are in a position to make some arrests."

Ro wondered if it would happen before Kelly announced Pembroke's resignation. Michael offered that Nancy Morris had not said anything about Pembroke when he had talked to her earlier. "Except to say it was very quiet with Senator Pembroke off on a surprise vacation."

"Laura, with Fred away, would that delay the FBI?" Crawford asked.

"The FBI and MPD are concentrating on more than Horowitz and the conspiracy. They want to nail down the chain of evidence on Mort's and Sherman's murder before arresting anyone."

Michael asked, "Wouldn't an arrest or two spook Senator Pembroke?"

"Senator Pembroke is expecting to be arrested," I said, looking to Crawford. "You agree?"

"I believe that's why he's taken Sally off alone. They have a very strong relationship. Once the tears, the anger, and the questions dry up, they'll work together and jointly tell their children," he said emotionally. "He won't run."

My great relationship with Jerry flashed through my mind. We were strong. We would be there for the other, no matter what. That thought caught me up. My heart was racing. "I have a brilliant idea," I said enthusiastically, "but only if you all agree." They laughed, and I got some fun-poking comments. I felt that relaxed everyone.

"This is very chancy. I bounce things around a lot with Jerry and Max. It may seem harebrained, but you sort of have to take it for what it is. Try not to reject it out of hand."

Ro smiled. "Is this how you won your Pulitzer?"

"We did a lot of it then, because we had very few hard facts as we have here. Try not to have strong ownership of your ideas, okay? First, I won't do anything with the tapes unless I have full permission from FBI SAC Davis and Captain Walsh. Okay?"

They nodded. I grabbed my water and took a large gulp, letting my preamble sink in. "I propose that the tapes be properly edited and played to Kelly privately."

Ro was the first. "That is a brilliant idea, Laura. I'm just not sure that it's a good one."

I laughed. The men followed, but Michael jumped in.

"I'd love for that to happen. But who'd play it?"

"Instinctively I have problems with it," Crawford said. "Ro and I couldn't do it. Tom would kill the messengers, deny everything, and probably threaten our careers, just for starters."

I grinned at him. "Other than that, Mrs. Lincoln, how did you enjoy the play? I'm thinking our publisher or managing editor would do it. There is precedence. They could call Kelly and advise him of an impending story. And remember, the FBI and MPD would be fully informed. This would allow them to have their people in place ready to pounce on Horowitz and the others when Kelly arrives at the *Star*. After the tape is played, the FBI would track Kelly, then wait."

"And this would be done without arresting Fred?" Crawford asked.

"At first, yes. If he has agreed to cooperate fully and will testify, the Justice Department might very well plead him out."

"He hasn't called me today," Crawford said. "I guess I should call his cell. When do you think all of this might take place, Laura?"

"Maybe tomorrow. Protection for Senator Pembroke and his family needs to be in place before Kelly has a chance to contact Horowitz. We're dealing with some very nasty people. My hope is that when we cut off the serpent's head, the rest of the snake will die."

"Being the bully he is, Tom may give up everyone to save himself," Ro said disdainfully.

I laughed. "Why, Mrs. Dalton, I am surprised."

We all laughed because of Ro's uncharacteristic statement. The tension-breaker felt good. Crawford agreed that Kelly would go belly-up. That set off a buzz of consequences and ramifications, until Crawford refocused our attention.

"Fred told me Friday that the whip and chairman of Appropriations were two others he knew of firsthand that had taken money. He knew there were others, but didn't give up their names."

"How will all of this affect your party's leadership?"

Ro answered, "Anticipating that imminent problem, Laura, a small group of us has met. We are prepared to nominate Harold Raines for majority leader. We'll work out the rest after that."

Crawford liked the idea of playing the tape to Kelly and not arresting Pembroke. Michael was all for it. Knowing Reed and Max, I felt we were on firm enough ground in their evidence-gathering to allow the paper to play our Mort/Pembroke edited tape to Kelly.

"Max already has one of Mort's killers in custody," I said, "and should have the second one soon. I don't know how the arrests of the senators will take place. After that stink in the House of Representatives about raiding a congressman's office, those of us on the outside feel many in Congress think themselves above the law, present company excepted, of course."

"I'm afraid, Laura, you are more right than you may know," Ro said somberly.

# 91

R eed and Max had agreed to my plan of playing damning portions of the tapes for the majority leader. The next morning at 9:15, I was sitting with Barton when he called Tom Kelly.

After the amenities, Barton told Kelly about the audio tapes implicating him in alleged illegal activity and that he wanted to give Kelly the opportunity to hear the tapes before the *Star* ran with the story. Kelly must have balked, because Barton firmly assured him the tapes were authentic and could be easily corroborated. Kelly must have eased off. Barton was nodding and asked the senator to pick a time to meet.

"Thank you, Senator. Yes, 2:00 in my office."

I called Max to tell him, but he hit me with his news without saying hello.

"NYPD knows the name of Sherman's killer. They matched facial recognition photos with the hospital's tape. They sent me the perp's photo, and it matches up with B&G's photos. FBI has put the perp at the top of their most wanted list. NYPD and MPD put out APBs as well."

I told Max that Kelly agreed to hear the tapes and when. Max said he'd call Reed.

Senator Kelly arrived on time, and Barton played him Mort's tape, edited so that Roanne's voice was not on it. Pembroke's tape was edited down to just his comments about the money and Mort being right. Riley, Lassiter, and I watched the meeting on closed circuit TV in an adjoining room. Kelly appeared calm, very much the actor. I thought Pembroke's comment about Mort's "being right" elicited the only flicker of emotion from him.

When finished, Barton asked if Kelly wanted to say anything, on or off the record. The senator denied the accusations without characterizing the tapes. As he stood to leave, he asked Barton what the *Star*'s plans were. Barton declined to say and again asked if Kelly wished to make a statement. He did not.

Max called me later in the day. "FBI agents were on Kelly from the moment he left the paper. He didn't head straight back to his office. At one point, his car pulled over to the curb, Kelly got out and made two calls from a pay phone. Dumb move. The FBI's parabolic microphone picked up his end of the first call, which was a message for Horowitz. That was confirmed later from the pay phone's records. Horowitz hadn't answered because he was in custody at that time."

"He's in custody?" I blurted.

"He was lunching with friends. FBI agents handcuffed and marched him out of the restaurant. I am told it created quite a stir. We picked up the male PI from Horowitz's firm who ran the two hit men, and we arrested the female PI who told Tina to get with Mort. Although a minor character, she is a link to the next person up the line. Kelly's second call was to Senator Pembroke. Again there was no answer. Kelly left a message for him to call back."

Riley and I spent the afternoon organizing our information. I called Travis and Rias. Both the German and Carmayan locations were deluged with cancer patients. Rias said the presence of the peacekeeping troops was the only thing preventing a riot.

He also told us that the cancer patients with appointments were immediately ushered into the rapidly filling airport motel for processing. He felt the Carmayans were doing the best they could with their meager resources, but might have to divert future flights to nearby airports in order to be able to sift out the tourists and the patients without appointments from the patients who had registered and been accepted.

Riley had Claire come in, and I brought her up to speed on Kelly. She was not happy at being left out of Barton's meeting with Kelly. Riley, to his credit, gently explained that it wasn't personal. He had given her all the senators except Pembroke, Crawford, and Dalton. Those three were mine.

I met with Health Editor Metzger at Barton's request because he had assigned her to get statements about Tutoxtamen from pharma critics and the health community. It would be front page. He had asked Grace Herman to read the Szymanski/Dalton Bill and to line up the Hill people and FDA administrators for their comments. I had Tutoxtamen.

At 11:00 Wednesday morning, Ro, Gavin, Michael, Harley, Rufus, who had already flown to New Jersey for Sherman's memorial service, and I met with Reed Davis and Max Walsh in a conference room at FBI headquarters.

Sherman had confessed to Harley about his duplicitous involvement with Horowitz before they'd left Carmaya. Harley's recounting of it was very close to our scenario. The pharmas had gotten their claws into Sherman when he was young and irresponsible.

Harley said, "Sherman hadn't been that person for twenty-five years. He'd used drugs and, for a short time, had sold them, but he'd never been charged or arrested. Horowitz learned of his drug activity and held it over his head. Sherman told me he thought that setting up the ambush would save the plant and send Horowitz a message. It did, but at too high a price. I wish he had consulted with me long before. He held himself fully responsible for the casualties and deaths and was prepared to . . ."

Harley choked and weakly asked. "Will any of that or the invasion details have to become public?"

"That'll be up to the prosecution or the defense teams," Reed said. "Senator Pembroke has returned, thanks to Senator Crawford. He has promised to cooperate with us fully. We've set up security at his home."

Max said. "NYPD has arrested the alleged killer of Sherman Rogers, and we have matched him up to what we had on the second man in Stroble's murder."

Reed added, "We know from the yacht's crew and guests that a man named Sam had been on board when the mercenaries were dropped off. When the six mercenaries didn't return to the yacht, he left, which was before the two from the hotel boarded. That confirmed their assertions they had only seen the crew and women on board.

"Thanks to Senator Crawford, the DOD counterterrorism experts, and the captured mercenaries, we now have a solid picture of the attackers' mission. The female guests and your Mr. Manchester have tied the pharmaceutical lobbyists to the yacht."

"We expect," Max said, "the Mort PI may be the link to the paramilitary people. His email and phone records are presently being scrutinized."

Reed said, "We're watching Kelly. We are holding Horowitz and that PI over for arraignment tomorrow morning. When Kelly is unable to reach Pembroke or Horowitz, we are hoping he will realize his predicament and lawyer up. The attorney general has told us to expend all our resources to show the American people that the United States Senate government is not for sale, even if some US senators are. The AG emphasized that every warrant had to be perfect. US Marshals will be used for the arrests. House and Senate leadership will simultaneously be informed of those arrests.

# 92

I was working with Riley later that day in his office when he was buzzed by his secretary. "Claire Rowley needs to talk with you."

"Okay." He punched the lit-up line. "What's up?"

He listened and by the changing expression on his face, it appeared to be serious. He said little, but did say I was in his office. "Okay, stay on it." He hung up.

He blew out some air, shaking his head and ran his fingers through his already-rumpled hair. "About ten minutes ago, Senator Kelly blew his brains out in his Senate office."

I was dumbfounded.

"According to Claire, it was at 3:47. Staff heard the gunshot and ran in. There were three sealed envelopes on his desk: to his wife, to the president, and a third with no name."

Kelly's suicide transcended everything else the rest of the day and evening. It would be tomorrow's headline story. Claire would write it. My long narrative would begin below the fold, as it should, and I worked on rewrites to include incriminating evidence I had not planned to include in this particular piece, which started with my first meeting with Senator Roanne Dalton.

Jerry and Tyler drove in to pick me up around 9:00. I was bushed, and Jerry let me relax.

Max called my cell a little after 9:30. "In Kelly's unaddressed letter, he confessed to taking huge sums of money from the pharmas. He listed his offshore bank account number and named Stanley Horowitz, Fred Pembroke, three other senators, four staff members, and two FDA officials—one being Kelso, whom Mort Stroble had given up.

"The FBI has arrested all except Pembroke. You knew Horowitz was already in custody?" I did. "They have all been booked and are being held over for arraignment in federal court tomorrow morning. I'll get you the time. After the Feds finish with their indictments, we will march Mr. Horowitz and friends over to the district court where they will be charged with murder."

# 93

The next morning, Jerry and I joined Max in the federal district court to see the arraignment of Stanley Horowitz; the pharma PI; the FDA people; United States Senators Majority Whip Hatcher, Appropriations Chairman Clarence, and Finance Chairman Jarvis; along with four senior staff, including the HELP committee's chief of staff. Tina's PI, who worked in Horowitz's firm, was considered a material witness and not present. Tom Kelly was named in absentia.

Kelly had stated in his open letter that Horowitz ordered the killings of Stroble and Sherman Rogers. I wondered if he really knew that.

The prosecutor charged, ". . . Mr. Horowitz of going far beyond lawful lobbying practices, of influence-peddling, mail fraud, bribery, and conspiracy to murder."

There were too many charges against the pharmas, and the judge would not grant bail to Mr. Horowitz. The defense team put up a fierce argument. They were rebuffed by the judge, who added the caveat that Horowitz was a major flight risk. He'd sort out the bail on the others.

The prosecutor then went on to name and charge all the others. They all pleaded not guilty, and bail was eventually set for them. Prosecutors and the judge were aware of local charges pending on the pharmas, and when the judge rapped his gavel, MPD officers arrested Horowitz and the PI for murder and marched them over to district court.

I learned later that at about the same time we were at the courthouse, another activity was taking place on Capitol Hill. Harold Raines was elected majority leader of his caucus. Gavin Crawford became chairman of HELP, replacing the interim chair, and immediately hired Nancy Morris as HELP's new chief of staff.

Raines put out a statement. "The public trust has been dealt a devastating blow. The United States Senate will cooperate fully with the Justice Department. Along with Minority Leader Olin Davis, we will seek a sweeping reform on lobbying. We are determined to bring forth legislation that will ban special-interest money, gifts, food, booze, partying, trips, and more. Senators and representatives are elected and staff is hired to represent all Americans. We are not sent here to party with those who bring business before us. It is our moral duty to rid Congress of this debauchery and lascivious living and to concentrate on serving the people."

# Epilogue

A typically hot, muggy Washington summer Saturday had been lessened greatly in temperature by a storm front associated with heavy thunderstorms tracking to the north of us. It was now a bearable eighty-seven degrees. Jerry and I worried we might have to move our small party inside and formed some contingencies, but so far it didn't look like we were going to get rained on.

Jerry, Tyler, and I were about to host a bar-b-que, a first in our new home. Max had arrived early carrying his large grill in his pickup and backed it to the edge of the deck. He would be treating us all to his pulled pork, North Carolina–style, topped off with his special fiery sauce made of vinegar, red pepper, ketchup, and who knew what else. We supplied a bucket of coleslaw and the drinks.

My emotions usually bounced all over the place after a big story, from euphoric to a lingering emptiness, but not this time because I had written several follow-ups and was planning for today's party for some new and old friends.

The federal prosecutor had asked those of us involved in the Carmaya adventure, the Senate/pharma debacle, and the murder of Mort Stroble to come in for questioning. Rufus had planned to fly from New Jersey to Carmaya after Sherman's memorial service on Thursday, but flew back to Washington instead. Ro had called to say she would have an escort to our party. I enjoyed the former governor and knew he and Max would hit it off big time.

I'd met with the federal prosecutor and FBI SAC Reed Davis right after our Wednesday morning meeting at the FBI. They'd interviewed me about

Rogers, Carmaya, and how I came to be involved with Senator Dalton. It had been all for background purposes, an interesting experience.

The ringing of our front doorbell announced the first of our guests, who were Ralph and Elaine Morgan. Gavin and Mariel Crawford came in on the heels of the Morgans. Gavin and Ralph had not met, so I got them all out on the deck and introduced Gavin to Max. Ralph and Max knew each other from our wedding.

Marsha Hines, whom we originally met during my serial-killer reporting last year and who now worked at Jerry's law office, had arrived alone, having taken Metro. Michael brought Nancy Morris. She and I laughed about our first very innocent meeting and how things had changed since then. I congratulated her on her promotion.

"Tyrell and I are taking her to the Palms next Saturday night to celebrate," Michael said.

Everyone was on the deck when I heard a loud, "Lawrah, you have company."

I went into the living room. "Roofuuss," I intoned. He gave me a bear hug, turning me slightly so that I didn't see Ro.

"We brought along a friend," he announced joyfully and let me go, aiming me at the front door. Ro and a man were standing in the threshold, grinning at me. She hugged me and said, "You remember Joe?"

Of course I did, I was just speechless.

"Major. Welcome." I extended my hand, which he shook, a little shyly I thought.

"Ms. Wolfe. The federal prosecutor wanted to debrief me." I guessed he felt he needed to explain his presence in the area, which he didn't. I was just happy to see Ro and him together, for whatever reason.

"Joe. I am happy to have you here. How's your mother?"

"She's doing great."

I looked at Ro. "Girl, you and I have to talk," and we laughed girlishly.

I wiped away my tears of joy, Rufus roared and headed for the deck as Jerry entered. "Hey Jer," he said, clapping Jerry's hand. "Where's the beer?"

"On the deck."

Rufus went out, and Jerry joined me with Ro and Joe.

I gave him a squeeze. "I told you, Jerry. This is Major DeMarco. I told you."

We all laughed.

"You didn't—how?" Ro questioned.

"The night after the dinner, I saw you two walking back into the hotel while I was talking to Jerry on my satellite phone. I don't know why . . . it could have been nothing, but I just had a feeling. I'm going to burst, I'm so happy for you," I squealed.

"The hard-nose reporter is a real romantic," Jerry said, nudging me. "Welcome, Major. I'm Laura's husband, Jerry Fields." They shook hands.

"Please call me Joe."

"Well, eh, should we join . . . who all is here?" Ro asked, taking Joe's arm.

"Michael, Gavin, Max . . . you'll get caught up on the others."

I ushered them out onto the deck and watched for Gavin's reaction to Joe. He was surprised. Ro, standing alongside me, whispered, "Well, at least it wasn't obvious to everyone."

I snickered. "I think it's wonderful. I think it's fantastic. Come on, meet everybody."

And so it went. Of course, we talked about everything and everybody who was involved in the Senate meltdown and about the proposed new Senate rules. I especially liked that all registered pharma lobbyists had been stripped of their credentials. A strong scrutiny was also going to be given to all lobbyists.

Ro took me aside. "I want you to know that yesterday Senator Raines, joined by the Minority Leader Olin, introduced a hard-hitting set of rules governing gifts, trips, any and all handouts, and a Public Integrity something or other. We're also instituting a new cooling off period of three years for all congressional members and staff who leave office or their job from working for anybody doing business with the government.

"The president issued some executive orders. One proposes the establishment of a new form of Ethics Committee. Its members will come from a rotation of federal judges, and it will be chaired by the chief justice of the Supreme Court," Ro said. "The majority and minority leaders jointly ordered Tutoxtamen hearings to be reopened immediately. Results from Germany and Carmaya will be admissible."

Jerry came over to us. "Come on, break it up. Max is about to feed us."

We joined the others as Max was saying, ". . . Mort's hit men were run by the pharma PI who may turn out to be the 'Sam' who oversaw the paramilitary operation that invaded the Rogers Pharmaceuticals's island. The FBI and CIA are still investigating the Carmaya incident and the use of the yacht."

"The attack went pretty much the way we broke it down," Gavin said. "The AMOP gear had been requisitioned—stolen—from their warehouse. I was surprised about Sherman's personal background and overall involvement, though."

Max held up a slab of ribs. "Hey, everybody, my North-Carolina, mouthwatering *bobbycue* is more than ready for the eating."

We all turned our attention to food.

I saw my friends enjoying each other. Rufus and Max were getting on well, as I thought would happen. Jerry had a long talk with Major Joe. I got back to Ro, eliciting her promise that we would make time for some girl talk. I then joined Gavin, Mariel, Marsha, Ralph, and Elaine.

Tyler was currently being held by Mariel. "I wondered why I hadn't heard from him," I said.

"Oh, he's delightful. I stole him away from Marsha."

"Is he dry?" He began twisting in Mariel's arms at hearing my voice.

"He seems to be. Right now, I think . . ." Mariel said, handing him to me, ". . . he wants his mommy, though."

I cuddled him and walked him around. He was having a ball. I eventually made my way to where Ro, Joe, Jerry, and Max were laughing about something.

"Your godson wants a little of your attention, Max."

He quickly wiped his hands and reached for him. "It's about time I start teaching him some of the finer things in life," he said, tickling Tyler under the chin and getting a squeal of joy in return.

Later, with the evening growing late and Tyler down for the night, Jerry had made a couple of pots of decaf. The rich aroma wafted over us. Ro and I were with the wives. Gavin was sitting with Michael, Nancy, and Marsha, probably engaged in a little shop talk that I imagined Marsha was eating up. Max, Ralph, Joe, and Jerry were leaning against the deck rail involved in who knew what, but it made them chuckle and laugh.

My article in yesterday's paper about Tutoxtamen and the real reason for the drug's not approvable had created considerable fallout in the Senate, House, FDA, pharma lobby, and a mass of indignation from all over the world. Others would be assigned to those stories, and my follow-ups would be on Harley Rogers and his pharmaceutical company.

He had told me he still planned to follow through with his promise to the Carmayan president: to maintain his mini processing plant on C-2, manufacturing Tutox there. He was also going to honor another promise: build a cancer hospital on the C-1. Rogers's main facility in Morris Plains, New Jersey, was already gearing up to resume manufacturing Tutox for worldwide consumption.

Following last evening's all hands editorial meeting with Barton, Travis, Lassiter, and Star editors I'd never met, Barton took me aside to say that Mrs. Osterman was anxious to schedule the official awards ceremony and luncheon for my Pulitzer.

Knowing me though, come my next day of work, I would more likely be anxious about what my next assignment might be and who would be giving it to me.

I did suspect, however, that my beat reporting days were behind me.

# Acknowledgments

One of my visits to Capitol Hill, in preparation to write *The Hill People*, was delightfully enhanced by good friend and former Assistant Secretary for the Majority US Senate Patrick Hynes, who arranged for and accompanied me on a personal tour of the Senate wing of the Capitol, regaling me with stories of how certain rooms aside from the Senate chamber were used by the senators.

I soloed on a later trip to Capitol Hill to learn about the three Senate office buildings: Russell, Dirksen, and Hart, which sit on Constitution Avenue north and east of the Capitol Building. I viewed many of the historic committee rooms and searched out who had oversight on the FDA and where those offices were located, which gave me the idea for where Michael Horne's friend, Nancy Morris, would work. That same solo trip became the one that Laura would take on her own exploration of the Hill.

I enjoyed a short, but fun collaboration with my oldest son, Graham, who holds degrees in chemical engineering and chemistry from NC State University and later earned his professional engineer's license. His expertise was vital to my understanding of what went into the construction of a small one-drug processing plant operation. He also reviewed and edited my copy on how I presented such a process in this book.

This is the third of my books to be republished by BQB Publishing. Death of an Intern, the initial Laura Wolfe thriller, was the first, and *Rude Awakenings*, a political thriller outside of the Laura Wolfe universe, was the second. Both of those books have received awards for mystery writing. I wrote a lengthy explanation of how I met the wonderful people of BQB Publishing in the acknowledgments for Intern, and how much I respect and enjoyed them all. I had come from a self-publishing world where no doors to the staff were open to me, the writer. My whole writing experience changed for the better the day I met Publisher Terri Leidich.

I know now that I had never worked with a real editor before Janet Green (www.thewordverve.com) was assigned to Intern and then again, at my strong request, to The Hill People. I wanted her to be boldly candid with me and not hold back on suggestions or demands. Jan's acumen and verve along with her ability to understand the thinking of my characters has made this whole rewriting experience something that I will always cherish. Jan is far more than an editor, she is a teacher.

Terri told me going into our association that after she and then Production Manager Lisa read my books, they would select the artist and editor best suited to me and my writing style. They have more than kept their word, for which I will always be grateful.